A Woman Undefeated

Born on the Wirral just after the Second World War, Vivienne Dockerty has always been a great storyteller. Her sagas are based on the amazing lives of her Irish ancestors and continue through each generation until her own autobiography in the 1960s.

Also by Vivienne Dockerty

Song for Ireland

A Woman Undefeated
Dreams Can Come True

VIVIENNE DOCKERTY

A Woman Undefeated

CANELO

First published in the United Kingdom in 2010 by Matador UK, an imprint of
Troubador Publishing Ltd

This edition published in the United Kingdom in 2021 by

Canelo
31 Helen Road
Oxford OX2 0DF
United Kingdom

A CIP catalogue record for this book is available from the British Library.

Print ISBN 978 1 80032 272 1
Ebook ISBN 978 1 80032 065 9

Look for more great books at www.canelo.co

Printed and bound in Great Britain by Clays Ltd, Elcograf S.p.A.

2

Foreword

I have never understood why my father didn't visit Ireland in his lifetime, as he always seemed proud to tell me that he was second generation Irish and all his ancestors were from the Emerald Isle. He would sing 'Danny Boy' and 'I'll take you home again, Kathleen' and other haunting songs that I never knew the titles of; he would show me how to dance the ceilidh and tell me stories of the ancestors that we were descended from. My favourite story was of how a Great Aunt had rowed up the River Dee estuary, with a handful of golden sovereigns sewn into the hem of her dress. I could imagine this doughty woman seeking a new life for herself, when things had got tough in her homeland.

One day he took me to a place called Denna Point, near the village of Neston on the Wirral and showed me the site where Irish immigrants camped out under a canopy of leaf laden trees, before setting off to the town of Birkenhead, or city of Liverpool, to find employment, or settled down to labouring jobs nearby.

I decided to visit this land of my childish imagination, to trace my heritage as far as it would go. I found an 'Irish stew' of spectacular scenery, quiet country roads, glittering loughs, tumbling waterfalls, mystical legends and learnt some of the island's turbulent history whilst I was there.

I feel sad that my father never made it to the Emerald Isle. He missed out on all the beauty that could have calmed his troubled soul. But he left me with a wish to write this story, the one that my Great Aunt Maggie would have liked me to tell.

Vivienne Dockerty

Chapter 1

The blackening clouds that heralded more rain, gathered menacingly over the west coast of Ireland. Blown in from the Atlantic they looked down upon the small hamlet of Killala, where a row of windowless cabins sat on the grassy headland overlooking the River Moy.

Maggie knelt at the side of her mother's bed in one of those poor cabins, deep in prayer as she rotated each bead on her rosary. She was oblivious to anything that was going on around her, so jumped in surprise when a gentle hand touched her shoulder. It was Jack, her childhood friend, who stood behind her, gazing down with sympathy in his eyes.

"Jack," she whispered, reluctant to even tear herself away for a precious moment from the task of praying on the behalf of her sick mother. "Yer not here again over the leaving, are yer? I've told yer I'll think on it, but not just yet."

She turned her face away from him and shifted her knees more comfortably, as her legs were beginning to feel numb. She wished he'd go, he was intruding into this time of peace and prayer.

He hovered, seemingly unwilling to wait until she'd finished her praying.

"What did the priest say?"

Maggie sighed wearily and dragged herself up to face him.

"He says there's little hope and to expect her passin' in the next day or so."

Jack nodded grimly.

"Aye, yer mother was never strong, never got over yer father and then young Bernie running off like 'e did." He put his large work-roughened hand out to steady Maggie, as she got up and took a few jerky steps. "Easy now. 'Ave yer eaten today or did yer give that broth me mother sent te Molly?"

Maggie's face brightened at the mention of her sister.

"Aye, I took a sup, but most was given to Molly. She can keep food down now the fever's broke. Wish I could say the same for me mother. She'll only have a little water, says her belly's past it."

She turned away, suddenly embarrassed. Jack had a strange expression on his face. As if he was drinking in the sight of her, like one would covet a rare picture on a wall. The look was unexpected. She knew from peering into the speckled mirror which belonged to her mother, that her face was drawn and her green eyes dull, that her long chestnut hair was tangled and her clothes were all raggedy. So why was he looking at her, like a girl he would wed if he could?

It was true that Jack's thoughts were following in that direction, he wanted to possess her, offer to wed her, take her away from this dying hamlet to a new life over the sea. But deep down he felt an anger. Anger at Maggie's blind and stubborn faith in the God she worshipped. The God who had allowed the main source of sustenance to the poor people of Ireland to wither and blacken for the second successive year. The God, who was allowing whole families to die slowly and in pain from the effects of the hunger in their lives. His shoulders drooped as his feelings turned to helplessness. Once he had gone from Killala, there'd be no one to look out for her. Jack didn't believe like she did, that God would be there to care.

Maggie knew that he was desperate for her to leave the hamlet with him, as leaving had been the only thing he had been able to talk about for the last few days. Recently though, his attitude had seemed to change from caring friend to possessive suitor. She knew she should be flattered. Any girl would be proud to walk out with such a strong young buck, but not Maggie. She had no intention of tying herself down at the tender age of sixteen.

She turned away from his gaze and went to lean over the wooden cot, where her sister, Molly, lay sleeping. She kissed the small child's brow, then listened anxiously to her breathing. To her relief it seemed better than it had been all day. She wasn't as hot, her waxy skin felt cooler.

Perhaps her fever was really on the mend.

Jack's manner though became insistent as Maggie rose from covering the girl with a threadbare shawl. He placed his calloused hands upon her shoulders and began to shake her gently.

"But Maggie, don't yer see, this is yer only chance of gettin' away. Once the winter comes you'll never be able to leave this place. The sea will be too rough, yer'll be cut off here in the snow and how'll you care fer Molly then? Look, come with us and leave yer mother and yer sister to the relatives. Your Aunt Tess would be up to looking after the pair of them and take Molly in after yer mother's gone."

He must have known from the look on her face that he had gone too far with his pleading. She shook off his hands and went to the cabin door looking flushed and angry. At that time Jack could have taken himself off to the ends of the earth if he wanted. Her duty was to remain in Killala and make her family as comfortable as she could. He followed sheepishly, knowing that he had pushed her too far, knowing that she could dig in her heels once she had made up her mind.

Words didn't usually come easily to Jack and it must have been a blow to his vanity to be shown the door, but Maggie knew where he'd be off to. He'd be seeing if his mother, Alice, could find a way to get her to change her mind. Alice could deny him nothing and would sell her own husband if it would please her son.

Maggie listened as Jack's footsteps faded into the distance. She knew that he was right. Life would become even harder now that the potatoes had rotted. There was no future for anyone living in the poor hamlet now. Most of the neighbours had gone, either left or succumbed to the fever that was raging through the land.

Her Pa had died three weeks before. He had been a fine strapping man until the hunger. Now his wasted body lay buried in the churchyard at Ballina, the nearest town, and it looked as if her mother would be joining him very soon. Her heart twisted in sympathy as she went back to sit by the sick woman. Her mother had simply lost the will to live, though why would she want to? What a desperate state her little family had found themselves in.

As Maggie continued her vigil, she began to think back over the years of her childhood. It had not been an easy life, as they depended largely on things they could grow. The most abundant crop had been potatoes. Rows and rows of the plant had grown profusely on their small piece of land, fertilized with seaweed gathered from the shore and manure from the wild ponies that came down from the hills. That had been until two years ago.

She felt sorrow as she remembered her Pa's words, when they had all lent a hand to plant the seed potatoes into their drills. He had boasted of the fine crop that they'd be having. Enough to sell at the market in nearby Ballina, with all of them having a rare day out. They'd buy new clothes, well, new to them from a stall on the market, as they couldn't afford Hegarty's, the outfitter's prices. And maybe there would be a bit of money left over, for a jug of porter from one of the taverns in the town. That was the measure of her father, he'd spend first on his family and then he would think of his own needs.

He had been a good man, a good husband and father. He hardly ever touched the drink, not like some of the men in the area, when sometimes it could be days before their wives would see them again. But that had been in the days before the famine came. Not many could afford to frequent a tavern now.

4

Her Pa had worked hard for his family, wresting a living from the ungrateful earth, or fishing from the small boat that belonged cooperatively to the people of Killala, or sold on some of their produce at the market and helped his neighbours when they needed a hand.

Maggie looked down sadly at Mairi, her mother. The woman lay on her palliasse waiting for death to release her from a cruel and heartbreaking world. She'd been a clean living and God fearing woman, who had only lived for her husband and family. Each Sunday she'd insisted that they all made the hazardous trek to Inishpoint across the headland, where they worshipped in a little church overlooking the dark Atlantic. Waves crashed onto the shore below, leaving seaweed and debris in its wake and fascinating them all, as they picked their way carefully along the narrow coastal path.

In those days Bernie, Maggie's young brother had been with them. He had always been a happy boisterous child, constantly getting up to mischief and setting Mairi's heart across her, when he ran too near the cliff edge. The cliff was dangerously eroded due to centuries of battering by the sea. They would attend Mass with the other 'cottiers', peasants renting small pieces of land. The staff from the Big House and farmers who were tenants on acreage belonging to the local landlord worshipped alongside them, all united in the purpose of worshipping the God who had given them their living and their homes. After church they'd wend their way back home for Sunday dinner, where tatties roasted slowly in pig fat and a rabbit simmered gently in the big pot hanging over the fire.

Mairi began to stir, which brought her daughter back swiftly from her happy memories. She looked upon Maggie with hollow shadowed eyes.

"Will you get me some water, child?" she said with some difficulty, in a voice so low that her daughter had to bend closer to hear her.

Maggie gave her a drop of water from the stone pitcher.

5

"Only a little now, Mammy. Just to dampen yer throat, too much will start yer belly aching again."

"Me belly's aching already, Maggie," Mairi replied, a rueful smile playing on her cracked and swollen lips. Then trying to prop herself up on one elbow, she tried to see how Molly was, who was still sleeping somewhat fitfully nearby.

"Molly's doing fine now, Mammy. Yer to lie back, yer need yer strength. I'm here to see to me sister if she needs me."

"Yer a good girl, Maggie," her mother said. "I couldn't 'ave wished for a better daughter, but I'll not be getting up from this bed again, I'll soon be joinin' yer Pa."

"Hush, Mammy, don't speak like that. You're sure to get better, I promise."

Maggie's words were meant to be comforting, but her heart felt full of despair.

Mairi sank back thankfully onto her straw filled palliasse. She knew it wouldn't be long before she went to join her husband in Heaven. She wasn't afraid of death, she welcomed it. Just the thought of seeing Pat's face again made her beating heart race. She knew she was being selfish, she should make an effort, try to eat, or her daughters would be left without her. But her thoughts were constantly with him, as she drifted in and out of consciousness. He was waiting, she could feel his presence. He was waiting to guide her to a pain free place.

Did Pat remember when she had been a young maid in Sligo? In the days when they'd been carefree, but he'd had itchy feet and an urge to see the world. He'd been good looking, a man any girl could fall for and follow to the ends of the earth. He was seventeen and had left his parents' land to seek out pastures new. The work on the land was just enough for his Pa and a younger brother, so his aim was a passage to one of the new colonies. But first he had to work to get some money for his fare. Any odd job he could set his hands to.

Seeing Mairi was Pat's downfall. He spied her as she scurried through her master's kitchen with her box of polishes and cloths. He looked up from where he was fixing a wobbly table leg and his heart was smitten. Pat thought she was the most beautiful colleen he had ever seen. One look at her pink rosy cheeks and her warm velvety eyes and he forgot his reason for being there. Mairi was impressed by Pat's handsome looks and boyish smile and decided to throw her lot in with this charming stranger. They were married three months later, from her parents' home in Sligo.

The couple still could have gone to the Americas if Mairi had been willing, but she was a home loving girl and from what she had heard about his home in Killala, it sounded much like what she had been used to before. She was welcomed heartily into Pat's family, especially as their marriage had brought the wandering son home. His father spoke up for Pat to the land-lord's bailiff, so a turf cabin was built on an acre of land. The neighbours brought gifts: a piglet, a chicken and a barrel of seed potatoes to give the newlyweds a good start.

They lived quite well. The pig was, in fact, a sow, and was always getting in the family way by the trotter from next door. Pat was a good shot with his father's gun and game was prolific; there was also a surplus of wheat in Ireland that kept flour prices low.

Life was good and Pat was happy to have settled down.

Mairi gave birth to Maggie in 1830, followed by the birth of Bernard in 1832. Then, Mairi remembered sadly, things started to go badly wrong. Another fine boy was delivered a year later, but three months on he died. There seemed to be no reason for his death. She had put him in the little wooden cot that Pat had made, when Maggie was born and the next morning when the family awoke, the poor little soul had gone. Her mother-in-law had said that it was just the will of God. Perhaps there was a shortage of cherubs in Heaven and the boy had been called to help out up there!

Mairi was not comforted by the thought. She believed it was the foul air in the cabin that had killed him, now that there were five people sharing and no window to let in fresh air.

From that day on, she kept Pat at bay when the urge to make babies came upon him.

The pain of losing a child decided her against being caught again. If it meant roasting in Hell for eternity, she wasn't going to go through all that pain again. Then as time passed by and she saw that Maggie and Bernie were growing into fine and healthy children, she welcomed Pat back to share her palliasse. A year later Mairi gave birth to twin girls, Collina and Bridie.

They wondered what on earth they had ever done to deserve the next tragedy. The family had tramped home in the pouring rain from their weekly trip to Mass. Both babies were well wrapped up, one in Mairi's shawl, the other in Pat's oilskin, but within a day of each other, two small souls had gone. She could still remember the tearing pain in her heart, as the two little coffins were lowered into the grave, on top of the coffin that held her tiny boy. Their loss affected her deeply. She lost weight and her pink cheeks were replaced with a pallor, her beautiful chestnut tresses hung limply around her shoulders and her eyes took on the look of deep despair.

Mairi felt guilty now, as she thought back to how she had put all the blame on Pat. She had blamed him for giving her children that so easily died; blamed him for his attitude that those dear little children could be easily replaced, if she didn't freeze in his arms when he came upon her. Then blamed him again when he gave her too much poteen at that ceilidh dance they had gone to. He had taken advantage of her befuddled state, so that she found to her horror she was expecting again. It had been the final straw. Mairi had raged at Pat, then wouldn't speak to him for days.

Now that he had gone, she wished that she had told him that she had been glad when little Molly had been placed into her arms. There had been so many tragedies in their marriage, so few good times. Now she longed to be with Pat again, to tell him how much she had cared. A tear trickled down her thin cheek and she whispered, "T'will soon be time."

Maggie was doing her best to keep her small family together. She constantly prayed for a miracle. A miracle that would save her country from the cruel ravage of famine; or a miracle to bring her mother back from the brink of death: or a miracle that would bring her brother, Bernie, back home to Killala as he was needed so desperately.

He had run away to sea six months before, and Maggie blamed him for her Pa dying the way he had. It was all Bernie's fault and she felt bitter. Her brother should have been there, facing up to his responsibilities.

Bernie had got a bee in his bonnet about becoming a sailor and travelling the seven seas. He had listened with growing excitement, as his Pa had told him tales of the beautiful clipper ships that sailed from the port of Sligo. He was green with envy when he heard that his Pa had almost sailed on one, to take him to a new life in the Americas. He couldn't believe that his father had wasted his opportunity, preferring to settle in the back of beyond, boring and predictable, living a quiet life and raising another generation there. The nearest Bernie had got to sailing on the ocean was when a neighbour, 'Old Joe', had taken him up the River Moy in a fishing boat. They had touched the Atlantic as they rounded Inishpoint and Bernie's heart had beaten madly, when Joe told him that if they sailed and sailed for a thousand miles across the vast and turbulent ocean, that they would reach the America's. A land that was there for the taking, where riches could be made by pioneers.

After a heated argument with his father one night, when Bernie asserted that at fourteen he was old enough to leave home, the boy had gone. He had sneaked out of the cabin door at night while the family lay sleeping. Mairi had worried and worried, so much so that Pat had thought her mind was becoming unhinged, so he tramped through pouring rain and hostile countryside, over damp peat land and boggy marsh, to look for their son. It took him three days to make it to Sligo. A fool's errand. His inquiries came to nothing. There were many young boys begging to be taken on by the packet steam companies. They were two a penny. Ocean life was far better than the poverty they had at home.

Pat returned to Killala a stricken man. He had lost his only son and for good measure he had caught a severe chill. The fever raged for many days, sending Mairi demented, as she treated him with her potions and kept vigil at his bed. Pat recovered, but was never strong again. For his family's sake he forced himself to plant a few rows of potatoes, but the work had nearly broken him and he took to his bed again.

Maggie was not at home at that time. She had been given the job of kitchen maid and general servant at the Filbey farm which was a mile up the track, near Ballalina. She was worked hard, but she ate well. Though the potato yield had been affected there too, it was not the farmer's main crop. He made his money from the barley he grew, which was sent to feed the people of England.

Home in Killala was like any other in the hamlet, a window-less dwelling made of turf blocks, small and mean, not airy and spacious like the Filbey farm. It had a large hole in the sod roof that let the smoke from the fire through. The floor was made of hard packed earth and a rug that Mairi had once woven, which was worn thin with age. The fireplace was the focal point of the cabin. Built into a deep alcove at the far end of the construction, it had wooden beams supporting an arch. Baked earth served as a hearth and upon it sat a primitive fire. Above this, dangling from an iron contraption knocked into the earth, was a heavy cooking pot suspended by smoke blackened chains. Nearby sat a big iron kettle that could also be suspended over the peat block fire.

The family slept on palliasses stuffed with straw, which in the daytime were neatly stacked to give more room for moving around. In the evening they were dragged out and positioned near the fire. It had been Pat's job to keep the straw of the palliasses free from bugs, by changing it regularly. Now the job had fallen to Maggie and as she sat by her mother's side, she could hear the whisper of insects creeping.

Her stomach began to rumble loudly, but she knew that there was nothing left in the place to eat. Her last meal, if you didn't count a taste of the broth from Jack's mother, had been eaten the day before, when she had stewed a bunch of nettle leaves that she had found growing near the cabin door. Drinking water filled her belly, but she couldn't be troubled to reach for the jar.

Maggie wondered idly if she should stir herself, maybe make it up the hill to the Filbey's farm? Her legs, though, were feeling wobbly and her eyes kept closing, as if her body wanted to shut itself down. She couldn't be sure of a welcome. There'd been no quarter given, when she'd begged time off from the mistress, after Pat had been put in his grave. She'd been told to consider where her duty lay, just follow the coffin and be back for milking time. Perhaps she'd been missed, perhaps Mistress Filbey would show her some mercy, give a little food, or pay her the wages that she was still owed.

Maggie's sister began to murmur anxiously, her tiny face crumpling in dismay.

"Want to go, Maggie. I nearly done it, but I know it will make you cross if I do."

"Don't worry little one, I'll help yer over," Maggie replied, relieved that her sister had woken and was able to speak. A stone pot was near at hand for use by the two invalids and with great effort, Molly managed to sit herself upon it.

Maggie began to feel guilty as she looked at the state of her. Her long hair was matted from lying in her cot for days and her calico bed gown was twisted and dirty, but to keep her clean meant walking to the well to fetch more water. Something that Maggie hadn't had the energy to do.

Maggie shivered as she tucked her sister back under the thin covering of an old shawl, another possession that had grown sparse and worn with age. The fire was smouldering, giving little warmth, and smoke caused no doubt by the earlier wind that had got up, was whirling around the hole in the roof. She reflected that Jack would be a fool, if he attempted to put to sea before the weather settled.

She looked down upon her dozing sister, wondering how they were going to manage once her mother had gone to her grave. Would the farmer give Molly shelter if she managed to get her job back again? Molly wasn't any trouble, she was gentle, trusting and loving and could probably help in some small way, little though she was.

But what was she doing, sitting there in a great depression, wallowing in uncertainty, when she should be trying to find food to make Molly well again? She got up quickly, then sat down, her head light with the sudden movement. Despondently, she muttered a prayer to be given strength to overcome all hardship.

The sound of Jack's voice came floating into the cabin, as he passed by with his father and brother on the way to their cottage. Alice, his mother, would no doubt have a fish to cook. Home for the Haine's family was not in a mean cabin like the rest of the hamlet. It was a small tied cottage on the boundary, still belonging to the local estate. A blessed two windowed place with a slate roof, leaving Maggie at pains to see, why they should want to uproot themselves.

Michael Haine's job as a ghillie was a good one. The family lived well. At least they hadn't been reliant on the potato crop and with Jack, his son, working too, there was plenty of money for bread. There had been turnips and kale aplenty in the Haines' field, until starving marauders had helped themselves one night. Had that made their minds up for them? Were they thinking now that the place wasn't safe?

She couldn't understand why Jack was being so persistent in taking her with them. Did he imagine that she would leave the place where she had grown and go with him and his family to a strange and heathen land? He had no right to interfere with her future. They were of no relation and she meant to keep it that way. Let him move out if he wanted, but she'd take her chances in Killala, which was where she was meant to be.

The thought of Jack trying to arrange her future spurred her into action. If she took it slow, stopped for a rest on the way up the hill, she'd be at the farm before nightfall. Filbey, the farmer, was a good man and he would help her if he could.

She checked that both her mother and sister were sleeping, tamped down the fire with ashes, then staggered along the track that led to Ballina. She could see by the watery sun that it wouldn't be long before dusk came, as it always came earlier at the latter part of the year. There was the risk of landing in a peat bog, as the well worn path was easy to follow only in daylight, and Maggie shuddered to think what would happen, without a lantern to guide her back. Her stomach started gurgling, reminding her of the reason for her journey. Physically weak she may be, but her determined spirit would push her on.

She pulled herself up a hilly incline, then paused for breath as her heart began to pound with the effort and her lungs worked overtime to drag in extra air. She rested on a grassy hummock, then looked down onto the headland where tillage land ran at the back of the dwellings. Normally at this time of the year, she would have seen the potato fields mounded into drills, in readiness for the next planting. All their pits would have been filled to the top, with enough newly picked potatoes to last the families until the next lifting, if used sparingly.

But now the haulms with the parasitic fungus, that had caused the crop to putrefy in a stinking black slime, stared back at her. The cottiers had been so certain that they would fill their pits to the top again. There had been hardship the year before, when there had been what the experts had called a partial crop failure, but with hope in their hearts and many prayers, they had looked forward to a healthy crop this time.

Each cabin was built about twenty feet from the next one, giving enough space to keep a pig or a chicken run. The hamlet was enclosed by a drystone wall, at the back of which ran the track to Inishpoint, the only way for the cottiers to get to church.

It could be bitterly cold on that headland, for all its shelter of the Oweniny Hills. The north east wind blew constantly in the winter, whooshing down to Killala Bay from the Atlantic and bringing with it icy pelting rain. Then the inhabitants of the lowly dwellings would huddle by their firesides, only stirring to replenish fuel or visit their potato pit waiting for the wind to change.

Maggie dragged her eyes away from the devastation and focused on the view to her left. The village of Killala, was away in the distance, where a row of fishermen's cottages could be seen perched on a hill. She gazed upon a derelict tower nearby. The structure had been a lookout for invaders, centuries ago. It had been out of bounds to the cottier children, its perilous position giving cause for concern. Parents had invented tales of the place being haunted, to keep their inquisitive offspring away. The ghost of a longshipman from Norseland lived there, they said, waiting for his vessel to return.

Bernie, her brother, had once spent a chilly night within that round enclosure, as a dare by his friends. He had boasted loudly that he hadn't been scared, because the longshipman must have gone back home!

Thinking of Bernie brought her hastily to her feet. Sitting there dreaming wasn't going to help in anyway. It had started to drizzle and she began to feel the damp seeping through her poorly clad body as she trudged along. The thick black shawl over her thin calico bodice and long black skirt was no barrier to the elements and the boots that she wore had belonged to her smaller footed mother, causing blisters to form on her uncovered toes. Normally Maggie went barefoot, as she couldn't abide her feet being enclosed, but her mistress was fussy about newly cleaned floors and liked her to wear boots while she worked up there.

Beyond a dense thicket nearby, lay a deep pool that was fed from a fast flowing stream. She could hear the sound of it chuckling and gurgling, as the water came gushing down the hill. This was where the children of the area would come in hot summer weather, to swim in the cool clear water, carefree and naked, posting a lookout for the parish priest in case he came wandering by.

She remembered with nostalgia, back to one summer evening when she would have been eleven or twelve. It had still been warm, when Maggie and her family finally finished their work for the day. They had been weeding between the rows of potatoes, which was back breaking and sweaty work. On impulse her mother had suggested that she and Maggie cool off in the 'Giant's Tub', as the pool had been nicknamed.

Usually her mother tried to maintain a certain dignity, when it came to showing off her private bits to her family, but that day she had thrown caution to the wind, when she saw that there was no one around. She was like a young girl again, splashing and frolicking with Maggie, like two sisters in a bath tub.

The fun was never repeated. Maybe her mother had later thought she had done something wrong? If she had felt it was sinful to show her daughter her naked body, all that had had to change. Now Maggie washed her in cool water from the well, with Mairi shivering throughout the ordeal. With her sunken breasts and the skin of her belly, hanging in folds over her piteous frame, Mairi was glad to return to the warmth of her blanket and wished that she could be left alone. There were bugs in the cabin, the air was filled with hidden dangers and she didn't want to feel pleasant and clean.

Maggie felt her tears begin to well, as she stopped for a moment to rest under the branches of an ancient oak tree. Tears were never far away, when she thought about the state that her family was in. Her heart felt heavy, unease began to grip her mind. What if the Filbey's turned her away?

Across the track were a row of fine cottages. These were proper stone built ones with grey slate roofs, the building materials having been carted from Foxford Quarries. They were sturdy and attractive with whitewashed walls and lattice windows. They had been built forty years before to house the farm workers, by a previous Filbey who had compassion for the men he employed. Not that they were lived in by farmhands nowadays. All had gone, taking their families on hazardous journeys to pastures new. Only one cottage was still occupied and that was by a woman called Widow Dockerty. She had no need to earn a living, she had two sons and a small income that helped her to survive.

One of the previous occupants of the cottages was Maggie's friend, Bridget Mulligan. Her family were the first to pack up their possessions and head for the port of Sligo, where they paid for quarters in steerage and took a chance on returning to Ireland as millionaires! That's what Bridget told her, as the two girls had hugged each other tearfully. The family was off to Chicago to join their Uncle Frank, who had emigrated five years before. They weren't sure what part of the city he was living in, but they'd find him. Chicago was probably as big as Ballina and they knew most of the people in that small town.

The cottage gardens had become unkempt, with the lack of attention that had normally been given to them. All except the end one. That garden was immaculately tended, with roses and honeysuckle-fronds growing round the door. Widow Dockerty lived in that cottage, a foreigner to those parts, but always ready for a chat with Maggie on her journeys to and from the Filbeys' farm.

Chapter 2

Maggie stood under the tree, debating whether to continue her journey or tap on the widow's door. She felt the need to talk and possibly be told of a way that would help her and her family to survive.

The decision was made for her, as the cottage door opened and a small slender woman, dressed in a black long sleeved gown, with her silver hair caught back into a bun at the nape of her neck, beckoned her over.

"The kettle's just boiled and I made a lardy cake this morning," Widow Dockerty said, as Maggie hurried into the cottage to get out of the rain. "Must have known you were coming, Maggie, though I'm surprised to see you on such a wet day. Take that damp shawl off and put it near the fire to dry or you'll not feel the benefit when you go out again… Muirnin, whatever is the matter? Come over and sit yourself in this nice comfy chair."

Maggie felt overwhelmed by the widow's kindness and felt the tears begin to flow. It was good to feel weak and childlike, whilst the woman listened to her sorrowful tale.

"It's me mammy," Maggie managed. "Accordin' to the priest she hasn't got long. If I could just make her a bit more comfy, get her to eat… I've done me best, the good Lord knows I have. Then Molly went down with somethin'… That's why I was passin'. I'm off to the Filbey's, ter see if I can get some help from them."

"There, there, Muirnin," the widow crooned, bending over Maggie, using her pinny which was hanging over a chair, to wipe away the tears. "Sit there and I'll get you a drink to warm you, and you'll eat a slice of my cake as well, my dear."

Maggie drank from a pretty china cup a little later, feeling somewhat better than she had before. The slice of cake had been disposed of in seconds and she eyed the plate hungrily that held the rest.

"You can have some more if you want it," said the widow, cutting another slice, after seeing the longing on her visitor's face. "I baked it for Johnny, but there's more than plenty and he's not expected for a day or two."

Johnny, Widow Dockerty's eldest, was a sea-faring captain on the cattle run.

"The last time I saw you, you were following your father's coffin to the grave side." Widow Dockerty said, breaking into Maggie's thoughts, as she briefly pictured the handsome young man that had just been spoken of. "Was it after that your mother took ill?"

Maggie nodded dully.

"Is there anything that I can do to help you, I have a little money tucked away?"

Maggie shook her head.

"I'm hopin' that Mistress Filbey will come up with the wages she owes me, though she seemed rather angry on the day I left. She said I was ter go to me father's funeral and be back that evening, but it nearly killed me mammy, all that traipsing backwards and forwards when she was feeling so weak. I couldn't just up and leave her, or leave her to look after Molly. If I can just get me wages, they'll tide us over 'til I can think of what next ter do."

"Perhaps your Aunt could care for Molly, just until you've sorted yourself out."

"Aunt Tess is to go and live with her sister in Sligo, though she may take Molly if I ask her to. She's the last of father's family now, the others left the land about two years ago."

Maggie stood up quickly, suddenly anxious to be gone. Talk of Molly reminded her of where her duty lay. There was nothing to be gained by pouring her heart out further to Widow Dockerty, but when she reached for her boots she found that her feet had swollen from the warmth of the fire.

She began to hobble around the room, gathering up her shawl and dragging her fingers through her hair in an effort to appear more tidy. Mistress Filbey was bound to scold if she saw what she thought was an untidy girl.

"Oh, it's goin' ter be dark before I know it," Maggie cried frantically. "I've stayed too long. Forgive me fer burdening you with me troubles. I'll have ter go. Oh, damn these boots."

She fled from the cottage door, barefoot. Her cheeks felt red as she realised that she had sworn. The widow hurried after the girl, shouting that she must return to borrow a lantern later. From the look of the clouds and the gathering gloom, darkness wouldn't be long. Then she went indoors, deciding to make a start on a nourishing stew that she could send back with Maggie for the invalids. She would be certain to stop by to collect the lantern, as the path to Killala could be treacherous at night.

Her thoughts were with Maggie, as she bustled around collecting the ingredients for the stew, then cutting up the rest of the cake for Maggie to take to her family. Tomorrow she would make another, as her eldest son was partial to lardy cake. The girl was certainly having her share of misfortune, though everyone around seemed affected in some way. How fortunate her own life had been, although she missed her husband, Con, dreadfully.

The couple had come from Galway, where Kathleen Dockerty had helped her husband to run a thriving inn. Most of his family, though, lived in Ballina and on their frequent trips to visit, the couple had decided that Ballina was where they would retire. They had bought the cottage from Farmer Filbey, who had welcomed the money, as he had cash flow problems at the time. Sadly, Con had passed away within a fortnight, the slow down in his way of life having an effect on his heart.

It was peaceful now, because Kathleen had no neighbours. It had been noisy, rowdy and chaotic at times, when the Mulligans and O'Rourkes had lived in the row. They had gone away to find a better life in the colonies and who could blame them, when the failure of the potato crop seemed to have touched most people's lives. She thanked the Lord that her two sons didn't rely on the vagaries of a harvest, both were shielded from that, thank God.

Johnny, her eldest, was a sea captain, who ran cattle from the Port of Sligo to farms by the River Dee. He came to visit often, to ensure that his mother was safe and well.

Her other son, Ted, had gone to live in England, running a successful tavern by the seaside, if the only letter she had received from him could be believed. He could be married with children for all she knew, as she had not seen or heard from Ted for many years. A daughter would have been different, she mused, someone like Maggie who had loyalty to her family. Daughters always seemed to stick closer to their mother's sides.

Her friendship with Maggie had begun with a passing greeting, when the widow had been working in the previously neglected garden. Maggie would linger by the garden wall, admiring the transformation that the new owner had performed. A pathway of crazy paving, which had been laid down by Con just before he died, now lead to the cottage doorway. Small orange marigolds lined the borders, with lupins standing majestically behind. Bushes of lilac frilled with white sat in corners, with clumps of phlox and marguerites mingling between. There were pink delphiniums and roses, and fronds of honeysuckle trailed above the door. A real cottage garden that fascinated the girl, as at home the land was used to grow their food. There was no room for the frivolity of flowers, but they used to have a herb garden that was quite pleasing to the eye.

A passing greeting progressed to an invitation to take a drink of tea. A luxury to the hamlet dwelling Maggie.

Sometimes, if she could sneak off from the farm, if her Mistress was upstairs resting, she would spend an hour in the comfortable little cottage. Her new friend seemed to welcome the company. The main attraction for Maggie, were the books that Kathleen Dockerty had brought with her from Galway. No one Maggie knew had such a collection. One book had pictures of Mary and Jesus and the print that the widow pointed out, was something called 'words'. Seeing the girl's interest, Kathleen helped her to read and copy and her pupil soon became an avid reader of religious books and poetry.

Her new found knowledge was hidden from Mistress Filbey, though, as a kitchen and general servant could never aspire to such a thing.

Kathleen, in her turn, developed a motherly affection towards Maggie. She had always wanted a daughter, but after Ted was born, no other babies had come along. Her own education had been limited, having been taught by a local priest who held a weekly class for his parishioners' children after Sunday Mass. That was if their parents didn't mind, as girls didn't need an education and boys were too busy helping on their families' farms. There were some parents though who had a broader vision, like Kathleen's father and she had been grateful that a whole new world had been opened up through books and poetry. To everyone's surprise, she wed an innkeeper and settled down to a happy married life.

—

The chill of the muddy puddles that Maggie had been splashing through, were balm to her aching feet. She soon sat down and inspected them, trying to decide whether to continue barefoot, or put up with the discomfort of the ill-fitting boots. She didn't mind going without a pair that fitted, it was something she had been used to all her life. There had never been the money for the luxury of being well shod. She wiped her feet on the hem of her skirt, thinking to herself that she probably looked like a scarecrow. Mistress Filbey was bound to scold her, when she turned up at the farm in a few minutes time.

First, though, she had to kneel at the shrine of Mary, the Blessed Virgin. The small statue was situated only a few feet along the path on a small wooden plinth. Protected as it was from the elements, by an arch constructed of local stone. Here, passersby could offer their prayers. A plea for the health of a loved one, a request for guidance in a matter that could not be faced alone.

Maggie tried to remember the prayer that Widow Dockerty had taught her. It was in Gaelic, but it had been translated into the English that Maggie understood, her parents having wisely decided that their children would only hear English spoken in their home. With the world changing around them, people travelling to foreign parts and stories of Irish uprisings against their English masters, her parents had accepted that maybe Gaelic would not be the chosen spoken word in Ireland in the foreseeable future.

She had a smattering of the old language and gazing at the statue, she prayed:

"A Mhaighdean bheannaithe, a bhanaltra an Ri ghlormhair
bi am' choimhdeacht san oiche agus fair sa lo me
am shui dhom, no mo lui dhom, am chodia mo am'
shuan, bi am' choimdeacht, bi thiompal, bi am fhaire gach uair."

"Oh, Blessed Virgin, oh, nurse of the King glorious,
Be at my protection in the night and watch me in the day,
at my sitting or at my lying me to sleep,
or at my slumber, be at my protection, be about me,
be at my watching each hour."

The words came easily, as she had said them over her mother and sister many times as they slept, hoping that the Holy Mother would intercede with Jesus for them. Her simple belief was that as much prayer as possible would alleviate their suffering, though hopefully her wages from the Filbey's would ease their plight as well.

The farm was quiet as she walked into the rough muddy yard. Usually there was a great conflict of noise, with cows mooing and hens squawking as they fought each other for grain; geese would be honking, dogs barking and the farmer shouting orders to his farmhands.

There was not a sound, except for a small black and white kitten, which, as he spied Maggie, rubbed his head against her leg, seemingly pleased to see her.

She decided that the Filbey's must be inside the farmhouse, so she squelched her way across the yard to the open door. She left her dirty boots beside the iron scraper and peeped her head around the door.

"Are yer there, Mistress Filbey?" she cried, feeling anxious as she looked around the empty kitchen.

She was used to seeing the big kitchen range shining. One of her chores had been to black-lead it daily, in an effort to keep it spotless. Now it stood dull, the fire had gone out and the woven reed basket, which usually held the peat blocks, was empty. The eight heavy kitchen chairs had been neatly returned to their places under the long well scrubbed table, a rare sight as the labourers were so untidy. There was an air of sadness about the place, the only sound the ticking of the clock that sat on top of the kitchen dresser.

Maggie felt a wave of weariness wash over her, so she pulled out one of the chairs and sank gratefully into it. She put her head into her hands in despair. What was she going to do now if the Filbey's had gone? Had she trailed all that way for no reason at all?

She heard a movement overhead, which gave her a great surge of hope that there was someone still in the building. She ran to the bottom of the stairs and shouted, "Is that you Mistress Filbey? Are you up there?"

She felt relief as the woman replied, "Maggie. I thought I heard someone, thought it was Mr. Filbey coming back. I'm here in the bedroom, come up if you will."

The girl ran up the wooden stairs as fast as her legs would carry her. Her heart had soared at the sound of her mistress's voice.

The farmhouse was a two storied dwelling. There were three bedrooms, one situated over the cow byre, one over the parlour and one over the kitchen where the Filbey's slept. A wise choice, as the room benefited from the heat rising from the kitchen. Maggie felt a sudden chill though as she entered the bedroom. She wondered if the damp air was already getting a grip on the place, or whether it was a sudden fear within her. Did the quietness of the place mean that the Filbey's were leaving? What was she going to do if that was the case? With no job and no future, she and her sister would possibly starve.

"There you are, Maggie," Mistress Filbey said, "I was saying to Mr Filbey only this morning that I wondered if you had heard that we were leaving. So, why have you come? To see us off, or is it that you think we owe you money? If that's the reason, you can turn around right now!"

Maggie's spirits sank when she heard her words. So what she had thought was true. They were going off like so many others. Abandoning the land they worked on, to try to find a better life for themselves.

"Where are you goin', Mistress Filbey?" she asked worried. "Is it somewhere close by so I can still work fer you? I don't mind travellin'. I'll let me Aunt Tess look after Mammy and Molly and come back ter see them when I have a day to meself."

The girl looked at her mistress hopefully. If they were only moving to another county, she could perhaps hitch a lift with a carter, or at least send money to help her family out with food.

Mistress Filbey glared back at her in answer. She had the same look on her face as when she was about to tear a strip off Maggie for some misdeed. Perhaps she had chosen a bad time to make her presence felt, when she could see that the Mistress was up to her eyes in packing and her husband not around to give a hand.

"Where we're going is on the other side of the world, Maggie," she began irritably. "'Tis hardly a day's walk from here. Well, which one is it? Come to say goodbye or do you think we owe you money? It's not like you to hold your tongue."

The Mistress was a small, thinly built woman. She may have been pretty in her younger days, but now her sharp, pointed face was etched with lines and her down turned mouth spoke of unhappiness. She was leaving the place that her husband had brought her, as his young bride almost twenty years ago. They had been hard years for the young Bessie Filbey. The youngest daughter of a slater, she had been unused to supervising the staff needed to run a small dairy and arable farm. She had been unused to the baking, preserving, butter churning and cheese making and the household accounts and marketing. It had taken sheer willpower and dedication and the assistance of her mother who had moved in for a while, to help the farm show a good profit and to learn quickly how to handle a lazy kitchen girl or dairymaid. All that hard work had been for nothing. They were going away to start a new life, leave this all behind them. It was a crying shame.

Her usual mode of dress was a dark homespun dress and a blouse of white linen, covered by an all enveloping pinafore, with a wifely mobcap on her head.

Today, though, she was looking different, with her dark brown hair hanging loose onto the white lace collar of her best blue linen gown.

She had been putting some clothes into a heavy oak chest before Maggie arrived. Now she let go of the lid with a bang. Before Maggie could get a word in as to the purpose of her visit, the Mistress looked at her with the gleam of battle in her eyes.

"That's it! You think we owe you money. Well, you had your three pounds for the half year, two months ago. Don't forget you also had free bed and board. Since then you've been more away from the farm than on it, with clearing off down to Killala. It's not my fault that your family is in the desperate state it's in."

Maggie felt a surge of anger at the woman's disgraceful words. Where was her compassion, why take on such a spiteful tone? She had done all that she had been asked to when she worked there, had worked her fingers to the bone and had earned every penny begrudged her. She knew though that she had to be careful, choose her words so that her anger and dismay didn't show. She had come to get help for her family and the woman could easily turn her away.

"It's me mammy," Maggie replied quietly, shuffling her feet in an effort to appear submissive. She knew that the woman would still like to feel that she was mistress and for once Maggie would have to swallow her pride.

"She's really poorly and Molly's not so good either. We buried Father, as yer know, three weeks ago and there's only me now for support. We've been eating the salt pork that we were keeping for winter, but now that's gone, we've nothing left at all. I was thinking that perhaps you could spare me some butter or cheese or a loaf of bread, or maybe some pennies to buy them with?"

Maggie trailed off her sentence, hoping that she hadn't over-done the pleading. The Mistress's face seemed to be softening, so she forged on.

"Not that me mammy can keep much down, but perhaps some crusts of bread for me and Molly? If yer can spare them?"

"Oh, yes, your father, that's why you left us, wasn't it? I'm sorry, Maggie."

The woman had the grace to look ashamed, but she had her own tale of woe to tell.

"We're in the same boat now. Filbey sold our last three cows on Monday. We've been living off one of the chickens that he kept back, before selling the rest to the Colooneys. When folk know that you're selling up, they beat you down to a price that they want to pay. He's up at Colooney's now, trying to raise money on the horse and farm cart, though God knows we need the cart for our journey to Sligo. It will take two strong men to lift our boxes on, though there's not so many strong men around today."

"I wish you weren't going, Mistress Filbey. What am I goin' ter do when you've gone? Where are yer goin' anyway?"

Maggie asked politely, not really interested in the answer, because now the mistress had said their boxes were going to Sligo, she was certainly going a long way away.

The woman's answer was given huffily, giving Maggie the idea that she felt it wasn't any of her business.

"We are staying with Sara, Filbey's cousin in Sligo, until our ship sails. We need all the money we can raise for our passage to Australia, though why he wants to go to some God forsaken place, full of convicts, murderers and fiends, I just don't know. What's wrong with the Americas, I keep asking? It's not that far away, a few weeks at the most. But no, he wants us to travel to the other side of the world, six months in some tub of a boat, then grab some land and try to ape the gentry. He's in his fifties, for heavens sake and I'm not so far behind him."

She sank down onto the edge of the bed, put her face in her hands and began to cry.

Maggie felt hot with embarrassment. Her mistress breaking down before her. This proud, no nonsense woman, a hard, determined person who had never shown emotion of this kind to her before! She had seen her anger, felt the cold silences, even felt a cuff around her head if the Mistress had been in a bad mood.

But she waited silently, bereft of any pity, until the woman had a grip on herself again. At least she was getting away from here, at least she had plans for the future. She was going away with boxes of possessions, and with chicken in her belly.

The Mistress wiped her eyes with a delicate lace handkerchief she produced from a fold in her skirt. Maggie could see that she was annoyed with herself for breaking down in front of an audience, but as she was never going to set eyes on her servant again, did it really matter now?

She continued to speak, in a plaintive voice.

"Do you know how much they are asking for travel in steerage? Ten pounds. That's for each of us and on top of that we have to pay extra for our water and food! Well, if Filbey doesn't raise any more money today, we'll have to borrow it from his cousin. She did well for herself marrying a moneylender, best kind of person to be married to in these troubled times! I'm scared to death when I think of the journey. We've worked this farm for nearly twenty years, barely making a living. The landlord's rent has always been a trouble to find and we've suffered too with the blight, having to pay for feed for the animals…" Her eyes began to fill up with tears again. "We've got to leave this place and take our chances in a world that we know nothing of. Who's to say that we'll even get there, with that great rolling ocean that goes on forever. We'll probably end up at the bottom of the sea with the fishes and the mermaids. Better to die at home in poverty, than end up in a watery grave!"

Maggie, as she listened, began to lose her patience. Watery grave or not, at least the Filbey's had the means to pay for their passage and time was running out. There was a large harvest moon showing clearly through the bedroom window and it didn't look as if she was going to get a penny piece from the wages she was owed. There was no food in the farmhouse, so she wasn't going to get even a bite of the left over chicken. So why was she standing there, having to put up with the mistress feeling sorry for herself? She decided to ask for assistance one more time and then she was leaving.

"Have you got any old clothes then? Perhaps I can sell them to the shop in Ballina?"

The Mistress answered sharply.

"All the clothes I've got, are either on my back or in the sea chest, Maggie. Why don't you ask for help from that friend of yours in the cottages? You've always run in that direction before."

"I don't like to ask her," Maggie replied defensively. "She's done me enough favours and I don't want to ask her for any more."

"No, but you'll come pestering me, not thinking how good I've been to you over these past few months. Your family would not have survived without the food you used to take home from here and that's what I said you could have. Lord knows what else you've smuggled out of here!"

She glanced at Maggie quickly, after she had made that nasty remark. She knew it had been uncalled for, as her servant had been an honest girl. The tension between them rose, with Maggie doing her best to curb her tongue.

Then a noise from below stopped them from saying what they were thinking.

"It's Farmer Filbey," the Mistress whispered quickly. "Mustn't let him catch me weeping. He's full of excitement and looking forward to his new life! Thinks I share in his quest for adventure. Downstairs with you Maggie and don't you dare let on!"

They were greeted by the small, stockily built farmer, who nodded to Maggie, as if she was still working at the place.

"Colooney says he'll give me four sovereigns, Bessie. I didn't think I'd get so much. He must have taken pity on me. He said he wants to try the horse out before he gives me any money, so he's offered to drive us in the cart to Sligo. That solves our transport problem. I told you things would be all right."

Colooney, was also a tenant farmer renting his land from the same landlord. Unlike Filbey, he felt no need to quit the area, his family having been farmers for generations, used to facing ups and downs in fortune. They had got by when the potato blight hit in 1831, diversifying into buying up the possessions of those who were on their uppers, selling at inflated prices to the dwellers of the nearby towns.

Filbey looked at Maggie as he finished his tale, as if he suddenly wondered why she was standing there?

"Have yer come to say goodbye?" he asked, the light of happiness shining from his eyes "You've left it a bit late though, haven't you? Did the Missis tell you where we're going to go?" His smile grew broad when Maggie nodded. "A nice long sea voyage, plenty of rest, then ready to take up the tools again in the far blue yonder. Have yer got anything to eat, Bessie, my love? My belly's fairly rumbling!"

He turned to his wife expectantly, then asked if Maggie would like to share a meal with them?

She could see from the frown on the Mistress's face that she wasn't welcome. The woman obviously had food tucked away, but she wasn't going to share her last crumbs with a servant.

"No, I'm just on me way, thought I'd come up to say goodbye," she muttered, feeling despair that, after all her effort, she was going to leave empty handed.

"You must have loved working here then, for you to trail all this way in the pouring rain just to say goodbye to us. Was it the land agent who told yer we were leavin'? Oh no, Maggie…!"

Filbey slapped his forehead with his hand, "I'm sorry Maggie, I'd forgotten. Yer daddy, yer went home te bury yer dad." The farmer came over to where she was standing and put his arm around her shoulder. "It won't be easy for yer, now we're going and what with him passing. How are yer managing Maggie? Yer won't have any money coming in."

"That's why she's here," his wife chimed in. "Thinks we owe her wages. She's not come all this way ter say goodbye."

"And do we owe her wages, Bessie? Because if we do we must pay all our debts before we leave."

"We don't owe the girl a thing. Anyway, it's taken all your time pestering folk to buy up our possessions, without us worrying about what we can do to help a servant girl. For God's sake, Filbey, we've got to think how we're going to manage. This money you've got us has to last a long time!"

"Perhaps we can help Maggie, in some small way?" came back his gentle reply.

He sat back down at the kitchen table, with silence hanging between them. Maggie fought back tears at the farmer's kindly sympathy, but she could see that his wife was annoyed that he wasn't taking her side.

"Me mammy's dying as well." Maggie decided to give it one last try. "She can't cope now me daddy's gone. After his funeral she took to her bed and all she is takin' is water. She doesn't want any food. And Molly's been ill. She got the fever, but she's better now and managing to take a little soup. The agent said we'll have to go, now that me daddy has gone and there's no one to see to the rent. I won't be able to pay it 'cos you're leavin', so I'll have no wages, will I?"

Maggie looked at the farmer expectantly, hoping that perhaps he could produce a magic wand.

"Oh, Maggie. Like I said, if we could help in anyway we would do so, but there's no point in keeping the farm on. We've been having problems finding the rent as well, even our barley yield brought us little this time. There's been a glut of it, so prices have fallen and you don't need me to tell you that our potato crop has failed. No," he shrugged his shoulders helplessly, "might as well do what others are doing and get out while we've still got strength in our limbs."

He sat looking thoughtful, while his wife busied herself polishing the table angrily, no doubt thinking that precious time was being wasted on her ex-servant. Time that they needed for finishing off their packing for an early start the next day.

"I've got it!" he suddenly shouted, making them jump at his words. "Bessie, what if we were to take Molly along? One less problem for Maggie and a nice addition to our family. What do you say to that? Bessie? Maggie? Would you agree?"

Maggie gaped at the farmer in shock at his words, but his wife suddenly had a huge smile on her face.

"Oh, Filbey!" she said. "That would be wonderful, a new life with our own little girl. What a perfect solution to Maggie's problems."

She turned a radiant face in Maggie's direction, but could see from her expression that she wasn't very keen on the idea. Once, in a moment of confidence, she had told Maggie that she had always wanted a family, but no babies had arrived for her and the farmer. After a few years she had given up hankering for what she couldn't have. She would be seeing this now as a chance to bring up little Molly. She had met the child once, a pretty, angel faced little dote.

"Let Maggie speak first, Bessie," Filbey's face had taken on a stern look. "Maybe it's not what she wants. It's only a suggestion, Maggie, but you know if we take her with us she'll want for nothing. We can promise she would have the best of care."

"Yeah, I know she would be treated well by both of you," Maggie said, gritting her teeth, thinking that the Mistress could go to Hell in a handcart before she'd hand her sister over. "It's just that I don't know what me plans are going to be. When me mammy goes I will only have Molly, though I don't know how we'll be managing. I'd be heart-sore to lose her if she went with you, especially to the other side of the world where I'd never see her again."

She was beginning to feel tired and dispirited. She could hardly think for the moment, never mind the next few days.

"The problem is I don't think she'd be fit fer travellin' and I'd have to see what me mammy says."

Mistress Filbey was, by now, really set on the idea of an adopted daughter and began to push any objections aside.

"We'll not be travelling from Sligo 'til the end of the month and will be staying at Sara's home 'til then. We could go down to Killala tomorrow and collect the child. Then, if we wrap her up warmly in a shawl and get plenty of nourishing food inside her, she'll be right as rain." She suddenly turned to Maggie, inquiring suspiciously. "It isn't infectious this illness she's had? We don't want to catch anything before we go on the boat!"

Maggie shook her head and answered that Molly had only caught a fever through a chill to her bones. Not having good food inside her and the poor conditions at home hadn't helped either. Mistress Filbey seemed content with that, though Maggie had been tempted to lie and say her sister had caught the yellow fever. That would have put an end to the Mistress's gallop.

"Give Maggie time to think on it, Bessie," Filbey broke in quietly. "You can see the girl is upset enough without us pressuring her. Like Bessie says, we'll walk down tomorrow and see how things stand. If you want us to take Molly, then we shall. Now, is there anything we could do for you before you head back home, Maggie?"

She nodded her head slowly. She had been thinking during this discussion that it looked as if she was going to leave empty handed. The Mistress wasn't going to be forthcoming with any food and she had made it clear that there weren't going to be any wages. She felt cheated, her living had gone and there was to be no compensation for the Filbey's emigration.

She wondered if her next request would be turned away by the old biddy, which is how she was beginning to think of Mistress Filbey, so she turned to speak to her more compassionate husband.

"Could yer give me that feather mattress from yer granddad's room, Farmer Filbey? I'm only thinkin' of me mammy..." she hurried on, thinking that perhaps she was asking for too much again. "It would make her last few days comfortable and I won't trouble you to help me. I can carry it down meself."

Filbey seemed surprised, but nodded his head in agreement.

"Aye child, help yourself. If an old mattress will bring a little joy into those eyes of yours, you can have it with pleasure. You know where to find it, though it's probably damp as it's not been lain on for years. You're welcome to it."

Maggie took him at his word and flew up the stairs to the bedroom at the end of the farmhouse. He was right, the mattress did smell rather musty, but her spirits rose as she thought of the pleasure she would feel, when she saw her mammy lying in comfort. She dragged it off the bed, thinking that if the rain held off during her journey home, she could warm the mattress by the fire before letting her mammy lie on it.

She smiled to herself wryly, as she thought of her own accommodation when she had lived at the farm. She hadn't been given a feather mattress to sleep on. Her mistress thought that servants shouldn't be pampered, and had given her the storage room by the scullery, which was just big enough to hold a truckle bed with a straw filled palliasse on it. Sometimes when the mistress was outdoors, she would creep upstairs and pretend that 'granddad's' room was her own room and would lie full stretched on the mattress to get the feel of it. She hadn't been frightened like some would be, that old man Filbey had died upon it, but loved that drowsy, cosy feeling that washed over her on a sunny afternoon.

Maggie stumbled down the stairs with the feather mattress jogging behind her, its sides bumping against the thick white-washed walls. Hearing the noise, Filbey came to ask if he could help her down with it. She would miss this kind man when he'd gone.

The couple stood together in the doorway, watching as Maggie careered across the farmyard half carrying, half dragging her hard won trophy. It was dark now, but at least the rain had cleared and the moon was so large it was taking up most of the sky.

She stopped for a moment to catch her breath and looked back to where Filbey had taken his wife's hand in his and was patting it gently. Maggie could hear his voice as he soothed her, his words so clear in the still of the yard.

"There wasn't much we could have done to help her, Bessie, but she'll survive. Look at her balancing that mattress, she looks like a lad except for that skirt of hers trailing in the mud. She's young, she's a fighter, she has youth on her side, Bessie. Not like you or me!"

Chapter 3

Maggie paused to catch her breath, leaning against the trunk of the same oak tree that had sheltered her before. A sleepy wood pigeon cooed above her and a rabbit darted past her legs causing her to stifle a scream. Her heart was racing madly anyway, as the burden of the clumsy mattress was beginning to take its toll. She began to wish that she had chosen something lighter to carry, but then chided herself for having selfish thoughts. This mattress was to make life more comfortable for her mammy. It could be her last act of love.

The thought that the earthly tie with her mother could soon be broken, brought a renewal of energy to her trembling body. She could see a light burning over at the cottage and remembered that the Widow Dockerty had offered her the loan of a lantern to guide her back home. Although she knew this track as well as any other in daylight, beyond the cottages lurked marshy bogs and peat land, a danger to any traveller walking after dark Swinging the mattress over her back, she trudged slowly to her friend's garden wall.

Maggie draped the mattress as best she could at the side of the cottage door. She peeped into the window to see the widow, pottering near the fireplace, talking away to someone that Maggie couldn't see. Curious to know who the visitor was, she craned her neck to see who her friend was talking to. It was Johnny, Widow Dockerty's eldest son! He was sitting in the padded winged chair, his long legs stretched out onto the hearth. In one hand he held a plate of stew, in the other a hunk of bread. She felt a surge of delight at seeing him. He had seemed a friendly man when she had met him before. Perhaps Johnny would see that she found her way home safely?

Maggie tapped lightly on the window. Johnny turned around to look, while his mother bustled across the room to the door.

"Maggie!" she exclaimed, when she saw the girl standing there shivering. "I was going to watch out for your return, but look who arrived not half an hour ago? Come in, come in. Whatever's that you've brought along with you?"

She looked past Maggie to where the feather mattress was leaning drunkenly against her cottage wall.

Maggie whispered that it was a feather mattress that the Filbey's had given her. She was beginning to feel shy now that she was going to be in Johnny's presence again. He had got up from his chair politely, when his mother had opened the door and had come to stand behind her, smiling in amusement when he saw Maggie's acquisition, no doubt wondering why she would be carting a mattress about in the dark and across the treacherous moor.

"Bring it in with you girl, it's beginning to rain again," Kathleen said. "It already looks filthy, but no point in making it worse than it is."

Both Johnny and his mother smiled at one another benignly, no doubt thinking that the girl must have been desperate to have accepted a castoff so obviously ready for the bonfire. Then Kathleen hurried over to the stew pot, while Johnny helped Maggie to carry the mattress in.

"I'd made enough stew for you to take to your mother and sister," Kathleen said, "but you can eat yours now before you go, if you want."

She was soon serving the ravenous Maggie with a plate of hot and appetizing beef and vegetable stew, while Johnny pleaded for a second helping.

"Mother is the best cook in Ireland in my opinion," he said, after she had put another steaming plate of stew in front of him. "That's why I hurry home so often to be at her fireside."

His mother was beginning to look her age though, he noted, as he sank back into his chair with a satisfied sigh. The hair that she wore in a bun on the top of her head looked whiter than he remembered before. Her skin was more wrinkled and rather lacklustre, though she still had her usual twinkle in her attractive hazel eyes. His dad had said that Mother had been a looker in her young days. She could have had any man in Galway, but she had chosen him. An odd match, his parents. She being small in height, gentle in her ways and educated and his father loud and brusque, a big bull of a man who could hardly add up his takings at the end of the day. Johnny adored his mother. It was just like her to befriend this bedraggled looking creature and just like her to be giving away food to the poor.

Maggie wouldn't have been happy if she had known Johnny's thoughts at that moment. She was in awe of him because of his status, admired his handsome looks and felt a stirring of excitement to be in his company again, because in her eyes she was a family friend. Her pride would have been severely dented if she had known his thoughts, though at that time she would have admitted to being needy and poor.

She searched for words, in between mouthfuls of satisfying dinner, to engage Johnny in interesting conversation. She didn't want him to think that she was brainless, or a foolish girl with nothing to say because of butterflies in her head. His mother came to Maggie's rescue, asking the outcome of the visit to the Filbey's, which started her off panicking again.

"Would yer look at me sitting here," she said soulfully. "Having all the comforts while me mammy and Molly are waitin' on me. There's no help ter be had at the Filbey's, 'cos they're leavin' fer Australia in a day or two. But I thank yer Widow Dockerty fer all yer kindness. Though if yer don't mind I'll be goin'. Got to get this mattress home. They'll be wonderin' where I've got to, I've bin hours away."

In fact she had only been away two hours, though it had seemed like a lifetime to her at the time. Johnny took his fob watch out from his pocket and glanced at it. It was just gone six. He was looking forward to a cosy evening of chatting with his mother and perhaps a bit of reading before he turned in. He had reckoned without the good heart in her, as she looked at her son in a quizzical way.

"Are you not going to help the girl down to Killala? Look at the state she's in. How can she manage that mattress, lantern and the basket of food I've prepared for her family? I'm sure you'd be happy with a bit of a hand, isn't that so, Maggie?"

"Oh no, it's no trouble," Maggie began to protest weakly, though her heart lifted at the thought of him accompanying her. "I can manage, there's a harvest moon that will light my way. Johnny will be tired having travelled all day from Sligo. It's not fair to ask him…"

Johnny could see from his mother's face that there was no use trying to argue. He and Ted had learnt whilst children, that their gentle mother had a firmer side. He let out a gusty sigh.

"She's right Maggie, I'll help you down but only as far as the river. You'll be fine once we get you down there. Fetch my jacket, Mother, dear, and the lantern, then I'll get out the apple barrow to carry the mattress. That will save our arms from aching and the lantern will guide me back if the moon disappears."

Five minutes on, with hugs and a promise to Widow Dockerty that Maggie would return in the morning to let her know how things were down in Killala, Johnny pushed the old hand-cart along the track. Maggie carried the lantern, as they walked through the dark shadows and eerie silence, occasionally interrupted by the rustle of a nocturnal creature pushing through the undergrowth sniffing out its food, or the hoot of an owl as it sat wisely in a tree. The track was narrow in places and the cart seemed to have a mind of its own, as it wheeled into a shallow peat bog or became entwined in thicket. The moon was covered now by fast flowing clouds and it would have been difficult to see without the lantern.

Not a word was spoken as they walked along, with Johnny wishing he was back in front of his mother's fire. He had been given a lift to Killala earlier by a travelling tinker, though the place where he had sat on the cart had not been under cover. He had thanked God that he had brought his oilskin with him, a necessary item both on his ship and in the pouring rain! A brisk walk had brought him down from the town of Ballina, where he looked forward to a good night's sleep after a home cooked meal. He hadn't reckoned to be escorting home this charmless girl, who now seemed to have been struck dumb.

Maggie was indeed feeling tongue-tied. Gone was the flush of elation at being in his company, replaced now with embarrassment at the scowl on Johnny's face. No doubt he was only there to please his mother, and wouldn't be wanting to spend his precious time with a young and ragged girl. She searched her mind for something to say that would break the silence, lighten his mood, make him see how grateful she was for guiding her back home. Instead her mind played tricks on her, making her dream of how life could be, if this man was always by her side.

Was he old enough to be her father, she wondered? It might be possible, as his dark curly hair was grey above his ears. He was probably in his thirties anyway. He was weather tanned and tall, with eyes the colour of the cornflowers that grew on the shore. He was muscular under his dark fustian jacket and walked with a rolling gait, which told of a man who went to sea. He would be a strong and caring husband. Look how he loved his mother. He would be the same with the lucky girl he made his wife.

Not like Jack. Maggie knew that Jack had plans that involved her marrying him. There was no way she could leave Ireland and go with him without marriage. A single girl would be frowned upon if there was no church blessing. For that reason alone, she was determined to stay on in Killala. She didn't love Jack. He had changed since they were children growing up together. Gone was the carefree boy who had teased her, played tricks on her, climbed trees and paddled in the sea with her. He had got in with a wild crowd from Ballina, liked to drink and brawl with the rest of them, stopped attending church and was uncouth and badly behaved towards his elders. Maybe he was thinking of changing his ways and needed a wife to calm him? Or was it his mother, Alice, who was at the bottom of it all? Was that really why Jack had asked her to go away?

The sound of water rushing into the 'Giant's Tub' brought Maggie and Johnny back from their reflections. They glanced at one another briefly and Maggie knew that now his duty was over, Johnny would turn away. She felt bereft. The future only held misery and anguish. This man would never look at her with yearning, she was a fool to let her imagination think that maybe he would.

He probably had a wife already, someone pretty, someone else he thought the world of, probably English and living on the mainland. He didn't always come to visit his mother on his shore leaves, perhaps he also had a family tucked away.

Johnny looked upon her as she struggled with the mattress, then helpfully handed her the basket of food. It seemed as if a sudden wave of concern had come over him. Was he wondering what was to become of the girl too? He had seen the procession of migrants on their way to the port of Sligo, seen their tattered appearance and the hopelessness in their eyes. Watched them as they crowded together on the quayside, waiting to be taken aboard any ship that would give them passage. Most were without possessions, as they had been sold to pay their fares. Maybe that would be Maggie's future if fate was to intervene.

The clouds suddenly parted to show a deep yellow moon. The rays from it cast a shadow on her face, causing her skin to have a luminous quality. Her eyes became deep pools. For a moment Johnny seemed trance-like as he stared across at her, shivering as he looked on something that perhaps touched his soul. Then the moment was over and he moved away, gruffly announcing that he must be heading back home. Maggie nodded in agreement and said her thanks. It seemed as if he wanted to say something further, but their time together was done. She watched him as he trundled the empty cart back up the track, then disappeared in the darkened gloom.

She waited until not a sound could be heard around her. When she was sure Johnny had gone, she flew behind a bush with her stomach churning and her bladder full. The relief of it all was bittersweet, as her body turned against her, rebellious of the good, rich food that she had eaten with such relish less than an hour ago. A little later, grimacing at the pain that was only just subsiding, she felt around for a clump of dock leaves, trying to avoid the nettles that were everywhere. Thus tidied, bare feet itching from the nettle she hadn't been aware of, she stumbled and bumped her way down the track back home.

As she reached the dry stone wall at the end of her journey, her eyes were drawn to the bobbing of lanterns that seemed to be clustered near her cabin. She wondered why and began to hurry, peering through the gloom ahead of her. Outside the cabin stood a horse and trap belonging to Father Daley. Her heart felt despair when she saw it. He must have been so concerned for her mother that he had driven over specially from Inishpoint, just to see how she was getting on. The priest was an important man in the eyes of his parishioners. A man to revere, as he had direct communication with God and was held in high esteem by the current owner of the acres; an earl from the landed gentry and one of the Kirkpatick clan. He had provided the priest with a manse and transport, to keep a godly eye on his tenants while he was away in his London home.

Jack came running as soon as he saw her, his face full of anxiety as he grabbed her arm. His action caused her to lose her balance and drop the mattress into the mud. Her body was shivering violently, no doubt from the bitter wind that was blowing and the terrible pain in her belly.

"What took yer so long?" he cried, his eyes awash with worry. "Yer mammy said that maybe you had gone to Filbey's, but that was hours ago. I was just thinkin' of coming up the track to look fer you."

He looked down at the discarded mattress and began to raise his voice in disbelief.

"What were you thinkin' of, dragging that thing down the track? You could have fallen into a bog or broken yer neck. I've been worried to death about you!"

Maggie suddenly felt annoyance. Who did he think he was? Why should he be hanging around waiting to lash her with his tongue? It wasn't his business what she had done with her day, was it? But maybe something had happened and he was there to break the news. Was it her mammy or Molly? She began to panic and made to move away, but Jack took hold of her hand, suddenly ashamed of the temper he was beginning to feel.

"Maggie, before you go in, I have ter warn yer. The priest is with yer mammy and things don't look good. Me mam and I took turns with sittin' with her before he came and we had Molly up to try out her legs. I told yer mammy about us going to England and I asked her permission for you and I to wed." He rushed his words then. He could see that she was getting angry with him for trying to hold her back. "We've always liked each other, always got on well together. Don't yer see that now we can always be together and be more than just friends!"

Jack waited for a reaction, but didn't care for the look on her face. What did he want? Did he expect surprise or even delight, that this was the opportunity she had been waiting for? To become his wife and escape from her poverty stricken world? It was her turn to look at him in disbelief, that he had gone to such lengths to get her, by seeking permission from her dying mother and in front of the priest as well!

He hurried on, trying to press his advantage.

"Your mammy said it was her dearest wish to see us settled together."

Maggie snatched herself from his grip, picked up the filthy mattress and dragged it through the open cabin door. She felt a cry of anguish rising up into her throat, as she saw her mother's palliasse, surrounded by the few people who had come to grieve for her. She heard an inhuman cry from somewhere, a rising animal cry, which caused the people in the room, to look up in surprise, then pity, at the wild eyed girl who had just joined them. Aunt Tess stood there with Molly in her arms, Father Daley knelt at her mother's side, Jack's mam and dad stood together looking sad.

"Here, I've brought her this, let her know a little comfort before she passes," Maggie cried in frustration, dragging the mattress over towards them. "Father Daley, Mister Haines, fer God's sake. Someone help me to lay me mammy on the mattress! Mammy, it'll be all soft and cosy for yer, I brought it all the way from the Filbey farm."

She sank to her knees heavily, whilst the two men took the mattress off her, reluctantly. It being only a gesture of kindness, as Mairi's soul had already flown away.

"She's gone. She's gone, hasn't she? Mammy, Mammy," Maggie began to wail. "Don't leave us now, please don't leave… Father, can she still hear me, does she know I came back? Mammy, please don't leave me now."

Gentle hands gripped her shoulders, as the sympathetic priest tried to pull her away.

"Hush child," he said. "Leave her now. Look she's happy. See the sweet contentment on her face as her soul flies off to Heaven. Gone is the grief and suffering she's had to put up with. Come now, let your Aunt Tess and Alice see to her body. Come with me and sit by the fire."

Maggie looked through her tears at her mother's body, seeing the premature aging brought on by the day to day shortages faced by a cottier wife, at the fading greying hair, the sallow skin the colour of parchment paper and the wasted form, so still under the blanket. Her mammy was better off in Heaven, than down here in the misery.

She allowed the priest to guide her to the hearth, where they both sat down upon the rug. The tears in Maggie's eyes had blocked her vision and her throat was beginning to feel sore. She dashed away the tears that threatened to fall again and looked around the room feeling wretched. Someone had been busy, she noted, had mended the fire which was now burning brightly, not smouldering as it had been before and because of this the kettle was bubbling and hissing, as no one had bothered to move it away. The priest's communion chalice and bread bowl sat by the hearth. The wine in the chalice glistening bloodily, as the flickering fire brightened up the dismal place.

Father Daley's words were soothing. This was the death that Mairi welcomed. She would be happy in the knowledge that her daughters would be cared for, now that she had agreed they should go away with Jack. Her troubled spirit was at peace and soon she would be reunited with Patrick, the husband that she had pined for every single day.

"What chance did she have?" Maggie muttered in response to him and then, to his surprise, she got up and staggered away. She tottered out of the cabin and into the cool air again, ignoring Jack, who was standing a few feet away, stretching out his arms so that he could comfort her; turned a deaf ear to Molly's wails and Jack's dad's words of condolence and began to take measured steps along the lane. She was like a sleep walker, not sure where she was going or what she was going to do, but her troubled mind pushed her to get out of there, or she'd be chucking herself over the nearby cliff.

She walked until her trembling legs buckled, sinking onto wet grass near a coppice, where she moaned in despair. She sobbed until her ribs felt raw and aching, her mind numb as she lay curled up like a babe, not caring that her clothes were soaking and her body was shivering from the cold. Her spirit had taken a shattering and at that time she longed to lie there, until she was united with her parents in death.

The sound of footfalls came to her ears a little later, signalling the approach of someone walking up the track. She had rolled herself into a hawthorn thicket, wanting to conceal herself and her misery from any passerby. Father Daley called her name softly, no doubt trying not to frighten the girl, but hearing his voice caused resentment. He would take her back, make her face the future and she wasn't ready for that. She lay there struggling with her conscience, but had she any option left?

"Maggie," cried Father Daley, firmly. "I know you're around here somewhere. Come out and we'll talk. No good comes of grieving on your own."

He stayed patiently waiting in the darkness, listening for a crack of twigs or branches to show that she had agreed to his command. He was glad when she trudged across to meet him, where he gathered her into his arms in his endeavour to give his sympathy.

"You've a lot of pain to bear, my child," he said, once her weeping had started to abate a little. "Two parents gone in the space of a month and a little sister to care for. But with the help of God you'll find that time is a great healer. And isn't it great that Jack is willing to marry you and take you into his care?"

Maggie felt beaten. The priest was a kind man and would only do what he thought was best for the members of his congregation. He obviously thought that marrying Jack was the correct and proper thing to do. She nodded her head against his chest in despair. It would have been a sin to argue with him, even if she had got the strength.

"The grieving gets easier, so I'm told, Maggie," he continued, "and your loss will be quicker to get over once you're settled in matrimony. You won't have time to think when you're caring for your husband and a family."

"Tell me Father, was it Jack that asked you to marry us?" She needed to know if Jack had been plotting to get his own way. The priest nodded. "Did my mammy say anything to you about it as well?"

"Why no, Maggie, your mother was in no fit state to talk to me when I came over today. It was Jack who told me of your mother's wishes. Why, what is it that's troubling you?"

His thin tired face showed his concern. "Is it because you feel it's indecent to marry, when your mother has just passed on?"

She hesitated before she answered. She knew that Father Daley had seen so much misery and death recently, with families split up and even murder committed for a bellyful of food. Marrying her to Jack would bring some light relief from the dismal duties he daily performed.

"I feel it would be more of a sin for you to travel unmarried," he admitted, "especially with two single men and Jack's father in the boat to England, even if Alice, Jack's mother, will be there. There will be times when you might see things that aren't for the eyes of the young and innocent, so I'm thinking that the perfect solution is for you and Jack to wed. He told me you would be leaving in the morning with them. And please don't worry about the burial of your mother without you. I'll see that she has a decent Christian funeral and is laid to rest with your father. Jack and his dad are putting together her coffin, even as we speak, child."

Maggie waited to feel the familiar stab of anger at Jack's interference, but surprisingly she only felt a sense of helplessness. If marriage to Jack had been her mother's dying wish, well so it had to be. It had begun to dawn on her that all hope of staying in Killala was being snatched away. She wondered for a fleeting moment, would it be a mortal sin to rush back up the track and take sanctuary at Widow Dockerty's? She was certain to be made welcome there.

But the priest's hand was firmly guiding her towards the cabin. She was a prisoner. A captive of her religion. No say in her future or control over her destiny.

Chapter 4

Alice Haines, wife of Michael, mother to Jack and Seamus, was a doughty little woman who only wanted the best for her family. For fifteen years she had lived in the little cottage near the hamlet of Killala, while Michael worked as a ghillie on the local Kirkpatrick estate.

Always in the back of her mind she knew the family could do better. She had taken a nosedive in status when she had married the charming Mickey Haines, twenty two years earlier, having been an assistant cook at a place in Westport. He had been working then for the big house on the outskirts, but unfortunately the old earl had died and the heir to the title let a lot of the staff go. Now the same thing was happening on this estate. The Kirkpatrick's didn't invite their house guests like they used to, when friends would come over from England to hunt and fish. They preferred to amuse themselves in London, after hearing, to their dismay, of the indigenous unrest. It wouldn't be long before Michael got his marching orders and the cottage they lived in was taken away. It was time for Alice to grasp her opportunity and grab the cooperatively owned boat that was lying idle on the shore. It was there for the taking by the Haines family. Who else was left who could manage a small boat on the seas or River Moy?

This was the chance that Alice had been waiting for. They could sail to a new life far away. It was just convincing Michael and her boys of it. Her easy going husband, Michael, was not a problem, he thought that they could live off the fish in any sea. Seamus, her youngest child at fourteen, could be swayed to her intention anyway. It was her handsome son, the fair-haired Jack that she might have trouble with. He wouldn't be happy leaving his homeland and saying farewell to his drinking friends.

Alice had wrung her hands at Jack's recent behaviour. She seemed to have no control over him nowadays. It was his cronies in nearby Ballina that seemed to call the tune. Jack had built up a reputation of being a 'hard man'. His work in the quarries at Foxford had given him muscles, he was tough looking and strong. Word had got round that he would fight any man for a prize winning purse. There were many takers, but luckily Jack always won. He loved the admiration from his fellow workers, loved to be the centre of attraction, but he spent most of his winnings in the ale house, treating the hanger-ons.

Alice knew, though, that Jack had an 'Achilles Heel' in the form of Maggie. She knew he had a gentle side and had always said that if he ever married, it would be to this young and innocent girl. He admired her devotion to her family, her determined spirit and tomboy ways. Not like some of the women he had come across, who used their feminine wiles and coquetry to try to snare him.

They would sail across the sea to Liverpool, then sell the boat to anyone who could give a bit of silver in return. Her men could work as labourers, on the many houses that would be needed for the immigrants who would be landing there. Alice would rent a house. She had a bit of money put by and she could let a room to boarders if necessary. Maggie could find a job in a gentleman's kitchen, as that was what she had been doing, learning her skills at the Filbeys' farm. She was bound to want a new life and to leave all this misery behind.

Alice had under estimated Jack's wish to leave his wild ways behind him. There had been too many contenders recently for his hard man title and it seemed to take longer to recover from the bouts. If truth was told he had been suffering a few headaches recently, so perhaps it was time to settle down with a good wife. He could sire many children. A quiver full would make him proud and they would look with admiration at their strong and handsome dad. The problem now was Maggie. How to get her agreement to be his wife needed careful thought. And what would they do with Molly, with her only being three? Did Jack really want to take on responsibility for a small child who didn't belong to him? Wouldn't the child be better with the aunt left in the hamlet? It was too much to expect that he took on the little sister, when he and Maggie would find it hard to be looking out for themselves.

Alice had a quick mind, she was a devious thinker and saw her opportunity while Maggie was away at the farm. She was there when Mairi took her last breath and there when the priest came in to say the final prayers. In front of Jack, God forgive her, she had told Father Daley of the dying woman's wishes, that Maggie was to marry Jack and travel across the sea. Molly was to stay in Killala with the aunt, who would be responsible for the child's welfare.

Clever Alice, Jack's wonderful mother, who usually got her way!

—

The boat didn't make it to Liverpool as had been the intention. Instead it was gripped by a frightening undercurrent as the sun began to show its first light of the day.

Jack and his father hastily swung the big cumbersome oars into action, whilst the fishing boat swirled around in the turbulent waters helplessly. They watched with trepidation as it was thrust unmercifully into the estuary tide of the River Dee. Both men were knocked backwards as the boat plunged sharply along its new course, leaving them all wide eyed and shaken. There was nothing they could do but sit there, as neither man felt strong enough to do anything more. The journey had been exhausting and fraught with danger, but as long as the vessel got them to safety, who were they to change Fate's hand?

There had been so much sea to travel. None of them had been aware of how long the journey had taken, though in a vague way the men seemed to think it was four or five days.

The first day had been one of appalling sea sickness for both Maggie and Alice, and they had taken it in turn to retch the contents of their stomachs up over the side. The two women had lain together on the mattress that Maggie had insisted on bringing with her, sharing a blanket under a tarpaulin and sleeping most of the way. They only felt like taking sips of water from the bucket, which was carefully stowed under one of the seating planks, and waved away the bread and cheese brought to them by an anxious Jack.

He and his father had tried to keep the boat hugging the headland of the north coast of Ireland most of the way, but this course of action had hidden dangers, mostly from jagged rocks that could smash a small vessel to bits. When a lighthouse was spotted along the North Channel, they stayed out at sea, where a strong head wind helped them on their way. There was much creaking and groaning from the valiant old boat, as its small white sail blew with a fierce intensity. But it had got them there to England, got them within striking distance of their destination, even if they had been blown off course at the end of the Irish Sea.

The men huddled together as the boat dashed along uncontrollably, anxiously debating what they should do if they saw a bit of land ahead of them. Hopefully the sea would become a little calmer, then the oars could be used to steer the boat ashore.

The outline of the hills in the distance began to take on a more definite hue and Maggie felt less shaken as she looked towards them. She had the oddest feeling that she had seen the hills before, but at that moment nothing was making much sense to her.

This was a dream that she was in the middle of. A nasty dream that maybe she would wake from and find herself back in the hamlet, caring for her mother and sister. Surely this couldn't be happening. Lying in the bottom of a smelly, wet and perilous boat with the Haines family, with her body feeling numb and with cold and hatred burning deep within.

She thought back to the hurried words of her marriage ceremony, spoken in Latin by the purposeful priest over a trembling bride, and a groom, who just wanted it over with. All the while her mother's body had lain on the granddad's mattress, covered with a blanket for decency's sake. Then Jack dragging her from the cabin, cruelly, she thought now, whilst Molly screamed that she had wanted to go too and Aunt Tess, white faced, but determined, had held on to the distressed little girl. She could have stayed, couldn't she? Fought Jack's insistence that she go along with them? But then, wasn't it what her mammy had wanted? Father Daley and Jack had both said it was so.

Her stomach began to churn at the thought of it all. The heartrending cries of her sister still ringing in her ears, the way that Jack had half carried her protesting body and almost thrown her into the waiting boat. The way that Alice had stood guard, as the men had gone back to the cabin to pick over scant possessions, which might come in handy in their new life.

Maggie began to tremble with emotion, as she remembered Father Daley's promise that he would take her mother's body to the Ballina graveyard, the very next day. These Haines' had prevented her from being there, prevented her from following the coffin, stolen away her right to the ritual of mourning and the knowledge that her mother's body had been safely and Christianly dealt with. Well, she would never forgive them for it, not one of them. Even if they had gone to the trouble of knocking up a wooden box, for her mother to be buried in decently. Whatever happened in her life from now on, she would remember what this family had done. Grief had turned to anger, but for the moment nothing could be done.

Alice had noticed that Maggie was showing an interest in the scenery and shuffled her body closer. They were passing a long narrow island, around two acres in width. Upon it perched a derelict building that might once have been a church. Around the island floated black, big headed creatures that looked like shiny dogs. One came so near to the boat, that Maggie leant out to touch it. She squealed in delight as it nudged her hand, then floated off again.

That encouraged Alice to put her arm around the girl's shoulders, whilst beginning to say that she was sorry that they had left Killala in the way they had. It had been the urgency of getting away on an early morning tide, but if it had been any different they would have stayed and helped to put on a decent funeral for her mother.

Maggie shook off her arm huffily and turned to look at the two smaller islands they were passing, so Alice shrugged. The girl would come round in time. She was sure to need some motherly advice in a strange and unfamiliar land.

The wind had begun to drop and the men began to take turns in rowing. Seamus, Jack's brother, was given the job of looking out for the sand banks that had begun to rise. The hills on the right of the estuary had now become mountains and with the vista being clearer, cattle could be seen grazing in the far off fields. To the left was rolling grassland and dark, dense woodland, with the occasional whitewashed cottage built along the shore.

A little way on, a fishing boat came into view, smaller than their boat, but a neat sturdy craft that bobbed and dipped in their direction. As the two boats drew closer, the man hailed them, probably intending to ask where they were bound. They gasped as one, when, as he did so, a flock of marauding seagulls swooped en masse, down upon the trawling net that the vessel was dragging behind. They all leapt up and waved their arms about wildly, nearly capsizing the boat in an attempt to help the fisherman from losing his precious catch. Then they sat down breathless, laughing with a touch of hysteria, a welcome diversion from the helplessness that they had been experiencing before he came along. The man smiled ruefully and pointed back in the direction he had come.

"Will it be the Irish settlement at Denna Point you're making for?"

He could see their weary faces, the brave countenances of the men, the worried looks on the women's faces and the mean chattels of a family without a home. He had probably seen many of these poor hopeful people before, as many Irish were leaving their homeland and trying for a new life in England. Directing Jack's dad to keep on until they reached the Denna Gutter, he said that the undercurrent would push the boat naturally into shore.

"The river thins out up there, see. 'Tis only high in the Spring. It's beginning to get choked with sampkin grass, so you'll be able to wade in and carry the women ashore."

He waved away their thanks and went on his way, with the seagulls whirling and swooping again and the fisherman poking a long stick into the air.

Jack shouted after him, "What place will we be?" But the man's answer was lost on the wind and under the shrieking cries of the seagulls, as his craft sped off pushed by the fast running tide.

Their spirits lifted a few minutes later, as a large village came into view. It was so different than anything they had ever seen before.

"Will you look at those wonderful houses," shouted Alice, as they all gazed with awe at the tall timber clad buildings interspersed with low whitewashed cottages. Grand personages walked along the promenade, leaving their carriages at the stone quay wall, so that they could take advantage of the healthy seaside air.

They could only stare and wonder. Only Alice whispered, "Is this to be our new home?"

"Naw," replied Jack's dad. "That place be only for fancy folk, not for the likes of us. We could only be their servants and they our masters. The river hasn't started thinning out yet, so we've still some way to go."

His words brought them back to earth again. Yes, they were common labourers, come to work for the likes of the people that they had just seen.

Maggie decided there and then that one day she would wear a dress like one of those that the women had been wearing. Surely they would all get jobs and make some money. Maybe she could save a little and get a pretty dress to attend church on Sundays, but then any dress would be better than the tattered rags she wore now.

She was brought back from her ambitions with a jolt, as Jack shouted.

"This must be the place. Look over there!"

After the big village, the scenery had returned to grass and woodland, but this had now given way to ugly mounds of discarded slag. Beyond the slag was a colliery with its machinery and smoking chimney, making the whole area look grim and austere. A coal sloop was tied up at the quayside and Jack steered the boat towards it. Maybe this was the place called Denna Quay.

A man ran out of the cottage that was built on top of the perimeter wall, shouting as he ran, "What's your business here? Get away, get away! This is private property. What's your business here?"

He was quite an old man, dressed in a worn black suit, and the occupants of the boat waited in trepidation as he puffed his way along the wall to where the sloop was tied. He looked down upon them and his angry face cleared into an understanding smile.

"Got lost, have yer? It must be the Irish settlement yer after. Sorry to be shouting after yer, but I'm the watchman here and I have to be careful. The settlement's just up the river there. Another ten minutes rowin' will do it. Tell yer pals though that I'll be waitin' for them, if they think they can start pinching any of the coal."

Jack thanked him politely and began to steer the boat back into the river. The men felt relieved that the quay hadn't been their destination, as none of them would have wanted to work down a mine. It was on land or fishing that they sought to earn their living or even building work in Liverpool, not entombed underground.

Feeling anxious and with bellies growling, since the cheese and bread that Alice had bought in Ballina for the trip had run out long ago, their spirits rose when the boat was pulled into the swollen gully, as the fisherman had promised. They saw a stone jetty a little further on and stared curiously above the sea wall, where a small group of people had gathered when the boat had come into view. Behind the group, tarpaulins had been erected into makeshift shelters under the cover of leaf laden oak trees. Cooking pots swung over open twig fires and children ran barefoot, clapping and shouting words of welcome to the newcomers. Everyone there looked like themselves, wild, tattered and unkempt. Sacking was draped around the shoulders of the unshaven men in their ragged clothing, hollow eyes stared from white pinched faces. The women looked no better than Alice or Maggie did, clinging to their heavy woollen shawls over thin calico dresses. At least the shawls gave some protection from the now biting wind.

The adults were not as forthcoming as the children, but one man, who must have been their spokesman, shouted, "What is yer business here?"

This time the question was asked in Gaelic, and for a moment the family all stared, wrong-footed. They had expected to be spoken to in English, as they were about to set foot on English soil. Then Michael, Jack's dad, found his voice and replied rustily in the old language that they were from Killala, that they were looking for shelter before the night set in and would be grateful until their dying day, if they could see their way to helping them.

On hearing that they were from the hamlet of Killala, and recognizing the Irish lilt in Michael's voice, a woman spoke quickly to the rest of the group and soon they were being helped ashore. The boat was tied up at one of the mooring rings and Alice and Maggie were lead to the warmth of a welcoming fire. Their chilled and aching limbs appreciated the luxury of a blazing fire and felt even better when the mattress appeared. What bliss after travelling on the cold and choppy sea.

A little later as the family sat around the fire, they were joined by their newly acquired neighbours. Their speaker introduced himself as Patrick O'Flynn and, with nods to the others, he gave their names as the O'Hara's and the Tierneys. Patrick explained that they hadn't made the crossing from Ireland as they had, but had all been given passage on a cattle boat which ran from Sligo to the Dee. The captain of the vessel, God bless him, had been a fine man, who had charged them nothing, as long as they didn't mind sharing the space with the cows. Who had cared about that, when they had free passage and a chance to settle in this fine and prosperous land?

As yet they still had to find work, but the nearest city, called Chester, was around twelve miles away, or so they had been told. This place was called Neston, or Little Ness as the locals called it, it being a few miles away from the main village beyond. They had been visited by the parish priest and a few nosey eejits who had never seen an Irishman before.

"Mebbe they expected us to have two heads or to be wielding a shillelagh, ready to beat them with it, I wouldn't know," Patrick had said wryly. "But we've been made welcome at the tavern over there and the missis was given some flatties by a local fisherman, in return for gutting the rest."

The Mayor of the village had seemed friendly enough, Patrick continued. He had got his men to bring down some tarpaulins for them to shelter under, but had warned them that they couldn't stay forever at the Point. He had suggested that the next time a brick cart came over from Liverpool to his quarry, one of the family's should hitch a ride and see what work could be had over there. There was a lot of building going on in Liverpool and labourers were in short supply. Going to Liverpool was a far better prospect for everyone, than staying in Neston and living off what the Parish could provide.

Patrick had laughed as he recounted the Mayor's words and said they were already getting parish relief of a sort. He had sent his wife out begging. She had been up to the big houses on the road out of Neston and the occupants had given her things, just so she would go away! Then a couple of his children had crept into a nearby farm and had stolen an old limping chicken and a few precious eggs, and the priest had opened his Poor box for them all as well. Of course, the money enabled the men in their number, to get acquainted with the local brew. It wasn't as good as the porter back home, but he was sure given time they would get a taste for it.

Patrick grinned after his explanations and winked a wicked eye, proffering a pot of the ill gotten chicken stew to the Haines', who fell upon this bounty, greedily.

It was getting dark by the time they had finished eating their fill and, yawning heavily, made their way towards the cover that had been allocated. Maggie listened to Jack half-heartedly as they settled on the mattress together, whilst he spoke of all the opportunities that they could have. Michael said that he was just glad that they had made it to safety and Alice said she was thinking of renting a house. Perhaps she would look at that village they had passed earlier. Maybe other folk would like to stay in such a beautiful place. She could take in paying guests, seeing she was still young enough to cope with them, and Maggie could help her. Maggie took no notice of the speculations and curled herself up beneath her shawl, hoping that sleep would come quickly to take away her resentful thoughts.

Sleep wouldn't come to Maggie, as she lay with Jack's body pressed up against her back. Her head was reeling with sudden anger at his thoughtless action. How could he treat her as if there was nothing wrong? Taking the step of lying beside her, without asking if he could.

A week ago the Haines' had been her neighbours. Jack had been a childhood friend, though his mother thought herself above the hamlet folk. What Jack had really done, she ruminated, was kidnap her. He had never given her the chance to turn him down. She may have gone along with the priest and been persuaded to go through with the ceremony, but Jack had only wed her because of circumstance. She would never forgive the Haines' for dragging her away from her birthplace, nor leaving her sister behind, who she probably would never see again.

She stared up at the leafy canopy above her, when she awoke from an eventual troubled sleep. Fingers of early sunlight began to filter through the branches, as she listened to the chirping of the little birds that sat amongst them and cows lowing in the fields behind. She sat upright, causing Jack to fall with a flop off the old mattress they were sharing. He didn't stir, still deep in slumber. She snatched her shawl away from his shoulders, annoyed that he had pinched it, attributing his action to her cold and aching limbs. She rubbed at her feet trying to get the circulation going, thinking longingly of the boots she had left behind at the Filbeys'. Even if they had been cramped and ill fitting, at least her feet would have been warm and cosy in the damp and chilly air.

She scrambled to her feet, wincing as pain shot up her legs and pins and needles cramped her ankles, then with her shawl pulled comfortably around her, she stepped gingerly over to the sea wall.

Across the estuary, shrouded in a light mist, stood rugged, craggy mountains. It was a majestic scene, that made her hold her breath as she took in the beauty of it all. The tide was out and in the distance she could see people walking in straggly groups, or riding what looked to be little ponies, or sitting in two wheeled carts pulled by donkeys. They were coming in Maggie's direction across the sands. She could hear the people singing, their voices rising and falling in lilting harmony. She watched in fascination, wondering at their uplifting voices, a haunting sound that she had never heard before.

A hand tentatively touched Maggie's shoulder as she stood there. She turned quickly, irritated that someone had spoiled her pleasurable occupation, piqued because that someone was disturbing her time alone.

It was one of the Tierney family. Jimmy, the elder boy. He grinned apologetically, then joined her to watch, as the musical people rounded the headland and disappeared from view.

"'Tis a wonderful place we've come to Missis, so it is," he said quietly. "I've stood here often in the mornings since we got here, drinking in the lovely salty air and watching those mountains in all their glory. Seeing the locals grubbing in the mud flats for their crabs and cockles, or looking out to sea when the fishermen set off on the tide. Those people you saw were from the Welsh side. Someone told me they come over for the Neston market, though they can only come across at certain times. Those gullies fill up pretty quick and I have heard there's been a few drownings. So, did I hear you're from Killala? We're from Mayo. From a little town called Westport. So that's why I'm glad we've come to this place, 'cos I wouldn't want to work in a city. Oh no, I prefer the smell of the sea air. No, city life is definitely not for me!"

Maggie glanced up at the young man and smiled at his earnest, tumbling words. For a few moments she had been lost in the wonder of the scenery and had forgotten her reason for being there. Jimmy had touched a chord in her dispirited heart, but she frowned when she remembered he had called her 'Missis'. That alone was enough to bring her back to earth.

She looked over quickly to check if Jack was still sleeping. He wasn't. He was standing a few feet away, glowering. His fists balled in readiness, it seemed he was about to lay this interloper on the floor. Panic gripped her and she wondered fleetingly if Jimmy could be the key to her escaping in the future? He had come over in the cattle boat, maybe he knew of its return. But for now it was her duty to humour her new husband, so she excused herself from Jimmy's presence and walked slowly away.

"What do yer think yer were doing, standing there for all to see. Engaging in conversation with the young bucko?" Jack hissed at her, jealously. His cheeks were aflame with anger and his eyes narrowed dangerously. "You're showing me up in front of the other folk. I was mortified to wake up and see you standing there." Maggie felt indignant. It hadn't been her fault that Jimmy had joined her. The unfairness of Jack's veiled accusation fueled her indignation even more. She answered quietly, hoping to show displeasure in her words.

"Get away with you, Jack, you eejit. What's the harm in me enjoying the scenery and listening to one who shared the beauty of the day? Am I to be yer prisoner now that I'm wed to yer?"

She walked back to their tarpaulin red faced and embarrassed, leaving the two men to sort out Jack's recriminations between themselves. Was this how it was going to be for the rest of her lifetime? Her every action decided upon with reference first to Jack? Not if she could help it. How was it that a few words spoken over them by the priest in Killala, gave him the right to treat her like a possession? She fumed at the injustice of it all.

She was desperate to relieve herself, seeing that the last time had been after supper the evening before, when the kind O'Flynn woman had shown her a clump of bushes to go behind. She felt anxious, though, in case Jack thought by her walking away to the coastal path, it was communicating a further determination that she wanted to be left alone. Indeed she did, wanted to be left alone by him forever, but common sense told her to be careful in her dealings with him. This was a foreign land that she had come to live in.

Maggie was saved from making things awkward by the arrival of Alice. Her mother-in-law had been setting up the kettle over the fire, which she and the O'Flynn mother had agreed to share.

"So there you are, Maggie," she said in a friendly manner, her round, untroubled face smiling with good will as she ambled over. "Do you want to take a walk with me over to the bushes?"

Maggie agreed to the suggestion gratefully, glad for once of the presence of another woman, or at least one sensitive to bodily functions, even though she was an enemy as far as Maggie was concerned. She glanced back at Jack, who was now walking along with his father. He smiled at her and shook his head ruefully, as if he was sorry that he had accused her falsely.

On the women's arrival back at the settlement it seemed they had a visitor. Two visitors to be exact, sitting astride their horses on the narrow, muddy track. The mayor in his official garb, with a gold ceremonial chain around his neck that glinted in the sunlight, and another man, plainly dressed in a brown striped suit, probably his bailiff.

The bailiff, a dour looking man, ordered the inhabitants of the camp to line up in front of them, neither man seemingly surprised that there was an increase of number in the motley group. News had reached them that the Irish were leaving their homeland in droves. In fact, the mayor was amazed that there was not a lot more of them, as he had heard that a captain of a cattle boat was giving free passage from Sligo, in an attempt to aid his countrymen.

The mayor was an elderly man, rather used to good living as the straining buttons on his waistcoat showed. He was of medium height, but seemed to tower over them from his vantage point astride his horse.

"I've heard there has been a bit of thieving going on," he said frowning. "And women pestering our gentlefolk for food." Some of the group shifted uncomfortably. "So, I want to know all your names, how many there are of you, and perhaps someone could tell me how you think you're going to survive down here, once winter comes along. As you can see by the leaves that are beginning to fall, the trees won't give you shelter and the tarpaulins are only on loan. Though it is our Christian duty to help the needy in whichever way we can, our village won't be put upon. So be warned that the wind on this headland can be bitter during winter and we've been known to have snow drifts as high as a man. Now, before I go, heed my next words well. You will live like saints or it will be the ASSIZES for any wrongdoer. Man, woman or child. This is a law abiding area and I mean to keep it that way!"

He shouted these last words, hoping that they would sink into the minds of the rabble, but it only caused a lot of muttering and raised tempers. A few hadn't grasped the import of the mayor's words, as their knowledge of the English language was poor. The O'Hara's in particular needed a translation, as they only spoke in their native Gaelic tongue. The bailiff rolled his eyes heavenward as he listened to their jabber. They were cluttering up this pleasant outcrop with ashes from their fires, using the branches of the ancient trees for their makeshift shelters, and no doubt using the bushes as a midden, nearby.

The mayor began to speak again and a hush descended, as the people realised he hadn't finished. Maggie could see that one or two of the women were beginning to quail at his bullish tirade.

"I had thought by now you would have moved on from these temporary shelters, but seeing as you haven't, I have asked around the parish to see if there is any work to be had. The Brown Horse tavern in the village is in need of a pot man and Farmer Briggs could do with setting a labourer on. There is a place for someone at my quarry and I'm sure my wife could find employment in the kitchen for a clean living woman." He waved his hand in the direction of the mine, then continued speaking. "I can also speak to the foreman at the coal mine, though they've got a few problems over there at the moment, so perhaps he wouldn't welcome workers from outside. Or you could always find employment in Chester, though I've no jurisdiction there. If you don't want to settle in the area, then you can hitch a lift on the brick cart. It goes from my quarry every morning to Liverpool, at half past five. Now, I'll leave my bailiff to take your names, while you think on what I've said. I insist you make decisions for your future, or I won't be answerable for the consequences. Now, I think I have done my part here, so I will bid you good day."

The Irish drifted back to their fires, except for the children, who took advantage of their parent's surly discussions, to clamber down to the shore and paddle in the oncoming tide.

Maggie sat silently with the Haines', feeling that whatever the outcome of their deliberations, it would mean that she would be borne along with them anyway. It would have made no difference had she joined the children playing in the water, as, just like them someone else would decide what she was going to do. She watched them splashing, laughing with glee without any cares, and her thoughts flew once again to her little sister. Her eyes welled up with tears as she remembered Molly's distressing cries. How she wished that Molly could have been among those carefree little ones. Maggie wondered idly, who it was that had decided that Molly should stay behind in Killala? Probably Jack, as Alice being a woman would know about family bonds.

She gazed at the waiting bailiff despondently, watching him sitting glum faced on his horse as he surveyed the scene. Tentatively she smiled at him, though her cheeks began to redden when he nodded back at her. She forced herself instead to listen, as Alice began firmly to try and get her way.

"No, Jack, not the quarry. I'm not having you mixing with tough, wild men and starting up your old ways again. You've a wife to think of now and one day a family. You'll do as yer told and try for that farming job, or you and I won't be speakin', do yer hear?"

Alice lowered her voice, as it became apparent that the other settlers had stopped their discussions to listen. Michael leant over and caressed his wife's hand. The family went back to talking in muted tones and Maggie lost interest again.

The next outburst came from the Tierneys. Jimmy had decided that he wanted to try for the pot man's job, as he saw his chance of getting away from his domineering mam. His mother was quick to realize that she would lose her son's wage and shoved Jimmy's father, because he wasn't insisting that the boy should stay with them. The father shoved his wife and then Brendan, one of the younger boys, attacked Jimmy, who he saw was the cause of all the palaver. The rest of the children began to howl, until the bailiff got down from his horse and bellowed for them all to be silent. He listened crossly, as the Tierney mother pleaded to her son that he should leave for Liverpool with them.

"Now listen you lot," the bailiff growled, as he faced the indignant parents and an adamant Jimmy. "I'm going to act like Solomon. If the lad wants to stay, he'll be treated alright at the Brown Horse. The landlord is a friend of mine and I'll keep an eye on him. If the rest of you are going to stay, I can fix it with the foreman at the coal mine. Lasses as well, they can be of help at the coal face too. Now, come on, I want your decisions as soon as possible. His Worship has gone to a lot of trouble on your behalf so make your minds up and let's have your presence off the shore."

He glared down at the scared looking children and peace reigned amongst them once more. He then walked over to Michael. Had a decision been made as to where this family was going to go? He had been surprised to learn earlier, as he had taken down the family name, that Maggie was married to the eldest son. He had assumed that she was a daughter and, hearing from Alice that the girl was sixteen, had shaken his head sadly. The bailiff too had a daughter the same age, and she was far too young to wed.

He seemed pleased to hear that Michael and Seamus were planning to use the boat to earn their living, and told them helpfully that there was plenty of plaice, flukes, dabs and sole to be caught from the estuary. There was a ready market locally or at Chester or even Liverpool, if they wanted to travel that far, though he didn't envy their choice of making a living. Now that winter was on the horizon, many a storm blew up the estuary, fuelled by the winds from the Irish Sea.

Alice said she might go along to the mayor's house. It would be regular money if the fishing was poor, as they would need to find a place to rent. They couldn't stay here at Denna Point forever. Maggie held her breath, waiting to hear what Jack's decision would be. Was he going to try for work at the quarry and would they need to rent a place too?

Jack asked the bailiff for directions to the farm. He was told it was a mile up a nearby country lane and he could go up anytime. Maggie was left to sit with Alice. Nobody asked what she would like to do and as the bailiff had said the farmer was wanting a labourer, not a couple, it was decided that Jack should go alone and not with a wife in tow.

Michael and Seamus went off to examine the hull of their fishing boat, to see if the extremities of the journey had weakened the vessel in anyway. Maggie listened half-heartedly to Alice as she excitedly prattled on. Did she care if her mother-in-law became a daily help at the manor or the wife of a fisherman?

Soon the settlement became a hive of activity as the O'Flynns prepared to leave. O'Flynn having decided to ignore the mayor's choices and seek a life on 'the tramp', hiring himself out on a daily basis, to anyone who needed a labouring man. Maggie thought that his choice would suit him. He looked as if more than a day's work would kill him and felt sorry for his wife and three small children, who were being dragged along with him. Their departure left the O' Hara's and the Tierney's, who sat around aimlessly, after Jimmy and the bailiff had set off up the Neston road.

She turned quickly, as Alice prodded her in the back in an effort to gain her attention.

"Well Maggie, isn't this grand? Glory be, we're lucky to have arrived when we did. Everybody settling to something and such a lovely place we've come to and it won't be long before we're nice and comfy in a little cottage somewhere. Did you see those neat whitewashed places as we passed that big village down the river? One of them would suit me nicely, so it would. It may be big enough to take in a lodger as well!"

Maggie nodded glumly. Not a word had been said by Alice to encourage or comfort her. It was all about herself. How could Alice forget so quickly that she had left her mother and sister in such a distressing way? Could she not see that her feelings were bruised and that she was incapable of sharing her excitement? Her only wish was to be back in Killala, with her parents alive and with Molly and Bernie and the potatoes growing in profusion on their little bit of land.

She looked at the older woman's round, flushed face, which was beaming with happiness. It was all right if you were Alice Haines, who hadn't had to suffer badly like the wife of a cottier had. She and Michael had always been better off, with him working directly for the gentry, while her family had been subject to the vagaries of the land. Maggie felt like screaming and violently slapping the smile off this person, who had contributed so much to her misery, and if she had to sit at her side much longer, then that would be what she would do.

"Hey up, look what we've got," cried Seamus proudly, as the boy and his father appeared from beyond the sea wall, just as Maggie began again to fall into despair. He flung the still flapping fish onto the ground near his mother, who hastily poked at the embers of the dying fire. Then, seeing Jack had appeared in the distance, Seamus ran over to meet him, grinning happily from ear to ear.

"Did you get taken on big brother? Did the farmer say he would take you on?"

"Whoa there, young-'un," Jack said breathlessly, having run back to the settlement, so eager was he to share his news. "Aye, he's taken me on and Maggie as well. Though he won't pay me any wages fer her, though they'll be gettin' an extra pair of hands." The two brothers walked back to join their family, who were waiting to hear what Jack had to say. "The wife said I was to go back to the farm with you, Maggie. You're to be looked over by her. I told her that you had worked at a farm in Ireland and if we're taken on, there's a cottage as well."

Jack threw himself down beside Maggie, panting with exhaustion as if he had run a mile. He kissed her cheek with exuberance and waited for her to ask him more. She looked at him dully, without betraying the annoyance she had begun to feel. So, she was about to be looked over. Like a thoroughbred horse or a prize winning cow. Would they check her teeth, look in her ears, test her limbs for quick reactions? God give her strength, or she would run from this nightmare yelling and screaming, because Jack was another who couldn't give a damn for her feelings at all. She listened to his boasting, as he turned away to look for admiration from his parents and envy from the immigrants who had not yet gone.

Chapter 5

"Come on Maggie, let's get our things together and be off. I want us to be settled by night time if we can."

Jack became impatient once his bragging was done, feeling no need to tell the others of the lies he'd had to tell. The farmer had been reluctant to take an Irish on, lumping Jack with the thieves who had helped themselves to a chicken or two. Jack had replied that he himself was an honest, hardworking man, who had worked his own farm as a tenant, but had fallen on hard times. All he now wanted was a chance to work on the land again and was hoping to do so at this fine and prosperous farm. He embroidered the truth. Well, they had grown vegetables on their small piece of land, and how hard could it be to milk a cow or clean out a stable? He'd probably be mending walls and clearing ditches anyway. It would be the sort of heavy work that the farmer was loathe to do and if it came to anything else he could ask his mother. Alice had spent her childhood living on a farm. Jack had gone all out to try to impress the man, even offering his strong young wife as unpaid labour. How could the farmer refuse the chance of an extra pair of hands? Jack, though, was now feeling anxious and he urged Maggie to hurry along. He would fill her in on what to say on the way back to the farm.

Before they left, Alice told Jack to leave any possessions and he could collect them later.

"It makes sense, rather than carrying them around with you," she said craftily. "Then we'll have reason to come up to see yer. We could help yer settle in, couldn't we, Michael? And yer never

68

know, the cottage might be big enough for all of us fer a day or two. And Maggie I've taken a liking to this old, but comfy mattress. Yer won't need it where you're going, yer know. The cottage will probably be furnished with a palliasse for you and Jack to sleep on, so I'll keep this for meself, to be sure. A bit of comfort now I'm getting a bit old in the bones."

An angry buzzing began to develop in Maggie's head, as she pushed Alice off the mattress and dragged it fiercely to her, shouting like a woman possessed.

"No, yer old besom, this is the one thing yer are not takin' from me. Yer've taken me freedom, parted me from me sister and brought me to a country that I'd rather not be in. I got this from the Filbey's as a comfort fer me dying mammy, God rest her soul. It wasn't meant fer you to lie on, yer big fat lump!"

She tailed off as she saw the astonished faces around her. This had been just the trigger to let it all go. Alice's face was a picture, whilst all around there was silence, as if everyone had turned into stone. Then Maggie began to weep with anguish as she realised what she'd done, sinking down to the ground with a groan of despair.

"Well," Alice began, standing over Maggie, menacingly, with her arms folded across her ample frame. "Well, I've never been spoken to like that in all me life. Yer want a good slapping, yer nasty little bitch. After all we've done for yer. Rescued yer from a life of poverty, given yer our good name and brought yer to a fine and prosperous country. Get her out of me sight, Jack, before she finds out what a good smack in the face feels like. And youse lot over there, get about yer business and keep out of mine."

Strangely, Jack didn't shout or even raise his voice to Maggie. He just scooped her up in his big strong arms, leaving Alice and the cause of their acrimony behind, and carried her across the field without a backward glance. Setting her down at the beginning of the lane, he continued to walk as if nothing untoward had happened.

If Maggie felt nervous in his company, she was astounded at his attitude. She waited for an angry outburst and trembled inside at the thought of what was to come. She decided to be penitent and began to say how ashamed she felt and sorry she was for shouting, then was amazed when he turned to her, with a hint of amusement in his pale blue eyes.

"That's what I've always liked about yer, Maggie, me darling. The way yer stand up to folk and then hit them right between the eyes. Me mother had it coming. She's never stopped fer a moment to think of how you must be feeling and neither have I when I come to think of it. I'm sorry Maggie, all I wanted was fer yer to come away with us. I couldn't have beared it to have left yerself behind."

Maggie was dumbstruck at his apology and even more so when Jack leant over and kissed her on the cheek. She had never known he had this depth of feeling, to make him scheme like he had.

She looked at him blankly, her mind warring with hate and admiration. He had torn her away from everything she held so dear to her, but she admired him too for following his heart.

She said the first thing that came out of her mouth, not sure how to handle his ardent declaration.

"She shouldn't have said she was keeping that mattress, Jack. It's mine, so it is, and she knew it. I brought it all the way from the farm for it to be a comfort for me mammy."

"I'll get it later if it means so much to you and when we've struck it rich and can afford it, we'll send to yer Aunt Tess and bring Molly over too."

He took Maggie's hand and they walked along the tree-lined lane that led to the farmhouse. The fields on either side, bounded by abundant hedgerows, lay ready for ploughing, harvest being over now and the hay stooks gathered in. Flocks of seagulls circled overhead, looking for last minute gleanings in the leftover stubble, while a couple of red squirrels darted up a tree trunk carrying acorn nuts, gathered in anticipation of their hibernation ahead. A field mouse scurried across their path and a bright eyed robin watched from a bough.

Maggie became anxious as the farmhouse came into view. What if the wife didn't like her? What if she was like Mistress Filbey, harsh and demanding, and her life became a misery? She looked back longingly at the view of the Welsh hills. Maybe Jack could be persuaded to move on if they didn't settle, now that she knew he had a tenderness for her. Surely he would want his new wife to be happy, both at the farm and wherever they were given as a home? Looking down at her appearance, from her travel stained clothes to her dirty bare feet, and the knowledge that her unwashed hair looked wild and wind blown, didn't help matters. The woman would have to be desperate to take her in this condition, or she'd have to be a saint. She hoped it was the latter and bravely carried on.

The farmyard was a hive of activity and Maggie looked with amazement around her, especially at the house. It was built of local sandstone, three storied with tall red brick chimneys. Two attic windows peeped out from under ivy clad eaves, above two bedroom windows that shone pristinely in the weak autumn sun. The front door was open and she could see that there was a kitchen on one side and a best room on the other, both having pretty curtains at the mullioned windows. To the right of the house was a dutch barn, to the left a cow byre. All built in the same sandstone, mellowed from the salt laden winds that gusted up from the sea.

On both sides of the cobbled yard, there was stabling for the great plough horses, pig sties and hen houses and little pens where long necked geese gobbled anxiously. The hens were allowed to roam freely, and they squawked and scratched at the soil in between the worn cobbled stones. The tall doors of the barn were open, revealing neatly stacked layers of golden hay, the product of many hours of backbreaking work for the farmer and his hired hands. A dog tied to a rope outside the farmhouse door, barked out a warning that there were strangers in his yard.

Farmer Briggs came hurrying to the door to see about the commotion. His face wore a welcoming smile when he saw who his visitors were. He looked relieved to see them, with it being so hard to find a local man who was willing to work for the wages of that time. Young people seemed to be drifting off to the cotton mills in Lancashire, where better money could be earned in return for a shorter working day.

Briggs was an easygoing, but hard working farmer. He had worked these twenty acres of good agricultural soil and ten more of pasture for twenty-four years. The farm had been in his family for generations, at least back to the Cromwellian times. He had never looked into how his ancestors had obtained it, some deeds of his forebears were best, in his opinion, left alone.

Briggs had no ambitions, other than to be a successful farmer. He had the loving support of his wife and five pretty daughters. He was a happy man.

He ushered them ahead into the kitchen, the place that was the control room of life for the workers and family. Here they ate their meals and took their orders. This was the domain of Mrs Briggs, where the cooking, preserving and bottling was done. Muddy boots and head wear were removed before entering, grace said at every meal time. The routine varied only by the dictates of each of the seasons.

Maggie quickly took in her surroundings. The place was similar to the Filbey kitchen, although the black leaded range was within a red sandstone fireplace and heavy woollen rugs lay on the stone flagged floor. At one side there was a solid pine dresser, with pretty glazed plates and ornaments upon it, together with a small wooden clock and a pewter jug that held a candle supply. On the other side of the fireplace, copper pans dangled from a wooden rack suspended from the oak beamed ceiling, besides flitches of bacon wrapped in muslin cloth. A pile of logs and tinder, lay in a willow weave basket beside the range and heavy red curtains were drawn against the gathering gloom. The room breathed warmth, as Briggs asked them to sit at the large well scrubbed table, where his curious children, who were already seated, had been told to carry on with their meal.

Ethel Briggs, who had been standing watching by the cooking range, looked flushed and weary after a day of meal time preparations. Her smile was welcoming enough, no doubt thinking that the couple would be nervous, faced with so many of the family in the room.

Maggie learnt later that she was younger than the eldest daughter, Peggy, who was getting married in four weeks' time to Dennis Phipps, a man who farmed sixty acres over Willaston way. Maggie was closer in age to Florrie, who had just left school and wasn't even courting. Still, as Ethel said to her husband later, it wasn't any of her business. The couple purported to be decently married, although she had noticed there wasn't a betrothal ring, but if Briggs assured her that they were decently married, then that was good enough for her.

Ethel's figure was ample and her life at the farm told well. She had a round, red-cheeked face and from under her white cotton bonnet, peeped small yellow curls. Her dress was of brown work-a-day calico, the cut of it doing justice to her broad hips and bosom, over which she wore a white all enveloping apron, for protection from her chores.

Her husband had a similar appearance. Still a youngish looking man, around his early forties, but his figure had gone as his wife's had. Her excuse being from the years of child bearing, his being from the love of food. He wore a coarse, linen collar-less shirt and brown breeches, with tightly buttoned gaiters around the calves of his legs. His waistcoat was of mole skin and usually he wore a black, wide brimmed hat, but not at the moment. His wife didn't allow men to wear headgear in her kitchen. It was one of the little rules she adhered to. Part of her attempt to keep respect and dignity within her family and amongst their workers too. Briggs didn't mind. Ethel had been a loyal and caring wife to him and what were a few little rules to him?

When the wife had mouthed her greetings, the daughters took their turn. They seemed surprised to see them there, as their mother would normally show any strangers into the parlour room. They had ear-wigged before though, when their parents were discussing taking on this pair, lately come from Ireland where the potato crop had failed.

It appeared that the Irish were dependent on the vegetable for their sustenance, though why they couldn't have chosen to sow a variety of crops as their father did, they were not very sure. But whatever had brought them to this shore hungry and ragged, as this couple certainly were, it was their duty as a Christian family to help them all they could.

"This is Peggy, my elder girl and Florrie, Olive, Emily and Ettie," Briggs said in way of introduction. "All good country girls who are helpful to their mother. Peggy is soon to be wed and will leave our happy home and that is why I thought you would be of help, Maggie. All this prancing around, getting ready for the wedding is taking the girls away from their daily chores. Now then, Ethel, what about a bite to eat for Jack and Maggie? You've made enough to feed a small army, I see. They can have a feed and then I'll take them down to Lilac Cottage. It'll be a bit musty down there at the moment, I'm afraid, as it's not been lived in since Joe Parry moved out a few months ago. But I'm sure once you've got a good fire going, you'll take away the smell."

He smiled at them amiably and suggested they help themselves from the vegetable tureens. One of the girls passed down a platter of carved up chicken and stomachs began to gurgle as the couple took their fill.

There seemed to be some whisperings amongst Florrie, Olive and Ettie. Their elder sister lifted her head to reprove them, but was invited then to join in. Maggie felt embarrassed. She could hear that the girls were talking about her, probably about the state she was in with her dirty appearance and rather objectionable smell. But wasn't it nice for them that they were sitting in pretty dresses, never having felt the pangs of hunger, with two solid parents to cater for their every whim?

When Peggy asked her mother permission later to leave the room, then reappeared with a blue woollen garment which she offered to Maggie, she began to feel a great deal of resentment. So she was a charity case as well? What else were they going to do for her, find a tin bath and put her in?

Then she felt Jack's hand searching for hers beneath the table, as he knew what she could do if there was a threat to her stubborn pride. His face wore a smile of acceptance and he thanked Peggy on his wife's behalf most profusely, saying that they would be grateful for anything that they were given, as they had lost their change of clothing to the sea. Their box had been swept overboard on the journey and he was most obliged for all that the family were trying to do. He said that his wife had also lost her nice black shoes and that's why she was barefoot.

Peggy went back to her bed chamber and brought in a pair of old leather shoes. She was apologetic for their worn appearance, but was sure they would fit Maggie, as they looked to be a similar size. Jack again thanked Peggy and asked her if she knew of anyone who had cast off clothes to fit him? It was said with the hint of a joke in his voice and everyone laughed along. It served to calm Maggie's resentment and put her more at ease.

Jack squeezed her hand at various intervals while they continued with their welcome and delicious dinner. He couldn't afford to let Maggie spoil things, not now that they seemed to have been accepted there. If she started showing her fiery side to this family, who seemed to be putting themselves out to be most helpful, then she would ruin everything. She would have to learn to pocket her pride. A job and a cottage, wasn't going to be offered to just anybody. He could see that he had been in the right place at the right time.

Maggie controlled herself and began to look with interest at each member of the family. Peggy had her father's colouring, but not his plumpness. She was a little shorter than Maggie, with straight, shoulder length sandy hair, pale blue eyes and a figure that was nipped in by a corset bodice above a plain brown skirt. She looked a friendly girl, occasionally looking over at the newcomer and smiling. Maggie began to feel so envious. She'd be having a proper wedding, not a mean affair like hers, and Peggy would have the loving support of her parents. Maggie had no one, no parents, no sisters, no one except Jack to care for her. And she wasn't even sure of Jack yet. She still felt wary. And prepared to stand her corner, if things weren't to her liking in the days to come.

Meanwhile, Jack was listening intently to the farmer, who was telling him of the work expected from his new employee. It seemed to involve a lot more than Jack had experienced in Ireland, having only ever helped his father care for the vegetables in their garden. Maggie listened with half an ear, smiling to herself as Jack nodded in agreement, when the discussion turned to crop rotation, breeding practices and the price of beef. Jack was only going to be a labourer, not take over the running of the farm!

Florrie was a little younger, perhaps around fourteen. Her long yellow hair was tied back in a dark blue ribbon. Olive, aged about twelve, was darker haired than the rest, with a long face and sticking out teeth. Emily, with copper coloured hair, a heart shaped face and lots of freckles was about two years younger, and the baby of the group. Ettie, had the face of an angel and shiny, golden curls. All the children, with the exception of Peggy, wore cornflower blue dresses, white pinafores and shiny black shoes. They had ignored Maggie during their excited chattering, though not unkindly, but it was family business this wedding of Peggy's. An outsider could only listen, and was not expected to join in.

It seemed that the meal was over, as the plates were being stacked and Ethel Briggs began to clear away. Maggie offered her help, but was told to save her energy. There would be plenty for her to do when she returned to the farm next day. Ethel looked annoyed when the farmer over ruled her, saying Maggie would need a day to see to her own affairs. The cottage would want a bit of cleaning and need to be set to rights to make it comfortable for the pair. Besides, the girl was looking weary and would need a bit of extra time in bed.

Ethel shooed her daughters off to make a start on washing the dishes in the scullery, as there was always plenty to do in a house of that size. There was the kitchen, the scullery, pantry and parlour and four good sized bedrooms above. Not to mention the dairy, housed in an outbuilding, which had to be scrubbed from top to bottom daily, after the butter and cheese making had been done. Some of the work she planned to offload onto Maggie. There was plenty for the girl to do. What with the making of the dresses for the wedding and the cake still to ice, bouquets to be made up and fruit for the damson wine still to gather, she could have done with her servant's help straight away.

–

Maggie, Jack and the farmer wended their way across the fields towards the coastline later. Patch, the dog, had been allowed off his rope and he snuffled and wriggled through the undergrowth ahead. Maggie felt as if every bone in her body was aching, through weariness or maybe the cold that was biting through her thin clothes. Whatever it was, she was looking forward to reaching their destination and hoped that she could sleep the night away.

Jack and the farmer strode out ahead, with Briggs pointing out his boundaries, marked by dry stone walls. They walked across a marshy meadow, where tall bulrushes sat in murky ponds; over stepping stones placed in a shallow stream; through a small copse of rowan, birch and elder trees, to a wooden slatted gate that opened onto a narrow rutted lane.

Maggie trailed behind, not seeing the purple hue of the clumps of wild iris, the last of the blackberries on the overgrown hedges, towering plants of thistle and marsh mallow, and bracken turned to autumnal brown.

Lilac Cottage was a ten minute walk from the farmhouse; a two roomed dwelling built in a hollow and sheltered from the winds by gnarled old oak trees. A slate roof came low over the eaves of the whitewashed walls and a climbing rose clung above the lintel. Small mullioned windows sat on either side of the stout looking door, where a previous superstitious occupant had nailed a lucky horseshoe. If the two men had been waiting for Maggie's gasp of admiration, as she joined them, they didn't get it. Had it been a hayloft, a pig pen or the floor of a draughty barn, it would not have mattered. All she wanted was to rest her weary body, close her eyes and sleep this nightmarish dream away.

Briggs was rightly proud of the dwellings he provided for his workers. The other two, Ashlea and Thistledown were along the same lane. All three had been improved substantially since his father's day, with a shallow pit privy and a spring water well. The roofs and thick stone walls were sound, no leaks or dampness would be found at any of his properties and he'd even put in a cooking range. The farmer frowned, as his new servant stood morosely, then turned to Jack who it seemed, was struck dumb. Jack couldn't believe his eyes and began to thank his new master profusely, then gripping Maggie's arm tightly, he explained that his wife was very tired.

"It's been a long day for me new wife, Farmer and she's not got over the sickness caused by travelling so far on the ocean waves. A good night's sleep and she'll be fit for anything. Isn't that so me darlin' bride? We can't wait to serve yer and yer good wife, Master. Tis thankful we are, fer this fine place to live, and God bless yer fer giving us this start."

Briggs looked gratified with Jack's appreciative outpouring and opened the door of the cottage to show the couple around.

"Joe Parry and his wife lived here before," he explained. "He got too old for working so I had to let him go. They've gone to live with a daughter the other side of Chester. Her place is too small for them to take their bits and pieces, so as you see they've left the table, chairs and sofa and there's a bed left in the other room too. There's some fruit still on the apple trees and you'll see there's a patch with cabbages and potatoes that your bride can use. Though you'll mostly be having your meals at the farm. And down the lane are your nearest neighbours. Sam Evans lives at Ashlea and the Tibbs live at Thistledown."

Briggs, now mollified, left them to settle in. He liked to be thought as civilized, and as someone who tried to be kind to his men.

Jack opened the back door to let some air in, then went out to look around. He felt he was a fortunate man, as he gazed at the orchard with its old gnarled apple trees, the vegetable patch which was sadly overrun with weeds, and the empty hen house which was rather tumble down. He knew it could be brought back to use again, with the loan of a hammer and some nails.

How he wished that Maggie was sharing his excitement, but she was sitting on the horsehair sofa, too tired to even listen, as he shouted happily to her. The view alone of the sea and the hills beyond, would have brought her a stir of excitement, if she had managed to drag herself to the door.

She was looking around the small living room, with weary red-rimmed eyes. She saw the stone flagged floor, the black iron cooking range, the spindle backed chairs, a round wooden table and an old rag rug that had seen better years. An enamel sink, a brass oil lamp, a battered looking pail, a tin tub and a besom, could be seen through the door that led to the lean to, but at that moment she didn't care. Her stomach was giving her the gripes again and she needed to lie down.

Chapter 6

Maggie lay in a dreamless sleep, having collapsed on the bed that had been left behind in the tiny front room. Jack had gone down to the shore to recover their few possessions. It was a chance to crow to his parents, over the good fortune he had been given by coming there.

It was a healing sleep, which gave Maggie's body time to recover from the fatigue it had suffered over the last few days. Mercifully her mind had also gone into shut down, not showing the images of her mother and Molly, that assaulted her senses most of the time.

A sudden tapping on the window pane brought her to a wakened state. Though not quite aware of her surroundings, she knew that the noise had intruded on her mind.

She gave a cry of fear, as a large shape loomed outside the window. It was not quite dark outside, so she could see that the creature had long shaggy hair, framing a heavy looking face and what looked to be a man's jacket on the upper part of its body. She sat up quickly, her heart pounding painfully inside her chest as she heard the front door opening.

"It's only me, Ruthie Tibbs, yer neighbour," her visitor said hastily, when she saw that Maggie had leapt from the bed and gone into the living room, her right hand balled into a fist in readiness, thinking that she was about to be attacked. "Is this 'ow you greet all yer visitors?"

"Only ones who peek through me window while I'm sleeping," Maggie retorted, smiling weakly as she sat down on the sofa, her legs having turned to jelly as she spoke.

The woman continued to stand in the doorway, staring down at Maggie in an accusing fashion, her arms folded over her pendulous breasts, tree trunk legs standing wide apart. She was dressed like a labourer, wearing a large black fustian jacket over a man's white collar-less shirt, brown corduroy trousers a little short in the leg and black down at heel boots, with the leather all cracked and worn.

"Honest, yer put the heart across me, so yer did," Maggie said, now that her pulse had returned to normal. "So yer me nearest neighbour. Ruthie Tibbs, did yer say?"

"You're not from round here though," said Ruthie, her voice suddenly taking on an accusing tone. "Are yer one of them immigrants then from the settlement, come to take our jobs and our homes? They say they're a load of left footers that's come over, brought their popeish ways with them as well."

"What do yer mean, a left footer?" Maggie inquired, not sure she liked this name that she was being landed with.

"I don't know," admitted Ruthie, a little warily, seeing that the new tenant looked annoyed and about to rise up from the sofa she was sitting on. "Just something our Solly, me husband, said. They're all left footers, them immigrants down on the shore."

Ruthie looked around her and Maggie smiled inwardly. She had suddenly realised that the woman was perhaps not a full shilling, as the eyes that were staring ahead had a blank expression. Though, to be kind, maybe she was just a country girl who was not used to choosing her words carefully, nor used to knocking first on a new neighbour's door.

Maggie decided that all she could do was try to be friendly, better that way than making an enemy of the poor soul.

"I've lived in Neston all me life," continued Ruthie proudly. "Me dad was the blacksmith before 'e was taken with the fever two years ago. They said it was the ale 'e'd bin drinking. 'E drank gallons of the stuff and water too. I'd bin wed a while by then and Solly wouldn't let me go to help 'im. Said me mam could manage, but she died as well. I never even went to his funeral, 'cos Solly said I had to stay down here, where the bugs are blown away by the estuary winds and our water comes from the fast runnin' streams." Ruthie paused for a moment, then looked at Maggie inquisitively. "You got any youngsters then?"

Maggie shook her head and was about to confide in her about Molly, but Ruthie settled her bulk at the side of her and continued to ramble on.

"Me house is bigger, but the same rooms as yourn, but with 'aving all the kids now we've had to make a bedroom in the loft. The little ones sleep in that bedroom." She pointed to the room, where Maggie had been sleeping. "And we have a ladder going upwards, back there." She pointed beyond the fire range. "That's where the older ones sleep. Our living room's bigger, so me and Solly sleep near the warmth of the fire."

Looking around curiously, she asked, "Have yer got nothing fer cookin' in?"

Maggie explained that Jack, her husband, had gone down to the settlement to collect her kettle and cooking pots.

"So, yer are one of them immigrants then?" Ruthie's eyes gleamed with triumph. "I thought yer was, yer don't speak like the folk from round 'ere. So, have yer come to pinch our jobs and our 'ouses? 'Cos if yer 'ave I'll get our Solly to ye. 'E'll sort yer out if I tell 'im yer not from round 'ere."

She stood up and towered over Maggie menacingly, but although she felt a bit intimidated, Maggie didn't show it. She was grateful to be removed from a bad and cloying smell. Ruthie gave off a mixed odour of sour milk, urine and sweat which was offensive to the nose. Maggie knew her own smell was bad enough, but these smells coming from Ruthie brought on a wave of nausea.

She bent her head to touch her knees, which Ruthie probably took as a sign that Maggie was frightened. There was a silence for a moment, as Ruthie stood glowering, then a little tousled head peered around the front door which was still ajar.

"Mam," said the small boy, who came walking into the room uncertainly, seeing a stranger sitting on the sofa, instead of Hilda Parry who used to sit on the sofa before.

"What do yer want, our Ernie?" Ruthie shouted, her attention taken away from her victim, as the nervous child came into view. "I thought I told yer to stay and look after our Katie, while Annie's away gettin' messages up at the Cross!"

"Katie's crying for yer, Mam, and our Danny's wet his breeches and I want to go and play with our Tommy."

"Get out of 'ere now and do as I told yer," bellowed Ruthie, aiming a blow at the cowering child's head. "I'll be after yer and give yer a clip round yer ear!"

Her voice came down a few octaves, as the ragged boy quickly fled, and she lowered her head to speak to Maggie in a confidential tone. "Can't 'ave a minute to meself with that lot, though I suppose I should be going now. It's getting dark and Annie, that's me eldest, will be coming 'ome. That little swine that's just been here is a bugger fer going missin'. Three days he was gone once and it was my Solly who found 'im. 'E were hiding out in a den the older lads had made, feedin' 'imself on scrumpin' apples. 'E had a terrible belly ache and was in the privy for hours. You'll see what it's like 'avin' kids once you get started," she said, nodding her shaggy mane and smiling in a knowledgeable way.

Maggie got up hastily as her neighbour ambled to the door, then stood outside the cottage while she listened to Ruthie's heavy footsteps disappear. She began to wonder where Jack had got to? He must have got lost with no lantern to guide him, not knowing the way from the shore. She trembled from the coolness of the air and the freezing bareness of her unshod feet. Remembering the shoes that Peggy had handed over, she went inside to find them, returning to stand at the door. There was no point sitting in the darkness or in front of an empty grate. She could wait instead for Jack and look at the stars overhead twinkling so vividly, in the clear night sky.

As usual her thoughts turned to Molly and her mother. Was it true that when you died, your soul would fly up to Heaven? Was her mother looking down on her daughters, as they lived their separate lives? Was Molly safe under the same clear sky? She sent a hope filled prayer, up to Him who is supposed to listen, that one day soon she would see her sister.

As Maggie stood there, wrapped up in her dreaming, she began to hear a sort of shuffling, clanking and heavy panting, coming from beyond the bushes that gave Lilac Cottage its name.

Jack appeared, weighed down by the mattress, the kettle and the cooking pot, holding a lantern in one hand, a dead fish in the other and wearing a look of exasperation. He couldn't see the funny side, when Maggie burst out laughing at the sight of him.

"You wouldn't be laughing if you 'ad to drag this damn mattress up that rotten 'ill," he chided breathlessly. "'Tis full of lumps and bumps and smellin' like a midden. Don't know why you want it, I saw there was a good enough mattress here on the bed. All right, all right, I know you got it fer a comfort for yer mother..."

Jack had the sense to stop mid sentence, as he saw his wife's grinning face turn quickly into a scowl. He was tired and ravenously hungry and was looking forward to eating the fish that his Dad had caught, after warming his feet in front of the fire.

His time with Alice had not been easy. She had nagged him into giving her his last few shillings, to help her rent a small house along the shore. She had said Jack had no need of the money now, with his meals and cosy cottage included in his job. Did he want his parents and younger brother to spend the winter on the shore at the mercy of the elements? With the O'Hara's and the Tierney's gone, there would be no safety in numbers any more. Did he want to hear about their frozen bodies, or find that their throats had been cut by marauding thieves? It was too bad of him to abandon his, when it was for his future that they had left their homeland.

Jack smiled to himself as he thought of Alice. She never changed, just took her advantages, when other people couldn't even see one.

He followed Maggie into the cottage, expecting to be met with a welcoming glow from within. Well, at least a fire, or some preparation of the vegetables he had seen in the garden.

He looked around in disbelief and asked her what she had been doing since he'd gone? Jack's face looked grim when she replied that she had been sleeping, but as usual she answered him in a confrontational way.

"So what am I supposed to use to get a fire going? And how can I see to cook a meal, seeing there's no candles? And why can't you cook that fish yourself, instead of expecting me to see to it? You may have dragged me away from Killala, but that doesn't make me yer damned slave."

"Oh, not that again, Maggie. Do I have to do penance for the rest of me life, because I didn't want to leave you in that desperate place all alone? You wouldn't have lived above a week, without money, food and a man to look after ye. Come on now, get over it and we'll have a good marriage, you'll see."

But she walked across to the lean to, took up the lamp and handed it to him and, with hands on her hips, she answered sweetly. "Well, Jack, if you can light this lamp from the candle in yer lantern, and gather up some tinder to make me a good fire, then I will cook the fish for you. But before yer do, let me make it plain. You were never doing me a favour, I could have made it on me own."

Later, after eating their meal of steamed fish and rosy apples, which Jack had picked from the trees in the garden, Maggie told him of their strange and fearsome neighbour. She told a good tale and had Jack laughing, as she mimicked Ruthie, prowling behind the sofa with a nasty look on her face. It lifted the tension that had grown between them and Jack was glad. It was time for bed and his wife was more relaxed. Maggie's eyes had begun to droop with the warmth of the hastily built fire and was looking forward to snuggling down, to catch up on her sleep.

She got up from the sofa and, taking up the oil lamp, made her way to the privy, asking him to make up the bed with a blanket, while she had a wash in the pail.

It was chilly in the bedroom when she joined him eventually. The fire had been dull and sluggish, and had only given enough heat for cooking and warming up the living room. Jack lay under the rough sacking that they had to pretend was a blanket, seemingly deep in thought or half asleep, as she settled by his side.

What did she know about love in a marriage, he was ruminating? Did she know what was expected now they were wed? Perhaps he should have asked his mother, but Alice had been rather bitter towards her daughter-in-law. Maggie wasn't like the painted women that he had met with in the taverns, or the whores who waited for a quickie after closing time. She was the girl he had known since childhood, the girl who was going to share his life forever more.

"Maggie," he whispered, making her wonder as he did so, why he was whispering, since there was no one to hear him, the nearest cottage being a hundred yards away. "Maggie, you know when people are married they have babies? Like yer mother had Bernie, Molly and you?"

"Hmm," she replied drowsily, having turned over to face the doorway, on the edge of a dream, hoping she could get into it without interruption from Jack, who had had all evening to talk if he had wanted to.

"Well, I thought we could make ourselves a baby tonight."

Pictures and images came quickly, as she thought about the making of a little baby. She remembered how alarmed she had been, when Molly had been born. To hear her Mother yelling and screaming, destroying the notion of a delivery by stork. She had linked the night time noises from her parents' marital bed, to the guaranteed certainty of a baby on the way.

Images flitted around her mind, their sow being caught by the next door trotter and the bull at Filbeys' farm mounting a poor little cow. It all seemed disgusting, shameful, degrading, like the monthly bleeding that had appeared the year before.

"I'm tired, Jack," she said, trying to make her voice sound regretful. "Whatever yer want me do, I'm sure I'll be too tired to do it."

She moved away, as again the vision of the little cow came uppermost. There was no way Jack was doing that to her.

"Maggie, turn around and look at me," Jack persisted. "I'm not goin' to hurt yer. Yer know I wouldn't hurt yer for the world. But the priest said words over us that means we should be makin' babies, so I think that we should stick to our vows."

She turned around reluctantly to face him with her face screwed up and her eyes kept closed, hastily pulling up the blanket over her shoulder blades. She shuddered as Jack lifted her skirt above her knees and started feeling around for her private parts. Her eyes flew open and she glared at him in the darkness. He was intruding on what had always been solely hers. She muttered between her gritted teeth that if he should hurt her, she would smack him one, whilst wondering if the priest had known of this palaver, when he had joined them together in matrimony.

He couldn't have done, she thought fleetingly, because Father Daley wasn't married, so how would he have known what Jack would do?

Her legs were pushed apart in a gentle caressing way and Jack prepared to mount her, all the time professing his fervent love. His hardened thing, that Maggie knew that Bernie had also, as she had often changed his rags when he was a baby, forced its way inside her. There was so much pain that she wanted to scream. Jack thrusted and grunted and kneaded her breasts as if they were dough, while she flinched from his onslaught until he was done.

87

She took her ravaged body to the lean-to, later, where the cool water in the tin pail reflected brightly in the moonlight and her body trembled as she searched around for a rag. A feeling of disgust then came upon her, as she looked upon the smears of blood and something else quite nasty, that were running down her legs. She winced as she scrubbed at her parts with the rough calico from her petticoat. Then saw that her feet had turned a startling blue.

Jack lay waiting, his legs stretched out to touch the warmth where her body had been. He felt shame that he had taken her in such a reckless way. She wasn't a woman who could be used for pleasure, then discarded. She was Maggie and he should have treated her more tenderly.

Maggie awoke next morning to find that Jack had left her. She was glad of the fact, because she felt that she could never look him in the eyes again. To do what they had done, in the bed that she was lying on, had been a revelation. She still could not believe, nor did she want to believe, that this was part of being wed. She wondered why her mother had never warned her? Surely she had known that her daughter would marry one day? Deep down though she knew the answer, Mother would have been too embarrassed to explain. It had been Widow Dockerty that Maggie had turned to when that bleeding had started. She had been given a stock of old linen and gently told it was Nature's way. There'd been no other details, no warning of what would happen when she married. No inkling of what would happen in the marital bed. Though, to be fair, it should have been her mother's place to tell her and she'd been too young for the knowledge at that time.

She snuggled down into the warmth her body had created, glad that she had not been required at the farm that day. She planned to light the fire, heat some water, wash again her tender parts, put on the dress that she'd been given by Peggy and then go out to look around.

She could hear the cows in the field next to the cottage, making enough noise to remind the cow herd that it was milking time. There was a frost on the bedroom window and her breath swirled mistily in the chilly room. She slowly counted up to ten, then with her shawl clutched around her, went on tiptoe into the living room.

A glad sight greeted her. The fire was still burning and the old black kettle steamed lazily on top of the iron grill. The room felt warmer and she lowered herself gingerly onto the sofa, while thinking on Jack's small kindness to her. Maybe it was his way of saying sorry? She didn't know, but was grateful that he'd cared.

It was a cleaner Maggie that emerged from the lean-to, later, to dwell on Jack's kindness again. She sat in thought on the sofa, thinking that if she could just get used to his demands upon her body, then this life might be worth living after all. They had work, a cottage to live in, and if Jack was to be believed, soon a baby to hold in her arms. She took comfort in the thought of a little baby to love and care for. Though she would trade it all for Killala and seeing Molly again.

She stood in the back doorway later, looking over to the mountains across the estuary. They could be seen to the left and the right of the orchard, their view uninterrupted over hedgerows and fields. It was a wondrous sight, with the clouds clinging low on the mountain peaks, the sun shining weakly onto a far horizon, ribbons of tide filling up the fast running gullies and figures bent over at their labours, on the nearest shore.

Maggie pulled her shawl around her shoulders tightly, shivering as the autumn air hit her body which was feeling clean and warm. It didn't seem as cold as it would have been in Ireland though. They would have been sitting around their fires by now. There were still a few vegetables and late roses growing in the garden here and rosy apples still clinging to the trees.

Looking at the apples reminded Maggie, that she'd nothing for her breakfast and no money to buy any food. She had little choice, but to visit the farm and throw herself upon the good nature of her mistress. Mrs Briggs was sure to be pleased to see her, especially as the farmer had given her the day to herself. It would look as if she couldn't wait to start working there. She wandered into the bedroom and sat upon the mattress to fasten the buttons on her shoes.

A small silver coin glinted by her right foot as she began her manipulations. Without a button hook, the job was awkward for an untrained hand. It was seconds before she realised that it was a coin, but she hastily picked it up when she saw what it was. A silver shilling. Perhaps one had fallen from Jack's coat pocket or had been left unseen by the auld ones, when they were clearing out their room.

Whatever, it now belonged to Maggie. She was off to the local village to find a baker or a grocer. Mrs Briggs could wait until tomorrow for her services, because her servant was going to grab her freedom while she could.

Chapter 7

Maggie became hesitant when she came to the gated field that would take her past the farmhouse. She dithered in case Jack might see her and ask where she was going. If she turned right and walked down the track to the shore, then Alice might see her and she didn't want to have a slanging match with her mother-in-law either. If she turned left at the cottage, she might meet up with Ruthie, someone else she didn't want to see. So she stood there, waiting for someone who could direct her to the village. Another neighbour maybe, a passing villager, a farm hand who could tell her the way?

In the branches of the oak tree up above her, sat two of Ruthie's children. Ernie and Tommy sat quietly watching her, waiting to see what the Irish woman was going to do. It seemed a good idea to start a spitting game. It would show this left footer that she wasn't welcome around here.

Maggie was surprised, as the first globule landed on her hair. She moved away quickly, thinking that it was a bit late in the year for cuckoo spit, or perhaps it was bird muck that had caught her unawares. Next came a hail of conkers which made her certain she was being got at, but not by anything two legged and feathery.

"Who's up there?" she shouted angrily. "Show yerself. If I get me hands on ye, I'll make yer sorry yer were born!"

She looked up into the branches, scowling as a burst of laughter came from above. Young Ernie showed his head and shoulders, obviously being shoved forward by his older brother, Tommy.

Feeling safe, Ernie began to make the most horrible faces, while Tommy mocked, "Oi, left footer come and get us if you can!"

Both boys gave out squeals of horror as Maggie put her foot onto the tree trunk, grasped the nearest branch and began to haul herself up. She hawked in her throat and spat as she reached them, the glistening droplet landing squarely on Ernie's cheek. He stared at her, trembling and frightened for his life.

"Let's get this straight, you young pups," she snarled, though inside her laughter was bubbling away at the sight of their scared little faces. "I might be a left footer, an Irish tinker, whatever yer want to call me. But you don't spit on me, or throw things, or I'll be the one to do the hurtin'. Now, if yer don't mind you can point out the way to the village, seeing as we're up here with the crow's nests and there's a lot of land to see."

Tommy, raising a shaking hand, pointed her in the right direction. Hopeful to make amends, he told her the quick way.

"If yer in a hurry, Missis, go past the gate, straight along, round the pond, and through the 'ole in the farmer's 'edge. It takes yer to the Burton road, and left will see yer in the village in the blink of an eye." He looked at Maggie with admiration. "Do yer want a hand at getting down or can yer make yer own way, Missis?"

Maggie laughed at his suggestion and shinned down the tree as if she were a monkey. Climbing trees with Jack and Bernie had given her plenty of practise. Though once her childhood was over, she never thought she'd have to use the skill again!

–

The road to the village was steep and winding, so she stopped to get her breath back on the top of an old stone wall. Beyond was a church, a large imposing building, shaded by tall elder and dark-leafed yew. Her spirits lifted when she saw the statue of Our Lady, reposing reassuringly outside the open door and realised that there were other people around who were

Catholics. So why did Mr Tibbs have a down on them? This church was a testament that their faith existed, so maybe it was the Irish that he didn't want around.

She hesitated, uncertain whether to take the path that lead to the church, meet the priest and make her confessional, or continue along to the village where perhaps she could buy herself a pie. Her stomach won. She would feed her soul on Sunday, now that she knew that she could worship here.

She passed a school, an infant school it said on the inscription, with the date of the building circa 1841, then a blacksmith, a row of thatched cottages, and the Wheatsheaf tavern at the bottom of the hill.

She loved that first sight of the village, with its little shops and the smell of baking bread, which drew her to the door of the baker, where she bought a penny pie. It was manna from heaven, with the crust all crisp and golden and the gravy running down the front of her dress as she gulped every morsel.

She watched the village people, as they scurried about their business. Mostly housewives carrying heavy laden baskets, or tradesmen walking along. Two young ladies stood talking in front of a shop called, 'Anne Rosemary (Tailoress)', pointing excitedly at the dress on display in the window. She sauntered along towards them, curious to know where their admiration lay, and sighed at the sight of a blue satin gown. It was an elegant looking creation with velvet trimming at the hem. Compared with Peggy's cast off, it was tip-top. Not home made or second hand, or made from a bolt of cheap lawn.

Maggie sighed, then moved away, feeling rather disconcerted. She should be glad she had decent clothing on her back, when yesterday she'd been wearing tattered rags.

She moved to the doorway of the grocer, her heart beating madly as she saw the queue. Would the man serve her if he knew she was an immigrant? Would he understand her when she opened her mouth to speak? She lingered on the doorstep, her mouth dry, unable to move her feet.

"'Tis your turn, girl," said a large and florid housewife, nudging Maggie inside the door from behind, in irritation. "Some of us haven't got all day, yer know."

Maggie stumbled in and hesitated. All eyes were turned towards her, looking at her curiously. She felt self-conscious and purposely began to examine the contents of the dimly lit room. There were sacks of flour, drunkenly supported by the shabby whitewashed walls, dark polished shelves storing stout stone jars, hooks on the ceiling with flitches of ham, crumbly yellow cheeses under pristine muslin cloth and blocks of salt and sugar, on the counter nearby. The coins in her hand felt sweaty as she waited for the grocer to notice her, whilst part of her mind wondered why she was even standing there.

"Yes, me dear, what can I get yer?" The smiling grocer was polite, as he wiped his hands on the long green pinafore he wore, over a white wing collared shirt and black trousers. He waited, as the young woman before him seemed to be trying to make up her mind.

"A twist of tea, a pound of flour and a cake of soap, Sir, if it's not too much trouble," she said, hurriedly, hoping that she had enough to pay him, though she was sure his prices must be similar to what her mother used to pay in Ballina.

"Certainly, Madam," he replied, somewhat tongue in cheek, as he had guessed from her accent that she was one of the Irish from the shore. "Will that be all, Madam?"

Maggie nodded and watched as he poured a small quantity of tea leaves onto the dish upon his weighing scales, then transferred the contents into a small fold of newspaper, which he twisted and presented with great aplomb to her. A small pre-weighed bag of flour followed, nicely presented in a brown paper sack and then a cake of soap wrapped in waxed paper, that he had sliced from a block with a well sharpened knife. She smiled at him shyly and offered the coins, holding her breath in anticipation that he would give her some change. He gave her back a sixpence, two pennies and a farthing and with

Maggie being able to breathe more freely, she nodded her head in thanks and began to walk away.

"Glad to see someone from that lot paid for their stuff, Ezra," the woman behind her remarked sourly.

"Isn't it a grand morning, Mrs Bailey?" was all that the grocer would say.

Heartened by her success in the grocer, though shaken that already she might have come across an enemy, Maggie turned her attention to whether she should save a little or spend all the coins that day. She turned each one over in her palm, not seeing the young head of Queen Victoria or the face of William the Fourth, but committing to memory the value of the coins and the weight of her good fortune. If she hadn't found the shilling in the first place, there would be no money for her to spend, so a pair of stockings and a pair of drawers from that hosiery shop on the corner, wouldn't be a waste of money as far as she was concerned.

If the truth was told she'd never owned either, so why not indulge herself today?

Later, as Maggie walked along the main street, clutching a pair of black woolly stockings and cambric drawers wrapped in a brown paper parcel and a little wooden hairbrush that she couldn't resist, she heard a bell begin to toll behind her. Then the sound of a bugle, loud and piercing, drowned all sound, so she lounged against the corner wall of the Greenland Fishery and waited to see what kind of distraction was being heralded. It was the mail coach, the horses lathered and snorting as they pulled the vehicle up the hill.

They came to a halt before the post office, a small house really, but an important place, because, for those who could read and write, it was their link to the outside world. Letters and parcels were handed in by the uniformed coach man, then the coach and pair were on their way again.

"Yer can tell the time by the mail coach," remarked a quavering voice at Maggie's side. She hadn't noticed the bent old man who stood near her, watching as the world passed him by. "On its way now to Willaston, then to the villages around. Been coming here now for twenty-six years and the only time I've known it late was during the blizzards, when they couldn't get the coach out of Chester that day. I was a clock maker then. Over there, see by the grocer, so I could tell if it was late or on time. Though I can hardly see a thing now, all shapes and shadows. My son has taken over me business, so now I have the time to dream."

Maggie looked at him sharply. It was as if he had been reading her thoughts, as that had been near enough to what she had been thinking too. That this day was for her pleasure and tomorrow there would be no time to dream. The old man looked sad as she bade him farewell and set off down the lane to the shore, but before she went back to the cottage she meant to gaze at the mountains again.

As she rounded the corner of the lane, she was startled to see a large two masted sailing ship dominating the scene. It took up all the space at the beginning of the old quay wall and was obviously of interest, as there was quite a crowd of people standing watching there. Propped against the side of the boat was a wooden gangplank and, at a signal, reluctant, bellowing cattle began to hurtle down into the sea. The water was shallow between the boat and the sand and as soon as the animals had found firm ground, they ran in all directions. It was bedlam, but a source of amusement for the onlookers, as they shouted their encouragement to the escaping cows. The smell of freedom had assailed the nostrils of the bewildered cattle, having been cooped up in the hold for twenty hours or more.

It all looked so exciting that Maggie quickened her pace towards the scene, until she saw who was overseeing the unloading. It was Farmer Briggs, shouting his orders to his farm hands, who were trying desperately to manoeuvre the animals up the steps of the seawall. She gasped and ran quickly to hide in an alley that she had passed by earlier. If Jack were to see her, there was sure to be trouble. He would take the view that she should be busy in the cottage, not standing on the sea front idling her life away.

Maggie waited with her heart in her mouth, expecting Jack to see her as the cattle were driven by. On hearing the sounds of the men and beasts get nearer, she began to wish she was anywhere but there. Then, suddenly there was a silence, causing Maggie to peer nervously around the corner to see where the cattle and men had gone. But then she saw a dirt track that ran at the side of an old building, once the old custom house, which gave a shortcut across the farmer's fields.

With a sense of relief she came out of hiding and looked over to the crew of the cattle boat, as they prepared to furl up the sails. Her spirits rose, as she realised that this might be the boat that was captained by Johnny. Wouldn't he get a shock when he saw her, thinking that he had left her in Killala, only a couple of days before?

She walked towards the promenade, her heart racing madly at the daring plan that was beginning to form in her mind. If Johnny was the captain, she was going to ask if he would consider taking her back with him. Life with Jack was not what she wanted. She had been coerced into this and these last few days had been a misery. She would return to Killala and beg work from the Colooneys, or any other tenant farmer who had not abandoned their Irish soil. She would find Molly and they would live together happily, instead of having to live with a husband who would be forever demanding his rights in the marriage bed.

Johnny came down the gangplank and walked with his head down in her direction. He was intent on reaching the tavern, where the landlord would be serving a meal. His crew had gone ahead to make sure a new barrel of ale was tapped in readiness. There were a few hours to burn before the tide was running and deep enough for the boat to leave its berth. Maggie stood there in his pathway, holding her breath as she waited for his reaction.

"Have yer forgotten me already?" she asked, innocently unaware that she was being coquettish, as he began to say "excuse me" in an effort to pass her by. "And here was me thinkin' you would never forget me face again."

He took a step back, seemingly astonished, his mind in confusion as he stared back at her. Did he know this girl or was she one of the local prostitutes he had used before? Her face was familiar, but her voice had sounded flirty. But wait, wasn't this the girl he had helped back at his mother's home? Bare foot and ragged, her long hair tangled around a weary looking face? Now her hair was all glossy, she was wearing a dress that wasn't tattered and wore black shoes on her feet.

"Where have you come from?" he asked in bewilderment, looking around him as if she had been conjured up from nowhere. "I left you back in Killala, but a few days ago!"

"It's a long story, Johnny, but take it from me not a pleasant one. If I'm not being a hinder, can I ask yer if yer'll take me back when the ship leaves again? I need to find out what happened to Molly. I left her yer see, I had no say in the matter."

Johnny shook his head, as if he couldn't believe what he was hearing. It was a shock to find her standing there, but he wasn't her keeper. Whatever she'd got caught up in, it wasn't up to him to sort it for her and what was she running from anyway?

Maggie could see he was taken aback, hardly over the shock of finding her in England before hearing that she wanted to go back home again. He looked as if he was having inner turmoil. He might risk the wrath of the ship's owners for bringing a handful of immigrants across the water, but returning to Ireland with a woman was a different matter. What was his crew going to say?

No doubt mindful of his crew, who would be waiting impatiently for his appearance at the tavern, he took Maggie by the arm and ushered her to sit on the sea wall. He demanded an explanation, urged her to explain what had been happening, all the time hoping that her story wouldn't take too long. She kept it short, telling of kidnap, abduction and forced marriage, and punctuated it occasionally with heart rending tears. Finally, not sure that she had convinced him enough to take her, she spoke again of her sister, hoping that the thought of Molly on her own in the hamlet, would swing his decision Maggie's way.

She ended her tale and waited hopefully, scrubbing away her sorrowful tears as she looked across at him. Had she given him enough of what had happened, to make him feel pity, make him help the underdog as he had before? Or should she promise reward for his kindness? A night in his arms might be easy for her.

But Johnny was frowning and his blue eyes looked concerned, as he gave his consideration back to her.

"If it's Molly that has yer worried, then I can tell you I saw a little girl with the farmer. They passed our cottage yesterday morning, as I was leavin' for the port. Filbey was carrying her and I'm sure she was smiling, though I couldn't see so well meself in the early gloom."

He watched, as the girl's face began to crumple. So, Molly had gone. What was the point of returning when her sister had gone so far away? At least if Molly had stayed with their aunt in the hamlet, there was a chance of seeing her again one day.

She took the liberty of hiding her face in the lapel of Johnny's jacket, so overwhelmed by his news that she didn't care. He patted her shoulder, feeling a little awkward. No doubt hoping that none of his crew would return to find out where he'd got to.

"I have a question to ask, Maggie," Johnny said a little later, looking sheepish, hating himself for having to ask it, but the answer would make things simpler from his point of view. He lowered his voice and asked her gently, had the marriage been consummated? Had she given herself to her husband, like she was supposed to do?

Blushing fiercely, she answered that it had been so. Though she qualified her answer by muttering that it had only been to make a baby, because the priest would have wanted her to.

99

"Then I can't take yer back to Ireland." He felt relief, though he wasn't sure why. "Yer married to Jack in the sight of God and until death yer must never be parted. I'm sorry fer yer Maggie, but yer must try to make the most of it. If I take yer back to Ireland, then I'll be guilty of a heinous sin."

With her face full of despair, she got up off the wall and stood apart from him. He tried to soften the blow by making her a promise. He would look her up, when he came back with the cattle the following spring. It would give her a connection still with his mother and he would tell his mother that he had seen her, in case she was wondering where Maggie had gone.

"I must go now, Maggie," he said gently. "My men will be thinkin' I've lost me appetite and they'll down my portion before it's gone cool."

He loped off without a backward glance, leaving Maggie bereft and feeling rather foolish. She had opened up her heart to someone, shown her feelings, hoping to be given sympathy from a fellow countryman. Though why should he, a voice inside her head gently scolded? "You're nothing to him, just a raggedy waif that had his mother's attention. You've foolishly woven a dashing hero inside your girlish dreams."

She sank down on the wall again, thinking glumly of her choices and wondering if Johnny would notice if she hid aboard his ship? If he found her, he was unlikely to turn the vessel around again. For the sake of his mother he would probably help her if he could. Or should she go to the nearest big city and find herself a job? She could hide away in a city, lose herself amongst the many there. Though she'd have to find someone to show her the way, if that was what she planned to do.

"And what if you're having a baby?" the voice inside her head said. "You couldn't manage with a tiny baby. Not in a city, all on your own."

Nothing much was left of the day. The heavens had become a dull blanket of cloud, getting darker by the minute as if there was to be a storm. Seagulls came flying inward, settling in rows on the house tops, a sign that they knew what was coming from the hills. She dithered, then decided, she'd make her mind up on another day.

She began to quicken her step. Following the dirt track, at the side of the old custom house, she reasoned, must bring her back to the farm. To the left of the track was a pit head. An eerie place with its inactive wheel, mounds of coal, empty carts and lack of noise from busy men. It was enclosed by a high wooden fence and a padlocked gate, so she strove to pass it as fast as she could, to the yonder open spaces and glorious coastal views.

Darkness was fast approaching as she came to a narrow lane. It was overhung by shady trees and her feet began to crunch on the carpet of their fallen leaves. A cottage lay in a hollow, but wasn't her cottage on a bit of a hill? Was this her neighbour's cottage, was hers along this way?

She needn't have worried, as Jack came into view as she rounded the next corner. He was walking down the lane with a lantern in his hand. His face looked grim and worried, but brightened when Maggie came into view.

"Jack, Jack," she shouted, relief making her run towards him as if the Devil himself was after her. "Jack, I'm so glad to see yer. I've been walking around for hours, wouldn't yer know it? I got lost when I decided to get some air. Then it started getting dark and I thought I'd never get to see yer again. I'm sorry I wasn't here when yer came home. Yer must be tired, yer've had a long day."

She thought her breathless words would please him, especially as she flung her arms round his neck as if she had missed him so. But he looked suspicious, as if he didn't believe her. More so, when he felt the bulge of her shopping, which was carried under her shawl.

He took her arm, not unkindly, but she felt the pressure tighten as he pulled her through the cottage door.

"Walking around lost fer hours? Is that yer story then?" He glowered at her, as she began to take her purchases out from beneath her shawl and put them on the table. "Then how come you asked the Tibbs boys the way to the village? They told me that they showed you which way. What's this?"

His eyes widened as he saw the woollen stockings, lace trimmed drawers, wooden hairbrush, block of soap, packet of flour and the twist of tea where she'd placed them. His tired looking face began to look grim.

"Have yer bin out pinchin', Maggie? God, our first few days in this fine country and yer about to get yerself thrown into gaol! What have I married, a brazen slut who goes taking stuff that doesn't belong to her? Maggie, I swear I'll do you damage if you've been out pinchin'!"

Her first thoughts was to confess that she had indeed stolen them, as Jack was working himself up into a frenzy, at the thought of her being a lowly thief. He might throw her out and then the decision would have been made for her. She could hide in Johnny's cattle boat. But her sense of pride and thoughts of the eighth commandment, spurred her on to tell the truth. Well, part of the truth anyway.

"Jack, how could yer think it?" she said, in a wheedling voice that sounded remorseful. "I had a bit of fortune. I found a shilling down on the quay."

She picked up two cups that were upended on saucers on the table and began to prepare a cup of tea. Her stomach was rumbling and she wished that she had bought herself some bread. Once she had added some boiling water to the tea leaves, she turned to face Jack, feeling wary.

"The truth is Jack, when I found the shilling, I couldn't wait to spend it, knowing that tomorrow I would be stuck down at the farm. I was desperate for some warming under clothes. It seems colder here than back in Ireland and I need to be warm for the winter days and I need to have a hairbrush to keep me looking tidy, as I don't want to become all tattered looking again."

She felt relieved, as Jack's face changed and a look of understanding crossed his features. Indeed he laughed and said he never thought he'd see Maggie Mayo in a pair of black stockings, never mind a pair of lacy drawers, and was sorry for jumping to the wrong idea of what she'd done. Worry for her safety had caused his anger, he had expected her to be waiting when he'd got home. He took her in his arms and kissed her lovingly and this time she knew not to push him away. They spent the evening happily, firstly sharing a meal of the eggs, bacon and loaf of bread that Mrs Briggs had sent with the new worker, knowing there was nothing at the cottage to make a meal. Jack told of his new found knowledge of farming and the work mates he'd met along the way and she didn't flinch when he took her in his arms that night. She had to learn how to live with her marriage and hoped to keep it that way.

Chapter 8

"Come on Maggie, it's cock crow! Get yerself up and we'll be away. We'll get a good breakfast at the farm if we shift ourselves. Come on, sleepy head, it's the start of a new day."

Maggie awakened to see Jack hovering at the side of the bed. His tousled hair glinting in the light of the lantern he was holding, his clothes all crumpled as he had slept in them again. He was sporting a grin from ear to ear as he watched her droopy eyed and trembling, woken up startled from a sleep that was deep and satisfying. She stumbled into the lean to and splashed her face with icy, tooth chattering water, then ran her new brush through her long, tangled hair.

Jack had topped up the fire with slow burning elder, so the room was still cosy from the night before. She listened to the wind that was howling around the chimney and wished she could stay in the cottage instead.

Maybe she could plead a chill or a headache, perhaps Jack would take pity on her if she said she was getting a cold? She turned to see him watching, as she stood at her ablutions in her lacy drawers.

"Oh, Maggie," he suddenly said with longing in his voice, looking at her bare young breasts, which she was wiping over with a damp rag, "I wish I could take yer back to bed. It's better now, yer getting used to me. Come here to me, me darlin' and let me feel yer body against me once more. Yer do me heart good, just the sight of yer…" And he pulled her close, his manhood hardening as he stroked her bare bosoms and kissed her neck and hair.

"Get off me, Jack," she cried in annoyance, pulling herself from his arms hastily, to run to the bedroom and put on her dress, stockings and shoes. He'd had his way twice, as they'd lain together that night, now the farm was seeming a safer place!

Childishly, she peeped under the bed to see if there were any more coins. Jack had swallowed her story of finding the shilling down on the quay. She resolved not to tell him that it probably fell out of his pocket, nor would she tell him of her encounter with Johnny, or the news that Molly had gone. This was knowledge she would keep to herself, not share the truth with anyone.

Maggie was glad of Jack's body though, when they set out into the gusting wind and relentless rain. The trees bowed beneath the strength of it all and he sheltered her as they walked in the early gloom, with his arm tucked around her protectively, as they hurried up the lane. The lantern was dispensed with after the flame flickered and danced, then went out. Jack kept cursing, but they kept on going, keeping to the stony track rather than the short cut through the boggy fields.

So much for the cock crow. The other hands were already there, sitting at the table eating their substantial meal. All eyes turned to look at the pair as they fell into the kitchen, which felt so warm after the bitter chill, and was filled with tantalizing smells.

Maggie with her wet shawl pulled tightly round her head and Jack, with his fair hair plastered down, his coat dampened and evil smelling, and his feet squelching in his boots, as they had let in the driving rain, stood there on the threshold feeling uncertain. It was natural for the farmhands' eyes to be all resting on Maggie, a woman they had never seen around the place before. Jack introduced her.

"This is my wife," he told them proudly, "and Maggie, this is Billy, Solly and Sam."

And with nods to Briggs and Ethel, Jack ushered her confidently to the table, where Ethel served up eggs and fried potatoes, with warm, refreshing milk straight from the cows.

"So, have you settled in now, Maggie?" Briggs asked kindly. "Got the cottage how you want it? All nice and cosy for the pair of you?"

The farmer made a fuss when he saw her. Her appearance would stop his wife from nagging him now.

Ethel Briggs looked up from where she was cracking eggs into a large black frying pan.

"Yes, and she can make a start on washing the crockery. She can take them through to the scullery now."

Maggie stopped chewing and stared at her new mistress, incredulous. Did she mean before she'd even finished eating, when there was still a couple of tasty sliced potatoes to go? But the others were standing now, waiting for their orders from the farmer. Including Jack, who was frowning as he looked at her. She swallowed another morsel quickly, then began to collect the greasy plates. She was back in harness, shoulder to the wheel, her holiday was over, she was a servant again.

–

The morning passed by quickly, as Maggie humped overflowing pails of water from the pump in the yard to the kitchen, boiled numerous kettles, scrubbed the place from floor to ceiling, then helped Ethel Briggs to prepare the food for dinner time. Not one daughter made an offer to assist them. Indeed earlier they had sat being happily waited upon, by the new servant at their breakfast time. Peggy's excuse was her appointment with the dressmaker, the other girls were on their way to school, but Maggie had the feeling that they had been instructed not to lift a finger. They had a servant now and she must earn her daily pay.

All the time she was watched and assessed by the mistress. Occasionally it was pointed out if she had skipped a bit of scrubbing, or peeled a potato too thickly, or the cabbage could have been chopped up more. To be fair, the woman did her share and they worked in relative harmony, until they stopped for a cup of tea at ten o'clock and Maggie nearly left by the door.

"That gown could do with a bit of a wash, Maggie," the Mistress remarked, as they tucked into a plate of homemade biscuits and a cup of elder-flower tea. "I'd swear that Peggy gave it you in a clean condition and it looks as if you have slept in it. Have you not a nightgown or a petticoat you could wear at bedtime? I insist you have certain standards whilst you're working here."

"I'm sorry Mrs Briggs at me appearance," she said, feeling like a lick spittle. "Truth is, we lost our change of clothing when our box was swept overboard. Until Jack gets his wages from the farmer, we have no money to replace them and this week I'll have to stock up on food."

Maggie felt resentment at having to square herself with this woman, who, if she could have given her eye teeth just to be in her shoes, she would. It wasn't her fault that she didn't have a cupboard of clothes to choose from. She wouldn't be working there if she had.

"Here, you can borrow Peggy's apron so that you can cover yourself for the moment," the farmer's wife said briskly. "I can't have you handling food in the state you're in, with me about to show you how to make a cheese. I like my servants to be clean and tidy. Cleanliness is next to Godliness, you know!"

Yes, she did know and she brightened when she heard that her new mistress was a believer. Maybe a Catholic woman, just like herself?

"Could yer tell me, Mistress Briggs, if yer attend the church on the road out of the village?" she ventured. "Only I saw it when I went for a walk yesterday."

"You mean St. Mary's or St. Winefred's?" the woman replied, helping herself to another biscuit as she spoke. "Both are on the road out of Neston. St. Mary's is the one we go to and all our workers are expected to as well. You can take the track up from the farm gates to the village and it's up the dip from the Wheatsheaf Inn. It's eight o'clock for the Sunday morning service and six o'clock at night. It's the rector there who will conduct our Peggy's ceremony, for which we've only another four weeks to go, I might add."

"Did yer say rector, Mistress?" Maggie prattled on, regardless. "We call them priests back home. Our priest, Father Daley was really kind to us. He married me to Jack on the night that me mother died. He said we…"

She stopped suddenly mid sentence, seeing that her mistress was looking at her with some sort of disdain.

"Oh, you're a Catholic then?" she sniffed, as if she had a bad smell under her nose. "A left footer. Well, I'm sure I don't know when your pagan services are. You can hear the noise of the bell at St. Winefreds tolling for the Masses all Sunday morning. You'll have to go along yourself and find out the times. Jack will still need to work on Sunday though. The animals still want seeing to, no matter what the day."

Well, that put me firmly in my place, Maggie thought resentfully. A left footer and of shabby appearance too. It's a wonder she wants to breathe the air we're sharing. She felt like getting up there and then and walking, but she knew that she couldn't. It would be difficult for her to get a servant's job again so easily.

Besides, what if she and Jack had made a baby? It was a thought that was constantly nagging her, and with that in her mind, she determined, she never would get away.

At midday came the workers, hungry as hunters from a morning spent in the fields.

Worn out and wet, with their clothes clinging, to Ethel's despair, and with her new servant waiting on the table, the wife put before them a substantial meal. There was no sitting or joining in for Maggie though, she was to eat her meal later when the men had gone. The men seemed to be getting on well in each other's company, 'Team working', the farmer called it, as he kept up a cheery conversation throughout the meal.

Maggie stood watching from her station by the kitchen range, noting that Jack seemed relaxed and happy as he wolfed down his meal. Not so, the man called Solly. His face wore a doleful look, perhaps it was because he had a long, thin face and a hooky nose. He had darting, thin-lidded eyes and his chin was dark and stubbly. Beside the open-faced freshness of the young man named Sam, Solly was an ugly man.

Sam must have been every mother's dream for their daughter. Handsome, good humoured and modest, while Billy, sitting on the chair beside him, was an elderly man. His face was lined and leathery, his brown eyes tired and rheumy looking, but he did his share of the farm work and Briggs was loathe to let him go.

A tremor passed over Maggie, when at one time Solly's eyes met with hers. It was a knowing look that he gave her, making her feel dirty and afraid. As if he was seeing her as an usurper, Irish scum taking work from a local woman. She hoped that he wasn't going to be unpleasant. They were, after all, going to be neighbours, but he seemed so different from his mountain of a wife. She decided to give Solly a wide berth if it was at all possible, feeling sorry for Ruthie, for being tied to such an unpleasant man.

She gazed at Jack, with his strong arms and good natured smile, his fair hair still plastered across his forehead, and decided that life for now wasn't so bad. He was doing his best to make a future for the pair of them, the least she could do was to work as hard as him.

The afternoon passed pleasantly, as mistress and servant worked together in the dairy, churning and patting butter and Maggie learning how to make a passable cheese. The woman seemed to have regretted her unchristian stance on the girl's religion and listened, seemingly sympathetic, as the girl poured out her woeful tales. She was rewarded at the end of the day with a basket of cold sliced chicken, another loaf and a large portion of crumbly Cheshire cheese.

So her spirits were high, as she walked back to Lilac Cottage, she had shown her mistress that she was not a shirker. It was late in the afternoon by this time and the sky looked as if it was on fire, a sure sign that tomorrow would be a better day. It would be Saturday and hopefully Jack would be given part of his wage. Maybe some of it would come her way.

Her mind was full of things that would be needed, especially a bar of carbolic soap, as the cottage was in need of a good scrubbing. Then a needle for darning, thread and a quantity of remnants to make the place look brighter, and basic things such as flour, tea and salt. The money may stretch to a scrag of beef, with vegetables from the garden for a Sunday feast.

She didn't notice the man as he stepped out of the bushes just ahead of her, as her head was down, whilst she hopped the muddy puddles left by the morning rain.

"Solly, yer put the heart across me, so yer did," she cried, when she saw him. "What are yer doing leaping out in front of me? Where's Jack? Is he still at the farm?"

Solly had a very strange look on his face. He was fiddling with his trouser buttons and shuffling around, as if he had a pain.

She felt concern as he stumbled down into the grass, and went to kneel beside him to see if there was anything she could do. He grabbed her at once by the hair and pushed her to the ground, all the while muttering, that he was going to 'tup the whore'. Her heart was racing wildly, as she realised what he wanted to do. It wasn't a friendly wrestling match that Solly was after, he was after doing what Jack did, though definitely not the same!

"Get off me, yer stupid eejit," she cried, her strength returning once she'd got her breath back. "What the hell do yer think yer doin', yer silly little man?"

She managed some scratching and kicking, until she threw him onto his back. Then kicked him in his tender bits, so he lay winded and in pain.

She stood there watching, breathlessly, concerned that she'd really hurt him, though she was more anxious to discover why he had chosen to lie in wait for her.

Solly clutched his manhood to him, as he gasped and uttered slimy sounding words that she hadn't heard before. It was really dark now and she would only be able to see his face if she were to lean across him. She decided to stay on the track, in case he was shamming again.

"Saw yer with that fella," Solly wheezed, "down on the sea front yesterday. Thought I'd have a go as well, seeing as Ruthie's turned the cold-hearted bitch on me. A man has to have some relief, or a man can go blind, yer know."

Maggie started laughing, albeit a little hysterically, but he looked so comical lying there. That this ugly little man, who was at least two inches smaller than her, should even think about trying to ravish her. Of course, he didn't know that she had been brought up with Jack and had Bernie for a brother. Both, who in their childhood days, she had given a bloody nose.

"Well, I hope yer've learnt a lesson from attacking me," she said grimly, after trying to get her feelings under control. "It was tough back there in Ireland and we weren't brought up to sit around. Years of toil have made me any man's equal, so think on that if you catch me alone again. And the man yer saw me with is a cousin. I was just saying goodbye to him."

"Then yer won't mind me mentioning to yer husband, that yer looked like yer were being more than friendly," he retorted nastily, squatting on his haunches now, still believing that she had been having a secret meeting with the man.

"Go ahead, but you'll end up feeling foolish, especially as I'll tell him that you've bin following me. Back home, Jack was a prize fighter, what they call a pugilist, and he won't take kindly to what yer saying about me. Remember I'm still his young and innocent bride to him."

Solly spat on the ground, then set off limping. Maggie gave him time to get ahead. He must have had a seizure of the brain to act in the way he had. Or did all men keep their brains in their trousers like Solly, waiting for a chance to force their will?

She resolved to keep her distance and treat all men with suspicion, though she couldn't see Sam or Billy behaving like Solly had.

–

"Bless me Father, fer I have sinned."

There was a silence as she got her thoughts together. Where would she start? What were her sins?

"Go on child," prompted the priest, no doubt thinking that he hadn't heard her voice before. Obviously one of the new Irish parishioners, who had slipped in late to Mass and just made it in time to take the Holy bread.

She cleared her throat and began.

"I don't love me husband like I should and I was forced into a marriage I didn't want." The priest listened for more, but Maggie had gone silent, trying to think of another sin. "I have bin rude to me mother-in-law and I should say I'm sorry, but she was at fault as much as me."

There was another long silence as she wondered if spending the shilling she had found and not sharing and not telling the truth to Jack was a sin? Or asking Johnny to take her back to Ireland, or kicking Solly where it hurt? She felt confused. Confession had been much simpler at home in Ireland, as she strived to be the perfect girl. Sometimes she had made up little sins just to tell the Father, but this time these were real. Grown up sins, not childish ones, and now she was nervous at what this priest would say.

Father Joseph O' Brien was from a little town in Tipperary. The third son of a draper, the business wasn't big enough to support another son, if he took on a family. It had been hard for this young man to leave the area that he had grown to love, to study theology in Dublin. He was a sensitive and caring person, with a clever brain, and if his family could have afforded the fees, would have had a distinguished career in medicine. But, instead of healing limbs and bodies, his mission was to heal the soul and mind. He was popular with his parishioners, especially old ladies, to whom he was especially kind. Joseph could hear from her voice that this young woman was hurting. She was away from her family and homeland, just like he was. He felt a certain empathy and her punishment would not be strong.

"Say three Hail Mary's and one round of the Rosary and try to work out what you can do to make your marriage better. Remember that your union is forever and you don't want to live in constant misery. As to your mother-in-law, think of the fifth commandment when next you meet."

Maggie dipped her head, made the sign of the Cross, then said thankfully that she would do so. The penance, after all, was not so strong. She went to genuflect before the altar, then skipped her way along the churchyard path. Soul cleansed, she was off to Parkgate promenade. Jack was working until three o'clock and until that time she was free.

–

She walked down past the English church and stood for a while listening to the singing. The road outside was full of horses, carriages and carts. Not like the church that she had just come from, where the congregation had been very small. She was wearing the blue dress with a stain on, so had thankfully slipped into the back of the church.

She stood outside the 'Anne Rosemary' dress shop, looking longingly at the colourful rolls of satin, bombazine and brocade. She dreamt of the dresses she would wear if she became rich and famous. Though how that would be achieved, she wasn't sure.

Moodily, she carried on, thinking back to the day before, when she had tackled Jack during his break at midday.

She had worked extra hard all morning, cleaning the family bedrooms, while the daughters were helping their mother in the kitchen and scullery. At dinner she had sat down with the others, while a meal of hot chicken and potatoes was served. She had thought that it was a sign that she had been accepted, and was eagerly looking forward to a little pay. Even Solly was in an up beat mood at the table, no doubt thinking how many tankards of ale he would be downing that day.

The farmer had then called his farm hands to order and produced his wooden cash box from a kitchen drawer. There was silence as each man, except Jack, was given seven silver shillings and they thanked him most profusely, as if receiving a pot of gold. It was Jack's turn next and Briggs made a speech to say how well the new man was doing. He was a hard and tireless worker, as the farmer had known he would be. Nothing was said about Maggie and no money came her way. When Jack followed the others through the door, back to the fields or wherever they were working, Maggie had felt her temper rising. Had she not worked herself to a shadow for the Mistress, in those past few days?

"Excuse me, Farmer Briggs," she began, trying to keep an even voice, though she wanted to shout that he was being unfair. All eyes turned to look upon her, from the farmer's wife, her daughters and even the little black cat, who had jumped on her lap looking for chicken crumbs. "Farmer Briggs, when I worked fer the Filbey's back in Ireland, it was usual fer the servant to get paid fer their labours. Would that not be so here at your farm, as I've worked very hard fer yer wife these past few days?"

He looked at her astonished, but was gentle in his reply, that he had given her wage to Jack, as had earlier been agreed.

"So, would you excuse me fer a few moments, while I catch up with him, Mistress Briggs?" she had asked. "I need some things from the village and t'will be too late fer the grocer shop, if he gives me my money tonight."

She didn't wait for permission. She flew out of the door as fast as her legs would carry her, a red mist of anger forming in front of her, as she began to shout after Jack.

He had been ambling along talking to Billy, on their way to finish the ploughing of a field they had started that morning.

Surprised, he turned back into the yard and left Billy to walk on. He could see that Maggie was upset about something, but she had been in a strange mood since Friday night, when she had pushed him away in bed indignantly.

"Where's me money, Jack?" she demanded loudly, once she had caught him. "Farmer Briggs said he had given it to you and I don't think that is being fair, do you?"

"Will yer keep yer voice down?" Jack said quietly. "They'll be hearing yer from inside the house. Yer sound like a fish wife and yer showing me up."

He took her arm and guided her towards an empty shippon.

"I need the money, Jack. We need something fer our dinner tomorrow, so we do."

He stepped back a few feet from her, as she eyed him belligerently. He knew that she was quite capable of taking a swipe at him after she had heard what he was going to say.

"Yer can't be trusted to spend our hard earned money wisely. Look how yer went and blew that shilling yer found and didn't even bother to share with me. I could have gone out that night and bought meself a flagon. A man deserves to quench his throat at the end of a hard working day. So, I've decided that I am going to handle our money and you can tell me what is wanted from the grocery."

Her eyes had begun to fill with tears when she had heard his words. Suddenly she felt weak and despairing and wondered what she was doing demeaning herself in that way? If he wanted to control the money, who was she to argue or disagree? She was his wife, his possession. A few words said by a priest had taken all her independence away. But she vowed that she would find some other way of making money and Jack could go to hell in a handcart then.

Maggie had left him looking nervous, as she ran back quickly to the farmhouse. Knowing her as he did, she'd have started plotting his downfall straight away.

Chapter 9

Maggie sat on the sea wall, looking out at the soothing ripples of waves as they ebbed and flowed creamily onto the shore. It was a lovely autumn day, crisp and cool, with the sun shining weakly and a refreshing breeze tugging at her hair. She turned, as she heard the sound of many people coming down the hill towards her. Now that the church services had ended, people were intent on promenading, or riding by in their vehicles, dressed in their Sunday best.

She felt calmer as she looked towards the Welsh mountains. The view was amazing, with its patchwork of coloured fields on the low land and the different hues of shading on the mountain peaks. It was worth all the tea in China, to be allowed this time to sit and stare.

Her mistress wasn't so bad once you got to know her. As a Christian woman she couldn't be. Noticing the girl's sudden pallor, she had taken her aside to say that she wasn't looking in the best of health. Maggie had gone red with embarrassment, but thought to herself that nothing ventured, was nothing gained. She'd gone on to tell Ethel that she had her monthly visitor again. With no money, rags or a thread and needle, she'd had to rip off a piece of her old skirt last night, to staunch the flow.

She couldn't speak with Jack. It was her problem and being newly wed she would have died at the thought of having to mention it to him. But was it fair that Jack was allowed to keep her money, because she was going to have this kind of problem every month?

Mistress Briggs had been very kind and motherly, calling on Peggy to help, but couldn't go against her husband and pay her servant herself, as she only did the household accounts. Peggy had been a life saver, furnishing her with all the things she needed and listening sympathetically to the young girl's woes. Her advice was to stand up for herself in the marriage, as that was what she was going to do when she married her betrothed.

Maggie smiled to herself as she thought back to her talk with Peggy. There was a world of difference in their circumstances, and she couldn't see Peggy having to argue for her pay.

"The top of the morning to yer, Mrs Haines. It is Mrs Haines, isn't it? You were down at the settlement for a couple of days." She turned to see a young man standing before her, who was looking rather uncertain, because she hadn't answered to her name. It had taken her a moment to wonder who this Mrs Haines was. Surely that was Alice, her mother-in-law?

"Oh, I'm sorry, Jimmy, I was thinkin' and dreamin' as usual and didn't see who it was standin' there," she said apologetically. "You were the one who went working at the tavern, isn't that so?"

"'Tis a wonderful place we're staying in," Jimmy nodded, as he sat himself down beside her. "I come here every morning before me work begins. Just to get the smell of beer and smoke out of me nostrils and breathe in God's fresh air, is a blessing. Before it starts all over again that is, 'til ten of the clock each night."

"Perhaps yer would have bin better with an outside job," Maggie commented. "You could have taken the farmer's job if you'd had a mind to."

"I know, I know," he gloomily replied. "But it was a sort of impulse that drove me there. That and with me mammy not wantin' me to have the pot man job. I did it to spite her."

"Are yer missin' yer family?" she asked, feeling sad for him, although at least he had a family to miss, whereas she had no one, if you discounted her sister and brother, as she might never see them again.

"Not at all, they're just a load of squabblin' eejits, so they are. But there is a person I am missin'. Eileen, me own true love. I had to leave her back in Westport. Her mother got herself between us, said she was too young to tie herself down to a man like me."

"Perhaps yer could write to her, tell her where yer livin' now? I could write yer a letter, if yer wanted me to."

Maggie spoke eagerly, knowing that probably Jimmy couldn't read or write and would, perhaps, pay a little money for the service. She would be happy with a sixpence, if he would agree.

"It's very strange you should say that, when yesterday I bought a prepaid letter from the post office, hoping that the landlord or a customer would write to her on my behalf. I hadn't got the courage to show that I was ignorant, so yes, I would be truly grateful for your accomplishment of a letter on my behalf." With that, he pulled out a dogged-eared missive from his pocket, followed by the stub of a pencil, which he handed over happily.

"Me talents need to be paid for, Jimmy," she advised him in a business-like manner, with the pencil suspended mid-air, while she waited for his reply.

He proffered sixpence, and once that had safely changed hands she said, "Now what do yer want me to say?"

That was the easiest money she had ever earned, she thought gleefully, as Jimmy went off whistling, his love letter gripped in his hand. When no one was looking she hitched up her dress and put the money in with her rosary, in the small pocket that she had found in her lovely new drawers. There were no shops open for trading on a Sunday, so there was nowhere to spend her coin. With a sigh of resignation she headed back. There was a scrag end of beef that wanted cooking, and perhaps she'd give her dress a wash.

"Coo-ee, Maggie!" came a voice from behind her. "Coo-ee, over here..." It was her mother-in-law.

Maggie turned to see Alice waving from the front door of a house nearby. One of a row of three, which had the vantage point of overlooking the sea.

She dithered, undecided whether to ignore her mother-in-law and make her way back to the cottage, but a little voice of conscience whispered that this was her opportunity to save herself from sin. She couldn't ask for forgiveness if she didn't forgive others, could she? And Alice was someone she had to forgive. But what was Alice doing there, instead of sitting under a tarpaulin down on the shore?

"Didn't Jack tell yer we had moved into this fine upstanding house then?" Alice said, looking at Maggie smugly, seeing her surprise when the girl joined her. "That's why his dad and him were out celebrating last night at the Ship. It was to thank Jack fer the money and us moving in. We got the place cheap. The woman who had it before has gone to live with her sister and there's three years left on the tenancy. And it's a boarding house, Maggie, just what I've always wanted! And we've even got a boarder. A Mr. Arlington has come to stay!"

Before she knew it, Maggie was being bundled through the door of Seagull Cottage. A dwelling aptly named, as the birds themselves were sitting on its roof. Alice hustled her from room to room, proudly giving each room a name and explaining each one's use. If there was antipathy on the woman's part, it had gone now, but Maggie fumed at the injustice of it all.

Where had Jack got the money to set his parents up in a boarding house and why was she not told? She'd have some answers later, if not from Alice, then certainly from her husband. If he had got money to throw about, then why take the job at the farm?

She would have loved to live in a house like this one, not dwell in a tied cottage with its ancient furniture and cold stone floors. This one had a parlour, with quality furnishings seemingly included in the deal. A family living room, a kitchen with an up to date cooking range, and water piped to the scullery, instead of a well or a pump in the yard. There were curtains at the windows and proper beds in every upstairs room. The views looked over the sea to the mountains, as far as Chester and to the islands in the middle of the estuary.

She was eaten up with envy as she looked around her, but Alice hadn't finished yet. Maggie was to take a cup of tea and stay, while Alice explained her exciting plans.

"I'm goin' to put a notice in the Boat House," she said enthusiastically. "That's where the ferry boats come in from Flint, across the estuary. I have heard that a coach takes the passengers over to Hooton Station and then they travel by that new fangled train. I thought, instead of travelling onward, they could spend a few days here and have bed and a breakfast with me. It stands to reason that our good sea air would be far preferable to a dirty city. And this is where you can be of help, Maggie. I need yer to write me a notice, while yer here. See, I've been and bought the paper. Just put 'Bed and Breakfast supplied at Seagull Cottage. Price fer a night from 1/3d.'"

"That seems a lot of money, Alice, fer a bed and a bit of breakfast. And would they have to share?" Maggie was astounded at what her mother-in-law was thinking of charging and that price was just for starters, it seemed. When Alice had built up a good reputation, her aim was to increase it, causing Maggie to make the comment 'that she couldn't believe her ears'!

It was afternoon when Maggie finally broke free of Alice's clutches, after swilling back endless cups of tea. She hurried along the shortcut, not caring about the beauty of the landscape, or the black mounds in the colliery as she quickly passed by. She was intent on finding Jack and hoped to see him along the way. Three o'clock could not come quickly enough for what she had in mind to say to him. How dare he sentence her to a life of servitude, when his mother would be living in a proper house, probably employing a daily woman as well!

She groaned when she saw Ruthie in the distance. Her neighbour had a shovel in her hand and seemed to be hitting out at something invisible. The children were hopping around her, shouting their encouragement, or trying to take the shovel away. Ruthie's trousers were tied up with twine at the bottom, and as Maggie approached, she shouted over that she was in need of a bit of help from her neighbour. She was catching rats and the 'little buggers', meaning her children, were all getting in the way.

"Yer have to be so careful, Maggie," she said, advisedly. "They try to bite yer bum when yer sitting on the privy. We've got a rats' nest somewhere, but I'm blowed if I can find it. I've been batting the straw in the loft up in the kids' room. One tried to bite our Lenny, but I managed to get it. I've got me trousers all tied up, because they can run up yer leg, yer know."

Ruthie looked all flushed and angry, glaring around her as if everyone was at fault. But, it was her next words that gave away the truth of the matter, Jack and Solly were up to something and she was venting her wrath on the rats.

"I hear that your man is a poogalist, Maggie. Solly came home last night and told me that he had been given important business by him. He's to set up meetings and hold the purse, which means he'll be round all the taverns passing the word. It takes me all me time gettin' wages off the bleeder. Look at me poor kids wearing parish handouts and eating whatever 'Lady' Briggs decides to send."

Maggie could only gape, she was so taken aback at what Ruthie had told her. First, Alice with her grand boarding house and now Jack resuming his fighting. Without a word or by your leave. There would be more than stew simmering for her husband, when he walked in later through the cottage door.

Ruthie went up and whispered slyly, "Has the cat got yer tongue, or is it that you're the last to know about it? Or were you too blind te see what's goin' on under yer pretty nose?" She turned away and banged two of her boys' heads together for fighting over the shovel, then, with a cackle of laughter, she shouted coarsely, "Or is it that yer too busy, letting him into yer drawers?"

Red in the face with embarrassment, or maybe anger, Maggie turned on her heel and fled to her own cottage. How dare Jack plot and plan with Solly? He had only met the nasty little man a few days ago and here he was getting all cosy with the enemy. She would have more than a few words now to say to Jack when he got home.

When she got to the cottage, it was to hear wood being chopped in the back garden. Jack had been stacking logs and tinder outside the lean-to door. He must have been home for a while, because he had also dug up the potatoes and had built up quite a mound by the cottage wall. He was about to cover them with a small tarpaulin, to ensure they would have a winter supply.

"Oh, yer know where yer live then?" Jack's greeting was scathing, as Maggie appeared at the side of him. "And I hear you've bin meeting men on the sea front, that's what Solly's bin tellin' me."

Unbeknown to Maggie, his words were spoken in jest, as Jack had believed that Solly was only being jealous, with Jack having a young and slender wife.

"And did he tell yer also that he lay in wait fer me the other day? Called me a whore and tried to do to me what you do to me at nighttime? I'd only bin passin' the time of day with Jimmy. Yer remember, the young man from the settlement?"

She dashed after him, as he ran the hundred yards to Thistledown Cottage. There were screams of fright from Solly as Jack dragged him out of his door. He shook the little runt as a terrier shakes a rabbit, until Solly shouted for mercy, which brought Ruthie out of her cottage to join in the din.

"Nobody touches my Solly without good reason," she shouted, hands on hips and glaring menacingly at the pair. "Whatever he's done I want to know about it. Oh, you're the man he's bin talking about. Yer should be ashamed of yerself, picking on him."

Ruthie stood there like a bull ready to charge at them, while Solly went to hide behind her bulk and peered around her sheepishly. It was a sight that made Jack burst out laughing. He shook his head in disbelief, then, taking Maggie by the arm, he marched her back to the cottage.

"'Tis a fine house yer've set your mother up in," she remarked later, broaching the subject carefully, as she was still in wonder at the way Jack had flown after Solly, in an effort to protect his wife and thinking that she may as well delay any of her challenges for the time being. "She had the courtesy of invitin' me in to look around it, seem' as it was me own 'usband that provided 'er with the means fer it."

"'Tis so," said Jack in agreement, not seeing her comments as anything more than that. "'Tis a fine house, which will be ours to live in when the auld one's pass away."

—

Maggie was kept busy after that fateful day, too tired to argue and too tired to daydream. The wedding of Peggy and Dennis was fast approaching and the farmer's wife was pulling out all the stops to ensure her daughter had the best of everything.

Mistress and servant were up to their armpits in pickling, cake making and checking the contents of the slow maturing elderberry and parsnip wines. They made meat and potato pies, roasted haunches of beef, pork and ham, sliced breasts of chicken, boiled legs and wings; while a fresh Deeside salmon lay on the cold slab in the pantry, with apple and blackberry pies and an assortment of little cakes and pastries by its side. The wedding cake was a work of art, a three-tiered fruit cake, covered in paste, then royal icing and decorated with a host of dried buds from the garden and pretty coloured ribbon purchased from the hosiery store.

No one was allowed to see Peggy's wedding dress. That would be collected from Anne Rosemary's the day before. Maggie thought it was probably a white satin, frothy lace concoction. At least that's what she heard Peggy discussing with her mother as she was passing the elder girl's room.

After the ceremony at St Mary's, the newly wed couple would be transported in a decorated farm cart back to the Briggs' barn. There, the eating, drinking and dancing would begin, after speeches from Peggy's father and the bridegroom of course.

But, in the meantime, preparation fell to servant and mistress, with Peggy and her sisters lending a hand when they could. There were little things, like laundering the table cloths and napkins and cleaning down the trestle tables, which were brought out from a dusty store, begging chairs from any neighbours who could spare them and sweeping out the barn. The outside workers were assigned the task of damping down the hay dust and transferring the bales under cover outside. There was the bridal bouquet to make, long and trailing, and four little posies for the younger girls, all made from lace, dried flowers, ivy and ribbon. The church was to be decked out in flowers, pew ends and garlands, though that job would be left to the church helpers, of course.

Throughout that time Maggie came home exhausted. Beside all the preparation at the farm, there was still the cleaning of her own place as well. And Jack had given up on doing the shopping, saying it was women's work and that he felt a fool standing amongst the housewives in the grocer's queue. He had however, stood his ground when she raised her objection to Alice being given all his money, when they could have run a boarding house together instead. Jack insisted that his decision had been the right one. His mother wasn't young any more, whereas they had years ahead. They still had time to make themselves a fortune, maybe even having their own farm one day.

He relented though and let her handle her earnings, with dire warnings of what would happen if she spent it on foolish things. That week he had given her three shillings and a sixpence, so with the sixpence she had earned from Jimmy, she had four shillings to spend.

The Neston Market coincided with an afternoon when Maggie had been given some free time, away from the frenetic activity at the farm.

Ruthie had told her about the bargains that could be found at the weekly market, where hawkers, peddlers and traders sold their wares side by side. It was as if the skirmish between Jack and Solly had never happened, although Solly now trailed Jack like an adoring puppy and Ruthie seemed to have forgotten what the shouting had been about.

Maggie, though, had not taken the incident lightly and was nervous if she crossed the fields on a gloomy afternoon. Jack had laughed at her fears, saying Solly was harmless and that if he hadn't believed that, then Solly would now be swinging from a tree. She had more to fear, he said, from the 'navvies' who were laying the railway track up at Hooton.

By the time Maggie had got to the market, the traders were beginning to pack up for the day. For most it had been highly profitable in the run up to Christmas, with housewives laying in their stores in case of bad weather, or buying thicker blankets and warmer clothes.

She could hear the sing song voices of the Welsh traders, who had sold all their pats of butter, large hens' eggs and crumbly cheese and were about to make their way back across the Queensferry border, leaving the local farmers to compete last minute, over their prices of vegetables or meat.

Maggie was looking for the woman who brought her wares on a barrow from across the water in Liverpool. Ruthie had said, that the woman went to the houses of the gentry, pretending to be collecting for the poor. She was in a way, because it was the poor who spent their coppers with her. Maggie was looking for a cast off dress, as Peggy's had become as tattered as the one she owned before.

"Orl right there, la?" asked Lily Dobbs, the proprietor and owner of the shabby wooden cart that Maggie spied at the back of the market. "Not much left in your size, queen. By the look of yer, yer need something worn by a tall, thin lady. Still, rummage through, there might be a bodice and may be a skirt that'll do yer. Not seen yer around before. New to Neston are yer? I've bin coming here from Liverpool fer years."

Maggie nodded and smiled, but didn't say anything in reply to the small, chatty, middle aged woman. She had come to search for a dress that was halfway decent, not to tell this woman the story of her life. Triumphantly, she found a black hard wearing looking skirt that would go with her old black bodice. She measured it against herself and found that it was just so.

"Cost yer sixpence, love and if yer like, I'll keep an eye out on me rounds fer someone like yerself, who would be willing to part with some of their things. I'm here every week. Real easy since the railway started to come along this way."

She wrapped the skirt in a sheet of old newspaper, and, after grasping Maggie's sixpence into her dirty palm and handing her purchase over, began to talk to someone else that had come to look at her wares. Maggie lingered a little longer, searching for a chemise and a pair of lace trimmed drawers, but then decided she didn't really want to buy them second hand.

It was good to have a little money and if she was careful it would go quite far, especially as they were still being fed at the farmhouse and given any leftovers to take home. She shuddered to think how Ruthie managed on Solly's earnings, that's if he decided to give her any of it at all. The mistress had told Maggie in confidence that she would never consider employing Ruthie for dairy work or even general scrubbing, having witnessed quite a few of her dirty habits over the past few years, though they were glad of her help at harvest time, as she worked as hard as any man.

Maggie rummaged through Lily's barrow a little longer, her heart twisting with sadness when she saw a little coat that would have fitted Molly. She wondered for the umpteenth time if her sister was happy with the Filbey's, cursing Johnny in her head for not taking her back to Ireland with him. She turned away from the clothing cart in despair. What was the point in dwelling on what might have been?

She wandered back to the high street, mindful of the need to visit the grocer on the way back home. There was yeast to buy, some candles, and a packet of tea this time, and she intended to visit the hosiery shop before she walked back home.

"There's one of them Irish passing by."

Maggie faltered as she stood on the step of the grocer, after hearing the accusatory words from within. Was it her that the woman had been speaking of? She quickly looked around.

The grocer stood behind his counter, embarrassed and nervously waiting for some reaction. She dithered. She accepted that she was a stranger, accepted that in a small community newcomers would be treated with suspicion, but she looked nothing like the skinny, dirty looking immigrant that she had been when she first arrived. Good food had filled her body out, gone was the haunted look she used to wear, her cheeks were rosy from walking in the chilly wind and her hair had started to shine. If her dress was a little shabby, she carried herself with a confidence that hadn't been there before.

Maggie cleared her throat, hopping onto the grocer's doorstep, ready to do battle with those within. Whatever they had against her, they could say it to her face. She saw the grocer fiddling with a display of jars on the counter, no doubt thinking he was going to witness some sort of cat fight.

"Have I done something to offend you, ladies?" Maggie addressed a couple of women who were standing there, fear flitting across their features, as they saw the Irish girl trying to keep her temper under control.

"Why no," answered the woman, who Maggie later learnt was called Mrs Adams. "We were just talking about the amount of fighting and brawling going on, since the Irish navvies appeared in our town."

"And that has got something to do with me?" Maggie raised one eyebrow at her inquiringly.

"Well, you are Irish and I were just saying, there's one of them now."

Maggie could see that the woman was feeling uncomfortable and probably wishing that she had not engaged in gossip with her friend. She began to cringe as Maggie gazed at her coolly, no doubt worried that the immigrant was going to put the 'ankarni' on her. The 'ankarni' was an evil eye, put on people who tried to hurt your pride.

Chapter 10

The incident in the grocer shop gave Maggie food for thought, as she waited up that night for Jack to return. She had held her tongue, as another customer tried to enter the shop, causing a distraction. The women had fled, not wanting a scornful lashing from the immigrant's tongue. Peace had been restored, much it seemed to the proprietor's obvious disappointment.

He beckoned her aside and explained why the two of them had taken a disliking to her and her sort. They were the wives of redundant colliery men and saw newcomers as a threat to their livelihoods. The Irish navvies who were working on the rail track nearby, were paid good money for sweaty, backbreaking work. They spent it freely in the taverns, while local men could only look on. Resentment caused fighting between the Nestoners and the newcomers, and the police had to be sent for from Chester, as the local bobby was unable to cope.

The grocer's words made Maggie think of Jack and whether he was involved in this fighting? If so, on whose side would he be? She had found it strange that Jack had given in on the matter of her wages, but believed that he had decided to put his trust in her. Had it been a smoke screen, to cover up the fact he was earning money again by fighting and keeping it to himself? Come to think of it, he had purchased a new shirt, neckerchief and corduroys, complaining that his old clothes were dropping to bits and not fit to be seen in. He'd worn his new clothes that evening, saying he was visiting his mother, though he'd call into the Wheatsheaf first and have an hour with the other men.

Maggie glanced idly at the newspaper sheet she had started to buy occasionally. There was nothing else to do whilst she waited for Jack to come home, except sit on the sofa and dream. There was a small piece written at the bottom of the broadsheet entitled, 'Rioting at Irish port. Many people killed.'

It seemed that a grain ship had docked at the Port of Sligo and as the cargo was being transferred to the warehouse, a crowd of hungry people had stormed it, trying to carry away as much grain as they could. The troops had been called in, shooting and wounding anyone who got before them and a local magistrate had been summoned to read them the Riot Act.

Her heart went out to those starving people. The article had caught her unawares. She had been too busy dwelling on her own despair. This was the plight of her fellow countrymen, left behind to face the hunger with little hope of being able to survive.

When Jack returned he found her sobbing, so he held her in his arms while she cried her sorrow out. Jack was angry, saying that he was of the opinion that no one could be bothered to help the poor in Ireland. The authorities were hoping that they would all just fade away, then the landlords would be free to do what they liked with the vacant tillage.

So another night went by where there was no sense in confrontation. How could she battle with Jack over the with-holding of any money while there was plenty of hostility back home?

-

The wedding of Peggy and Dennis came and went, with Maggie finding herself with more time on her hands. She still had to appear at the farm every morning, but the Mistress was content to let her go at dinnertime. Maggie was glad of it, though her shorter working hours reflected in her wages. But it meant she could do lots of exploring around the village, along the coast and up Liverpool Road to the hamlet of Thornton, a pleasant little place with its own village green. She grew stronger and healthier, more than she had ever been in all of her life.

So, she felt it was rather strange to find her head down the privy hole when she got up one morning. She hadn't eaten anything unusual, though the bigger portions she had been having she put down to the chill of wintry days, and trying to put some fat on in cold weather to help her ward off coughs and colds. Maggie resolved to go and see her neighbour. Ruthie would know what was wrong, being well used to illness, with all the children that she had.

Panic was making her heart beat faster later that morning, as she began to imagine she had white throat, tuberculosis or even cholera. She even sneaked a look into the mistress's bedroom mirror, checking her tongue, neck and throat.

It was all quiet at Thistledown cottage when Maggie knocked at the door. She had never been inside Ruthie's dwelling place before. There had never been any need to, as her neighbour seemed to spend her days outdoors.

It was strange not to hear the clamour of the children from within and she wondered if perhaps one of them was ill? Had they been carted off to the isolation ward, poisoned themselves with Deadly Nightshade or drowned themselves in the estuary? Her imagination was working overtime as she pushed the cottage door open and peered into the room.

Had the family upped and left, telling no one of their departure? Maggie looked at the living space, devoid of any rugs or furniture, just a couple of dirty looking mattresses lying on the un-swept floor. Although the dull looking cooking range which was in need of house-wifely attention, still threw out a little warmth, there was no kettle above, gently steaming, no pot or pan holding a hearty lunch time soup. Whatever had made them take to their heels had not occurred in the last half hour.

She heard a noise. A snuffly noise. It seemed to be coming from the room nearby. She tiptoed in and saw the palliasse, where a small, thin boy lay with dribble down his chin.

Maggie turned away. He was, what was known then as a spastic. An outcast, a child to be kept away from public gaze. No wonder Ruthie kept herself to herself, not making any friends.

Maggie dithered. Should she stay and keep the poor mite company and hope that his mother would be returning soon? Surely the child hadn't been abandoned? Ruthie would never be so cruel.

The noise of excited children chattering and Ruthie's loud boom broke into her thoughts as she stood there, so she quickly ran up the path, to stand nonchalantly by the gap that once was filled with a gate. It would be best if her neighbour didn't find her lurking by the cottage door. She watched as the family walked along the lane, dragging a log and a fir tree behind them.

"Cooee, Maggie."

Ruthie began to wave her free arm madly, her children copying exuberantly behind. Maggie let out her breath in blessed relief and counted. Tommy, Ernie, Danny, with Annie carrying Katie, trailing behind. All looked healthy and sound.

"Maggie, we've bin to the woods and got our Christmas tree and yule log and Mam's taking us to the market tomorrer. I can't wait for Christmas Day."

Ernie ran ahead of them all, abandoning his part of the fir tree, to joyfully dance around in front of her, then jig up the path to the cottage excitedly. Ruthie came waddling as fast as her enormous legs would carry her, leaving the tree in the middle of the lane, in her haste to catch up with her unruly son. Maggie stopped her mid-flight, laying her hand on the arm of her breathless neighbour.

"I know about your little boy, Ruthie," she said quietly, as she realised that was why the woman was on the run. "I've been here a while and couldn't help but hear his movements as I stood knocking on yer door."

It was as if Ruthie had had the wind knocked out of her. She leant against the rickety fence that surrounded the cottage and didn't say a word. The rest of the children stood waiting nervously, waiting for the storm that usually erupted when their mother was reminded of her poorly son.

"Then come in and meet him," she said at last, resignedly. "Annie get his chair from the lean-to and put Katie on the floor."

They all walked into the cottage and watched as Annie pushed a battered Bath chair in front of the fire. Ruthie brought it to life again with much rattling of the poker. The family gathered round to feel the heat, as it had been cold in the woods looking for their fir. Then Annie walked in from the bedroom carrying her disabled brother. His legs were thin and wasted and his large head lolled on his too small shoulders, but he managed to give them all a lopsided smile, when he saw his siblings standing there. Then his words tumbled out, all of a jumble, but the children seemed to understand as they all gathered around.

"This is our Lenny," explained Ruthie, in a very kind voice, completely different to the tone she usually used with her other children. "He's our second eldest boy, next to Tommy. Ernie came after him. Say hello to Maggie. He can understand yer Maggie. It's just he gets so excited talkin', that his words come out all jumbled. He's a clever lad really, isn't he kids? But his legs don't work, so he spends a lot of time on the palliasse. Solly says that one day he'll make him a little cart fer the kids to push him around in. But he'll never manage to make one. Always too busy at the farm."

Maggie's heart felt full of sympathy for Ruthie and poor Lenny and she asked if there was nothing that could have been done for him by the hospital or doctors when he was born?

"Like what?" Ruthie said scornfully. "Nelly Fleming, she was the midwife attending me at the birth, she told me just to let 'im go, not feed 'im or anythin'. But, me tits were giving me 'ell, full of milk and really 'urtin', so I put the little runt to me breast and let 'im have a go. There was nothing wrong with 'is appetite, 'e took the lot and wanted more. Then Nelly said later, that p'raps I should put 'im in the asylum up at Clatterbridge,

133

when 'e didn't grow much or begin to walk or talk. I said that she should go to 'ell. No one was taking 'im away from me. Our Lenny 'as just as much right to be on this earth as me others. No, I don't have any truck with any doctors, because they'd only want to take me boy away from me."

She looked over to her children and Maggie couldn't believe the wealth of love that came into her eyes. Big loudmouthed Ruthie, a giant of a woman who most people feared, had a heart as soft as a feather pillow as far as her children were concerned.

Her mood, though, suddenly veered and she shouted to the children to go and play outside. There was nothing for it but to do as they were told. There was no furniture to sit on, no rug or toys they could play with, unless there were possessions hiding in the lean-to.

"If yer wondering why we've nothin', yer can blame our Solly," Ruthie said, once the children had left, as if she had been reading Maggie's thoughts. "The little sod has sold the lot over time. Me mother's thing she called a chiffonier, the Welsh dresser, table and chairs, her rugs, nice beds, and everything. He said the kids would only break them. Probably true, but I really wanted her things. He said the money he got would go on me folks' burial. Though I never saw sight nor hair of a penny of it meself. Oh, except he did get our Lenny that Bath chair."

She stroked her big hand across her son's head and adjusted the blanket that had been thrown around his shoulders. His thin body was only dressed in a flannel shirt and a pair of corduroy breeches. Like the rest of the children, he was bare-foot.

Maggie's eyes filled with unshed tears and she turned away, hoping that she could disguise her sudden emotion. She'd forgotten why she had visited in the first place and planned to make a quick escape.

Ruthie suddenly reminded her.

"What were yer doin' lurking round me door, anyhow? 'Ad yer come to take a cup of tea with me, like the gentry does? Only yer didn't leave me yer callin' card."

Maybe it was said as a joke, but her words only served to make Maggie feel humble, when she weighed up her worries against the worry that Ruthie must carry daily in her heart.

"Ruthie, I was wonderin'. Have yer heard if there's bin any sickness? In the village or in the cottages around?"

"Why, is there something I don't know of, some disease that people are catchin'?" she asked, as Maggie's words began to sink in. "Yer know we had a typhoid outbreak around here, a couple of years ago?"

She looked at Maggie fearfully. Her parents had died of that infection. Had it come back to the area again?

"I was sick this mornin', Ruthie and I'm never ill," Maggie blurted out. "Even when I was in Ireland and we were so weak with hunger, I never caught as much as a chill. I've been worrying about meself, thinking that I've caught some terrible plague."

"Sick in the mornin', is it? Have yer thought yer might have caught? That means yer might be expectin' a little babby, that's what happens to me sometimes. Though I don't always know when I'm expecting. Sometimes they just pop out, with me being so fat, yer see. Our Katie appeared one day when I was sittin' on the privy and there's lots of little Tibbses buried under the apple tree. Some just arrive when they're not ready, not formed properly, or just born dead."

Maggie felt horrified as she listened to her neighbour, pleased that she might be having a baby, yes, but the thought of all those little children buried in the cottage garden, made her eyes fill up with tears again.

"How can yer bear it, Ruthie? All those poor little souls waiting to be born, then having to go back up to Heaven again."

"I dry me tears and get on with it. Solly's always ready to get his twig up me, so it starts all over again."

What a life, Maggie thought sorrowfully, as she wandered back towards her cottage. Her own happiness seemed to be wrong somehow, when she thought of the troubles that her neighbour had to bear. Yet, there she was, helping her children to get ready to celebrate Christmas, though Maggie couldn't see what a fir tree had got to do with the annual festival of Jesus's birth.

In Ireland, it was Mass on Christmas Eve or Mass on the day and a gathering of the family for a special meal. Small gifts to mimic the presents given to the Holy baby, though not as generous as the gold, frankincense and myrrh that the Lord had received. More likely a knitted scarf or socks for the men, a handkerchief embroidered with the person's name, a polished stone or a necklace made of shells. All given lovingly and just as gratefully received.

She lay on the sofa later, her mind churning with this new found knowledge that Ruthie had given her. She thought back to the time when her mother was expecting Molly. Had she been sick, as Maggie was?

She found she couldn't remember. Poor Mammy, at least she was at peace now, with no more heartache to bear. Though she'd never know the pleasure of holding her first grandchild, Jack's mother would be the grandma now. What would they call it and where would it sleep? Who would help her with the birth?

Her musings had to stop when Jack came in. She went to heat his dinner, it was vegetable stew again. The mistress had got a bit stingy with the leftovers that she allowed her workers to take home since the expense of Peggy's wedding, and wasn't adverse to telling them that they should be grateful for the meals they were given at the farm.

Maggie had begun to feel worried. How was she going to work and look after a tiny baby, when she was sure to lose her job as soon as she was too big to carry on with it? The baby was as much Jack's responsibility as hers, she fretted. He was the one who had seemed intent on giving her a baby and it looked as if he had got his wish, or so it seemed.

"Jack, Ruthie thinks I might be having a baby," she ventured, sitting back as they finished their meal, to see his reaction. It was one of disbelief, incredulity and happiness all rolled into one, as he took her into his arms, laughing and crying with surprise and delight!

"Are yer sure? A baby? Oh, Maggie, you are me dearest one."

After the initial excitement though, Jack's mood became sober. He lead her to the sofa then told her the truth. He had been getting Solly to drum up support for a fighting match, just as Ruthie had said, while meantime Jack had been getting in some practise with local contenders for his big day. It had been a series of contests and he had won every one. Proudly he went into the bedroom and brought back a money belt.

To Maggie's amazement, he poured the contents into her lap. There were sixpences and shillings, a few sovereigns, and even a white pound note!

"This is for our son," he told her, as tears of emotion welled into his eyes. "To give him the best start in his life with good clothes, good food and the best schooling. And this is only for starters, Maggie. When I win the big one, he'll never go short of a thing."

She suddenly became fearful, searching his face for bruises, healing cuts and slight abrasions, then realised that she was looking at him properly for the first time. This man who had taken her away from all that she held dear in Ireland, was risking his life for the good of their son. It struck her that perhaps she was beginning to love him now, because she cared that he could be hurt through his fighting. Would he listen if she begged him not to put his life at risk, or did he believe that this was the only way to riches, not content to live out their years working on someone else's farm?

"Do yer know when the babby is expected, me darlin'?" Jack was asking, breaking into her thoughts when he saw the softness of expression on her face, presumably interpreting it to be a satisfied one. She couldn't answer, she had no knowledge of how or when a baby arrived. All she knew was that it involved a lot of screaming and grunting. Maggie, like Jack, was completely mystified.

"We'll ask me mother," he said. "She and Dad will be so happy when we see them on Christmas Day. Which reminds me, here's ten shillings. Get presents for the family and something fer yerself as well."

That night they cuddled up together, Jack too frightened of hurting his baby to assuage his manly need. He was so happy he could hardly sleep, but he also had a niggle on his mind.

"Maggie, could yer do somethin' fer me tomorrow?" he asked quietly. "I'm really worried about the money belt. I'll bring home some sacking and you can sew me a few bags, then I'll go to the village and get a couple of bolts fer the doors."

-

Next day, Maggie stood in awe as she looked at the coloured lanterns that festooned the many market stalls. There were people selling holly, ivy and mistletoe from round wicker baskets, though she couldn't see why the shoppers were buying it, when it was free if they were to walk into the countryside. Geese, capons, chickens and rabbits hung upside down on one farmer's stall, with homemade cakes, biscuits and sweets on another. Whipping tops, dollies, necklaces and woolly hats sold out rapidly, while the voices of carol singers, vibrant and warm, sang popular tunes of the day.

It did Maggie's heart good as she stood and listened to the good-natured bartering of vendor and customer, and saw women laden with Christmas fare. With the smell of chestnuts from a smouldering brazier and ginger-snaps available from a rotund man, Maggie's first Christmas was about to begin.

Knowing the second hand clothing trader now as 'Lily with her barrow', Maggie watched as the woman stomped her feet to get the feeling back, and rubbed her hands, which were cold from the chill in the air. She saw her taking nips from a small bottle in the pocket of her apron. A swig of French brandy which her seagoing son had brought her, in an effort to keep her limbs from turning to ice.

"Last Neston market afore Christmas," Lily started shouting. "Last chance te buy a present fer a loved one."

Maggie smiled to herself when she heard her. Lily was making sure she returned to Liverpool with an empty barrow and plenty of money to tide her over until after New Year.

Well, she had plenty of money this time to spend with Lily. That is if the barrow held what she had in mind.

She had been dreaming all day of a cloak made of velveteen. One that would cover her from head to foot and keep her warm on frosty days. It had to have a hood and hopefully be trimmed with fur, and it didn't matter about the colour, as long as it was cosy for the cold, draughty days. She shivered under her shawl as she looked through the few items left on the barrow, her heart sinking as she realised that Lily must have sold a lot that day.

Her trawl found her nothing. Just a pair of young girl's pantalettes, a black fringed shawl only suitable for wearing at a soiree, a frilled lace bonnet, two red flannel petticoats and a pair of black leather boots. What a disappointment. She had been looking forward to this moment all day.

"Nothing there fer yer, queen?" asked Lily, seeing Maggie standing there, looking forlorn. "Yer should have come earlier, I was full te nearly overflowing this morning. I really have done a good trade today." She rattled the money bag that she kept hidden under her coarse cotton apron. "Wharrabout these boots? Will these not fit ye? They look as if they could be your size."

"No, I was after a cloak. It would be warmer than this tatty old shawl I'm wearin'. Though I might come back later to try on the boots, as these shoes I'm wearin' have seen better days. I'll take that lacy bonnet fer me mother-in-law and one of the red petticoats. I think it would fit me neighbour's girl."

"I knows where yer'd get a cloak, but it'll cost ye," Lily said helpfully. "That fancy shop in the High Street had one in the winder. Didn't yer pass it on yer way?"

Maggie replied that she hadn't. She had come along the coastal path, a favourite way to reach the village, as she could look across to the mountains, breathe in the salty air and watch the sea birds as they ducked and dived in the waters of the sea.

With her hopes up, she couldn't wait to leave the market and sped along the High Street as if her bottom was on fire. Just to see it, maybe touch it, this cloak that she really wanted that was only a few minutes away. And Lily was right, there was a cloak in Anne Rosemary's window. By the side of a grey satin day dress trimmed at the cuffs and hem with ivory lace. It was a dark blue garment, plainly cut, with no fur on the hood. More a cape than a cloak really, because it didn't look long enough to touch the floor. But it was made of the velveteen she wanted and it had pretty fringes at the bottom of the hem. There was no price though, nor on the dress, so she probably couldn't afford it anyway.

Maggie looked through the window and saw an elderly, white haired woman stitching in the room beyond. If I don't ask, I'll never know, she thought and with the woman looking quite approachable, she took a deep breath and walked in.

"Can yer tell me the cost of the cloak in the window, Missis?" she asked nervously. Even to her own ears, she sounded coarse. She tried again, this time trying to modulate her words with an accent more refined. "Sorry. Could you possibly tell me, how much does the garment cost in the window? I'm interested in purchasing the cloak."

She saw the woman smile gently to herself before she looked up from her sewing, no doubt thinking that this must be the young girl that she had heard the grocer next door speak about. She pointed to a seat nearby and asked the girl to sit herself down.

"It's quite expensive, Madam, I'm afraid," she said, treating Maggie to the same courtesy as if she was an alderman's wife. "'Tis the best quality velveteen and has the price of seven pounds."

Betty Brown (Anne Rosemary was her trading name) watched as the girl blanched at the price, then cast her mind back to what it had been like when she had been Maggie's age. When she had aped her betters, copying her mistress's clothes when she was a lowly sempstress in one of the gentry's homes. Her rise in status to a shop owner had only been due to her father, when he had left her his money in his will.

He had been a sea captain, who made his money selling goods that he had brought home from foreign shores. There had been enough left after he died for her to rent the shop and the accommodation above it. She was clever with her needle and made a good living, though her eyes were not as keen as they had been, and her bony fingers sometimes gave her pain.

Maggie got up to go. Seven pounds. It would take her half a year to earn it. The ten shillings that Jack had given her didn't seem to be so much any more, so she thanked the lady for her time and walked away despondently. One day I will afford a cloak like that, she promised herself, and the dress in the window as well. It just needed Jack to keep on winning the fights that he had planned.

"Excuse me, before you go, could I ask you a question?" Miss Brown, asked kindly. Maggie turned back quickly at her words. "How are you with a needle? If you bought the material and I showed you how to cut it, would you be able to make it up yourself? It is Christmas after all. Goodwill to all men."

Maggie could have kissed her. Of course she was good with the needle. Didn't she used to have Mistress Filbey at her back, watching over her stitching, making sure she did a neat hem?

"How much have you got to spend, dear?" she continued, getting up from her treadle and walking over to join her customer.

"Only nine shillings. I'm sure it wouldn't be enough for such good quality velveteen."

She had been lovingly stroking the garment whilst Miss Brown had been talking, as the hem was hanging over the back of the dais of the window display. But Maggie knew if she parted with all of the money, there would be hell to pay from Jack and none of the presents he had sent her to get.

"What about a length of woven wool that I have on the end of a roll?" the owner continued. "It's black and not as pretty, but it's hard wearing and will last you for years. You can have it for six and five pence and I'll throw in the thread that you'll need."

Maggie's eyes began to fill up with tears. She realised that she had made a friend in Neston that day. When she looked back down the years it was to that moment, when Betty Brown gave her a new direction to her otherwise humdrum life. It was arranged that Maggie would return next day and if Betty wasn't busy, they'd make a start on the cloak.

Chapter 11

It had to be said, it could have been the best Christmas that Maggie had ever experienced. It started well, but slowly went downhill. At least it was one that Maggie would think on for many years to come.

Dressed in the new cloak that Betty and she had worked hard on, and wearing the only slightly too big boots from Lily's barrow that she had run back to purchase, she had walked along the lane to Ruthie's. Oh the joy she had felt, when she handed over a fruit cake she had made herself, the red flannel petticoat for Annie, a dressed dolly for Katie and a penny for each of the boys. It was Christmas Eve and the children were flushed with excitement. She could see that they had decorated the fir tree with paper lanterns and shells dangling on twine. They had been with their mother to the market, and were looking forward to the biscuits, sweets and fruit she had bought them and the capon that Briggs had sent from the farm.

She had felt a lump in her throat at the reaction of Annie to the petticoat. The child had put it on straight away and danced around the room. She had been dressed in a cast off summer dress of very faded fabric. With a tight fitting bodice and a full skirt, it looked quite incongruous in the setting of the bare, empty room. There was nothing on Annie's feet, which made Maggie want to shudder. The memories of her own barefooted days had long since gone. She wondered why Ruthie had never knitted the children stockings. How much did it cost for needles and wool?

"Yer the proper Lady Bountiful, arn't yer?" Ruthie had observed, looking scornfully at Maggie, who had changed from the raggedy immigrant that Ruthie had chanced upon only weeks before. "Yer all dressed up in yer cloak and button boots, with nowhere else to go. Well this year my lot are gettin' proper presents. Our Solly has bin workin' hard making them things from bits of wood. He's whittled a flute, a wooden top and a set of little animals. He's made a wooden box fer Annie and I've stuck on some shells. I managed to find a little jacket on Lily's barrer for Lenny. When Solly finishes the cart he's started making, the lad will need one to keep him warm. And he's given me five shillings from what Jack give him, fer fixing things up."

Maggie's ears pricked up when she heard her husband being mentioned. The children were playing a noisy game and most of what Ruthie had been saying she couldn't understand.

"Yer mentioned Solly's bin fixing somethin' fer Jack, Ruthie?" she shouted above the din. "Jack's bin so busy nowadays, that all he does is fall asleep when he gets back home."

"That's because they've had to catch up with all that ploughing. Farmer couldn't decide which fields and which crops he was going to sow. The ground was like iron, because of all the frost we've bin havin' lately. He's fixed up a match with a man named Feeney. He's the undispooted champion from Liverpool, Solly says. The purse will be worth more than twenty pounds, and there'll be a lot of people coming from far and wide."

Trust Ruthie. Maggie had had to go to her neighbour's to find out what was going on. Though all the words in the world wouldn't stop Jack from fighting. It was his dream to make big money, especially if he was going to have a son.

Earlier that night, Jack had made her feel so very guilty. He had produced a little parcel, all wrapped up in coloured paper. Inside lay a golden wedding ring. He took it out and put it on her finger, saying that she had to have one to wear, now she was expecting his child. It was a perfect fit, though Jack said it could be altered if it had been necessary. All Maggie had got for him was a muffler. She had blown all the ten shillings he had given her, mostly on herself. Though he had complimented her on the neat stitching and cut of her new cloak, she had the feeling he was disappointed. Maybe even thought she'd been extravagant, but as he had kept her short of money all those weeks before, it had been difficult to stop. She had felt ashamed when she thought of Ruthie, who had been pleased with the money she had got from Solly and had blown the lot on her family.

The next day had been Christmas and she proudly wore her new black cloak, new boots and new wedding ring to Mass at St. Winefred's. She wore her shabby blue dress under her lovely cloak, but no one in the congregation could see that she was not dressed as she longed to be. Outwardly she looked like a proper English housewife, with her long chestnut hair pinned into a curly bun on top of her head, similar in appearance to the other young wives who attended the service with their families. Gone was the weary looking ragamuffin, to be replaced by a woman who wore her clothes with dignity. She felt as good as any person in that community. With Jack in his Sunday best, and Alice, Michael and Seamus, who accompanied them, looking tidy and neat too, no one would have known that they were immigrants. Their first Christmas Day in a new country together and Maggie felt they were fitting in very well.

A choir sang 'Hark the Herald Angels Sing', their voices soaring to reach the rafters, then 'Come All Ye Faithful' and 'Oh Little Town of Bethlehem'. It was a wonderful morning and the emotion of it all had Maggie in tears. If only her real family had also been there, it would have felt like Heaven on earth.

They had scrunched their way through hard packed snow, on the way down to Seagull Cottage. Flakes of snow had begun to lie while they had been in church, which had made the scenery look magic. The hills over the sea were white tipped, as were the waves that crashed onto the shore. It looked as if a storm could be brewing, but it didn't really matter at all. They would be warm and cosy, eating a good Christmas dinner, courtesy of Farmer Briggs, who had supplied the bird.

Her mother-in-law, looking even plumper than she had in Killala, and wearing a heavy brown skirt, cream high-necked blouse, brown boots and a smart brown cape to complete the outfit, linked Maggie's arm. Holding onto her companionably as they walked along, peering into the High Street shop windows as they passed them by, Maggie told Alice of her good fortune. Finding Betty had been the best thing that could have happened to the girl. As usual though, Alice, always looking for the main chance, tried to get in on the act.

"Yer say she's getting' on a bit, this lady who has the dressmaker's?" Alice's eyes gleamed after she had heard Maggie's words. "Have yer thought about the future? What about gettin' in and make it so she needs yer, then yer might be able to take it over from her one day?"

Maybe Alice and Maggie had more in common than the pair of them thought, because that had been exactly what Maggie had been thinking. A dressmaker's establishment in the village could be made very profitable. Given that Jack might assist her with the purchase, seeing as he had helped out Alice with her house near the shore.

"She's a long way off retirement, is Betty," Maggie replied, not wanting to put her ambition into words, in case there was a malevolent spirit listening. "But I was thinkin' that I perhaps could be her apprentice. I can sew very well and she says she doesn't mind showing me how to do things. But, I'm stuck workin' at the farm every mornin'. That was part of the deal when the farmer took Jack on and now that I'm expectin'…"

She didn't get to finish her sentence, as Alice hugged her with such delight that she nearly lost her balance. Jack turned around from where he was walking with his brother and dad and wagged a finger.

"I knew yer wouldn't wait until we opened our presents, as we agreed. I should have had a bet with yer, how long yer could hold yer tongue!"

He was grinning as he said it though. He had been bursting to tell his parents, but they had agreed to wait until they got to Seagull Cottage.

Alice was so elated that she danced around, much to the surprise of other folk that were out for the morning air. She was also counting on her fingers, announcing that it would be an August babe.

"Oh Maggie, I'm so happy," Alice cried. "What a wonderful time to tell us, on Christmas Day and all. This is the best present yer could give us. This will be a Christmas to remember after all".

So it took all that time for a baby to grow inside you, Maggie mused, after all the excitement had died down. She would ask Alice more about it later, because she had lots of questions on her mind.

They had their festive dinner in the parlour. Just the family, as the residents that Alice was now looking after, had gone to visit kith and kin. The bed and breakfast idea that Alice had originally planned had been abandoned, after the packet ship ferry from Flint to Parkgate had been closed down. There had been a couple of drownings and people were loathe to risk the passage when a coach into Chester would connect with the Birkenhead train. Alice had managed to attract three clerical workers on a permanent basis, making her weekly income for full boarding to over thirty shillings. No need for Michael or Seamus to stir a stump now, but they still went fishing when the weather was good. Alice was glad to give her boarders freshly caught fish and they thought her cooking was the best around.

Maggie felt pangs of guilt as she passed over the presents to the family, though Alice was delighted to receive the newly goffered lace cap, which Maggie had laundered at the farm and Michael and Seamus seemed happy enough with the woollen gloves she had bought them. She felt that she should have spent more from the money that Jack had given her. She hoped it was because she wasn't used to buying presents and didn't know how much to spend that had made her spend so little on them, but she did so love her cloak and boots that the pangs of guilt soon passed by.

Seamus seemed very anxious to leave the table as soon as the last morsel was eaten.

"He's got a friend from up the promenade," Alice confided. "A young lad the same age as himself, one of the sons of the inn keeper at the Ship. What they get up together I don't ask, so it will be just the four of us fer puddin'. Then I've got something to tell yer, but I wish I was goin' to tell yer something else."

It was said in a very mysterious manner. Even Michael seemed uncomfortable as they sat eating their plum pudding for dessert. Then her bombshell hit them.

It seemed that Mr Arlington, he was the first lodger who came to live there, was a clerk who worked in the office of the Estates manager. It had come to his hearing that all the land, buildings, colliery and leases were up for sale. It wasn't general knowledge as yet, but Mr Arlington felt it was his duty to alert his landlady. She might be offered a chance to buy her lease, or the house might be sold to a buyer over her head. With a place down the coast named New Brighton, being purpose built for the pursuit of leisure to attract the people of Liverpool, it had been thought that Parkgate would become a ghost town, only attracting bird watchers and walkers.

So the owner of all this vast estate wanted money to set up another seaside town. He had his eye on a place on the Welsh coast, with a long, wide beach and plenty of land to build hotels. It had a natural deep water harbour that would attract the packet ships from Dublin. Not like there, where the estuary was becoming so silted that even the cattle boats had difficulty mooring. If a buyer didn't appear in the next three years, it would all be sold at auction. Mr Arlington was gloomy, because he would be out of a job as well.

"I wouldn't worry, Mother, dear," came the drowsy voice of Jack, who was feeling the warm effect of the brandy that his Dad had plied him with. The second bombshell landed… "My fight with Feeney will see you right, there'll be plenty of money then."

He didn't know what had hit him, as his mother leapt around the table and began to lay into him. He fended her off by pinioning her arms against him, laughing as Alice tried to slap him.

"Perhaps I should send me mother to tackle Feeney, eh, Maggie?" he said, still smiling at the little woman's fury. "See where I get me fighting spirit from? You'll see him off won't yer, Mother? A big man like him trying to hurt yer son."

"It's no laughing matter, Jack," Alice said soberly. "Especially as yer've a babby on the way. How's Maggie goin' to manage without yer, if yer leave her behind to bring up a son?"

"Maggie will manage very well without me. Isn't that so, Maggie? She'd have her freedom at last from a marriage she doesn't really want and plenty of money to live on."

She could only sit there red faced and full of discomfort at his words, while Jack's parents looked embarrassed and shook their heads disbelievingly.

They say 'When drink's in, truth's out'. Had Jack been right with his surmising? Although Maggie had tried to live by the rules of a Christian marriage, all along he had not been fooled. Though she hadn't wished him dead like he was suggesting, of course.

Maggie felt sick to her stomach and wanted to vomit. Jack had seen through the charade that she acted out each day. He knew from their childhood that she was naturally not submissive. It hadn't been easy to be the servile one, in a friendship that had begun when she was ten.

She got up quickly and ran to the scullery where she chucked up her dinner and plenty of bile.

Yes, she would remember that Christmas. One for straight talking, but would she ever look directly into her husband's eyes again?

They managed it somehow, they had to, didn't they? They had to keep their marriage going, without resorting to ugly words and inflicting pain. They had their baby to look forward to and a living to earn, and the months went by without that Christmas being referred to again.

Though Maggie did haunt the priest in his confessional box for many weeks to come. Her rosary beads became well used, as she daily atoned for the guilt she felt.

The weather didn't help to make their spirits lighter either, with snow on the ground for days on end and a difficult trek to the farm each day. There was nothing for the men to do, except pull out stranded cattle and sweep the snow from the yard. The mistress took the opportunity for an early spring clean, whilst moaning all the while to her husband that at least one of the staff was earning her pay. The rest just idled, eating their heads off whilst waiting for the thaw, which would surely come any day.

At night time, Maggie made amends to Jack, sewing little sacks by the light of a flickering candle. He filled six of them. Counting his money into them like a miser and stuffing them into the feather mattress away from prying eyes. She didn't know how much he had put in there, because the counting had been done in the bedroom alone.

"Here, get some stuff from that shop yer always on about and make us a pair of curtains for that little room," he said, handing Maggie a few shillings one evening, when he'd got home. "I'll have a pole cut by the weekend fer yer to put 'em on. Yer never know who cuts through this way, or who maybe is hanging around."

She smiled to herself as he said it. Had the bare window mattered when she had complained? There she was in the tin bath once a week, but there had been no curtains talked about for privacy then.

She hadn't seen Betty since they had made the cloak together and now Maggie had an excuse to call in. She decided to go to the village after work next day, as the thaw had come and the mistress's house was shining like a new pin. Her spirits lifted, as she imagined running her hands over Betty's rolls of fabric, picturing what kind of garment each bolt would make. A flower sprigged dress, tight bodice and overskirt, or a walking out dress with flounces round the hem. There were all sorts of things she could tackle with a needle, but for now, a pair of thick curtains was within her skill.

—

It was late one night in April, that an urgent knocking came to their cottage door. It was Solly. Out of breath from running, he couldn't get his words out, until Jack had sat him down with a tot of brandy. Then came the news that Feeney was imprisoned in Walton Jail. The fight was off and would be so until Feeney had done his time. Was it relief that Jack was feeling as he listened to the tale? Or would the love of money be his master? Maggie couldn't tell.

"How long are we talking? What was his crime?" asked Jack of Solly. The little man could only shake his head sorrowfully.

"Dunno, I got told this from a man I was drinkin' with. One of the navvie's workin' on the railway line. But, p'raps there's another we can arrange a fight with? Reg McKeown is a crowd puller. Though they say he's dirty, not many men have managed to beat him up to now."

"And what about the money? Same bets as on Feeney, or less would yer say?"

Solly looked more cheerful.

"If we arrange it fer the evening of a wage day and I put word around the navvies and the quarry men, we should have enough interest. The colliery men are back at work as well, only sack fillin' to begin with until the new owner opens a seam, but I could go down after work tomorrer and tell 'em as well. Though are yer sure about this, Jack? Why not wait until we hear about Feeney, find out why he's in and how long they'll be keepin' him?"

"Naw, I'm itching to getting back into it, Solly. Look at me muscles going to waste, I'm going soft. Yer know the last fight yer got me? T'was like tackling a man with one eye and one leg. No, I'll keep me reputation intact until I meet with Feeney, then the purse will be an even bigger one. Try to fix it on the floor of the quarry, there's more room there than round the back of the Bowling Green tavern."

"Jack," Maggie began, as she had been allowed to sit on the discussion, "is it wise to be fixing up such a big meeting? If the authorities get to hear of it, you'll be in big trouble. Maybe Feeney has been put away for that very reason?"

"Keep out of it, woman," Jack snarled, playing to his audience, showing Solly that he, for one, had his wife under control. "Go to the bedroom and stay there 'til I tell ye. This is men's business and you've heard all yer need to know."

Maggie was ready to give him a mouthful in retaliation, but shrugged her shoulders and did as she was told. If he didn't want to heed her warning, then so be it. She had the babe to think of, but what she didn't want was for its father to be in prison when she gave birth.

She sat on the bed, smoothing her hands over her expanding stomach. When she went next time to Betty's, she would buy a dress length. The seams of her skirt were taut and pulling, and it wouldn't be long before she couldn't wear it at all. She thought back to the talk she'd had with Alice on Christmas Day.

It seemed that the baby built a little nest inside its mother's innards. As the baby got bigger, so did the belly, then the baby got so big, it had to come outside. Alice had said that then the baby had to burrow, just like a rabbit coming out for air. It would come head first down the tunnel where a woman passed water. She would know that the baby was coming because she would have a lot of pain.

"Like when yer go to the privy because you've got the gripes," Alice had told her. "But it's worth it when yer get to hold yer little babe. Look at the size of me, giving birth to my two giants, but if I had me time all over, I'd go through the pain again."

Well, if little Alice could do it, so could she, Maggie thought. Another four months and it would all be over and Michael Patrick Haines would be there on show!

She picked up her needle and a reel of thick white cotton, thinking that she may as well do one of those jobs that she never seemed to get around to. It was sewing up the hole in the mattress, where Jack had put his money sacks. It was difficult trying to hold the two thick seams together, as her fingers kept slipping again and again. In her exasperation she gave the mattress a little shake and, to her surprise, a little stream of silver fell onto her lap! Silver coins that looked like shillings in the bedroom's gloom. Gathering the coins into a fold in her skirt, she got up to bring the candle nearer to examine them, whilst tutting with annoyance at her needle skills. It was obvious that the job she had made on the money sacks had been a little slapdash, so she felt around in the mattress, to make inspection of the others she had made.

But it wasn't hessian that her fingers were touching, it was muslin. Her heart began to beat wildly as she touched another little bag. What else could there be hiding in the mattress, beside a few little bugs? They had lain on the mattress for months, thinking it lumpy and uncomfortable, but she would never have dreamt of throwing it out. Jack was always grumbling, threatening to buy a new, clean mattress, but hadn't been willing to risk her wrath.

She began to hear movement in the living room. Solly was getting to his feet and making for the cottage door. She swiftly put the silver into her skirt pocket, vowing to investigate further when Jack had gone to work the next day. Only pausing to comment on how flushed she was looking, though it wasn't from drinking brandy like he and Solly had, Jack eventually crawled into bed. They would both be looking bleary eyed in the morning, as Maggie was far too excited to sleep.

The next morning she pretended that she wanted to be sick again, assuring Jack that she would follow on in half an hour or so. She rushed to the mattress and began her search. In ten minutes she had discovered seventeen little muslin bags, all filled to the top with silver shillings. There were twenty coins in each and the necks were fastened with twine. The stitching was clumsy, not the work of a woman. More likely Granddad Filbey, who had passed away at the Irish farm.

There was nowhere to hide the precious money, it would have to stay put until she came up with a plan. She couldn't believe her find and began to tremble with excitement at the thought. No waiting for Jack to tip up any money, no being frugal and doing without. She had seventeen pounds that she could call her own, as she was certain that she wasn't going to share it with anyone. She wanted to jump for joy and dance about! But her good sense eventually came to the fore and told her to be careful. It would be best to put the bags and the sacks all back, and restore the mattress to its lumpy self again.

Maggie hurried along the farm track later, busy with her thoughts. The trees that had been stark and bare for what seemed like ages, were back in bud, with primroses in profusion all around. Spring had arrived in Neston, new life beginning everywhere.

She could have a new life with seventeen pounds. She could go back to Killala and start afresh there. She had enough for the rent of a cottage and the care of her little baby, but she knew that she wouldn't leave her husband, now that his baby was on the way.

Perhaps she would buy a smart baby carriage or some shop bought clothes. She hadn't begun to make his little outfits yet and their baby would need lots of toys. Or maybe a cradle. Jack had not got round to making one like he'd promised. He had said there was still plenty of time. Good old Granddad Filbey and all his precious coins. If he was watching from his perch in Heaven, he would be able to see how happy she was.

"But what will Jack's reaction be?" a little voice in her conscience began to say. "He'll think yer've stolen his precious sacks and then yer'll be in trouble with him again."

It came to Maggie like bolt from the blue. She'd take a trip up to Betty's again!

Chapter 12

Maggie stood hesitantly outside the door of the dressmaker's shop the next day. There was a young woman inside being measured and she felt that Betty, or Miss Rosemary, as she had been told to call her when she had gone to buy the curtain material, wouldn't be pleased if she just barged in.

She decided to waste some time in the grocer's. There were lots of things to look at in Ezra Williams's shop, items that she had never seen before. He kept a block of brown stuff on his counter that she had heard housewives call 'brawn'. It was weighed on delicate silver scales and sold at a half penny for an ounce. There was a sack of aromatic coffee beans, large tins of cocoa powder, tins of sticky treacle, packets of yellow suet, bags of oats and since the railway line had come to the Wirral, a basket full of oranges imported from a place called Spain.

Ezra Williams seemed to have a soft spot for Maggie, maybe because he was an incomer to the village as well. He and his wife were originally from a small village in Wales, but with a legacy left by a sheep farming uncle, they had decided to buy this grocer store in Neston which had providentially come up for sale. Ezra was now a widower in his late forties, as his poor wife had succumbed to the epidemic that had raged through the village a couple of years before. His business kept him busy and took away the bitterness he had felt for months, after his beloved Joan had died.

With the help of a local woman who came in to do his cooking and his laundry, life was beginning to be a bit more pleasant, especially as he had joined the choir at St Mary's, which meant he was at practise Thursday nights and singing his heart out twice on Sunday.

This soft spot he had for Maggie was shown in little ways, when she went in to give him her custom. She had been one of the first to taste an orange, courtesy of Ezra, when she had gone in to buy a loaf, or an extra ounce of sugar or tea was given, served with a smile and a bit of gossip now and again.

So she waited as Ezra served his customer, knowing he wouldn't mind her staying until Miss Rosemary was free.

"She'll be that new woman that's staying at the Brown Horse," explained Ezra, glad to have a snippet of gossip to pass on, after Maggie had told him that Miss Rosemary was busy with a client. "I've seen her a time or two passing by and one of my customers said she's a relation of the new landlord at the Brown Horse. Doesn't seem to be short of much, dressed to the nines. Always sporting one of those posh parasols, come rain or shine. Don't know what she is to him yet. Daughter maybe, or sister, maybe his wife? I heard they've come from across the water. I think he was a landlord somewhere over there, but with me not being a drinker, I can't find it out from the horse's mouth. And I hear your man is being touted as the winner of the fight between him and Reg McKeown. Not that I hold with men beating each other within an inch of their lives, but I can't help but hear how the betting's going."

"Oh, I take no notice of what Jack's up to, Mister Williams," Maggie replied, trying to sound indifferent. "He's come home with a cut eye once or twice, or his cheek and jaw swelling with the bruisin', but I can't stop what he is doin'. He'll not listen to me. I just worry that Farmer Briggs might say something and we'll be out of the cottage on our ears… Oh, I think Miss Rosemary is free now, I've just seen the new woman."

She dashed out of the shop and into the dressmaker's, where Betty was putting away some rolls of fabric that she had been showing to her client.

"Maggie, how nice to see you again," she said, pleasure written over her tired, lined face. "What is it this time? A new dress, or help with the seams on your old one?"

"I've come to see if yer can help me with a problem that I've found meself landed with, Miss Rosemary. No, no, it's a nice problem that I'm havin'," she finished hastily, as she saw Betty furrowing her brow. She didn't want to cause the lady any anxiety. She was a decent soul. Probably the only person around that Maggie could take a problem to, especially as she had felt overwhelmed that a genteel lady such as the dressmaker would even want to bother with a common Irish girl like herself.

A little later she found herself drinking tea out of a pretty china cup in the dressmaker's tiny kitchen, with the lady herself mulling over what she had just been told and what course of action she could recommend.

"So do you have a plan for this money you have found, dear?" asked Betty kindly. "Seventeen pounds is a lot of money for a young girl like you to have. If I were you I wouldn't go making any large purchases. Not only would your husband be suspicious, but so would a lot of other people. They would wonder how you came upon it and if it was lawfully gained."

"Yer mean people would think I'd pinched it," Maggie said, dolefully. "Though that would be right, how else would someone like me be in possession of such a grand sum?"

She watched Betty hopefully, whilst thinking what an elegant person this lady in front of her was. A little stooped with age maybe, but tall and slim, dressed in a beautifully cut day dress of dove grey, her pure white hair swept up into classical curls that were immaculate. She had deep blue eyes, set above high cheekbones, with a wide and generous mouth, which was turned down now as she dwelt on the problem.

"Perhaps you could bring it to me for safe keeping," she said briskly, once she had arrived at her decision. "That is if you would trust me with such a large sum. I do have a bank account in Chester and once a week I take the coach with the money

I have earned from my commissions, do a little shopping and have a little lunch. Or maybe you could accompany me to the city and we could lodge your money in a new bank account."

She looked at Maggie eagerly and the girl saw from her face that she would welcome her company.

"Me with a bank account, Miss Rosemary?" Maggie replied, quite astounded that she had come up with this answer to the problem. "It sounds wonderful, but can yer honestly see a bank wanting to deal with a person like me? I mean, look at me. Except fer this grand cloak yer helped me make and me pretty boots, what is there underneath it all? A fat, shabby immigrant, with tatty hair and a voice as common as muck. They'd laugh at yer, walkin' into a fancy place with the likes of me. No, I'll have to think of some other way of hiding it, or just leave it with yer good self. And how would I get the time to come a banking with yer anyway?"

"Oh, Maggie, don't sell yourself short," Betty admonished. "Yes, they say clothes maketh the man, but that cloak you have on covers all irregularities. Furthermore, a woman in your condition would cover herself anyway. She wouldn't be showing her dress underneath and you could always give your hair a good brushing before we go. But yes, you are probably right that it would be difficult for you to get away from your responsibilities, and the gossips would wonder why you were travelling with me. So, I have decided I will let you borrow my reticule. You can hide it under your cloak, then at an opportune time you can take the money from the mattress and bring it back to me. I will make you a receipt out, my dear," she ended, taking Maggie's worried look as a sign that she wasn't so sure.

"No, that's fine with me, so it is. I'm just workin' out when will be a good time. I'm ever so grateful fer yer helpin' me the way yer are. If yer can keep the money 'til after the birth of the babby, then I can think again of what I'm goin' to do. Perhaps yer could give me a little when I need it, fer baby things, yer know? Although I think me husband may provide some of the things."

Their discussion was put aside then in favour of planning a new dress to cover Maggie's ever expanding stomach and, of course, a little genteel gossip concerning Madeline, the new woman who had come to reside at the inn.

—

Maggie groaned to herself later as she came within sight of Lilac Cottage. Alice was outside, walking up and down impatiently, clutching some papers in her hand. She had only been once before to visit and Maggie was sure it had been to satisfy herself, that her son wasn't living in a hovel. Though if she'd had any opinions when she had seen the barely furnished rooms, she had kept them to herself.

"There yer are Maggie," she fussed, when she caught sight of her. "I thought you only worked mornings at the farmhouse. I've been standing here waitin' fer the past hour. I've had that big woman from the corner asking me my business and her smelly kids draggin' a cart past me with an idiot child lollin' in it…"

"Oh, that will have been Ruthie Tibbs and her children, Alice. I had to go up to Anne Rosemary's. This dress of mine wants letting out, but we've decided on makin' a new one instead. It will be gathered under me chest to take account of me bigger belly and 'tis a very pretty fabric, sprigged cotton in yellow and green. I'll be up there every afternoon until it's finished. Miss Rosemary is very good to me. We'll work on it together if she's got the time."

She ended her announcement proudly. Even Alice couldn't claim she had a friend as grand as Miss Rosemary.

"Well, that is as maybe, Maggie," Alice said, ignoring the boasting and waving a letter that she carried in her hand, "but I have more pressing problems than you having a dress made. I got this this morning and as you know me eyes aren't good, so I brought it over for you to read. I need yer to tell me what it says. I know it's from the landlord's office, because it says at the top Regent Estates and that is who Mister Arlington works for, but I can't wait fer him to come home for his dinner, so I came to you instead."

Maggie had to smile at Alice's words. So she was good for something, even if it was because she could read. She unlocked the front door of the cottage and ushered her mother-in-law through it, then busied herself with raking the fire embers, so that she could make her a cup of tea.

Alice sat fidgeting with the tassels on the end of her shawl, no doubt annoyed that Maggie hadn't read those things called words immediately and was taking her time fiddling with cups and saucers while she waited for the kettle to boil.

"It says here that yer can buy Seagull Cottage off them fer one hundred and thirty pounds and you must make yer mind up about it by the end of July," Maggie advised her at last, when she decided at last to read the missive. "You must send them a letter of intention saying if yer want to buy it, then pay them a deposit as a sign of good will. If they don't hear from yer, or yer don't intend to purchase, the place will go on their list fer auction and yer have to sort out a new lease with whoever eventually buys."

"Oh no," moaned Alice. "So it's come to this already? We've only bin in for a while. Mr Arlington told us it would be up to three years before we had to do anything. By that time I thought we would have a big lump saved. What are we going to do, Maggie? I love that house. It's become a real home to me and Michael. It means we'll have to start again somewhere else and at our age it seems unfair!"

She started nibbling her nails and looking at Maggie expectantly, hoping for some sympathy, at the very least. But there would be no sympathy coming from Maggie. She had a long memory and it was time to even up old scores.

"I can't see yer findin' that kind of money. Jack hasn't got a bottomless purse and yer were lucky that he gave yer the rent when he did. Now we've a babby on the way te think on, we'll need every penny we can get and there'll be nothing to spare fer anyone. You'll have to go after a job cleanin', like yer said yer would in the beginnin' when we got here, and Michael and Seamus will have to spend more time fishin' or find employment in other ways."

Alice stood and drew herself up to her five foot nothing, glared at Maggie and told her where to stick the cup of tea.

"I knew I wouldn't get any sympathy from you," she spat. "I only came fer you to read the letter, not have yer tellin' me what me and mine can do. I built that business up and now I've got a steady income and I'll not chuck it away for the want of the purchase price. I know from Michael that Jack has money put by and this fight in the offing will bring in more than twenty guineas, I've heard. I'm sure Jack'll let me have it, as he wouldn't want his mother on the street, if the new owner isn't prepared to lease."

She scurried from the cottage and down the lane to the shore, without even a backward glance, leaving Maggie fuming. The woman couldn't even ask after her health and that of her coming grandchild, it was all about Alice and nobody else! It would serve her right if they were thrown out of Seagull Cottage. Playing the grand hostess to her piddling boarders, who the hell did she think she was?

Though Maggie felt a bit of dismay later, as she busied herself in the garden, hoeing between the lines of vegetables that Jack had sown earlier in the spring. So it was definitely on then, this fight that she had heard Jack and Solly discussing, and Alice already had her eye on the proceeds of the purse.

Suddenly remembering her own hoard tucked away in the mattress, she had to rush inside and put the little muslin bags into Miss Rosemary's reticule. If Alice was looking for money, she supposed by law Jack could hand this over to her too.

She abandoned her afternoon in the garden and walked as fast as her ungainly body would go. Her seventeen precious secrets would be having a new home to dwell in from now on.

"Why are you suddenly interested in the fight with Reg McKeown?" asked Jack, as he sat on the sofa later, after his meal of Irish stew. Maggie had tentatively broached the subject after serving him his favourite dish, though he had spoiled the pleasure in the making, by saying his mother's Irish stew had a better taste.

"I'm askin', because yer mother was here today, wantin' me to read this letter she's got from her landlord," Maggie replied curtly. "They want one hundred and thirty pounds fer the purchase of Seagull Cottage and she seems to think you'll be buying it for her from the proceeds of the fight. Seems to me the money is more important now than her son's well being. That's why she came away from Ireland wasn't it, 'cos she was worrying over yer getting into trouble with the authorities as well?"

"Oh, I knew it wouldn't be because yer were concerned about me," replied Jack, rather nastily, turning the tables on his wife's verbal assault. "Well, yer won't get yer wish to become a widow fer a long time to come, Maggie. I'm going up in the world and me mother can have anything that she wants!"

"What do yer mean yer going up in the world? How can a purse of twenty guineas buy a house like Seagull Cottage, and seeing as now you've said it, I'm not hoping to become a widow just yet. I've a child to consider and every child deserves a father. I've had to throw me lot in with yer Jack, because yer made me do it, but that doesn't mean I wish yer ill."

"I know, I'm sorry fer the words I've just said to yer, but yer not the girl I remember from Killala. You've become a hard young besom and I'm frightened to speak to yer sometimes in case we have another row. Come and sit by me and let me feel our little babby. It looks like you'll be having two of them, you've got so big in the last week or two."

They sat together companionably then, while he caressed her stomach, gasping with delight as Michael Junior kicked his hand, neither of them thinking that the baby might be a girl. Jack waited a few minutes, enjoying the contentment, before he explained his plans for securing riches, knowing that Maggie wouldn't be happy with what she was about to hear.

"A man was sent over to meet me in the Wheatsheaf, last weekend. He is the personal agent of Lord Charlie Belsham, who is looking to become a patron or sponsor of a pugilist willing to be trained. This man, whose name is Richard Mannion, said he would come to the fight arranged for next Friday night, between me and McKeown, and whoever wins will be asked if they would like to work for this lord. It means training meant to get the best out of me. I would tour the North of England and take part in the circuit bouts and go to a place in Liverpool, where I would get as much sparring practise as I like. All my expenses will be paid fer by Belsham. Oh, and he could provide a house over there, so we might have to move."

Maggie's reaction was one of disbelief. This was Jack talking. A farm labourer, who did a bit of fighting now and again after last orders. Just to earn a bit of extra money and keep his muscles and body in trim.

She looked at him in amazement, noting his broad shoulders and the determination on his strong and healthy face. He had shaved off his beard and cut his hair short in readiness, but why should he want to stake his life against fighters who could kill him with a fatal blow? The answer came back readily, as Jack continued on.

"Mannion was telling me of others that have been backed by patrons such as Lord Belsham. I would be his first, but he has friends who have made a fortune taking on fighters such as me. It has to be organized just so, with spectators paying gate money. That's split between the two contenders, so we each get a share. Then there's the betting, which relies on how many spectators are there. If it is publicized properly, thousands will turn up to it, not the few hundred that's expected at next week's fight. Then the winner pays his sponsor from the proceeds of the wagers, or something like that, and the more fights yer win, gets yer a better reputation. Who knows, one day I could become the All English Champion, and I've heard he lives like a King!"

Jack paused and looked to see how his wife was taking it. He could see she was stunned with his revelations and, he probably thought, a bit in awe. But she wasn't, she was thinking how foolish Jack had become.

"So, yer want me to uproot meself and foller yer around the country, with a babby strapped to me body and reliant on yer fancy backer fer a roof over our heads. What happens if yer have a losin' streak? You've been lucky up to now, with just a few bruises and cuts. What will happen then, when yer brought back half dead on a wheelbarrow? Farmer Briggs won't keep yer job and this place for yer. Nor will he let me stay, a woman and a babby on her own."

Her voice had begun to rise with sheer panic. She had started her nesting period in the pregnancy and the cottage was now the place she had to call her home.

"I suppose all this has been discussed with yer mother? She seemed to think you'd be helping her out with another loan. It is a loan? You'll get the money back for the good of our son one day, won't yer?"

"Me mother only knows what me dad will have told her. Me dad is going to be me manager now. I can't trust Solly, he's in his cups most of the time and he's not a man that I care to have as a go-between. Dad will make sure I'm gettin' a fair deal from Mannion and Belsham and we'll keep a room for him at the new place in Liverpool. Of course I'll get the money back from me mother. When she dies the house will come to the eldest son, with Seamus inheriting anything else she has. Anyway, who's worrying about the money I've given to me mother? We'll have the life of Riley once I get known in the fightin' world."

"I still haven't said I'm coming with yer."

"Will yer listen to yerself, 'I still haven't said I'm coming with ye'," Jack mimicked. "Yer me wife and don't forget it.

You'll live in a grand villa on the outskirts of Liverpool, you'll see. Lord Belsham will come a visiting and he's not going to call at a hovel, now is he? You'll probably have a maid to help and to answer the front door for you. Twenty guineas will be chicken feed. It'll be two hundred guineas each time, or more!"

He hugged Maggie exuberantly. She supposed he was hoping to be given a smile, but she felt a shiver rushing through her body and folded her arms around her stomach protectively. This wasn't the right time in their lives to think of uprooting. Anything could happen. At least here at Lilac Cottage, they had a roof over their heads. They ate good food and Jack was a hard and willing worker at the farm. To throw his lot in with a patron, who perhaps would tire of his new venture, or want to put his money into a more profitable scheme, was sheer folly. There was no sense in even trying to change Jack's mind though. He was self-willed and stubborn, just like her.

Maggie felt as if they had started on the slippery slope next day, when the mistress asked if she could have a word. It seemed that Florrie, the second to eldest girl, had finished school now that she was fourteen and was looking for employment locally.

"I don't want her to go into service," the mistress explained. "She did quite well at school, knows her letters and her numbers, so we would like her to find something in the village. Or failing that become a pupil teacher, if a position was to come up at the Infant school. Meantime, Maggie, without wanting to sound rude, you are getting a bit clumsy now your time is nearly due. Florrie can help me, while you take some time off for resting and we can talk again after your lying in. That is… if you are still with us." The mistress broke off and looked at her servant meaningfully.

"What are yer saying Mrs Briggs? Do yer think something will happen to me and the baby?"

Maggie looked at her employer fearfully, wondering at her words.

"No, no, Maggie," she replied reassuringly. "Everything will be fine with you and the baby, don't you worry. It's not you that I'm thinking of. It's Jack I hear there is a fight on Friday night at the quarry and Briggs has said if Jack doesn't turn up for work on Saturday morning, it's his last warning and he's out on his ear. Oh, didn't you know that some mornings, he's not been able to even lift a spade?"

She broke off, when she saw that Maggie hadn't a clue what she was talking about.

"Surely you've noticed the state of him, when he's come home to you at night?" This was said with some disbelief.

"I'm usually in bed when he comes in from the tavern, and fast asleep when he gets up for work," Maggie explained. "And if I'm honest, I don't care what he does when he gets with his cronies. It's his body and he won't listen to me."

"Well, you will be caring, my girl, when the farmer tells him to remove all his possessions and quit that little cottage," she warned. "Then you'll be at the mercy of your mother-in-law and let's hope she'll help you out!"

Chapter 13

With her mistress's words ringing in her ears, her final wages and a layette of knitted baby clothes under her cloak, courtesy of Peggy, Maggie trundled up the muddy track to the village. She was on her way to see Miss Rosemary, to collect the new dress that the dressmaker had been finishing off, with Maggie not being very proficient in the smocking part of it.

She was amused to see a big cage-like thing, hanging on the door of the clients' changing room, when she got there.

"That's for underneath the crinoline gown that Miss Madeline has asked me to make her," Betty explained, as she saw the girl raising her eyebrows at the absurdity of it. "Depending on how wide you want the skirt to be, you can add as many petticoats to make it stick out. Miss Madeline doesn't want more than three, or she would never get through the Brown Horse's front door. So she has asked me to make a wheel of thick plaited horsehair, which will go around her waist, two plain muslin petticoats and another with flounces. The sleeves of the bodice have to be what she called a pagoda style, and the over skirt must be four tiered, with a fringe sewn on every hem! I'm glad you called by, Maggie, because you can help me with the stitching of all the flounces and frills she wants on it. Do you know how much material will be used for all this? The bottom of the skirt alone will take ten yards!"

Her voice was raised in disbelief, as she gave Maggie a run down of all the work that was involved. She considered it an unattractive change in modern fashion, she preferred the Empire line, with its high waist and simple leg of mutton sleeves. Made in silk, satin or crepe, not these new materials that she was going to have to get in, organdie, tulle and tarlatan.

"At least your dress is ready, Maggie, it's hanging behind the kitchen door," she said, wondering why the girl wasn't working at the farm that day.

"Oh, thank you, Miss Rosemary. I've bin frightened of burstin' out of this one, there's nothing left to take out any more in the seams. So where does the woman get her fancy ideas from? What is she doing in Neston? Has she told yer any more?"

"Only that she has been used to shopping in the big stores in Liverpool and her uncle took her down to London for a few days. She says that the crinoline is what everyone is wearing there. She brought me a likeness to copy, but I hope it doesn't catch on in this neck of the woods, the stitching that goes into it is a nightmare. Do you think you would be able to help me out over the next few days?"

"I've got all the time in the world, Miss Rosemary," Maggie answered, feeling delighted that she would have somewhere to come each day. "The farmer's wife has told me to start me time of resting, which I'll gladly do. See, her daughter, Peggy, has knitted these baby things for me."

Maggie proudly produced the crocheted shawl, containing a few little items from under her cloak.

"Oh, they are beautiful," sighed Betty, as she examined the perfect white bootees, matching mittens, bonnet and little matinee coat. "The pattern of the shawl is the same throughout the whole layette. She's a clever girl, is Peggy Briggs."

"Peggy Phipps now. I did hear a whisper that she was expecting, but I haven't heard any more, so perhaps she wasn't. Perhaps she made this lot fer her own little babby, thinkin' she was. I was very surprised when the mistress gave them to me."

"We should be thinking of making a few baby clothes together, Maggie, and you will need to buy some towelling, so that we can cut the material into squares. If you don't mind me saying it, this is the time in your life when you really need your mother. I wouldn't know the first thing of how to change a baby, or how to feed it, or what to do when it cries."

"Yes, I still miss me mother and me sister, Molly," Maggie replied sadly, "but I know how to change a baby when its cloths are dirty, because I used to help Mammy. I think I'll need to make at least a dozen little dresses for him, so I'd be glad if you could search out any remnants for me, Miss Rosemary. Plain and simple will do fer Michael Patrick, no smockin' on the top. Accordin' to Alice, I've still got three months to go, so I'll have plenty to keep me busy, you see. It has to be said, the farm work was gettin' too much fer me, havin' to lug this big lump around."

"That's what I like about you, Maggie. You have me smiling on the darkest of days. Now, I have a little proposition, which I have been mulling over since you entrusted your money to me. But we'll have a cup of tea first before we discuss it. I am sure you will like what I have in mind."

"But why would yer be doin' this for me, Miss Rosemary?" Maggie exclaimed, as the dressmaker outlined her plan later. "It isn't as though I'm related to yer or yer've known me very long. I must say I'm grateful, but I might not be here more than a month or two. Jack has come up with grand ideas about his future and I suppose I'll have to foller him."

"Well, my dear, to answer your question before we discuss the why's and wherefores, my father left me fairly well off, as the result of many of the investments he made. Being a sea captain gave him access to items that you would never see on a local shop's shelves. He brought back bolts of cloth from the Orient, spices, wood carvings, china, furniture, tobacco and spirit from Jamaica, and made a lot of money selling the goods on to willing purchasers in Liverpool and the cities around.

"My mother and I had a comfortable life from the proceeds, enough for me to give up my job as a sempstress with the gentry, and eventually I was in a position to buy some property.

I've always felt a little entrepreneurial, must be the blood of my father flowing through me. If I were a man there would have been nothing to stop me forging ahead and creating great riches, but it is always difficult being a woman in a man's world. However, I see a need in this community for a money lending service, as I have just explained to you. Your seventeen pounds could be put to good use while you have no need of it. And hiding behind the name of Sheldon Loan Company, no one will know that it is a woman behind it all. I will say that I am the company's agent and all transactions will be conducted from here. Then when the company grows, and I am convinced it will, you can take over. Especially when the little one has gone to school."

"It all sounds wonderful, so it does Miss Rosemary, and whatever yer say I'll go along with, but yer still haven't said why you've chosen me. Yer could use yer own money to set up a new company."

"Let's say it's because I'm going soft in my dotage, Maggie. I've lived a lot of years on this earth and one thing I have learnt, is that you've got to grasp the opportunities as they are given to you. I admire the way you've stood up in the face of adversity. You were not a willing participant in Jack's flight from your home country, but you've made the best of it. You're a young girl of, what, nearly seventeen years, without parental guidance in a strange and foreign land. When you handed me the money that you found in that mattress, I thought this is a girl to whom the fates are going to be kind and I would like to be part of it as well. So, here's the ledger, 'Mrs Proprietor of the Sheldon Loan Company' and we'll have a shop bought cake to celebrate."

Maggie came out of the shop later with her head buzzing. Betty had shown her how the ledger would be kept. The customer's name at the top of the sheet, with columns for loan given, payments made, interest and loan repaid. There was a declaration at the foot of each page that the loan would be repaid in a certain time or extra interest would be added.

Then a place underneath where the customer made his mark or signed their name. Betty had even worked out the interest to be charged on each amount borrowed, and was going to speak to Ezra Williams, who moaned about running a slate for his customers, and was sure to be willing to send any would-be borrowers to the dressmaker's shop next door.

Betty had expressed the opinion that the people most likely to become Maggie's customers would be the wives of the colliery workers and possibly those of the quarrymen too. The men of both these employments seemed to frequent the many taverns there were in the village, leaving their families short of money for clothing and food. It was a traditional thing, to piss your earnings down the open drain at the end of a hard week's graft on a Friday.

There was something wrong with a man who wanted to do anything different. He must have got religion or become a member of the Temperance Society, and had no business to be working alongside working men. So, the taverns and inns were full to overflowing at the weekends and the wives needed just a bit extra to tide them over for food and other things.

Maggie loved the name that Betty had chosen and had asked her why she had given it that name? Sheldon, it transpired, was connected to the family.

"It was my mother's maiden name, Maggie, and it is in memory of her that I hand it on to you. She would have made an excellent business woman had she been born into this century, but, unfortunately for her, it was not to be. Even now, single ladies such as myself are made to feel inadequate somehow, because we are not married and producing babies. But God gave women brains as he gave them to men. We just need opportunities, and that is what I am giving to you."

Maggie stood for a while studying Miss Rosemary's window display. She wasn't really seeing it, because her mind was in such a whirl. The Sheldon Loan Company. She was the proprietor of a loan company! Not just lowly Maggie Haines, married to

Jack and with a baby on the way, but someone with seventeen pounds to cast like bread upon the water, and one day that figure would be even more!

She hugged her secret to her, reluctant to return to the four walls of the cottage, when she should be dancing, shouting, telling the world of her good fortune. Telling everyone she met that today hadn't been an ordinary day! That Miss Rosemary, tailoress to the community, had just handed her a golden future and that life would be very different now than how she had imagined it to be. But who would believe her and who could she trust with the knowledge? There was no one around her that would wish her well.

Maggie strolled down Parkgate Road, trying to make her mind dwell on something else and trying to keep the absurd smile from bursting all over her face. A walk to her favourite place might serve to encourage it, as the view from the hills alone always seemed to calm her soul. Her thoughts flickered back to when she had last sat on the sea wall, when Jimmy, the pot man, had got a letter from his lover back home. Did he still miss his beloved Eileen or had he gone to Liverpool to be with his folks, or was he waiting for the cattle boat to take him back to his roots? Of course, Johnny! He had said he would be returning to this sea port the following spring and how amazing was it, that Killala and her old life was only being remembered at this time. It had been weeks since she yearned for the hamlet, weeks since she yearned to go home. Her fear now was that the life she had made in Neston could also be easily snatched away.

Betty had pooh-poohed the idea when Maggie had spoken of Jack's plans.

"I can't see him throwing up a perfectly good job for an uncertain future in the world of the pugilist," she had said reassuringly, "especially as he has the added responsibility of you and the child."

She had a lovely way with words, Maggie thought, feeling a little more comforted. But Betty didn't know Jack as she did.

If he'd made his mind up on something, then he wouldn't be shifted at all.

-

It was a beautiful May afternoon, the kind of day that started badly with mist over the river, but the sun had come bursting through the clouds by midday. Maggie wasn't the only one who sat on the sea wall, whilst she contemplated the latest developments in her life. Ruthie Tibbs's girl, Annie, had come wandering along. She looked lost and uncared for, passing Maggie unseeingly, so deep in her thoughts was she.

She gave a jump of surprise when Maggie laid a kindly hand upon her shoulder. Annie hadn't wanted anyone she knew to see her in the place she liked the best. Away from her dominant mother, her pig of a father and the demands that her siblings made upon her too.

"Why, Annie, what's the matter with ye?" Maggie asked, startled at the miserable face that the girl was showing.

"Nuthin'," she replied, turning away dejectedly.

"I like to come here too, when I've a lot to think on," Maggie confided. "Why don't we sit together and look out over the wonderful sea?"

"I want to sit on my own," came back her quick reply.

"That's fine with me, Annie, but if yer change yer mind I'll be just a little bit away. Perhaps we could go to the shop over there later. I believe they make the best ice-cream and I could treat yer to some before we go home."

But the girl just sat there, staring morosely out across the sea, so Maggie decided to leave her alone. The girl had made it obvious she wanted it that way.

She had always pitied Annie. It couldn't have been an easy life, living as she did in poor surroundings, with loud mouthed Ruthie and Solly, the little weasel. She had nearly always looked subdued, with none of the excitement of childhood during the times that Maggie had come across her. She was still wearing the faded dress she had been wearing at Christmas, but now the bodice was straining across her chest and the hem was up around her knees.

Maggie looked across to where a fishing boat was tying up, the skipper shouting to his mate to be careful with the rope he was putting around the capstan, as he had nearly upended a passerby. Unbidden thoughts of Johnny came rushing back to her. His curly black hair, his cornflower blue eyes, the way he walked and smiled. All of these things paraded themselves in front of her. Irrelevant, pointless thoughts and she couldn't understand why they had come to her. Johnny had made it plain that he didn't want to know her. Had abandoned her to Jack and Neston, as far as she was concerned. Come to think of it, after the immigrant settlement had been disbanded, she had not heard another voice that had held the Irish brogue. Perhaps Johnny took his cattle boat now to Liverpool. Certainly there had been no more new stock in the farmer's fields.

She felt a touch pressing on her elbow. It put an end to her musings when she saw it was Annie standing by her side.

"I'd like that ice cream now, if yer don't mind, Missis. I've never had one, but that Florrie at the farm says she's had many, so I think I would like you to get me one to try."

Dear God, Maggie thought, the child was willing to be friendly for the sake of tasting an ice cream. A lump came to her throat and she dashed away the tear that came into her eye.

"Sit beside me, Annie, and tell me what is ailing yer. Do yer see a lot of Florrie? Is she a special friend?" She patted the space beside her and Annie came to sit at her side.

"She used to be me friend, until her mam sent her to the charity school, but my mam wouldn't let me go, 'cos it took me away from things. She said she needed me to look after her babies, and why would I need all that learnin' anyway. Dad said that when me mam had finished havin' babies, then it would be my turn. But I don't want to be like me mother. I want to get away from Neston, maybe go to Liverpool, get a job over there and have some peace on me own!"

She turned a tear-streaked face towards her and Maggie looked back in horror at her words. What did she mean it would be her turn having babies? What could Solly possibly mean by his insinuating words?

"Yer don't mean that yer father has been laying his hands on yer, do yer?" Maggie asked gently, holding her breath, waiting for an answer that might mean she would have to do something to the little turd. She would strangle Solly if Annie had been interfered with, remembering back to that time in the fields, when he had wrestled with her. Maggie breathed more easily as Annie made her explanation, but began to listen more closely to the now talkative girl.

"Naw, the only time I get touched is when he clats me round the head for speakin' back at him. He did climb on to me palliasse once, when he got lost, he said. It was one night when he came in drunk, but me mam hauled him down the ladder and clatted him round the ear instead. No, yesterday I heard them talkin'. Dad is so excited about this fight on Friday night. Yer know, the fight that your Jack is havin'? Dad said it was going to make a big difference to the way he lives his life, but Mam got angry with him. She knows if he gets any money, he'll just drink it away in the pub. I mean, look at me dress. Missis Briggs give me this, one that Florrie has grown out of, and that petticoat you bought me was sold as soon as he could get it off me. He said if Jack loses the fight, then he's going to sell me to the gypsies…"

"The gypsies?" Maggie squeaked. "You mean those travellin' people that don't have a home? Here? I saw some once passin' through Ballina, that's near where I used to live, by the way. Do they have gypsies in Neston? Why would he want to sell you to them anyway?"

"I think it was more of a threat to me mam, than really meanin' it. He thinks I should be bringin' in a wage by now. He calls me mam a lazy, fat cow, who could manage without me if she would just stir herself. But, as I said to him, 'I don't want to stay and work in Neston, and I'll keep away from the gypsies when they do their yearly visit to the Ladies Day Fair.'"

"Oh, is there to be a fair soon, Annie?" Maggie inquired eagerly, glad to change the subject, if only to cheer the girl. "I've never bin to one of them, though me mother told me she had once."

"Well, I'll tell yer all about it, when we've had the ice cream and we're walkin' back to the cottages," Annie replied, slyly. She had had enough of talking for one day and her mother would be wondering where she had got to. She'd probably get a back hander anyway for disappearing again.

Maggie brushed her hair until it shone when she got back to the cottage. She changed into her brand new dress, admiring the way it fell into billowing folds from underneath her enlarged breasts. A picture of domestic contentment, she thought, hoping that Jack would see the same. Enough to take his thoughts away from his hopes of a fighting future and come to his senses.

"Did yer hear that Missis Briggs has finished me, Jack?" she asked, when he came loping through the back door.

"I heard Maggie," he replied and sat himself on the sofa beside her. "Farmer Briggs told me this afternoon in the fields."

Jack was looking rather weary. He told Maggie it had been back breaking work clearing the cabbage field of weeds, so that they could start again with the winter seed. The crop had been gathered the day before and loaded onto the cart for the market. He was looking forward to a night in with his feet up and wondered why his wife was looking so blooming and clean. He hoped that she wasn't going to start her back biting all over again.

"You should be pleased that you'll have time to yerself," he said. "There'll be no time fer anythink when Michael Junior is here to stay. Come on, let's get it over with, Maggie. What's eatin' ye?"

"It's just that Missis Briggs said that if yer didn't turn up for work on Saturday after the fight, that you'd get the sack. It hasn't been the first time that the farmer has had to warn yer, or so she said. You know we'll lose the cottage and our living…"

She began to weep a little, thinking it might impress him. The gentle pleading and a few sorrowful tears should make him want to change his ways.

"Maggie, I've made me mind up, yer know I have. All the crying in the world or Briggs's warnings is not goin' to change it." Jack put his arms round her now shaking shoulders. "We don't need Briggs and his measly wage, nor his cottage that is no more than a hovel. I can use me fists to earn a livin'. I'm good at it and when that agent sees me on Friday night, I'll prove that I'm worth the patronage. McKeown doesn't stand a chance against me. I've heard he's a dirty fighter, but now I have that knowledge, I'll be careful and pull me punches sparingly. No, I'm after the good life, Maggie, and you'll be with me all the way. You'll have shop bought clothes, not something you've had to cobble together. Though I have to say, you look very good in the one you've just made for yerself," he finished hastily.

"And what if I don't want to come with yer to this new high life yer promising?" she asked despairingly. "I've settled here in Neston. You're the one that dragged me here and just when I'm thinkin' that it's me home fer ever, yer draggin' me off again."

"Oh, is there no end to yer whining, Maggie?" Jack began to raise his voice in exasperation. "Don't yer want fancy clothes, a shining new house, with a servant to answer the door? Yer must be mad to want to bring our child up in this poverty. No, I've made up me mind. Be ready with yer bits and pieces on Saturday morning and I'll borrow a handcart. We'll be staying at me mother's until things are finalized. Then yer can please yerself. Stay with me mother by all means if yer want to, but we are definitely not going to be workin' at the farm."

So, that was all there was to be said on the subject, Maggie thought, as they spooned the broth she had made earlier into their mouths. Both of them were churned up inside and she was glad when Jack put his coat on and said he was going for a walk. Though it was a pity that they had never taken the air together like other couples. She would have liked that sometimes, linking arms and taking the air along the promenade.

Maggie looked around the living room sadly. This had been her first real home. One of her own, she amended hastily, her real home was in the hamlet of Killala. How she longed to be back there. Was Jack really expecting her to pack up all their possessions and go to live at Alice's house? How were they going to manage with all the lodgers? Was there room enough for them? It had probably been discussed already, and rested on the amount of money Jack had secreted.

Chapter 14

Maggie couldn't believe her eyes later after Jack had gone on his walk, using the opportunity to stealthily pull out the draw string bags and count Jack's money. She found twenty gold sovereigns in each of them, amounting to £120! How had he amassed such a grosh of riches and where could he have taken his winnings to change them into all those coins? It was a mystery. Surely the wagers taken would be paid for in shillings, not in gold!

So, already his fighting had been more than an exchanging of blows with a local opponent. Jack's father had obviously taken a great deal of trouble to make the fights into proper events.

Maggie straightened up with difficulty after carefully placing the money bags back, wishing, not for the first time, that her confinement was near to the end. The waddling around like a bow legged duck was getting harder, with another two and a half months to go if Alice was to be believed. She decided to say nothing about the money bags to her husband. Other than to remind him that if they were thinking of leaving the cottage, then he would have to move his wealth to his money belt. Or take it to Alice, of course. Maggie didn't think that any of his money would be coming in her direction.

Next day, the evening before his fight with McKeown, Jack acted as if nothing was out of the ordinary. As usual, he got up at the crack of dawn. Putting on his work clothes and pretending to set off for a full day's work at the farm was his way of shielding his pregnant wife from the truth of the matter. Plans were already well advanced, but Maggie didn't have to know.

He made his way to Seagull Cottage, where his mother provided a breakfast of sliced ham, eggs and steak, before he ran a circular route around Neston and Parkgate. Later he rested on the bed that Alice had proudly made available for her pugilist son, until Michael, his father, said it was time to get up again.

Unknown to Maggie, the parting of the ways had already occurred between Jack and the farmer. There had been a lot of strong words from Briggs, as he had assumed that the Irishman had been grateful for the start he had been given. A job and a cottage was not to be sniffed at and it would take some time to find a replacement amongst the local men. Straight talking hadn't worked. Briggs reminded Jack of his responsibilities.

Talking to Jack, trying to get him to stay with the life that they had both become used to, hadn't worked for Maggie either. So she had busied herself until bedtime, preparing the next day meal's vegetables, then showing Jack the little garments that Peggy had knitted for their baby. Anything to keep her from shouting and crying out, that he was a great big stupid fella to be throwing away this life.

Later she had lain beside him, marvelling that Jack could sleep. While she lay wide-eyed, contemplating all the horrors that could possibly happen. The future was uncertain, so much rested on Jack's capabilities. No one could predict the outcome of his performance or his skill.

-

To keep a secret from Ruthie Tibbs in itself, would be a test of endurance. Though she didn't make an appearance at Lilac Cottage until the next afternoon. Ruthie surprised Maggie as she came wandering out of the privy. She'd been feeling a few unsettling pains, though why she didn't know.

"That will be yer babby bedding in," explained Ruthie knowledgeably, when Maggie confessed to having pain. "I had to get Nellie Flemin', the midwife, in once. Around the same time as you are, 'cos I kept thinkin' that me and the babby was about to be parted. She told me it starts putting its 'ead in the hole and likes gettin' itself comfy. It will probably go quiet now, gettin' its strength fer the birthin'. Not that you'll be able to get much restin'. Now that yer leavin' the cottage and the farm."

Maggie looked askance at her neighbour. Had Jack already told the farmer that this was going to be his last working day? How had Ruthie heard about their moving? It was like she had a second sight, or some way of divining other people's thoughts.

"Thought I would come to see if there is anything that yer thinkin' of leavin'. Those curtains ye made would fit me windows and maybe that mattress yer brung along. Yer won't need yer kettle and pans neither, 'cos yer'll be sharin' with Alice, I'll be bound. It's alright fer some, married to a fine fella whose goin' places. I hope he's not goin' to ferget our Solly, once he's over the water in Liverpool."

It must have been Solly, giving his wife the latest on Jack's plans, Maggie thought. Surely Jack would have waited until he had got his pay that evening, before telling Briggs that he was to go. Even so, she began to feel a little nervous, with Ruthie hanging over her like a spectre at a feast and the possibility of the farmer being angry.

"Don't suppose I'll see yer much, once yer settled in Seagull Cottage," Ruthie continued, nodding her head sagely. "Can't see that fancy Alice wantin' the likes of me visitin' fer afternoon tea and scones. Which reminds me, will yer be takin' them little cups, and what about that blanket? Did they come with the cottage or can I have them? And have yer told Nellie Flemin' of yer movin', or is yer mother-in-law to be at the birthin' instead?"

"Ruthie," Maggie said, worried. "I'm not feelin' so well and I've a mind to get into bed and stay there until tomorrer. Jack should be bringin' a handcart first thing in the mornin' and what we don't put on it, yer can have. If yer would, ask Nellie to come down to Seagull Cottage if she can manage it. Alice has not mentioned a midwife being at the birthin', but it won't harm fer her to visit as well."

Ruthie lumbered away, reluctantly. Maggie felt as if she'd just been run over by a horse and cart. She lay on the bed and pulled the blanket over her, her last thoughts before she slept, being of wondering where Jack had hidden his money belt. If Ruthie was to be the recipient of the feather mattress, she would have to make sure it was empty of Jack's wondrous wealth.

She closed her eyes. A little sleep was welcome, just until Jack came home to change out of his working clothes.

Was it a dream or could she hear a man shouting and was that the thudding of fists on the front door that she could hear? She sat bolt upright, glad of the closed curtains she had pulled across the window before sleeping, adrenalin coursing through her body, as sleep fled in an instant when she heard the noise!

"We know yer in there, Missis. It's the Po-leece. Open up I say, or we'll begin to break your door down."

Holy Mother and all the Saints! Maggie got off the mattress as fast as her ungainly body would let her, trembling from head to foot as she did so. How she managed to get her shaking fingers to turn the key in the lock, she never knew.

It was Ernie Higgins, the local man from the constabulary, all puffed up with importance, with Farmer Briggs at his side. Higgins was sweating profusely from his harassed exertion and the farmer was staring at her, indignantly.

Maggie looked at them both in total bewilderment. What were they doing there and was that Ruthie and all her kids at the top of the path, looking over balefully? And what time was it? She had gone to bed with the sun still peeping through the tree tops and now the moon was glinting from a starry sky!

Ernie Higgins could have been a prize fighter himself, with his squashed in nose and brutish face which looked to be older than his forty five years. He was the last of generations of 'burley men', whose job had been to look after the hedges and common land of the area. He had been promoted in 1840 to look after the good men and women of his village and he took his work very seriously, seeing that he had been chosen by a jury of local businessmen and shopkeepers. Chosen for his height, powerful muscles and his towering frame, he was head and shoulders above ordinary men.

"Is Jack hurt? Is that what you've come to tell me, Farmer?" she asked, still trembling slightly at her recent shock, but determined to be in control and face up to whatever was going to present itself. "Or is it that he's dead?" she asked further, seeing that Briggs was hesitant and waiting for Higgins to speak.

"We haven't come about yer blessed husband," replied the policeman. "Though we should be throwing him into prison for all the trouble that he's caused today. No, it's this one's man we've come about…"

He jerked his thumb in the direction of Ruthie, who, for once, was looking very nervous. Not daring to come down the path to Lilac Cottage, in case she herself was whisked away.

"I've got Tibbs in the lock up in the village. When yer see that husband of yours, 'cos I can see from lookin' that the rumour is correct and he's been taken somewhere else, tell him, if he wants to press charges on Tibbs, he's to present himself to me by Tuesday morning. The magistrates sit once a quarter at the Mostyn Arms Hotel and until then Tibbs will reside in Park Street. Not a pleasant place for any person to have to stay in, being damp and smelly, but I'm sure he's been up to things in the past that I've been unaware of, so a few days incarceration will make up for the times he's got away."

"But what's he done? Why have yer put him in prison?" Maggie asked in bewilderment, looking beyond to where Ruthie stood crying and the children were starting to howl.

"He was caught red handed by a fellow policeman. We had to bring in twenty other men from the Chester police force, to cope with the numbers that turned up to watch the quarry fight. There must have been three hundred and fifty workmen, from the railway, the colliery and the quarry, including all the followers that came with McKeown from Liverpool and, of course, all the local support for Jack. It seems that there was a lot of money in the purse and Tibbs was caught running away up Neston High Street, as if the devil was at his tail.

"My man challenged him. Well, what was a lone fella doing, running up the High Street, when every man was at the quarry watching your Jack? It appears Tibbs was going to hide it. It was his responsibility and he was going to keep the money safe. But your father-in-law tells a different story. Solly has been hanging around, since Jack's father has taken over the promoting and overseeing of everything, including the handling of the money. It was Jack's father who said to hold on to him, since Jack was being carried away on a handcart, the last I saw of him. Though he won the match fair and square. Reg McKeown wasn't up to much, by all accounts."

"And what are you here fer, Farmer Briggs?" she asked, relieved to hear that Jack was being taken care of and it seemed that Solly was only getting his just desserts.

"Constable Higgins came first to the farmhouse to tell me what had happened, seeing that Jack and Solly are both my employees. Well Jack was, so I decided to accompany him. But what I would like to know is, what you are doin' with a lock on my cottage door?"

She was saved from having to answer him, as Ruthie came shambling up to the doorway, pushing her way through, crying and pleading with whoever would listen that Solly would never steal money away from Jack and that it was all going to turn out to be a terrible mistake.

"He said to me that he was the holder of the purse and that 'is job was one of great importance," she cried. "Please Sir, let him go, or we'll all be in the Workhouse. He needs his job and our little cottage. Solly ain't a bad man to me and the kids at all."

If it wasn't all so serious, Maggie would have been in danger of collapsing into hysterical laughter. Ernie Higgins was standing there, so full of carrying out rightful justice. Briggs was puffed up pompously, vexed that two thirds of his workforce, if you didn't count Billy, were causing him untold displeasure by their actions of that night and Ruthie, her big strong neighbour, zealously declaring how good her runt of her husband was. It was all too much, she had to end it, or she would run the risk of being carried off to the asylum.

Maggie drew herself up and squared her shoulders.

"Gentlemen," she said, "could I just remind yer of the condition that I am in. I've heard enough from both of you and I think the best thing would be to wait until cock crow. I will have gathered me possessions together, Farmer, and will have quit yer cottage. I believe I will be stayin' at Seagull Cottage on the promenade, until such time as our removal to Liverpool. So, Constable Higgins, yer can see me husband down there. Ruthie, I will see yer in the mornin' too. So good night to all of you."

With that, she shut the door firmly on all of the astonished faces and resolutely turned the key, to sit down on the sofa trembling. Whether it was from the cold night air, or from all the agitation she wasn't sure, but probably it was from relief that Jack hadn't been fatally injured, as she had feared at first he might have been.

It was Seamus who arrived the next morning with the handcart. There was no sign of Jack and, in answer to her surprised questioning of his whereabouts, Seamus mumbled that his brother was resting back home.

The day promised to be a warm one, but Maggie needed to wear her cloak to cover up the money belt. She had found it where Jack had tucked it, under the mattress on his side of their bed.

With Seamus gone, and after taking the few possessions she didn't need to her neighbour, Maggie wandered around the cottage to reminisce. Going back to the time when she had come as a reluctant bride to the place.

But Lilac Cottage had become her harbour and her shelter. Here she could close the door and turn the key, and the beauty of her view from the garden could be compared with no other. She wandered into the orchard, where fruit from the trees and vegetable patch had kept them adequately fed. She began to think of the future then, with a sense of unease. Wouldn't life be perfect if she could have been allowed to stay on here without him!

She decided to take a different route to the promenade, without incurring the pleading look in Ruthie's eyes and the tearful faces of her children, which she would if she were to pass Thistledown Cottage on her way. There was nothing she could do to help the release of Solly and, if truth was told, it served him right. It would be the kind of thing that Solly would do, if he thought he could get away with it. He was a shifty character, creepy and slimy, and she felt sorry for his family. She hoped that the few possessions that she had sent down to Ruthie might bring in a little silver to tide them over if Briggs evicted them and put another family in.

–

Such a scene met her eyes as she came around the corner of the promenade. Outside Seagull Cottage was a grand looking carriage, with two snorting greys tossing their heads in the air. A small group of people had gathered, not because they had never seen horses and a carriage before, but probably because they were curious about who the Irish woman had got inside.

On the outside of the shiny vehicle was a coat of arms, which suggested that the visitor must be nearly royal. Maggie's heart gave a leap of alarm. It must be the patron that Jack had spoken of, a man called Lord Charlie Belsham. He'd be sitting in the best room discussing his protege's future, and she wasn't even there to get a look in. She could imagine Alice in there fussing, plying his lordship with homemade cake and coffee served in fancy cups. She'd be made to stay in the background, while her future would be decided yet again.

Maggie pushed her way through the throng into the hallway, and found herself being propelled into the kitchen by Alice, demanding to know what had taken her so long?

"The lad's been here for ages," she said snappily. "He said yer were only minutes behind! His Lordship is, at this moment, deep in negotiations with Jack and his Dad. Did yer know that my son won the contest in only nineteen rounds? No, yer didn't. Well, yer would have done if yer had come down like yer were meant to yesterday. Didn't Jack tell yer to come down and sit with me? We could have done some knitting and kept each other company while we waited fer the outcome." Alice was so agog with all the excitement, that she didn't wait for Maggie to reply and eagerly carried on. "Did yer see his carriage and those beautiful, well-trained horses? Wait until yer meet his Lordship. Talk about handsome, he's like a god. And the clothes he's wearing. Straight from the best tailor in London, I'd say, and perfect teeth. White and gleaming, like pearls from an oyster. His manners are faultless. Should have heard the way he spoke to me when I asked him if he would like a cup of coffee or tea."

"And what did yer serve him with?" Maggie asked, trying to keep up with her animated flow, but Alice didn't answer, as she listened to the muted sounds of conversation coming through the parlour wall.

"I think he's for the off now, Maggie," she decided as she heard a chair being pushed back and a man's voice coming near. "You'll have to be presented to him. He knows Jack's a married man. Go and stand by the front door and look as if yer just comin' in."

Maggie did as she was told. It wouldn't have done, her starting a row with Alice, not at that moment anyway. She'd find the time later, if what had been discussed was not to her liking. For now, she would be gentle and biddable. The kind of wife that a pugilist could be proud of, whatever that was supposed to be.

"Lord Belsham. May I present my daughter-in-law, Mrs Margaret Haines," Alice said, picking up her aitches and making a great sweeping movement with her arm. "She was away on a little business, on the occasion that you had chosen to call, but providentially she is with us now for an introduction... Mrs Margaret Haines."

Maggie had to stifle a giggle that rose up in her throat at Alice's lengthy presentation. It was as if they were in the sumptuous surroundings of a palatial drawing room, not in the narrow hall way of a seaside boarding house.

Lord Belsham must have sensed the levity in the situation, as he bowed to Maggie most formally, then winked with a twinkle in his other eye, as he straightened himself up.

"Charmed, I'm sure," he said briefly. Then turning to thank Alice for her hospitality, took his leave. He whistled up his coachman when he got outside, as the man had seized the chance, in his master's absence, to buy his Missis a pot of shrimps from the seafood shop that had recently opened, further along the road.

Lord Belsham was everything that Alice had said about him, Maggie thought distractedly, as she prepared to follow her mother-in-law. Charming, handsome, lovely teeth and a well fitting suit, but a man the same as any other.

Jack was lying on what his mother called the 'chase lounge', still in his knee length breeches from the night before, with a blanket thrown around his shoulders. His left eye was closed, his cheeks and jaw were a mass of darkening bruises. His knuckles were scraped and raw from the constant pounding that he had given McKeown and his calves had gone numb from the sneaky kicking that his opponent had inflicted when the referee's head was turned away. McKeown would have won hands down, if he had been allowed to fight in the way that he had earned his reputation. But last night had been different. Each man knew that in the audience sat a philanthropist Lord and his agent, Richard Mannion. The rules had to be adhered to. No punching below the waist, no blows to be administered if the opponent fell to the floor. Wrestling was allowed and vicious, brutal beatings, but not biting or kicking. That was frowned on. So, McKeown lost the match in the nineteenth round, when a skilful body blow from Jack had him clutching convulsively at his heart.

Down he went, with his supporters groaning in concern all around him. He didn't get up, just lay there, while his second flapped a wet rag over his face and upper body, in a futile attempt to try and revive him. The crowd went mad. An almighty roar shook the sides of the quarry and Jack was carried shoulder high. Until his father insisted he was helped to get his son home and in a safe condition. Each man who had placed a bet on Jack wanted to come and shake his hand or clap him on the shoulder, but Mannion, the agent, took charge and had his fighter whisked away.

Jack looked up from his makeshift bed when Maggie entered. He smiled at her ruefully, but no wife was going to prevent him from enjoying his acclaim.

"So here I am, Maggie," he said, speaking with difficulty through his cracked and swollen lips. "You see before yer the champion of the quarry. Holder of a purse amounting to forty-five pounds and heir apparent to the entrepreneurial ways of Lord Charlie Belsham. We've to have a place in Toxteth, a large Georgian dwellin', would yer believe, with an allowance to dress meself in a very gentlemanly manner, a carriage to ride around in and a percentage of the purse. So, what do yer think now, my beloved? Want to climb aboard this wagon of luxury with me, or are yer still intent on staying in Neston, with yer dressmaker friend and wonderful view?"

His words were delivered with a hint of defiance, mocking her gently, whilst Maggie kept her anger within. Now was not the time to challenge Jack to a wrangling match. Let him think he was the great wondrous hero and his family bow down to worship him.

She would have a few days to think things over, there were more pressing decisions to be made without Jack.

Chapter 15

"Now come on, Jack, I think it would be wise to have yer back in bed again," said Michael, after his son fell back, weakened by the excitement of his visitors. "Plenty of rest is needed to let yer mother's magic potions work on yer innards and yer bruises start to heal."

He and Seamus hauled Jack up from the chaise longue and began to help him to the stairs, while Alice prattled on about the treatment she had been giving her son.

"I've put arnica ointment on his bruises and a concoction that the chemist gave me to heal what he called internal bruising. Such a helpful man. Him from that place on the corner, next to the Brown Horse. Said he'd heard that me son was the local champion and to call back any time if I needed more advice."

"Don't forget to give me mother the money belt," Jack shouted down, as he rounded the top stairs and onto the landing.

Maggie drew her cloak aside, to reveal to Alice that it was there around her thickened waist.

"Jack, what about this business of Solly Tibbs? Don't yer know they've got him locked up in the local prison?" she shouted back to him from the foot of the staircase. There was silence, then she heard him say to his father.

"You sort it, will yer? I'm too weary to be gettin' involved. Yer know what she's like when..."

"Jack's dad will be down in a minute, Maggie," said Alice, kindly for once, seeing that her daughter-in-law was flushed in the face with the embarrassment of becoming a snubbed wife. "Come, let's go into the kitchen and I'll make yer a nice cup of tea and yer can give me Jack's money belt. I'll have to find a hidey hole for it until Monday, then I can go by where Mister Arlington works and pay it into the bank. Isn't this all so excitin'? We'll have the house paid off and we'll never have to worry about money again! Of course I know it isn't all of it, but I did put a deposit down on the strength of Jack winnin' against McKeown. But that's not a problem, I have me own little nest egg. I knew it was a good move to leave Ireland… now what were yer sayin' about Solly Tibbs?"

Jack's father walked into the kitchen, his face grey with fatigue and worry, looking older than his forty-seven years. Maggie glanced over at him as she sat at the wooden table, sipping her tea and finishing off a slice of currant cake that Alice had placed before her.

It wasn't that she was thinking of Solly in his time of need, she was thinking of his poor wife and kids. Here were the Haines', gloating over their good fortune, but sitting in Thistledown Cottage was a woman who could be facing eviction, and no good fortune would be coming to her.

"The thing is, Maggie, it wasn't Jack's money that Solly tried to make off with," Michael explained. "It belonged to a bookie from Liverpool. We've got a different system now the fights are organized by the agent. I went around taking a percentage of the wagers, when Jack had been declared the winner. Solly didn't know this, because Jack was waitin' to see if his Lordship was going to become his patron first. Then he would have been let down gently, with a bit of money to ease his way. It makes sense that I've become Jack's manager, I've plenty of time on me hands, as yer know."

"Yes, but what is goin' to happen to his family if they lose their breadwinner?" Maggie asked bluntly. "There's no way the farmer will let them stay at the cottage and they've a sick little son called Lenny to think on. He could be put in the asylum."

She looked in turn at Alice and Michael. Surely they would have compassion for Ruthie's hapless brood?

Alice, of course, could only see what was best for her. She shook her head, saying it was none of their concern. Michael, though, was more softhearted.

"Was the money handed back to the bookie, do yer know, Maggie? When the policeman handed Tibbs over to Constable Higgins?"

"I don't know," she replied. "I shut the door on the lot of them, when they all appeared ranting and raving at the cottage. Surely it's up to Jack. It was his fault that Solly ran off with the money, being that the temptation was put in front of him to steal. Are yer sure he didn't know what yer were plannin', and was making sure he was paid fer helpin' Jack all this time?"

"No, I think it was just greed on his part, but I could have a word with the constable. Now that the bookie has gone back to Liverpool, if he's got the money and isn't here to put a charge against Solly, I think they'll let him go. Though he will have a black mark against his name."

Maggie sat back with a sigh of relief, then went up to the bedrooms, wondering where Alice had decided they should sleep. She peeped into the front room with a nice bay window and saw Jack lying comfortably on a big bed that looked out on the beautiful view.

Seamus, Jack's brother, who was keeping him company, seemed pleased to see her when she entered, but made an excuse that he was hungry and would see her later on.

"He can't wait to get back to that friend of his," Jack explained. "I've upset all his plans for the day. With sending him up to get yer this mornin' and then Mother presenting him to Lord Belsham. He can't wait to tell Danny all about it, 'cos his dad wouldn't let him come to the fight. But Seamus was the bottle bearer, so he was on the front row!"

"Jack, are yer really alright?" she asked, worried. "Those bruises look terrible. You've taken a bit of a beating by the look of yer. Shall I leave yer to rest, come back after yer've had some sleepin'. Maybe I should go."

"Maggie, yer should have seen the other fella. This is nothing. I'll be right as rain in a coupla' days. Did yer give the money belt over? I can rest easily once me mother's got it, 'cos we'll always have a roof over our heads if I never got another fight."

"Jack…" Maggie was going to talk to him about the house in Toxteth, but she never managed to get her words out.

"If yer goin' to go on about Solly, ferget it. Dad will do all me worryin' in future and he'll sort it out. Let me tell yer more about me plans fer you and the babby. I want you and me mother to go into Chester and get one of those perambulators and a little cradle. When yer up te it. Me hands won't be up to making a cradle for a while yet, and now we can afford the best of everything fer the little chap. And yer can get yerself some shop bought dresses, Maggie… I know yer not happy about what I'm doin', but this is me chance to make a name for meself."

"Jack, let's discuss it after I've had the babby, shall we? It's a big move to the city, when yer know I've always lived in the fresh air and by the sea. That's what I want fer me babby, not livin' on top of one another in a dirty, smoky place. Let's wait and see what happens, shall we? I'll go down and help Alice in the kitchen. She'll be tired with all her excitement. It's not every day she has a visit from a lord. I'll bring me things up later, not that I've brought a lot. I let Ruthie have the things that I didn't think I needed. Even me pan still had stew in it, since yer didn't think to tell me yer weren't comin' home. Alright, alright, I'm goin'."

She finished her sentence quickly, when she saw that his face was wearing a scowl.

They were in the middle of supper, when there came an urgent knocking on the front door. They all groaned, because a kind of peace had descended on the household. Mr Arlington and the second lodger Mr Peel, were away for the weekend and the third lodger had removed himself temporarily to a room above the Ship Inn. Alice and Maggie had agreed that they would walk together to St. Winefred's the following morning, so had begun to discuss the priest and how his sermons were spoken from the heart.

Michael got up to answer the door and came back to the kitchen with Constable Higgins in tow. He stood in the doorway officiously, frowning a little at Jack, who had continued to sit in his chair, having been helped downstairs earlier, whilst both Alice and Maggie had virtually stood to attention at the mere sight of the man.

Michael asked politely if the policeman's visit was regarding the arrest of Solly Tibbs and Higgins agreed that was what he had come about.

"I won't have these goings on in my village," he started imperiously. "Tis bad enough that we have these gangs from the railway supping in our taverns, without hordes of people crowded on the quarry floor. If it happens again I'm going to call on the might of the Cheshire constabulary and then you'll all be sorry. The organizers will go to gaol, if I hear of it happening again."

"I can assure you, Constable Higgins, that it won't be happening again, at least on our part," replied Michael softly, trying to diffuse the situation, as he could see that Jack was looking grim. "My son is to be sponsored by Lord Charles Belsham and will be removing to Liverpool, as soon as accommodation can be found that is suitable. All fights in future will be supervised by his agent, a gentleman by the name of Richard Mannion, and we have been told that these events will be held in designated sporting areas, not on the floors of quarries and at the back of inns."

"Well, that is as may be," said Higgins, feeling that the wind had been taken from his sails, "but what is going to happen to this miscreant I have in the lock up? It appears from further questioning of this Tibbs fellow that he had taken the money from a bookie. The man has now disappeared, of course."

"Yes, I'm sorry I've not been to Park Street to see you over this matter. As you can see my son here has been badly beaten and we have been attendin' to him. Then we have had a visit from his Lordship this morning. You probably heard that his carriage was parked outside. From both my son's and my point of view there will be no charges against Tibbs. He is free to go, unless you have anything else you want to charge him with. So, have you finished with us, Sergeant? Could we get on with our puddings now? I'll see you out if you've finished."

Michael closed the front door firmly on the astonished policeman and, as he walked back into the kitchen, they all began applauding.

"Here, yer could have been on the stage with all that acting, Michael," Alice said. "Never dropped yer aitches once and yer sounded just like Lord Belsham… 'You probably heard that his carriage was parked outside!'" Everyone started laughing at her antics, as Alice mimicked her way to the oven, where she took out a gooseberry pie.

Maggie looked around and thought that for the moment life could be quite comfortable, especially if she were to become a biddable daughter-in-law, which, for now, she was prepared to be.

"Would yer like to walk with me and Michael to the village later?" asked Alice, the following Monday morning, as Maggie sat with Jack in their pleasant bedroom. "Only I thought the exercise would do you and the baby good and, with us carrying such a large amount of money, it would be safety in numbers."

"And don't ferget yer need to ask about one of those actuary fellas while yer there," said Jack "I'd come with yer meself, but I think anyone seeing me face would run a mile. Maggie just showed me in the mirror and I'm not a pleasing sight to see."

Although the three of them smiled at his little joke, it was true that Jack looked a sorry sight. His bottom lip was cracked and swollen, sporting a deep purple tinge and now that his face had been bathed by Alice, jagged cuts could be seen on his cheekbones, which were turning navy blue. His face was puffy from under his eyes, right down to his jaw and there were angry marks all over his torso, which he had kept partially uncovered. But, his spirits were high and no one was unduly worried. There was plenty of time before he would get his next match and the healthy sea air outside would soon put him right.

"I'd like to visit Miss Rosemary if yer don't mind, Jack," Maggie asked. "She was terribly busy last time I saw her and I promised I would help her, once I had finished at the farm. If yer were agreeable, once I've finished helpin' Alice with the chores each mornin', I'd like to go and help. I'm sure she would pay me, or at least let me help meself to the remnants, so that I can get on with makin' things fer the babby in me spare time."

"Well, I don't know," replied Jack, considering. "Mother, what do you think? Is it wise to let Maggie go off each day in her condition, without one of us being with her at this time?"

Alice also stood and thought about it, no doubt working at some little plan in her mind. Maggie held her breath, because if the answer was no, Jack and Alice would be suffering with chewed off ears from her later, because she had already made her mind up that to Miss Rosemary's she was going to go!

"We were only talking about it at Christmas, weren't we Maggie, about becomin' an apprentice at the dressmakers?" Alice said with deliberation. "The woman's gettin' on in years, Jack, and if things don't work out fer you both in Liverpool, Maggie could buy that shop off her, or buy an even bigger property and go into competition. But, fer now I can't see it harmin' her to sit fer a couple of hours each day doing a bit of needlework. So, we'll go about two o'clock, Maggie, because everywhere closes fer lunch at one."

-

"Maggie, you're here again. Come to help me out, I hope," Betty remarked, delighted, as the girl slipped into her shop after saying goodbye to Jack's parents. "I've been inundated with people wanting lengths of material to make their own outfits and I've had three orders for walking dresses that have to be completed by the end of May. Now that you are here, take your cloak off and I'll make you a cup of tea, then we'll talk about what needs doing."

She paused for a moment then looked at her thoughtfully. "You have come to help me haven't you, not just come to check up on your investments? Happily, your seventeen pounds has all been lent out!"

Maggie had to lean against the door post when she heard her words, as she couldn't believe her ears! Betty put down the garment that she had been stitching and asked her to follow her through.

"Come and sit down, my dear. The weather is really warm, especially for you in your condition. I can show you the ledger later on, but your little venture has certainly taken off. What with the Ladies' Walking Day coming up and the colliery being on short time again."

"I'm really surprised, Miss Rosemary," Maggie said shakily, as she was so overwhelmed that her money had been loaned out so quickly. "Are yer sure yer don't mind takin' the trouble to do this fer me? Only you've such a lot to do already with yer own business, without havin' to think of mine."

"No trouble at all, Maggie," she said airily. "In past years I've sometimes run a weekly club, so that the poorer people could pay me a little off their purchase, a bit at a time, but I always ran the risk of having to chase up defaulters. This way they think they are dealing with an important loan company, especially having to sign their names at the bottom of their agreement. They'll be nervous of a visit from a big brute of a fellow, if they don't make their repayments. It is the same for Ezra Williams, he's pleased to pass on the information regarding the Sheldon

Loan Company, because he finds it hard to say no when he is asked for food stuffs to be put on the slate."

"Yer haven't told him that the money we're lending belongs to me, then?"

"No, indeed not, Maggie. Ezra will have the same thoughts as other men. That a woman's place is in the home, not involved in such a masculine industry as a loan company. Dressmaking or shop work, yes, he can just about deal with. No, I said that I am the agent temporarily, until the company finds suitable premises in the village."

"Good," Maggie replied thankfully. "And if yer don't mind, Miss Rosemary, I've bin thinkin' that I won't be takin' any of the money out. You know, like the interest or whatever yer call it. Jack made such a lot of money from the match he won last Friday, that it is time he began supportin' me. I'll keep this as a little nest egg, in case I need it at a future time."

"That is fine with me, Maggie, and now you can tell me all about what happened with that business involving Solly Tibbs. We'll have that cup of tea and then we'll sit and get on with all this stitching that I've taken on. I hope you'll keep your promise and come in every day."

—

The first Thursday in June arrived, dry and warm, and the spirits in Seagull Cottage were high, as they all looked forward to experiencing the joys to be had during Ladies' Walking Day. Maggie had heard that a procession would begin from St. Mary's on the High Street, with the leading members of the district and wives and daughters of humble working men walking around the streets of Neston as one, carrying staves garlanded with bounteous flowers and a red rose pinned on each chest. Later these staves were to be placed as pew ends during a service to celebrate the aims of this benefit society, then tea was to be provided in the school room, with slices of homemade cake and sticky buns. A fair was to be held on the fields that backed onto the village and dancing in the evening had been organized on the green behind the Golden Lion. Non-members were charged an admission fee, the proceeds of which went to club funds.

The family walked excitedly up the Parkgate Road, behind crowds of others who were intent on having an enjoyable day. They chose a spot to stand at the crossroads by the drinking fountain, so that Maggie could sit on the low stone wall, if it got too much for her.

A cheer went up as the procession began, marching slowly down the hill from the church. The Band of Hope led the way, with an uplifting tune, which, of course, none of the family knew. But Maggie did recognize the material of some of the dresses that went wafting by, especially the pink and green satin walking dress she had worked on. It sort of made her feel part of it all, a sense that brought on an inner glow.

Jack had suggested that, after the procession was over and people had gone into the Anglican church, they took advantage of this quiet time to wander over to the fair. They all agreed it was the best thing to do and that there would perhaps be somewhere to sit and have a little refreshment.

Maggie remembered Annie telling her of the gypsies and she looked around rather fearfully as they walked into the field. Though why she was worried, she didn't know, when she'd got the local champion fighter at her side!

She had noticed the deference from the people who had recognized Jack, from his drinking cronies and other people who knew him. She had to admit to a sneaking pride at being beside him, especially as he kept insisting on introducing her as the Missis, telling all and sundry that he was a father to be!

Maggie glanced over to the gaudily painted gypsy wagons that were drawn into a circle over by a clump of trees, but her attention was soon caught by the swing boats, hobby horses, fire eaters and shooting galleries. With a fortune-teller, coconut shies, guess the weight of the fat lady, and a hot potato stall, there was plenty to do and see for everyone, but first they made for a little roped off area where they could sit at a table and drink home made lemonade.

Later, Alice and Maggie watched as Jack and Michael tried their hand with a rifle, both winning a novelty ornament at the shooting gallery, a china dog and a pretty little pot pony. Both would gain pride of place on the Seagull Cottage mantle piece. Then they went to guess the weight of the fat lady, where Maggie thought, unkindly, that if Ruthie ever needed a job, this would be the one. Her ex-neighbour was even fatter than the lady on show! Unfortunately, they were all well out in their estimates, so sauntered on to look at other things.

They couldn't believe their eyes, when they saw the man who was sticking a flaming sword down his throat. No wonder he drank a bucket of water afterwards, probably to put out the fire! They looked at the fortune-teller's tent and bickered between themselves, over whether or not to go in and have their palms read. But Madame Petunioni already had someone with her, so they would have had to have waited anyway. It was long enough to make them decide that none of them wanted to see into the future, and surely it was against their religion anyway.

The church service at St. Mary's over, a surge of people came running onto the field to sample the delights, as they had. It was time for them to go, though they had lost sight of Seamus. He was last seen disappearing with Danny, to enjoy the thrill of the swing boats. But now the boy was coming up to fifteen and nearly a man, Michael decreed he was allowed a little time from under the noses of his parents. Maybe next year, he said, when the baby had arrived, Jack and Maggie could stay longer and partake in the evening dancing. The grandparents would be only too happy to take the baby off their hands. Even if they had moved to Liverpool, they would still be over to visit, he was sure. Especially as Ladies' Walking Day was an annual event to enjoy.

If only life could always be as perfect as it was now, Maggie thought a few weeks later, as she sat comfortably on the window seat in the bedroom, looking out over the estuary to the Welsh hills.

She felt settled, more than she ever thought she would, considering that she had Alice as a mother-in-law. Both women were getting on famously, as Maggie left Alice to make all decisions, especially considering it was her household.

She helped as much as her bulky body would allow her, but only that morning a visit from Nellie, the midwife, had confirmed what she had been thinking, that the baby was on the way. She had a constant dull ache at the bottom of her back and during the night had frequently been passing water in the chamber pot.

It was as well Jack was away with Michael, visiting a prospective property for the couple to live in; being put up in a good hotel while further discussions were taking place. It seemed that Mannion, the agent, had found a coach for Jack and soon he'd be busy with his training each day.

Jack had banned her from visiting Miss Rosemary's a couple of weeks back and she was only allowed to walk the promenade as far as the Boat House. The rest of the day was spent with her feet up, sewing ribbons into the neck seams of the little baby gowns.

It was the first day of August, her birthday. She wondered hopefully, as she sat there, if Michael Patrick would make his appearance that day.

Chapter 16

Michael Patrick Haines, did indeed put in an appearance on her birthday. Well, at least his head did, on the stroke of midnight. Nellie decided that she would count his birth as having happened on the first of August, so that mother and son could celebrate their birthdays together. It would make life so much easier!

It had been a quick delivery considering it was the first one, according to the midwife, though Maggie didn't feel as if it had been that quick. The pushing and grunting had seemed to take forever and the pain was, at times, unbearable, but looking at her chestnut haired son lying in his perambulator, a present from his proud grandparents, purchased at the finest shop in Chester, it didn't now seem that bad.

Michael Patrick was now almost three months old, growing more handsome by the minute. Or so it was said by people that she passed by in the High Street, when she took the pram and its passenger out for his daily walk. She had decided to call him Mikey, as it was all so confusing having two Michael's around. And because he was a baby, the name wasn't so grownup, and better than Mick, which sounded like an Irish navvie's name.

She had higher hopes for him than that, when the time came for her grown child to choose employment. A track layer, or a tunnel digger were not the jobs she had in mind.

Jack had been over the moon when he had returned to Seagull Cottage. He had arrived two days after the birth, excusing his absence by saying he would have only been in the way. To his mind, the process of delivering a baby was essentially only women's work. Far better meeting his son when the child was all cleaned up and cheerful, than pacing the floor and having to listen to gruesome noises from the wife in the bedroom above.

Although Jack had arrived back pleased to hear that everything was fine with his wife and little baby, he was full of what was happening now he had met Billy Jackson, his coach.

Billy had once been a fighter on the Northern circuits, who'd retired when he found that his hearing was going and been hired by Lord Belsham to train this raw recruit. He had already started Jack on his strict regime. Three hours daily devoted to exercise and an intake of food that would keep his muscles strong. Jack had to cut out his favourite sustenance of potatoes and bread. He could only drink beer on special occasions and never even sniff it if a match was only days ahead.

The house in Toxteth was far better then he had expected. There was a parlour, dining room, family room, kitchen and scullery on the ground floor, three bedrooms and a good sized bathroom on the first. With attics that could be accommodation for a live-in cook and a general maid should he require them. Jack thought that Maggie would think she had died and gone to heaven when she and the little fellow moved across the water to Liverpool, but that weekend when he came home, she had shown no enthusiasm at all about seeing the place and three months later, Jack's patience was wearing thin.

During the first week of September, Jack decided to move into the Toxteth house alone. The cook and the maid he decided to have were supplied by an agency, providing an excellent service to their new master, though Alice said when she saw him that Jack was beginning to look thin. Michael stayed over, when there was business to discuss with Richard Mannion and Lord Belsham had paid a visit already, to check the house, the staff and his new investment.

Alice, of course, had been over and given everything her blessing, like Maggie knew she would. She chided Maggie on her return, saying that the child and herself were missing out on a very good life. Alice had enjoyed looking at the highly glossed quality furniture, the excellent amenities and the fact there was a bathroom off the first landing. The house as yet, had not been fitted with pipes or a geyser to heat up all the water, but there was a maid there, she said, who looked capable of bringing buckets of hot water up the stairs.

Alice had enjoyed interfering with the cook's menu and loved bossing the hardworking maid around. She couldn't understand why Maggie was more than content to make her home at Seagull Cottage, though she had to agree there was a beautiful view.

It was not like the view that faced number 23 Westminster Street, Toxteth, as an identical house stood across the road, Maggie had heard.

She wasn't missing Jack, not even by one iota, and at the weekend, during his next visit, she was going to tell him exactly that!

Jack stood before her in the bedroom. Alice had taken young Mikey away to the kitchen. Perhaps she had sensed there was going to be a confrontation that day. Jack was dressed in the very latest style to be considered fashion. Maggie, by comparison, looked shabby, as she had only just managed to get back into the old dress that Peggy had given her.

Jack's frock coat was dark blue in colour, high collared and double breasted, with cut away tails. Underneath the coat showed a high collared, white frilled shirt and a pale blue cravat at the neck. With this he wore buckskin breeches in a pale cream shade, a pair of black shiny riding boots and under his arm carried a high beaver hat. What a transformation for the man who had landed at the Irish settlement just under a year before! He had given his fair hair a centre parting and slicked it down with a sweet scented pomade.

He had travelled by the railway, as the horse and carriage that had been spoken about, had not materialized as yet, and so he had caught the ferry across to the station at Woodside and finished his journey by train.

Maggie realised, as Jack began to speak, that if he had ever belonged to her, she had lost him now. This was not the boy she had known in Killala, he had grown beyond that. He walked now with confidence and assurance, in fact he had developed a bit of a cocky strut. He seemed to be enjoying this life of his, so full of danger, with its luxury and all the trappings that went with it. She did not want to share this life of precarious living and she had told him just that.

"Of course yer can live in this house as long as yer want to," Jack had said expansively, after she had told him of her decision. In fact, it was quite possible that he was more than a bit relieved. He hadn't shouted or become the dominant husband, just accepted her wishes, as if he'd been expecting them. "As mother of my child you are very much entitled," he continued pompously. "It will be the child's house in the future anyway. But should yer change yer mind and yer want us to become a family again, then yer only have to ask. Though whatever business I get up to in the future will be my affair. Just remember, you are the one who rejected me, but we will still be married in the eyes of the church."

He went on to mention an allowance that would be paid to her for personal needs, though it was to be spent primarily on the child and not to be frittered. She wanted to tell him where to stick his money, but thought he would be mortally offended by it, so she held her tongue. Things were going exactly how Maggie had hoped they would go. She would be free within reason, to do as she liked, and Jack could have his freedom too.

"Have yer ever loved me, Maggie?" Jack asked sadly, after he had finished acting out the role of 'the big man'. "Don't yer remember the good times when we were children? You, me, Bernie and Joey Mulligan from the cottages, digging in the rock pools to bait the end of our fishing rods. Playing knick-knock around the cottage doors and jumping in the river at the Giant's Tub. I always thought that when I grew up and took a wife, you'd be the only girl fer me."

"But don't yer see, Jack," she replied gently, "yer lookin' back at our childhood with fond memories. Yer thought yer could just drag me away from me roots on the strength of it. I'm only a simple cottier's daughter. I don't want this life of luxury yer've taken on, or a big pile of money. Living quietly in this lovely place, with me cherub of a son, is enough to satisfy me. And if I ever want something different, I'll do it meself. I won't need you to help me. But to answer yer question about love, Jack. What is love? I do care fer yer. Enough to worry about what yer lettin' yerself in for. I love little Mikey, because I'm his mother and I'm here to protect and defend him. The love I think yer talking about gets confused with making babies and Mikey is the only babby I shall ever want. Now, don't let the weekend be spoiled by the both of us sulkin'. Mikey still needs yer in his life."

Their separation had obviously been discussed over the weekend with Jack and his mother, as on the Monday morning, Maggie was told to move her belongings into the smaller back room.

"Yer don't need the space, now that our Jack'll only be making short visits," Alice told her, tersely. "There's enough room in there fer Mikey's cradle and a single bed fer you. Me lodger, who's bin residing at the Ship Inn, wants to come back again."

"But that's not fair, Alice," she protested. "I'm still married to Jack and he said nothing about me having to move out of the front bedroom and losin' me beautiful view."

"Well I'm tellin' yer, see. Like it or lump it! He's told me yer marriage is over, so yer should think yerself lucky that you've still got a roof over yer head. Yer only here now fer the sake of the baby, as far as I'm concerned. Yer just a nursemaid, Maggie.

That is all yer are to our Jack now, if yer don't want to be his wife."

"I didn't want to marry Jack in the first place," Maggie shouted out in anger. "It was you and him that plotted to get me away!"

"Oh, stop playing that old tune on yer fiddle, Maggie. I'm tired of listening to it. Living in Killala indeed. Why don't yer go back there then and see what state the country's in? Then perhaps you'll be thankful fer the life yer've got here."

She flounced off, and for the next few days there was a hostile silence between them. Maggie did as she was told and moved herself and Mikey to the back room. She mourned though for the view of the Welsh hills, as the side wall of another house was all that she could now see. Maggie couldn't believe how Alice had changed in her attitude. Her mother-in-law had been so kind, helping Nellie at Mikey's birth, accompanying her to St. Winefred's, when it was time to give thanksgiving for a healthy baby and to have her 'churching' done. There had been angry words only on one occasion, when she and Alice were discussing who were to be the godparents at Mikey's christening. Maggie had wanted Miss Rosemary to be godmother and Alice was dead set against it. It seemed that godparents had to be from the same religion. Catholic in Mikey's case, but Miss Rosemary attended St. Mary's. It just wasn't done, Alice had raged, when Maggie had insisted that she should choose her friend. Catholics and Protestants were like oil and water, according to her mother-in-law.

Maggie had stuck to her guns, pointing out how well they seem to mix in Neston. Look at the way all religions were mixing on Ladies' Walking Day. That had been the only time that there was discomfort in the household, but Alice chose the people in the end. Seamus and a couple from the St. Winefred's congregation, whom Alice had decided were her bountiful friends.

By the following Wednesday, Maggie couldn't stand the atmosphere there any longer, nor could she bear the smug look on the face of the lodger, as he had moved his belongings back. She decided to take Mikey for a walk in his pram, drop in on Ezra, then maybe discuss her options with Miss Rosemary. She could be relied on to give Maggie good advice about her future and, after three months at Seagull Cottage, it was time she stopped idling her life away. Perhaps if she made a start by helping the dressmaker, she would begin to feel needed and useful again.

"Oh, Maggie, just the person I wanted to see," Betty said, coming into the grocery shop when she saw the baby carriage outside Ezra's. "I am hoping that you are also going to spend a little time with me. Hasn't Michael grown since I last saw him?" she continued, as she helped her carry the little vehicle over her shop doorstep.

"Come, I'll help you push him into the kitchen. He's fast asleep, so we can talk quietly and, before we do, I'll make a cup of tea."

She listened sympathetically as Maggie told her of Alice's churlish behaviour, after she had heard that the couple were to go their separate ways. Betty appeared shocked at first that they had decided their marriage was over, but she didn't condemn, or openly take sides, knowing that Maggie would not have been happy with a city life.

"From my point of view, your decision could perhaps be a godsend," Betty remarked, after handing the girl a handkerchief, to mop away her bitter tears. "Christmas is nearly upon us, as you know, and I have very many commissions, what with evening gowns and winter visiting wear. And, I don't know where Miss Madeline gets her money from, but she has asked for another of those crinoline gowns!"

"I could do with making meself a warmer dress, too, Miss Rosemary," Maggie said, brightening once she heard of a way of changing her future. "But now yer come to mention it, I'm dreadin' Christmas too. It would be to my advantage if I could get away from Alice and came to help yer each day. Though it might be a problem with Mikey. He isn't always so peaceful as he is now, yer know. I dare say I can rock him to sleep while we're walkin' up the hill each time and I'll try to keep him awake in the mornings, before I come here. Yer won't mind if I hide away in the kitchen when I need to feed him, will yer? 'Cos I don't think he'll take to one of those new fangled milk bottles I've seen in the chemists and it will be a while before I try him on a bit of mashed up food."

"Of course you will have to bring the little one," Betty replied, looking pleased, that she would be getting some company, "and if you could do the plain stitching, I could spend my evenings cutting out and seeing to all the twiddly bits. I have to confess I am finding it difficult to keep my stitches as small as they should be. Your eyes are so much younger than mine and of course I will pay you for all of your time."

"You will not!" Maggie said, indignantly. "Look how yer helpin' me money to grow and I can't help thinkin', that you'll find just the right amount of material fer me to make me dress. No, I need to keep busy fer the sake of me sanity."

Betty smiled and put her arm around the girl's shoulder. "It's a great pity when a relationship flounders, my dear," she said, "but I can see both sides of the story. You want a simpler life than Jack aspires to and neither of you want to compromise. From what you have told me in the past, your marriage was never one to have been made in Heaven. You were forced to leave your country in such dire circumstances. All that was bound to make you bitter towards your husband, but I have to say I admire your tenacity. Many girls would have simply gone under with what you've had to go through."

"I'm tougher than people think I am and I'm a good actress," Maggie replied, as Betty sat down in a chair in front of her. "I put it down to me faith in the good Lord Jesus. He guides me when I'm in need of Him. I'm sure the reason I'm sittin' here now is because He sent me."

"Oh, Maggie, what a lovely girl you are," Betty exclaimed, her cheeks pink with pleasure, at her words. "He must know that I would never do you a bad turn. You've helped me out when I've needed you too and I'll always be grateful."

It was arranged that Maggie would begin to work every afternoon from the following Monday. Before then, Miss Rosemary was going to put on her 'thinking head'. She had a plan of action in mind, which would not only fulfill a need that she thought Maggie could probably assist her with, but it would give her time to look at her own finances too.

'Never trouble trouble, because trouble will always find you,' was a saying of Miss Rosemary's, Maggie thought, as she wandered slowly back to Seagull Cottage later. Living as she did, having to walk on eggshells when Alice was around, she was finding it very hard to keep her mouth shut. She would have loved to stir up her mother-in-law to anger and be shown the door. Then perhaps Jack would be moved to pay for somewhere else for his wife and child to live, though Maggie couldn't see that happening. Both Alice and Michael would be loathe to lose their grandchild, and Alice had once hinted when the tension was at its highest, that Maggie could always move away to work, leaving Mikey in their hands.

"Ah, Maggie, yer back at last," greeted Michael, as she eventually walked up the path of the boarding house in the gathering gloom. It was late and Mikey would soon be wanting another feed.

"Maggie, I need to speak with you," Michael said, grimly. "It is something that concerns you and Jack. Take the baby through to Alice, as I've asked her to look after him."

Worried now, Maggie did as she was bidden, but couldn't fail to see Alice looking at her, quizzically. Fleetingly, she wondered why it was Michael who wanted to speak alone, as it was Alice who would be putting in her oar usually.

"Jack has asked me to tell you that he wants to come and stay after this next match. It is planned for next Friday. It's quite a small affair, to be held in a warehouse off the Dock Road in Liverpool. We think about two hundred and fifty people will attend, as it is a ticketed event and they have been selling quite readily. Of course all the stevedores and seamen will be trying to get in as well, but he has to take on this contest to get him ready for the Northern circuit. He will need time to recover, as he has an even bigger event planned for the last week of January. Alice says you must move back into the big bedroom, because we have to keep up appearances. She doesn't want it to get about that you and our Jack are estranged. Mr Dickinson will move into the back bedroom, as he doesn't want to go back to the Ship Inn at what will be the noisiest time of the year."

Maggie looked askance at her father-in-law. Trust Alice to come up with that one and send Michael to do her dirty work! She bent her head to show Michael that she was considering it, while he moved about uncomfortably, as the silence between them grew.

Ah, poor Michael. He hasn't changed, she thought. He was still under Alice's thumb, still looked to her for guidance. Why, she probably even chose those smart clothes that he was wearing, and noticed that his hair at the front was getting very thin.

What did she think about sharing a bed with Jack again, she pondered? Would he expect his conjugal rights? Did she want to sit around the family table at Christmas time, after worshipping together at St. Winefred's? Would she be able to be a good actress during the season of goodwill?

"I'll have to think about it, Michael," she replied, undecided. "Of course Jack can come here to recover. It's his home, isn't it? And I know Alice will want a decision fairly quickly, because she will have to make arrangements with her boarder, so I'll think quickly on it. I'm presumin' that this move into the front room includes our Mikey as well?"

"Well, we were thinkin' that Michael can come in with us," Michael replied. "It will give you time to be alone, yer know, if there's anything yer want to discuss together."

He began to appear nervous and started fiddling around with the collar on his shirt. She smelt a rat. So that was it, a reconciliation. Was it Alice's idea, so that she could get Maggie living across the water at the house in Toxteth? Or her son's idea because he wanted to try and get back his unwilling wife?

She turned, as she heard a movement in the doorway. Alice was standing there sporting a smug smile on her face, as she held Mikey firmly in her arms. She was up to something, Maggie thought, worried. Something that was going to catch her by surprise. She got up and snatched the baby from his grandma. She would go off to the bedroom to sit in privacy with her child.

–

The next day, bright and early, instead of waiting until the afternoon like she had agreed with Miss Rosemary, she hurried Mikey into his outdoor clothes and set off up the road to Neston.

It was a cold day, with a bite in the wind, and the sky looked as if it could easily snow. The waves that normally only came within fifty yards of the promenade, were crashing and foaming angrily, thundering against the promenade wall, only a few feet away. Maggie felt an empathy with them, as that was how she was feeling in herself that morning.

She had lain awake most of the night, listening to her son's steady breathing, thinking over her conversation with her father-in-law. Something was niggling. What, she wasn't sure, but, Maggie was feeling angry, because somewhere along the line, she sensed there was to be some sort of a set up. Maybe Miss Rosemary could help her to unravel it all.

She banged on the door of the dressmaker's shop. It wasn't even near opening time, but Betty had always told her that she got up with the lark. True enough, the lady herself came to the door, dressed, as always, immaculately, as if she never went to bed in a nightie at all.

Her smile of welcome made Maggie feel as if she was dropping anchor in a harbour, where she could be sheltered from the storms of life that she was experiencing.

Mikey was wide awake, so he lay in her arms while Betty listened patiently to the latest twist in the tale.

"Yes, it does seem something is afoot," she agreed, when Maggie had finished. "I have a feeling it concerns the baby too. I wonder if they are trying to scare you off, make you feel as if you've got to leave, but they are saying that young Michael here should share the accommodation with the grandparents, over Christmas time? You see, knowing you, you'll be thinking that you won't want to spend Christmas in a fraught atmosphere, pretending to be part of a happy family. But, you wouldn't want to deprive Jack of having his son with him, so of course you'll say that you will leave him there. That's what I think they are banking on. By saying you will be sharing a bedroom with your estranged husband, it will frighten you off. Leaving them to accuse you of being an uncaring mother, by abandoning your baby son at Christmas time!"

Maggie was stunned by what she thought were Betty's prophetic words and stared at her in shock, feeling her heart pumping madly as she took in the meaning of it all. She pulled Mikey more closely to her, causing him to give a little cry of alarm!

"What am I going to do, Miss Rosemary? Are yer saying that Jack can take the child off me? Where would they think that I'd be going anyway?" Her questions tumbled from her mouth, wildly.

"If you were to leave the boy behind and say, come to me, as I'm sure they know I'd take you in, I'm not awfully sure where you'd stand with the authorities. According to the Law, you must seek permission from his father to take him with you, as

I think you and the child are still considered to be part of his chattels and goods. No doubt it is your mother-in-law who is at the bottom of it all."

"Shall I write to him and see what he's got to say for himself?" Maggie asked. "Or I could wait until his return? I thought that maybe you and I could celebrate Christmas together this year. I know we go to different churches, but we could eat our dinner here. I could buy a bird from the market and make a plum puddin'. It would be grand, Miss Rosemary, even if I have to stay back there and share a bed with Jack. That's what I'll do," she ended hurriedly. "I'll call their bluff. Say that I will move into the big bedroom, share his bed, have Christmas there at Seagull Cottage, and see their reaction then. I can't wait to see Alice's face when I get back there and tell her. But, is that all right with you if we have a festive meal together? They can't take me child off me then, if I'm only away fer a couple of hours."

Chapter 17

She worked her fingers to the bone that following week. Stitching seams, stitching hems, inching sleeves into the shoulders, stitching carefully around the neckline. Her needle flew on each occasion that she went to the shop in her effort to assist Betty. Even her dreams were filled with stitching dresses. Green ones, blue ones, with masses of frills to be put onto cream or white petticoats.

At least it took her mind off Jack's impending visit, stopped her thinking of what he might say. Alice had been dumbfounded when Maggie agreed that the plan of moving bedrooms was agreeable to her.

Alice had pasted a false smile on her face, forcing herself to be friendly, even including Maggie in the following weekend's plans. It tickled her that she was one up on Alice, but inwardly she was quaking at the thought of what was to come. Betty found her staring sometimes with a vacant expression in her eyes. She would tap her on the head and tell her to stop dreaming. Time for that, when all the clients had come to collect their gowns!

Betty had arranged all her fittings to be done in the mornings. It would give all her ladies the peace and quiet that they were entitled to, instead of having to listen to a crying babe, if Mikey was restless in the afternoons. Sometimes Betty would leave Maggie to mind the shop and carry on with her frantic stitching, while she would walk the pram and its little passenger around the village streets. She told Maggie she enjoyed it.

Learning a little of what it would have been like if she had married and had children of her own.

Saturday morning came soon enough. It was time for Maggie to move back into the front bedroom. The lodger had left early to visit some friends in Liverpool and Alice had asked his permission to move his possessions, so between the two women, everything was quickly done.

To Maggie's surprise, a single mattress was placed near the double bed. Seamus had brought it down from the attic earlier on. Alice explained that Jack couldn't possibly share his bed with Maggie, in case her movement in the night would inflict more pain on him.

"Then why all the insistence that I move back in, Alice?" she queried. "If yer don't want us to sleep together? Yer really are the limit sometimes, I just don't understand."

"Appearances, Maggie, appearances. Don't forget we are a Catholic family and if the priest got to hear of all these shenanigans, he wouldn't be very pleased!"

They sat together at lunchtime over a light meal of bread, cheese and a cup of coffee, waiting for Michael, who had gone to fetch Jack in a hired carriage. He didn't want to impose the sight of a bloody looking prize fighter on the public, as they would have if, instead, they had come by ferry and the train. He had said they would arrive in Parkgate around eleven in the morning, so Alice started twitching, as the clock on the kitchen wall showed it was just past two.

"Where've they got to? Typical men, probably stopped off somewhere, instead of coming straight back here," she fidgeted.

"Well, maybe there's been a problem, Alice," Maggie answered. "The carriage didn't turn up maybe, or perhaps they've had snow in Liverpool. The sky has been very grey this morning, they could have had snow over there."

"Or maybe something bad has happened to Jack," replied Alice in a shaky whisper. "There's no way of letting us know, except by letter, and you know that Michael isn't good with a pen."

"Listen, I can hear Mikey crying," Maggie said quickly, as she wasn't about to get drawn into her mother-in-law's uneasiness. "I'd better go and feed him. Perhaps if yer were to find something to do, instead of sitting here worrying. Maybe make a start on dinner? When I've finished with the babby, I'll come and help yer. The men will need feeding when they eventually come."

Maggie sat on the bed and opened the buttons of her bodice, glancing down proudly at her outfit as she began to suckle her child. She had managed to make the dress in time for this occasion, the bodice being full of pleats and tucks, with leg o' mutton sleeves and an ankle length gathered skirt. Shorter than what she had been used to, but it was an up and coming style. She had chosen a deep purple colour, in thick velvet material, which seemed to bring out a deeper hue in her normally light green eyes.

She had also taken a lot of time in fixing her hair. It was now parted in the centre and brushed into a cluster of curls, that she had wound into place at the back of her head and settled with a ribbon of matching purple. On her feet were a type of ballet shoe, again fastened with purple ribbon around the ankles, criss crossed and fastened behind.

Maggie wasn't sure why she had made such an effort. Except perhaps because on Jack's last visit, she had felt so dowdy, compared with his peacock self. She had also made a cambric nightdress, stitching by candle light while Mikey slept. It was time she had one, she couldn't keep sleeping in her chemise and drawers. She was a mother now and might need to visit the kitchen in the dead of night and come across one of the male persons in the household.

Strange that it had seemed so important to get the nightdress finished, especially now, when Jack and Maggie were going to share the same room again.

She heard a knocking on the front door, just as she had finished feeding Mikey. She assumed it was her father-in-law, having forgotten his key. She began to rock the baby in her arms, as he looked as if he would go to sleep again.

—

She heard a voice coming from below, although it didn't sound like Michael. Nor were there noises she expected, like the sounds of giving assistance to a weary, worn out Jack.

"I'll have to go to him!" she heard Alice cry, to whoever it was she had been talking to.

Maggie rushed down the stairs, as fast as she could with a sleeping baby in her arms. There in the hallway stood a thin young fellow, aged around fifteen. He was dressed shabbily in cast off clothing, looking white faced, the pallor of a city boy who doesn't get very much to eat.

Alice was putting her heavier shawl around her shoulders and trying to pull her lace cap off at the same time, to change it for her ornamental hat.

"He's gone and done it, Maggie!" she cried, when she saw that her daughter-in-law had come down the stairs. "Just like I warned him! Got his self knocked out cold in the twentieth round, lying like a statue now in that great big house of his. The doctor's bin called, accordin' to the boy here. He'll have nobody to nurse him. Michael won't be of any use to him now!"

"Alice, calm yerself down, will yer?" Maggie said, taking stock of the situation, as there was nobody else there to do so. "Yer can't go racin' off across the water on yer own. Shall I go and find Seamus? Perhaps he'll come with you? Yer don't know this boy from Adam. It could all be a made up tale. Has he asked yer fer any money? Tell me, young man," she said, looking at the young boy sternly, "how did yer know where to come to and how come yer know about Jack?"

The boy straightened his back and looked at Maggie steadily.

"I'm Jack's bockel bearer, Missis. I woz there at the fight. I took over from yor Seamus, when 'is mam 'ere said she didn't want 'im to go. Michael asked me to bring a message over, when the doctor bloke said Jack couldn't be moved. 'E woz only te travel as far as 'is house in Toxteth. Michael give me the price of the ferry and the train 'ere. That woz fun, I've niver bin on a train afore. 'E said 'is Missis would probly come back wiv me and she'd pay fer us goin' back. Oh, an 'e said I was te be fed with sommat afore we set off."

Maggie thought that she had a terrible way of saying things, but this boy's way of speaking meant she had to tune in her ear. Alice looked as if she was going to pieces, so it was Maggie who went to the kitchen, to make her a cup of tea and see what was left from lunch time for the boy to eat. She put Mikey into his grandmother's arms, hoping she wouldn't drop him with her trembling, but determined not to let Alice make things even worse, by not being strong when it came to helping Jack.

Holding Mikey seemed to bring Alice to her senses. She handed the baby back and bustled off.

"You will have to see to any of the boarders who come in for their meal, Maggie," she said in her agitation. "They were making themselves scarce today, but Mr Dickinson may come back. What's yer name, love? I can't keep callin' yer the bottle bearer? Oh, it's Fred, is it? I'll go and put some things in that valise Michael bought me fer Christmas, Maggie. I don't know how long I'm goin' to be away. That's the problem. Will yer wait up fer Seamus? No, go and get him after I've gone. You can't stay here on yer own with these male boarders. He'll be at the Ship Inn. Tell him he can bring Danny around as well if he wants to. There'll be enough roast and vegetables fer everyone."

"Alice, yer know that Jack has a cook and a maid livin' there?" Maggie said. "Won't one of them be able to nurse him, instead of you rushing over to him?"

"Typical! Just what I would expect from you, Maggie. It should be you that's rushin' over to Liverpool, and what's more you should be livin' over there with him!"

—

Maggie managed to get through that weekend, though how she did she'd never know. It was true what Alice had said. Though said in spite, the woman was only letting her know where she thought her daughter-in-law's place should be. It made Maggie feel guilty and with it came flashes of Jack's cut and bloody face before her, every time she had a minute to think.

She fed the boarders as best she could, knowing that her standard of cooking was not as good as Alice's. Seamus, after being told of the situation, was extremely supportive and helped her out as much as he could.

There was only one time that she had any problem, when Mr Dickinson asked for his bedroom back. She controlled her tongue, though wanted to be scathing. Words like 'kicking a man when he was down' came to mind, but she told him politely that Alice and Michael would be bringing their son back home.

She was just getting Mikey settled in the pram on the Monday, in readiness to set off up the hill to Miss Rosemary's. It had snowed overnight, the kind of snowflakes that didn't settle for long, but left the ground slushy. She saw Alice come slithering around the corner. Her face was angry looking. Someone was about to get an earful. Probably me, Maggie thought.

"Come in and make me a drink, will yer, Maggie," she said when she reached her. "I'm perishin' cold after that journey. Bloomin' trains. Nasty, draughty contraptions, and then I had to wait half an hour at Hooton, fer a trap to bring me back again!"

"I was just goin' up to Miss Rosemary's, Alice."

"Let her wait, I've got something important to tell ye. Aren't yer interested in knowin' about Jack?"

Maggie wheeled Mikey's pram back into the hallway and left him sleeping, while she followed resignedly. Alice was shivering, so taking pity on her, she went to the kettle, which was steaming gently on the hob.

"Sit down there fer a minute." she commanded, pulling out one of the kitchen chairs.

Maggie did so, while Alice changed her fancy outdoor hat for the lacy thing.

"Well, when I got to the house in Toxteth, the doctor had gone and that maid they got from the agency was seeing to Jack. She was wipin' his forehead and spoonin' some gruel into his mouth. Oh yes, he's come round by the way. Though I believe he took a nasty clout! Anyway, as I said, this young woman seemed to think it was her place to be caring for him. I said to her, 'Kitty May, what do yer think yer doin', yer the housemaid, not a nursemaid!' Well, yer should 'ave seen the look on her face, she coloured up, left the room, then said she was off visiting her mother. It was a good job the cook was still there to see to us." Alice paused for breath then continued to prattle.

"I said te Michael after, that I thought there was something funny going on there. I mean, it's not her job to be carin' for me son. Only me should be able to do that or a paid professional woman. Michael went all sheepish, I know when he's hidin' somethin' from me. I've known him fer more than twenty-five years. Well, would yer believe, the next morning, when Jack was able to sit up a little, (ye should see his poor face, Maggie, talk about being beaten to a pulp), he said that he thought I should come back over! He said with me havin' a business to run, I was needed by the boarders. I said, 'What about gettin' a professional nurse in to look after you' and he said he would make do with Kitty May! It appears she looked after her father, when he had the coughing sickness, so she's used to lookin' after poorly people. I said, 'I don't think so. What about doing personal things, fer you?' Michael then spoke up and said he would help with bathing Jack and seein' to 'you know what', so I said if I wasn't needed, then I would go. You know, 'that one', had a look of triumph on her face when I said goodbye this morning. Michael said how could anything be goin' on between them, when there was the cook and himself as chaperones?"

"Is that what yer thinkin', Alice, that they've formed a relationship between them?" Did she feel a sense of relief and hope that what she was saying was true?

"That's what I'm thinkin', Maggie, and it isn't right. He'll always be a married man. Oh, I wish you'd think again and go back with me son. We had some happy times when we all lived here as a family."

"But Alice, yer know all the reasons that Jack and I are not together," Maggie said, gently. "And if he's found someone else to love him, then I'll be happy for him. It's not as if they live over here and would be flouting themselves around fer everyone to see."

"It's a sin fer yer to even be thinkin' that way, Maggie! By all the saints, would yer listen to yerself. If you were me daughter, I'd wash yer mouth out with water and a bit of soap!"

–

Over the next few days, Maggie decided to distance herself from Alice's ranting. She seemed to have taken a personal affront that her daughter-in-law was the cause of things 'going on' in Jack's Toxteth place and she couldn't wait for her husband to get back, so that she could give him a piece of her mind. He was letting things happen under her nose and he should be full of shame.

It seemed to Maggie that Alice was finding 'the goings on in Toxteth' more important than Jack returning to good health, and she worried for his future, because he had another fight planned in another month. And what was going to happen to the plans that Alice had for Christmas? Maggie still wanted to spend the day with Miss Rosemary, as that was what she had promised to do.

It was nearly time for the annual Christmas market and Maggie was looking forward to it eagerly. To buy gifts for little Mikey was her greatest wish, although she knew he was too young to appreciate them.

Then Michael came home and there was bitter feuding, though the couple tried to keep their quarrels quiet, so that the rest of the household couldn't hear. It seemed that Jack wasn't going to be coming home at Christmas. He was better now and would be resuming his training. He had sent Maggie ten pounds, to spend on whatever she wished.

Whatever was being said between Michael and Alice, Maggie didn't want to know and was glad to be out of the house. When she had asked Alice for permission to have her Christmas dinner with Miss Rosemary, it was freely given. Though she was told very firmly that Mikey had to spend his Christmas day with them.

Strangely enough, Alice also expressed a wish to look after Mikey more often. She had said that Maggie could leave him with her in the afternoons, her excuse being that now the weather had turned chilly, with a biting, blustery wind, Mikey would be better off staying in the warmth with her. Maggie was quite surprised, as Alice had asked her in a pleading tone, which was very unusual. Whatever the reason, she was glad to be given breathing space of her own.

—

The Christmas market was everything that she remembered and more. This year though, Maggie had plenty of money to spend on presents and was dressed more like the type of person she had always aspired to be. A young English gentlewoman, demurely dressed, with plenty of coins in her bag. She wore a pelisse around her shoulders. It was padded and from the same heavy velvet as her blue velveteen, but she had to wear her button boots, because on the day she visited the market, the wind was very raw.

"Well, Missis, I'd a niver 'ave recognised yer, if yer hadn't 'ave come up to me and said 'ello," said Lily, standing in the same place with her barrow and with a few more lines upon her face. She was stamping her feet in a pair of big old boots and this time her hands, under her thick black shawl, were caressing a bottle of gin.

"Wot can I do fer such a finely dressed young lady? Not a lot here fer yer on me barrer this time, I'll be bound."

"Oh Lily, it's lovely to see yer again, so it is," Maggie cried. "I've bin workin' hard at me job at the dressmakers. Do yer remember yer sent me there, when I was after buying a cloak? Well, since then I've given birth to a wonderful little boy named Mikey and we don't live at the farm any longer. We live on the promenade down by the sea."

"Aren't yer wed to that fighter, Jack Haines? Only me son went to a fight on the dock road a few weeks past and someone said the fighter 'ad a wife and kid who lived in luxury, Parkgate way."

"Hardly luxury, Lily. Jack bought the property fer his parents to run as a boardin' house. He had to work very hard to get the money and I still 'ave to work."

"Better than standin' here on a cold winter's day, eh, queen? Now is there anythin' on the barrer yer'll be wantin', 'cos I'm sure yer must be gettin' on."

Maggie felt stung by Lily's attitude. Just because she had pulled herself up by her boot straps and had made something of her tattered life, didn't mean that Lily had the right to begrudge her. Though, as she walked away empty handed from the stall, she felt sorry. Maggie was beginning to feel extremely blessed with what she had in her life and if truth were told, it was Lily who had sent her to the dressmakers in the first place. She resolved to go back to the barrow, when she had finished shopping. There had been a small black shiny reticule that had caught her eye, and she had been just about to purchase it for Alice. If it was still there, then she would buy it. It would bring a smile to Lily's face and Maggie knew that Alice would love it.

Maggie handed over the capon she had bought to Miss Rosemary. The good lady was just shutting her shop and told her that she would purchase the vegetables next day.

Then Maggie went to Ezra's, to get the ingredients for the plum pudding. She planned to make it that evening, as it was Christmas Eve next day. She spent the following morning wrapping up the presents, including Alice's reticule, that couldn't be left on Lily's stall, even if the owner was ill mannered. She finished off the parcels with pretty purple ribbon, left over from the dress she had made.

Satisfied with everything, Maggie settled herself to look out of her bedroom window. There had been no mention of her moving to the back bedroom again, of which she was heartily glad. There seemed to be an unspoken understanding between her and Alice, though nothing was ever going to be the same again.

–

Christmas Day saw Betty and Maggie sitting very much at ease with one another, having enjoyed a good cooked dinner of Christmas fayre, including Maggie's moreish pud.

The family had gone to church together, including Mikey, who had been clucked over by the women of the congregation and had been given a golden sovereign by his godparents. Alice had loved her reticule, saying that she would treasure it always, Michael was given a cheap silver chain for his fob watch and Seamus was given a striped waistcoat, which he seemed very taken with. She had decided only to tie a brightly coloured bauble to dangle from Mikey's pram, but had bought him a little woollen jacket and a matching bonnet, to wear over his little gowns. It would be a while yet before he began to wear breeches, probably when he was three. Maggie thought the tradition of breeching was namby pamby, but to do it earlier could have caused a disagreement between Alice and her.

Maggie had bought a gift for Miss Rosemary and there was one for her too. The parcels sat side by side on the living room chiffonier, as they both felt embarrassed initially, as to who would open them first. They decided to open them together and were both amazed to see that they had chosen a similar theme! Maggie had bought a wooden casket, ornately carved with little birds, with sheets of good quality paper and envelopes inside. It had cost her more then all of the family presents put together, but it was something she had to buy for her friend. Betty had bought her an ornately decorated silver ink stand, with a silver handled quill and two spare nibs. They were both taken aback at their choices and flung their arms around each other, spontaneously.

They sat together later, nibbling on a mince pie each. Alice had them sent over, with the compliments of the season to Miss Rosemary. The dressmaker and Alice had only met once, when Alice had called into the shop to look at some fabric, as Maggie had said she would get round to making her a dress one day.

"Well, that was very nice, Maggie," Betty said, as she put her cup and saucer down on the occasional table nearby. Maggie agreed that it was.

"Now, I want to talk to you seriously about something," she continued. "I've given it a great deal of thought after you told me the situation regarding Alice and her making you play musical bedrooms. What I would like to know, Maggie, is if you and Mikey would like to live with me?"

She couldn't believe her ears! Miss Rosemary asking her and Mikey to move into this place? She would like a shot and began to say so, but Betty put a hand on her arm and said she had better explain.

"I'm not talking about moving in here, dear. You can see there isn't the room for us all. No, I shall use these rooms for storage. I want to move to Selwyn Lodge. You, Mikey and me!"

Chapter 18

Selwyn Lodge! She had passed that house often on Burton Road, when she used to take a shortcut through the farmer's field. It was a grand building, in its own grounds, and the back of the house looked on to the sea. Maggie looked in awe at Miss Rosemary, but managed to ask, weakly, "That house belongs to you?"

"Yes, it is our old family house. It is named Selwyn Lodge after my father's mother's family. Her ancestors came from Wales and my father did very well with his business interest. Not only did he leave me the family home, I also own some cottages on Parkgate Road."

Maggie whistled through her teeth at that information. Who would have believed the dressmaker had her own shop and all those properties!

"And that is where you, Mikey and me are going to live?" she queried, still feeling stunned.

"That is if you want to, Maggie. It is in rather a dilapidated state inside at the moment. You tend to find that when people rent your house, they are not as careful in its treatment as they would their own. It also needs some modernization, as it needs a bathroom putting in. As regards refurbishment, you could help me make new curtains, bedspreads, and anything you think we need to make our lives more comfortable. It won't be straight away, because I have to give notice to the couple who live there. The reason why I've decided to make some changes in my life is purely selfish. I'm not getting any younger. No, no dear, I don't mind telling you, I'm the wrong side of sixty. Sometimes at night when I'm on my own here, I get frightened. Being so close to all these inns and taverns makes me nervous, and what if I was coming down the stairs in the morning and fell?"

"So you want me to be like a companion and live in with yer?" Maggie said, thinking that the prospective job sounded very pleasant.

"Well, I suppose it would be something like that, but I would not call you my companion. You have become like a daughter to me. You seem to be the only person that I could say, hand on heart, cares for me. Except Ezra, I suppose…" she finished hastily.

"I don't know what to say, Miss Rosemary. You've stunned me. Me, Maggie Mayo as was, livin' in a grand house on Burton Road. All I can say fer now is that the good Lord looks after his own!"

"Yes, I heartily agree with those sentiments, though there might be a few problems achieving our aim. Firstly from the point of view of your marriage. You were telling me that Jack didn't come over as expected. Do you know why that was?"

"Oh, they'd had a falling out over something, him and Alice," she replied. It was best for now to keep Alice's suspicions to herself.

"I did make some inquiries on your behalf, when I went to see my solicitor in Chester. He seemed to think that if your child's welfare has been tantamount in your arrangements, then Jack has no call to litigation, should you take Mikey away from the family home. I thought perhaps we could find a nursery maid for the little fellow and leave you free to help with my next plan. I thought that maybe you would like to take over the running of my shop and my other interests too. Of course, I would not be sitting at home idle, but I would like to be a little more in the background. Put my feet up, as they say!"

Again, what could Maggie say? She was seventeen years old, had been in this new country just over one year, married with a baby, and here was this wonderful woman offering her things that if she had lived in Neston for fifty years, she would never have achieved on her own.

"Do you think you would be up to it, Maggie?" Betty broke in, as she saw that the girl was wearing a look that was pensive.

"Well, I'm sure with your backing and encouragement, I could do anything I put me mind to, Miss Rosemary. I just can't take everything in that yer tellin' me!"

"Maggie, I am sure you will rise up and overcome all adversities. Now we'll have another sherry to put a seal on it, and in future you are to call me Betty, not Miss Rosemary!"

—

The shop was quiet over the first few weeks of January and Maggie was able to make a dress for Alice. It was similar to the ankle length skirt and figure hugging bodice, that she wore herself nowadays, but in a dark shade of green. Alice was very pleased with the result and thanked her profusely.

Her in-laws were on tenterhooks again, because Jack wasn't really back to full fitness. The next match which was to take place in Southport, was nearly upon him, but he had been getting bad headaches again. Michael decided to ask for an interview with Lord Belsham, to speak on behalf of his son. The interview took place in the suite of rooms at the Adelphi Hotel, that His Lordship always reserved for himself when he had business in the city.

He was not an uncaring man and listened to Michael fairly sympathetically, but he was beginning to think that he had been unwise in his choice of protege.

"I think that we must send Jack to see my consultant," he had said. "He has a practice in Rodney Street and if he pronounces your son as unfit, we will have to think again about my patronage. I could not be held responsible if Jack did not recover from this show in Southport. My father would be hopping mad and there would be an absolute stink. So, if my consultant says he isn't up to it, we will pull out or get a stand in. I am toying with the idea of transferring my interest to the America's anyway. Railroads maybe, or I might get back into the sport again. New York or Chicago. I've heard that the fighting is just as strongly supported over there."

Michael had come back a few days later, to say that Jack would be coming back home for further recuperation. The house was to be closed up for the time being in Toxteth and the cook and the housemaid would be going back to the agency.

His words threw Maggie into panic. What of her plans to move into the grand house with Betty and look after Betty's business interests too? Just when the future was looking more rosy, Jack was moving back to his parents' home again.

While she waited in trepidation for her husband's return, Maggie still worked every afternoon at the dressmaker's. As she was stitching away on the finishing touches to an evening gown, the front door opened and a client inched her way in. It was Miss Madeline. She had hoped that one day she would get to meet this young woman, to see the person for whom she had worked on her huge crinoline.

The first thing she noticed about Miss Madeline was her glorious red hair. It wasn't carrot coloured, nor what an onlooker would call ginger, it was in between that, maybe titian. It was shiny and bright, tied up into a Roman style at the back of her head, which cascaded into bubbly curls, and was adorned with pale blue ribbons.

She had what could be called a heart shaped face, which sat upon a long neck, though the look was probably the effect of her hair being tied up. Her nose was pert and her brown eyes were fringed with curling lashes. Her skin was creamy white with a few freckles here and there.

She was only a little taller than Alice, which made her about five feet two. She had on the second crinoline that Maggie had worked on. This was the one with four layers, each with a fringe sewn on the hem. It was in two different shades, royal and azure blue.

"Hello, may I speak to Miss Rosemary?" she inquired, as she stood in the dressmaker's doorway, leaving it open wide. "Oh, you must be Maggie, the girl, I am told, who spent all that time on my crinoline. Such fine needlework, I have to say."

"Miss Rosemary has gone to Chester, to the fabric house. Can I be of any help to yer?"

"I have another dress in mind that I would like to commission. It's for my forthcoming marriage. We have to see the priest, of course, before we can set a date, but maybe May or June, we thought. Apple blossom colours and in the style of a milkmaid."

"A milkmaid?" Maggie replied faintly.

"You know, a low shouldered bodice, with lots of stiffened white petticoats and a creamy fabric pinned up into wide loops above it. On each side of the loops would be little green ribbons made into bows. If you have some paper I could sketch it for you. Or would you rather I called back when Miss Rosemary is around?"

"I think yer should call on her tomorrer. I'll tell her of your intention when she gets back."

"Very well. Perhaps I'll see you again when I come for my fittings? I am pleased to have met you, Maggie. Good day."

Maggie couldn't help laughing when Miss Madeline had gone. A milkmaid outfit indeed. The crinoline was taking its time, thank goodness, to catch on in Neston. Would a milkmaid style gown ever become the fashion of the day?

When Betty came back, she was intrigued to hear that her young client from the Brown Horse was getting married.

"I didn't know that she had a beau," she said. "She has never mentioned one to me. Her conversation is usually about the fabrics I can get in Chester and fashionable styles. Sometimes she has brought in her sketches to show me. I believe she gets very bored in the quarters her uncle has given her. He won't allow her to go into any of the public areas, so she must get very lonely, poor soul."

"Has she told yer any more about where she came from?" Maggie asked curiously. "It seems very strange, the way she suddenly popped up, as if out of nowhere."

"All I can surmise from the little she has told me, is that her father had a position of importance on a landowner's estate. She went to a private school and wanted to go to some place in Paris to study, but her father said enough was enough."

"Oh well, if she's going to be coming to see yer over this milkmaid's outfit she wants yer to make, she'll probably say who she's goin' to marry to yerself."

-

Jack came back to Seagull Cottage at the end of January. Maggie was half expecting that the single mattress would be brought down from the attic again.

Alice was in a flurry of excitement, dropping little hints that once Jack was back again with them, everything would be right again. She had made an enormous meal for his welcome dinner. A steak and kidney pie that oozed with gravy, cabbage and fluffy potatoes and a custard pie for dessert. She had put on her best outfit to show Jack how his wife, Maggie, had come on in leaps and bounds with her needlework.

Maggie put on her purple dress, the one that Jack should have seen the last time. Her nightdress was draped across the counterpane on the double bed, high necked and long sleeved. Enough to cool any man's ardour, especially her husband's, she had thought.

They all sat down around the table after their satisfying meal. Jack seemed a little on edge, but Maggie put it down to him feeling uneasy with his mother. Though Alice had chatted enough for all of them, she had, it seemed for the sake of her son, put the past away.

Maggie thought that Jack must have really suffered from his injuries in his last bout, as his nose was slightly crooked, one of his front teeth was cracked and he had a scar under his left eye from a deep cut that hadn't healed very well. He was pale and he had lost all his healthy colour and she noticed that now and again the side of his mouth twitched. His attire, though, was still splendid, dressed as he was like a man who had made good.

"So have yer thought what yer'll do now the fightin' is behind yer, Jack?" asked Alice, shooing Maggie away, as she got up to take the plates to the scullery.

"No, you see to Mikey, Maggie. I'll do the dishes later on. Would yer look at him, Jack? Hasn't he grown? Six months old now and can pull himself up to get a good look around him and Maggie doesn't have to be on call so much, now that he can eat a bit of porridge and a biscuit mushed up with a little milk. So, have yer thought of goin' back to see the farmer and see if he'll take yer on again? Not that I'm wanting you and Maggie to move out to live in a cottage as before. I thought mebbe you could get work with him when he needs yer, or any farm if it comes to that."

"Leave it, Mother," put in Michael, seeing Jack was searching for an answer. His son had only been home an hour or so and already Alice was questioning him.

"I'm not sure what I'll be doing yet, Mother," Jack finally answered. "Maggie, I was wondering. The weather seems to be settled into a bit of sunshine this afternoon. Shall we put Mikey into his pram and walk along the promenade?"

"That would be lovely, Jack," Alice spoke for her daughter-in-law, her face beaming with happiness. "Maggie, go and change Mikey's cloths, while I put this nice warm blanket in for him to lie on, and put that little coat and bonnet on him too. It may look a sunny afternoon, but it'll be cold in the wind today."

"She never changes does she?" remarked Jack, as the couple walked along the promenade towards the Boat House, with Maggie pushing the pram and Jack linking her arm companionably. "It must have bin difficult fer yer these last few months, living here with Alice, but yer were given the opportunity to come and live with me."

"It hasn't been so bad and think on, it was me who decided to stay here, and now yer back anyway. Is it to be for good?"

"What makes yer ask that, Maggie?" asked Jack, looking at her questioningly.

"I think I know yer quite well by now and yer won't settle back ter farm work, will yer? A few more weeks when yer've forgotten all the pain and sufferin' yer've just bin through, yer'll be lookin' for another match again. Whether it be here in Neston or elsewhere, I can't see yer settling to scratchin' a livin' again. You've tasted some of the high life and soon yer'll want some more!"

"How very all seeing of yer," her husband replied, cynically. "As it happens, I wouldn't be happy with goin' back to where I started from and I have the feelin' that you wouldn't be happy sharin' my life either…"

"Don't say that, Jack!" she cried hotly. "You're the father of me son. I just didn't want to leave where I was settled, where I was happy as well. And as it happens, I was right to stay here, because you've had to come back here again."

Jack looked at her strangely, then started making cooing noises to Mikey. Whilst walking back to Seagull Cottage, he didn't speak at all.

Maggie was busy the rest of the afternoon, helping Alice and seeing to the baby. In the evening, Jack and his father went to the Ship Inn, leaving her all jumpy and nervous and worrying about sharing the double bed. It was all very well for Jack, he could go to the inn and have few drinks to settle him. She wished that Alice had some sherry in the house, so that she could have a few glasses to settle her worries as well.

At ten o'clock, Maggie sat on the bed, all wrapped up in the voluminous nightdress, as Jack carefully put his good clothes into the wardrobe, then stood before her in his underwear.

Her heart was beating painfully in her chest and she hoped that he couldn't hear it.

She looked away when he sat beside her on the bed, especially when he put his arm around her shoulders. She was glad

236

that he couldn't see her embarrassed face properly, as she had half turned away from the candlelight.

"Maggie, there's somethin' I want to tell yer," he said quietly. "Me father knows, but not me mother. There's a chance I'll be leavin' England, forever. Nothing is certain and that's why I came home to get me head around it. I was intendin' to see if you and me could make another go of it, but somethin' has happened meantime and I think I've made up me mind."

"What is it Jack, is it something to do with…"

She was going to say Kitty, the girl who was Jack's maid at Toxteth, but he had interrupted and started to explain that Lord Belsham wanted someone to look after his interests in America. Find a man to sponsor like he had sponsored Jack. Be an agent like Richard Mannion, he supposed.

Jack squeezed her shoulders gently and said, "Do yer remember when we spoke of love and yer said perhaps I was confusing love with making babies? Well, yer was right. I was lonely without yer in Toxteth and I took Kitty May into me bed. I knew I was doin' wrong, being married to you an' all, but I felt rejected by yer and she was so willin' to share my bed. Well, when everything went wrong and I was felled like a tree along the dock road, she was so good to me. Looked after me as if I was a little baby. Then me mother came over and she knew. I suppose mother's have a nose fer these things and she told me to get rid of Kitty. I couldn't do it, send her back to the agency on me mother's say so. The girl didn't deserve such treatment and so mother took the huff and came back home. One thing led to another and Dad went to see Lord Belsham on my behalf, and here I am waitin' fer me orders, because what I haven't told yer yet, is Kitty is expectin' a babby."

He looked away from her as he said it. Dropped his arm from her shoulders, as if he was expecting a blow.

Maggie looked askance at him. She couldn't believe what she had just heard. Kitty May was having his child?

"So she's made me mind up," he continued, mumbling a bit now, as he had his head bowed in contrition. "I'm taking the job in America and she'll be comin' with me. Not that she knows any of this yet. I went to her house on Scotland Road and it's a hovel that she and her family live in. Eight younger brothers and sisters all squashed together in two damp rooms. Her father died last year, so Kitty and her mother hold the family together. Her mother was mad when she saw me, said Kitty has been sick as a dog, three days on the run, and the people she works fer now are very concerned about it."

"Well, all I can say is I wouldn't like to be in your shoes when yer tell Alice. Yer'll be the black sheep of the family and you'll be glad to get away."

"Yer takin' it very well, what I've just told yer, Maggie. Isn't there a tiny scrap of love in yer heart fer me?"

"I told yer once before, Jack. I'll worry about yer always and wonder how yer are, but all this havin' babies isn't the life that I'm wantin'. I'm glad you'll have Kitty, 'cos I wouldn't like it if yer were on yer own so far away. But I'm surprised yer went against yer marriage vows. We might have got over our problems in the future, but we certainly can't now."

Jack turned away, looking guilty. It seemed there was nothing more to say. But when he put his arm around her, as they settled down in bed together later, she snuggled up beside him and held him close. This marriage of theirs would bind them together forever. He was bound by their Catholic faith to never divorce. She could still have the status of a married woman, but answer to no one in the future, but herself.

—

An unspoken alliance seemed to exist between Jack and Maggie over the next few days. If the weather was favourable, he made a point of walking out with her and their baby and they'd stroll around the village, along the coastal roads and even visited Miss Rosemary's shop. He was polite and courteous to her friend, when in her company, but Maggie could see a certain tightness in Betty's face, and her smile didn't quite reflect in her eyes. She assured her friend that Jack was only visiting and she would be back soon to help her in the shop again.

Jack asked later why she had said that to the dressmaker. Surely it was none of the auld woman's business how long he stayed at home? She told him that they had to get a story together, for when he had gone from there. Once Alice heard the reason for his departure, she would never be able to hold her head up again.

Each day Jack intended to say something of his plans to his mother, mention the possibility of working again for Lord Belsham, then maybe later say it could be in America, and finish up that his lady friend was expecting. But, he couldn't do it, as he knew the truth would break Alice's heart.

Jack kept saying to Maggie, that the biggest wrench in his life was going to be leaving all his family, especially Mikey, his little seven-month-old son. He intended to work very hard to make a lot of money, then he would come back and visit them all again. One of those times was when they were out walking, passing the house named 'Selwyn Lodge' and the grandeur of the building had caught his eye.

"That's the kind of place I want to live in, Maggie. I would think that I had it all if I lived in a place like that. In fact, I would be proud to live in any of these swanky places along this road."

"I think yer'll have to wait 'til yer mother has passed over before yer come back," Maggie told him, keeping it to herself that she might be living in Selwyn Lodge herself one day, "though she'll probably swing at the end of a rope when she finds out what yer up to, then yer won't be here to buy a swanky house at all."

Maggie had said that tongue in cheek, but she was glad she wasn't in Jack's shoes. Alice would kill him when she heard his plans. Of that she was very sure. In the end, Jack took the coward's way out and left all the telling to Michael.

Mikey had been causing a few interruptions to the households' sleep at night, due to teething and restlessness, so Jack had taken to sleeping on the chaise lounge in the parlour. Though, for appearances, he usually started off in the marital bed, then sneaked away downstairs.

On his last night at Seagull Cottage, he had been particularly loving as they had settled down to sleep. She had been aroused by the little kisses he had placed on the nape of her neck, and she had turned in a friendly fashion, to snuggle into him. She had felt a wild desire to turn and face him, as stirrings of something, she knew not what, began to stir in her private bits. Would it matter if, for one last time, she allowed him to do the things he used to do? She lay there, rigid with tension, feeling her body begin to burn with a passion that took her by surprise. Then she heard Jack, softly snoring beside her and chastised herself for being such a fool.

Could she really have coped with another baby, while her husband was with Kitty May on the other side of the world? She drifted off and soon it was morning.

"Come on, you two sleepy heads, it's time yer were up. You should be gettin' a job, Jack. Yer've bin lollin' about fer far too long!"

Maggie scrambled up to a sitting position, as Alice pushed her way into the bedroom, bearing a tray and talking stridently. Mikey pulled himself up in his cradle and began to wail at the sound of her voice, so Alice handed Maggie the tray with two cups of tea on it, then went to the cradle and scooped her grandson up.

"Has he been teethin' again, poor little soul?" she asked, shaking her head. "I've told yer Maggie, yer should get up to the chemist and see if he's got something to put on this poor little mite's gums. Where's Jack?" She looked across and saw that her son wasn't lying in the bed. "Couldn't stand the baby's wailing then? Typical. Has he gone out, gone out fer a run?"

Maggie knew then why Jack had been so loving. She shook her head at Alice and said she didn't know where he had gone.

Suddenly they both heard Michael, shouting for Alice from down below. She handed Maggie the baby, saying she would see him later on.

After Maggie had fed Mikey, changed him into his day-wear and got herself dressed, she suddenly heard her mother-in-law come pounding up the stairs. This time Alice was waving a letter, with Michael close on her heels. Maggie draped a light shawl around her shoulders, she had a feeling she would be sitting on her bed for a while.

Alice threw the letter at her, as if it was about to burn her fingers. Her face was puce with anger and her body was trembling, as she raised her voice.

"Don't tell me what Michael has been tellin' me is true! Read it out, will yer, and let's get to the bottom of it. This letter is from Lord Belsham, Maggie. See, look!"

Maggie's fingers began to tremble also, as she opened the very expensive looking envelope and read the written words out loud to her in laws.

> *Dear Jack,*
>
> *Thank you for agreeing to be my agent in Chicago. I enclose a draft that can be drawn on my account in Tithebarn Street, for any expenses you incur before you go. Your passage has been booked. A double cabin, as requested, on the SS Methuselah, leaving Liverpool on the 27th February. Please would you send a telegraph to Richard at his office, on your safe arrival. I will be following on in the middle of March, so would be obliged if you could reserve a suite of rooms for my visit. Of course at the best hotel.*

Lord Belsham had signed it with his compliments and a flourishing signature, but by the time Maggie had got to that part, Alice was in a swoon beside her, looking very agitated and distinctly unwell.

"So, he's gone and done it then," she moaned, then she put her head into her hands and began to cry. Michael fluttered anxiously at the side of her, patting her shoulder and saying that all would be well. Maggie got up, as her baby had filled its cloth and she needed to change him, while Alice was getting over her shock. It didn't take her long, and within minutes she was shouting.

"Yer both were in this together. You and Michael, yer knew he wasn't goin' to stay here and settle down. What was it? Were yer waitin' fer this letter to come? Neither of yer seem in the least surprised!"

"Hush, Mother," soothed Michael. "The lodgers will probably be still eatin' their breakfasts, I haven't heard the front door shut."

"Never mind the bloomin' lodgers!" she spat. "What I want ter know is what you two have bin up ter and why I am the last to hear of it?"

"Jack didn't want to upset you," Michael answered. "He knew that yer were goin' to be upset anyway, so he thought it was best if he waited for the letter to come. Yer know he wouldn't have settled down to our kind of existence, not now he's tasted the fruits of the high life."

"And you, Madam…" Alice shot a look of venom in Maggie's direction, seemingly content with her husband's explanation, but having to put the blame on someone. "Yer've bin pretendin' that everything's rosy between yer, taking little walks together and proudly showing off yer little son."

"I had no choice, Alice…"

"Never mind yer excuses. Well, we'll all have to get ourselves dressed in our best and go after him. No son of mine is going off to the other side of the world, without him saying goodbye to his family."

"But we don't know where he will be staying, Mother," Michael answered, no doubt thinking they'd all be off on a fool's errand. "We can't just go off to Liverpool, it would be like a dog chasing its own tail!"

"Ah, but you know where this office of Mr Mannion is, so we can go there and ask of his whereabouts. Come on now, the pair of youse. Michael, run up to the Cross and see what time there's a trap leavin' fer the station and Maggie, get a basket together for the baby and put in plenty of changing cloths."

"Alice," Maggie said gently, waiting fearfully for the bombshell that would surely explode when Alice heard her words. "Alice, I don't think yer know that Jack is going to America... with Kitty May."

Chapter 19

"Kitty May?" gasped Alice, her eyes narrowing with this new information, as she struggled to take in Maggie's words. She dashed away the tears of frustration with her palms, as she looked at her daughter-in-law in disbelief. She repeated, "Kitty May? Isn't that the name of the little baggage that was looking after Jack at Toxteth, when he was ill? What is she to Jack? Why's she goin' to the America's with him?"

"She's expectin' his child, Alice," replied Michael gravely, then flinched as his wife started hitting out at him with wild, flailing fists, screaming that it was all his fault for not keeping an eye on their son.

Maggie decided to make for the door and let them get on with it. Up to now Mikey had been turning his head as Alice or Michael spoke, wondering at all the excitement, but she could see that his bottom lip was beginning to quiver.

"Stop there, Maggie," Alice commanded, as she saw what Maggie was about to do. "I want to know what part you played in all of this. No, wait, Michael and I will go down to the kitchen. See to the child and then come down to me."

She stalked off with Michael trailing behind her, looking so miserable that Maggie's heart went out to him. Michael would take the brunt of Jack's foolishness, though somehow she felt she would be getting it in the neck as well.

She took her time seeing to Mikey, bathing his squirming bottom in the bowl full of water that she kept on a small table in the bedroom. She dressed him in clean clothes, then brushed her hair until it shone.

Alice and Michael were sitting at the table with Seamus. It seemed that the poor young man had been told the sorry tale, as he looked as if he'd been getting the sharp edge of his mother's tongue as well.

"Here yer are, Maggie," Alice said, sounding quite friendly. "Come, little Mikey, come and sit on Grandma's knee. There's a bit of porridge left in the pan, Maggie. Give him that and then we'll talk about what we're goin' to do about all these shenanigans."

Maggie did as she was told and made herself a cup of tea, then brought the child's bowl of porridge to the table, where she set about feeding the little fellow. Alice didn't exchange a glance with her once, whilst she spooned the mixture into Mikey's mouth. There was an uneasy silence in the kitchen, as the three concerned members of the family waited for Alice to speak.

"Well, I have to put the blame firmly at Maggie's door," she started in an accusing tone. "If you had been a good wife to me son, we wouldn't be sittin' here with this problem. You've made no effort to keep him by yer side and now yer've let him go off with some little whore."

"Alice, that's enough," reproached Michael gently, whilst looking at Maggie apologetically. "Kitty May is not a whore, she's goin' to be the mother of yer grandchild. And as fer Maggie not bein' a good wife to our Jack, how do we know what goes on behind closed doors? No, the blame has to be laid firmly on our Jack. He's never been content with livin' the simple life like we do. He's always bin chasing rainbows. After the crock of gold!"

Alice sniffed and said, "Yer always taking the side of the underdog, aren't yer? Where would she be if she had insisted on staying in Killala? Yer should have bin grateful, Maggie, fer what we've done fer yer and worked harder at yer marriage. Anyway, it's done now. We've got ter think of a way of making sure there will be no scandal. I mean, if the priest and me friends were ter find out what our Jack's done, I couldn't go to St. Winefred's again. I would be hangin' me head in shame!"

There was a silence while everyone took in the importance of her words. Maggie sipped her tea, feeling aggrieved. As far as she was concerned, she had been a good wife to Jack. Especially as the marriage had been forced on her anyway.

"I've got it! We'll pretend he's dead! Read the letter again to me, Maggie. What day is that ship he's goin' on, sailin' from Liverpool?"

Alice threw Lord Belsham's letter over to Maggie, who now, having finished feeding Mikey still on Alice's knee, had moved to Seamus's side.

"We'll all go over on that day and come back wearing funeral clothes. And when I've finished with the pair of them, Jack will be wishin' that he was dead."

"Yer can't do that!" they all said in unison. Even the baby looked up in surprise, as if he had understood his grandma's words.

"Why can't we? He'll be dead to us," she retorted dramatically. "We'll get up really early and creep out of the house before the lodgers get up. Michael, you can see if Sam Cottrell, the cabbie, will do a special journey fer us. Yer can tell him we'll pay double if he helps us catch the first train. There's no time, fer you to make us any outfits, Maggie, and it would draw attention if Michael and Seamus went to the tailor for their funeral wear. After we've waved off the ship, we'll go into the city, to one of those big department stores, and we'll get shop bought clothing. Then we'll come back and say that Jack has dropped dead in his lodgings and his landlady went ahead and had him buried in a Liverpool cemetery. We'll all have to walk around miserable and wearing dreary clothes fer the next six months or so and you, Maggie, can't breathe a word of it to that Miss Rosemary. Nor Seamus, either to Danny or his parents, do yer hear? The lodgers will believe us, 'cos I was always saying that I worried about Jack, that he might get his headaches back again. Now, what was the date again, Maggie? Oh yes, the 21st."

"But Alice," she began to say, because she thought her mother-in-law was carrying everything a bit too far.

"Can yer think of any other way to stop a scandal?" Alice challenged. They all shook their heads at her, numbly. Nobody could.

The following afternoon, Maggie returned to Miss Rosemary's. She was tired, as she had slept fitfully. Mikey had been restless in the night and Alice's plan kept creeping into her mind. Not even the beautiful view out of her bedroom window could lift her spirits, or the snowdrops that she had seen in someone's garden, as she walked along.

Betty remarked, when she saw her, that she was looking peaky. If Maggie didn't mind her asking, was it because the separation hadn't been resolved with Jack? Or was it because Maggie had changed her mind about the move to Selwyn Lodge?

"No, we're still havin' a separation," she answered truthfully, "because he still wants to carry on with the fighting. I told him that me and Mikey might be movin' out."

She had to keep her head down over her sewing, so that Betty couldn't see her face. Betty would know that she was lying, because she was apt to colour slightly with a sense of guilt. It was only a little lie that Maggie was telling, as it had been Jack who had decided to go his separate way.

"I thought you looked so happy together, when you called in to see me the other afternoon," Betty continued, as she sat opposite tacking the seam of a jacket.

"Jack likes to appear that he is playing happy families. Mainly fer his mother's sake, who would like nothing better than for us to give it another go. I kept telling him that he should give up the fightin', if he wanted to spend more time with me and Mikey." She got up quickly to make a cup of tea for them both, as she felt she hadn't been telling the truth again.

"Work will be starting after Easter on Selwyn Lodge, or so I've been told by Mr Freeman, 'Master Builder'," Betty called

247

through, as Maggie filled the kettle with water from the rain barrel outside the kitchen door. "And we are to have piped water. Imagine that! Such an innovation. Piped water to the kitchen and the new bathroom!"

Maggie wandered back into listen, as what Betty was saying was very interesting.

"My tenants have found a place to rent on Chester Street. A smaller dwelling, but infinitely more suitable to their needs. Now, Maggie, we will probably be inundated over the next few weeks with commissions. This is the time of the year when local farmers dig in their cash boxes and treat their wives to a flowery bonnet or new gown. There is an Easter Parade from Neston Cross on Good Sunday and the best bonnet is chosen by the Crow man. I'll tell you all about him later, he's just a bit of fun. I don't know where the tradition of the Crow man comes from."

-

The day drew near when Alice's plan was going to be put into action. Sometimes Alice would be full of excitement, because she was having a day out in Liverpool. Sometimes she sat staring vacantly into space, as if she was practising for the day of doom. Seamus kept saying that he didn't want to go, he would rather be spending the day with Danny.

Maggie didn't want to go either. As far as she was concerned, Jack and her had already said goodbye. What was the point of hanging around the dockside, just so she could have the chance of seeing Jack and Kitty, off on their voyage across the Atlantic? It would only bring tears before midnight for all concerned. Then there was her child to consider. He could be cold, hungry and crying while highly strung adults waited around.

In trepidation, she mentioned her feelings to Michael. He was sympathetic as usual, but asked her to see Alice's side of things as well.

"Let her have her day, Maggie. It will help her to get over the loss of Jack quicker. 'Tis saying goodbye to her son, who she will probably never see again. In her way, she's tying up all the loose ends before she embarks on becomin' a grieving mother. I see what yer sayin'. You've probably already said goodbye ter Jack and can shut the door on his memory and move on."

Maggie kissed him on the cheek for being so understanding. Nobody would wonder about Michael's feelings, he was losing his son as well.

"Yer've always got te have yer own way, Maggie," was Alice's reaction after supper the night before the journey, when she had made her mind up finally that she wasn't going to go. No one could make her. Even Alice would be loathe to try to drag her there. "I knew yer didn't want to come with us and see Jack off. You thought you'd wait 'til the last minute, when all me plans were made."

"I don't want to go either." That came from Seamus, who had planned to go fishing with Danny, as they could see from the sunset that evening that the following day was going to be a good one.

"Well, fiddlesticks te the both of yer," Alice said, sounding aggravated. "But, don't ferget, when I come back with those mourning clothes, yer goin' te have to wear them. If they don't fit, it won't be my fault, because yer refused to come with me and try them on. Now, this is the story that you've got to stick by. Me and Michael went to visit Jack at his lodgings before his big fight, planned for next Saturday. We got to his lodgings and we were given a big shock. It seemed that Jack had bin gettin' headaches again and when the landlady knocked on his door one morning, to see why there had bin no noise from his room, she found him lying on the floor and he was dead. There was no papers in his room to say if he had any relatives and if there had bin she couldn't read them anyway. So, she searched through his pockets and found he had some money. Then she called a policeman, who was walking past her front door, and he went fer an undertaker. There was enough money on Jack to bury him and that's where he is, in a Liverpool cemetery."

"And I bet the landlady pocketed the rest of the money," Seamus commented sourly.

"There was no landlady, yer daft eejit, that's the story we want believin'. Now, you two, we'll come back after we've seen Jack and his strumpet off and they've both had a piece of me mind, then we'll go up to Lord Street to one of the big shops. Then, when we come back I'll be cryin'. I will be anyway. If the lodgers are here, it will be even more believable, 'cos you, Maggie, will rush up the stairs in tears. Seamus, you'll say, 'Oh no, not me dear brother!' and then you'll run out of the house, saying yer've got to tell Danny. Then me and Michael will sit down and tell the lodgers the made up tale. Got it? Now we'll all go to bed, we've got to get up early in the mornin'."

Maggie made the lodgers their breakfast next morning, fielding questions on the whereabouts of Alice, making beds and doing the cleaning, and getting the vegetables ready for the evening meal. Everything was done from habit. Her mind was far away. She saw a clipper ship loosening its moorings, sailing off with the wind gusting and the sails unfurled, taking Jack and Kitty off to a new world. Would she have liked to have been in Kitty's shoes, she wondered? Put her life into Jack's hands? A man who had probably taken advantage of his housemaid anyway. An innocent young lady as she had once been. The answer was 'no', and Maggie felt an overwhelming sense of pity for the girl well up inside her. At least, though, his actions had made her a free woman. She was glad of it, but stopped her work just for a moment to whisper, "God speed."

Maggie couldn't face working at the dressmaker's later. There were more lies to be told and she felt wretched. Mikey had been so fretful that her head was aching from his cries. She pushed the pram up to the village, intending to make her excuses, then go for a long walk in the weak February sun.

Betty understood and said it could also be all the sewing that Maggie had been doing. Perhaps she should be resting her eyes instead, though she was glad Maggie had called in anyway, as Miss Madeline had been in for a fitting for her wedding dress and, would Maggie believe it, her client appeared to have put on weight!

Maggie walked slowly out of the village, intending to walk past Selwyn Lodge on Burton Road. She wanted to see it for herself again, the house where she would be living soon. Though, first she must visit St. Winefred's. She hated the deceit that was to be forced upon her by her mother-in-law and heartily wished she could be rid of the sin.

But, how to do that without getting the priest involved, was beyond her. Though he was bound by a vow of silence to keep confessions confidential, it wouldn't stop Father O'Brien from knocking on the sinner's door! She decided to tell all to God in front of the altar and was thankful that she was alone in the church.

Feeling better, she wheeled the sleeping baby across the lane and stood in front of Betty's house, to remind herself of her good fortune and where her future lay. The garden was enormous and full of early daffodils, and the lawns looked well tended, with shrub-filled flower beds. Tall trees shaded the large sandstone house, though it had an air of neglect about it, as if it was waiting to be loved. There was no smoke coming out from the tall, narrow chimneys, the windows were dirty, and wooden guttering broken off.

She walked down the lane at the side of the house and whistled with amazement at what she could see. Attached to the back of the house was a narrow glass building, which appeared to run horizontally. It seemed as if there was a garden inside it also, as she could see green foliage and small bushy trees. The hedged off garden stretched down to a screen of sycamore and elder, beyond which were fields of meadow land. In the garden was an arbour, a splash of yellow from a forsythia and a little gurgling brook, with a small paved area for sitting out. Maggie's spirits soared as she gazed in wonder, feeling that she couldn't wait to start her new life!

A chilly wind blew up from the estuary, so she decided that she would walk back slowly along the main village street. She planned to look into the window of the bonnet maker's shop, in case Alice brought her back a hideous hat, then back to Seagull Cottage to await the return of her eccentric in-laws.

Dusk was falling as she came onto the promenade, whilst the birds, that the house was named after, sat on the roof above, flapping and squawking as they settled in a row.

She heard voices, as she lugged the pram into the hallway. Michael and Alice were back already, sitting at the kitchen table drinking cups of freshly brewed tea. Alice pushed past her in bad humour, muttering as she did so that she was going off to bed. Michael just shrugged and signalled quietly that she was to let her go.

"There's no talkin' to her, Maggie," he explained, as she joined him at the table. "She's been cryin' on and off since the ship weighed anchor this mornin'. We got to the gate at Huskisson Dock, in time to see the clipper slip its moorings and sail off down the Mersey. It shattered her. All the way on the train she was tellin' me what she was and wasn't going to say ter our Jack. She kept askin' the man on the dock gate after, 'Are yer sure that was the ship that's crossin' the Atlantic? Me boy's on that and I haven't bin able to wave him away.' The man told me, it had bin an exceptional spring high tide and the captain probably took advantage of it. It seems there's a lot of competition at the moment amongst the passenger ships, each trying to cut down the sailing time from here to the America's."

Michael paused to look at her kindly, then got up to look at Mikey in his pram.

"Maybe yer could make a start on gettin' the lodger's meal together. I'll take Mikey into the parlour and keep an eye. Give her a few hours on her own. She'll come round, yer can be sure of it, and we'll all be at the receivin' end of her tongue."

Maggie couldn't resist peeping into one of the boxes that Alice had left on the table after he had gone. There were two hat boxes and two brown paper parcels there. She was relieved to see a black coal scuttle shaped bonnet, not a hat with feathers and bows. Alice had chosen well. She hoped that her mourning clothes would be just as simple, with no frills to the bodice, or flounces on the hem.

A tear stained Alice, all meek and humble, came down to the kitchen later. Her re-appearance timed for when the lodgers would be there. She had left all the explaining to a weary looking Michael, and graciously accepted their sympathy and condolences. If they wondered why Maggie, the new widow, sat silent and white faced, there was no comment made, except for a shuffling of embarrassment on their part. A lovely young woman bereaved, at only seventeen!

That evening a family meeting was called, after Mikey had been put to bed and the dishes cleared away. Alice, as usual, had something very important to discuss with the family. Not about Jack or the day's events, no, it was their finances. Now Jack was gone, who was going to bring the money in? She and Michael could manage on what the lodgers paid them, but Maggie would have to ask Miss Rosemary for wages now.

She wasn't an apprentice any more. Alice could see that by the outfits Maggie had been making. Seamus was told he had to stop racketing about with that friend of his. He was nearly sixteen and most boys of his age were down the colliery shaft or in the quarry and certainly not spending their days fishing, unless they were fishermen.

Maggie thought of the interest she was earning from her money lending service. Should she begin to draw a weekly wage from that? At last count it had stood at thirty-seven pounds and five shillings. More than double the original seventeen pounds she had given Betty, all those months ago.

She could see that Alice was waiting for an answer from her, fiddling with the strings of the parcels as she did so. Alice had brought them in from the scullery, where she had placed them out of sight of the lodgers' prying eyes.

"Mam, I've bin' meanin' to tell yer something," Seamus piped up. His voice sounded wobbly. From the upset of his brother leaving or being nervous of his mother, Maggie didn't know. "Me and Danny have decided we're goin' to try fer jobs on them clipper ships. We were talkin' today about it and Danny wants to work as a galley boy. He likes helpin' his dad with the cookin' at the Ship and I could be a person who looks after the cabins. A cabin boy, or maybe someone who helps serve the dinners. Anyways, that's what we want to do."

He bowed his head after his hurried explanation, waiting for the tirade that would surely come. Or at least be ready for the blow that would probably land on his head. Michael and Maggie waited with bated breath for the raving that would surely follow, and were surprised when Alice put her head in her hands at the table and quietly said, "Do as yer want son. Yer will do anyway."

She lifted her head then, to glare in Maggie's direction, accusingly.

"And I suppose you want to leave us too, Maggie? Take our grandson away from us, the only reminder we have of our Jack."

"Not so, Alice, at least not yet," Maggie replied, feeling put on the spot, but she had no indication from Betty when Selwyn Lodge would be ready for occupation. "I think it would be better if we all stayed together fer the time being. Present ourselves as an united family. Try to live as the bereaved would do. It will only be a nine day wonder anyway. I'll speak to Miss Rosemary about a wage and give you something to pay fer food, at least fer Mikey and me. Now, do yer think we could try those dreary clothes on? If mine don't fit, I'll have to get crackin' with me needle."

It was hard to keep up appearances over those next few days. It was easy for Alice and Michael, who had only the lodgers in their lives and Alice decided that they were not to go to church that Sunday, anyway.

Maggie was out when the priest called down to Seagull Cottage, after he noticed the family were missing from Mass, but whatever was said he seemed satisfied, because he didn't call around again. No, the hardest thing for Maggie was playing the bereaved widow in front of Miss Rosemary. Betty, her dearest friend, who had listened, advised and sympathized and given her the chance to improve her life. Many a time she wanted to blurt out... 'It's not true, it's just a charade!' but she felt she couldn't do that to Alice. So, she put up with being looked at with sympathy, or stared at nosily when she walked by. People even came in the shop, on the pretext of looking at material, though it was merely curiosity on their part.

Word got round quickly in Neston village.

"Jack Haines, the local fighter, yer know the one that won the match at the quarry? Well, he's gone and died. A blow ter the head, it is believed. His wife works at the dressmaker in the High Street. You'd think she'd stay at home behind drawn curtains, but there she is flaunting herself, would yer believe?"

Whether it was the gossip surrounding the fighter's wife, or a genuine desire to have a dress made, it brought Mrs Briggs into the dressmaker's shop and renewed their acquaintance.

"I thought it must be you, when Solly told Briggs that Jack, the man who used to work for us, had died," she said sympathetically. "And when he said his wife was working at Miss Rosemary's, I said to the farmer, 'I must go and comfort the poor creature and take her some of her favourite cakes'. Here, I baked them especially this morning for you."

Maggie could only nod her head in gratitude, as she looked upon the Maid of Honours the farmer's wife had brought her. It made her want to bow her head and cry. It had been the second time that day, that goodness in people had been shown to her.

Most touching of all had been when Ezra had stood in the shop doorway, smiling at her hesitantly. He had been clutching a small posy of violets in his big beefy hands.

Chapter 20

The family kept away from the Easter Parade. It wasn't done to indulge in frivolity in times of bereavement and Alice had heard the gossip regarding Maggie still going out to work. She decided that the family would lie low over that weekend. Though she did insist that they went to church on Good Sunday, where they sat quiet and sombre for all to see. Alice and Maggie wore black veils over their faces, though Maggie privately thought it was carrying things a bit too far. She was beginning to get rather impatient, counting the months when this play acting could be laid to rest.

The following week, Miss Madeline announced that her nuptials were to be on the second Saturday of May. It couldn't be any earlier, because the church was tied up with Lent and there was also to be a celebration of the children's first communion.

At the dressmaker's shop, the needles had flown again, as Betty and Maggie worked on little plain white dresses and matching lacy veils. Betty had said it would do them good to watch Miss Madeline's wedding, though they'd keep their distance in the churchyard. She would find it satisfactory, listening to the comments of the watchers, regarding the unusual dress and the bride's ten foot train.

Maggie told her that she didn't really feel like going. In her black dress, pelisse and sober bonnet, she felt she looked like a crow. Madeline, on the other hand, would be looking blissful in her wedding dress of starched white tulle, over many petticoats and covered with a looped creamy crepe, flounced with pale green ribbons and peachy bows. A real eye catcher, not like the normal dress that local brides wore, of simple white satin and a demure floor-length veil.

Maggie was feeling really miserable with the life she was now leading. She and Alice had been rowing, because the lodger had asked for his bedroom back and Alice had said that it was his right to move back in, because Maggie was only paying money for her board. Then Mikey started crawling, sometimes hovering at the top of the steep stairs, uncertainly. She was so convinced that one day he was going to fall right down them, that she had demanded that Alice provide a gate. Alice only grumbled and asked her where Maggie thought she could get a gate from? It never was a problem when she was rearing her boys.

Maggie fired back angrily that it was because the dwellings at Killala never had stairs!

–

Maggie supposed that the happiness of the wedding might lift her spirits, so on a beautiful sunny afternoon, she and Betty found a place under some yew trees in the church yard and waited for the bridal vehicle to arrive. There must have been over fifty curious women waiting with them. The wedding of this outsider had been eagerly speculated upon, especially as this was the woman who fancied herself in a crinoline!

"I've got a secret to tell you," Betty whispered, as they both looked at the wedding guests, who were disappearing into the church. "The young lady is expecting. She told me when she came for her final fitting. Only because she knew I could tell. That's why she wanted so much material in her underskirts. It appears that her father wouldn't give his permission to marry, so she had to wait until she was twenty one. She was lucky that her birthday fell whilst she was only up to the five month period, or she would have given birth to an illegitimate child, and that wouldn't have gone down well with the church."

There was a hush amongst the chattering women, as the carriage carrying Madeline and her beau arrived outside the church. It was an open topped barouche, pulled by two matching, garlanded white horses, with the driver all dressed up in a black top hat and matching tails.

The crowd looked on in amazement, as the bride began to step down. Her dress was so enormous that the man and his driver took several minutes to get her onto the first step along the pathway and then had to set about fixing her very long train. Her face was totally covered, but she radiated such happiness and sparkle that Maggie found she had a lump in her throat. This was the kind of wedding she would have wanted, had she not been so callously forced. A dream of a wedding with a handsome beau, that was never going to happen in her life, she thought sadly.

She looked over to the man who was walking beside Madeline, though it was hard to concentrate on his appearance, because Betty was worrying to her, over the threat of rips and plucks to the enormous trailing train.

He looked familiar. He was all dressed up in a dark blue frock coat, over a white frilled, high-collared shirt, with which he wore a matching blue stock. His trousers were narrow and black and strapped under the instep of his fine shiny shoes.

It was his dark curly hair and suntanned face that came crashing back into her senses. It was Johnny, looking tall and lean and grinning happily with Madeline on his arm. As he passed the two women by, he looked unseeingly into the crowd and Maggie saw those wonderful cornflower blue eyes that she remembered from before. Vaguely, at the back of her mind, she thought of her old friend, Widow Dockerty. Would she have managed to make the journey, all this way to see her son get married? Probably not. Last time she had seen her, the lady was beginning to look quite old.

"I want ter go now, Betty," Maggie said, feeling despair wash over her. "I don't want to watch any more. I think I'm gettin' a headache, it could be the glare of the sun in me eyes."

"Oh, Maggie. What was I thinking of? Suggesting you came to watch the wedding when it's not long since you lost your Jack. This must be really upsetting for you! Come, we'll go back to the shop and have some refreshment and, on the way, I'll tell you where Mr Freeman, the builder, is up to with the renovation of Selwyn Lodge. This will cheer you up. He said that we can probably move in at the end of August. That is if the boiler he has ordered is fitted in the bathroom by then. I thought on Monday afternoon, we could finish our work early and go along to measure up."

Maggie couldn't understand why she was feeling so low in spirit. She lay in bed later, listening to the gentle breathing of Mikey, knowing that she was so lucky to have the care of her little son and the chance of living in a wonderful house in the near future. But, seeing Johnny again had unsettled her. It wasn't as if they had meant anything to each other. Rather, she could still flush up with annoyance against him, because of the uncaring way he had treated her that day. She supposed it was seeing him and Madeline walking up the church path together, making all the girlish dreams she had once had, vanish into thin air. Most girls had dreams of being whisked away by a knight in shining armour, riding a white horse, but her dreams had been of a handsome sea captain, who had swept her away on board his ship; who had taken her back to the small hamlet of Killala, to live with her mother and Molly again.

-

After they had locked up the shop on Monday afternoon, Betty and Maggie set off down Burton Road, to visit Selwyn Lodge. Betty was full of her plans for each room of the house, but Maggie only listened half-heartedly as they passed St. Wine-fred's. She gazed upon the doorway of the church and vainly daydreamed, that it had been her coming out on the arm of Johnny, though she would have worn a more simple dress for the marriage ceremony.

"They've gone on their honeymoon to Chester," Betty said, after she had noticed her inattention. "Madeline told me it was to a little hotel on the road out to Mold. What's bothering you, Maggie? Are you remembering when you got married to your husband? It is best to only think of the good times, I find."

"I can't remember many good times, Betty. Not after we were married anyway. Oh, I know I have Mikey, and I love every inch of him, but to see Madeline all dressed up, being wed to such a handsome man, made me see what I had missed out on. She really had the wedding of her dreams."

"What I have found in my life, Maggie, to ensure my daily sanity, is always be thankful for what the good Lord sees fit to give you. Be glad of the day and don't look for things that you may have had, or can't have. Now, when we get to the house, I'll let you choose your bedroom, but I hope it won't be the one that I have got my eye on!"

Maggie couldn't believe it when they stood in the hallway of Selwyn Lodge. To think that she would be going to live there soon. The hallway was as big as her old cabin in Killala, wooden floored, with a three-candled sconce hanging from the ceiling. The stairs leading up to the first floor were made of mahogany, as were the bannister and spindles.

The first room that she was shown, to the left of the hall, was the drawing room. It had a high ceiling, finished off with smooth white plaster and cornices, a crystal candled chandelier and a huge oriental rug. Its rich pattern, in blue and green, was edged with many cream fringes. The next room to see was the dining room. This had big wide doors that lead on to the place that Betty called the conservatory, or winter garden. It had been her father's favourite room, filled as it was with plants from India, Siam and South America, which he had brought back from some of his many voyages. Here in this little warm oasis, most of the plants had survived.

The conservatory looked on to a paved area, where Betty said they could sit in the summer months and have afternoon tea. Beyond was a lush, verdant lawn, with many yellow and pink roses and other pretty flowers in the beds that lined the garden. A pretty arbour, where honeysuckle fronds trailed all over, gave a focal point to an entranced gazer such as Maggie. From a fast flowing brook that ran through the garden on its way to the sea, came a constant source of water. It was because of this that they would be able to pump water into the house, as it came from a natural spring. The trees at the bottom of the property were there to hide a rather hideous feature, the colliery. Betty said it could be seen from the view out of the back bedroom windows. She advised her to avert her eyes, should she choose to sleep in one of those rooms. It wasn't pleasant to look upon the slag heaps and the winding wheel.

The kitchen was large and airy, with a flagged floor and plenty of space for working, eating and being warmed by the kitchen fire range. Here, in the past, someone had been busy making rag rugs, as there were two, a blue one and a red one, and neither worn thin.

The builder had knocked down the outside privy and built a small extension, which now housed a store room and a scullery.

"Do you want to see upstairs now, Maggie?" Betty asked, trying to keep in the excitement Maggie could see she was feeling. "We did have five bedrooms, but because of the new bathroom, now there are only four."

Maggie just nodded, she was still having difficulty taking it all in.

"What's in there, Betty?" she asked, as they began to climb the stairs to the upper rooms. There was another door that Betty hadn't opened, it was on the right of the hallway, as they had come in.

"It used to be the living room, but the couple who lived here never used it. They either sat in the kitchen, or in the dining room. It is rather damp, as it doesn't benefit from the sun. The drawing room, which we will use instead, has a side window, which lets in the light. I'll show you later. I'm thinking of having that room entirely re-plastered and the chimney swept in the future, but not yet, as there are plenty of rooms for just us three. Come, we'll have a look at the bedrooms now. One for you, one for Mikey, one for me and the other for whoever gains our employment, though I may leave it empty, just for the use of visitors, and we'll have two daily women coming in. There's an attic as well, which could be converted to another bedroom. At the moment it holds the family furniture, those that hold special memories for me."

The view from the bedroom that Maggie eventually chose was as wonderful as the one she had at Seagull Cottage. The room was large and airy and it was decided that Mikey would share it, as he was too little to sleep apart from his mother at that time. Betty had her old room, the one with the colliery view, but, as she said to Maggie later, it was possible because of poor coal production, that the place would be shut down soon.

"We'll have such fun, Maggie, choosing all our furnishings, and a trip to Chester in the next few weeks wouldn't come amiss," she said happily. "Maggie, whatever is the matter, dear?"

She had seen Maggie's face crumple. It was all too much for her. She was overawed with all she had seen and her emotions came flooding to the fore. Less than two years before, she had been a simple cottier girl. Her only thoughts were of keeping hearth and home together and the worry of where she was going to get their food. Now, here she was in that awe inspiring house and about to discuss fine and quality furnishing, when all she had ever been used to was a turf built cabin and a palliasse to sleep on.

"I'm sorry, Betty. 'Tis this place. To think I was just a simple Irish girl and now yer askin' me to live in a place so grand. I can't get over yer generosity. I'll do whatever yer ask ter make yer proud of me, but don't ask me to choose things fer the house. I can go to the hardware shop and get us a ladle, pots and pans and spoons, but that is me limitations. Why don't yer ask Miss Madeline to help yer? She's an eye fer this kind of thing I'm sure, with all her designs and sketchin'."

Betty was most concerned at her reaction, and most understanding.

"I'm sorry, Maggie. We've arrived at this moment from different directions. I wanted you here for company, never thinking about your feelings and the life you had before. Certainly all of this must be very daunting for you, coming from your background, as you have. I'm expecting more from you than I should, so we'll go now to each room and I'll make a list of what is needed. Then we'll lock the place up and go back to our respective homes. We've got a lot of sewing ahead of us, especially as soon it will be Ladies' Day!"

–

Ladies' Day again! Where had the last year gone to? It brought back memories of Annie to Maggie, and her fear of being sold to the gypsies, the rifle range where Jack and Michael had won two ornaments and the fortune teller's tent, with Alice and her reluctance to have their palms read. That happy day, when Jack was treated as the local hero and they had said that next year, they would dance together behind the Bowling Green. She had never had sight of Annie since and had only seen Ruthie once, haggling over the price of an article from Lily's barrow. Maggie preferred to push the pram along the smooth surface of the promenade, so didn't follow the coastal path where she used to walk before.

She was irritated beyond belief that her widowhood must continue. Alice had decided that the family could only be allowed to watch the Ladies' Day parade that year. Their relationship was becoming strained, because Mikey had begun to take his first steps and was climbing out of his cradle. Alice had refused to consider a barrier at the top of the stairs, as her lodgers would be inconvenienced, she feared. Maggie controlled her anger irritably, counting the weeks to be got through before Betty and she flitted, then Alice could take all her petty laws and whistle!

–

The crowd was as large as the year before, even though the sun was staying behind the clouds. Spirits were high and everyone was in holiday mode. When the women of the Ladies' Club passed by, she could pick out even more of the outfits she had made that year, especially on the daughter of a local alderman, who had decided to follow the very latest fashion, the hated crinoline. The skirt was a cerise pink colour in a zig zag patterned cloth, with a plainly cut cherry bodice, and she wore a dyed pink ostrich feather in her leghorn hat. Maggie had spent many hours on that stitching and winced when she remembered the creating of it all!

A movement by the Brown Horse Tavern caught her eye, not least because standing there was another follower of fashion. It was Madeline, and with her was a man that Maggie had never seen before. He looked much older than Madeline, at least by a good fifteen years. This must be the uncle that Betty had told her of. Johnny, her husband, must have gone back to sea. From where Maggie stood, she could see a family resemblance and wondered if this man was Ted, Johnny's brother. He was thickset, with dark, straight hair, and his features were similar to Johnny's, but not as handsome. She turned away, as a rush of jealousy threatened to engulf her. But why? What did it matter that Madeline was married to Johnny? Men were awkward and stubborn, could be threatening and dangerous when they couldn't get their own way.

Not all men, though. Michael was gentle and Seamus was a dote, and Maggie's father had always been kind to her, but Jack had not been everything that a wife could wish for.

Thinking of Jack seemed to have conjured a letter up from him, as a few days later, Alice came up to her bedroom, waving a missive in her hand.

"This has come from the America's, Maggie. Open it, quick. Must be somethin' about our Jack!"

Maggie's heart sank. It seemed there was going to be no getting away from him, and here she was, planning, to move out of his house in a month or so.

"It says it has been written on his behalf, by a scribe named Mr Reilly," Maggie said, looking at the strange writing closely.

> *Dear folks,*
>
> *We have settled in a place called Evanston, which is a small town outside Chicago. It was a very long journey from Newark. Chicago is on the shores of Lake Michigan and has a population around the size of Liverpool. We live in a room above a chandler, but hope to move soon nearer to the city. Lord Belsham came to visit and he has given me a small allowance to help him with his affairs. I know you do not think well of me, but you are often in my thoughts.*

Maggie paused and looked at Alice, who was beaming happily as she listened to the words.

"Is there an address? How did he finish it?"

"There's no address and he finished his letter by saying, 'From Jack, yer son.'"

"See, he's homesick. He'd rather be home with us. I can tell by his letter. If it wasn't fer that Kitty woman, he'd be home here with us. Still, this letter gives us hope that he might come back one day!"

"So, what will yer say if he does come back?" Maggie remarked dryly. "That it was all a mistake, that Jack wasn't buried? He's bin raised like Lazarus and to our bosom returned?"

"Yes, if I have to," Alice declared stoutly. "But he won't, will he? Because he knows you don't want him and he has to stay there anyway, to look after His Lordship's affairs."

Maggie got up quickly, busying herself with Mikey in an effort to keep her annoyance from Alice. This charade was going to blow up in their faces one day. She hoped to be gone and settled in her new life when it did!

Maggie had already chosen a length of material in pearly grey, in readiness for the day when she could throw off her mourning shackles. She was even toying with the idea of making herself a crinoline! The fashion was beginning to catch on, at least with the younger women of the community, and Betty was thinking of taking on an apprentice, someone who was willing to do all the straight stitching of the many layers and hems involved in the making of a crinoline.

"We could do with thinking more of our domestic requirements also, Maggie," she had said. "I'm not very good at cooking, I left that to my mother and, being a woman on her own, I have usually bought my needs from Ezra, or the bakery. You made a lovely plum pudding at Christmas time. Are you good at savouries and that sort of thing?"

"I'm the same as you, Betty. I can make a simple stew, make a roast, but that is all yer would get if yer left me to the cookin'. I leave Alice to it and the shopping, and the lodgers are always sayin' what a good cook she is. Perhaps we should ask her to move in with us?" she finished, mischievously.

"No, Maggie, I don't think so! We will ask Ezra first, if he could ask amongst his customers. Someone might be willing to give us a few hours each day. There's no point putting a note in his window, because a lot of people aren't able to read. We'll ask him to say that Selwyn Lodge is looking for a cleaning woman and a cook and to call in here for an interview. Then, we must think about a nursemaid for Mikey, for you won't have Alice on call when you move in with me. I was thinking that when he is a little older, we could make that front bedroom into a nursery. Though, it won't be until I've got rid of the damp in that room downstairs. There would be plenty of space for a little bed, wardrobe and a chest of drawers. There'll be room to play and a bed for the girl who would look after him. That is if she wanted to live in. Maybe, next time I'm in Chester, I'll look around for a Domestic Agency. They will come with references then. I don't want just anyone coming in."

Maggie's mind had quickly flown to Annie, when Betty brought up the subject of Mikey's nursemaid. It was true that once they had left Seagull Cottage, Betty would expect her to take on greater responsibilities, and with Mikey being at the age of exploration, he would have to have someone with him every minute of the day. She remembered that when she had seen her last, Annie had been complaining that her father had been looking to her to bring some money in. Maybe he had carried out his threat and sold her to the gypsies, or had married her off to someone locally. It was quite a while since Maggie had been to Thistledown Cottage and she wondered if she should visit again?

She mentioned Annie to Betty, saying that the girl seemed happy to look after her small siblings. She had seen her look after Katie and Lenny, who were part of Ruthie Tibbs' tribe.

"Do you mean the daughter of that man who stole the fighting purse from Jack?" Betty asked suspiciously. "The one whose mother is a great big loud mouth? Maggie, dear, you'd never get the woman away from our house. I was thinking of that young daughter of Farmer Briggs, I think Florrie is her name? She will be used to looking after her siblings also, because I think there were five of them, weren't there? Everyone was a girl!"

"Yes, but Annie is in more need of a job, Betty," Maggie stuck to her guns. "The family is very poor and there's only one farmhand's wage goin' in to it. Florrie will be wantin' something more than a nursemaid's job. She went to the local school and can read and write, by the sound of things. I think we should give Annie a chance, I think it is only fair. And Ruthie won't become a nuisance. Knowing her as I did, she'll be overawed by Selwyn Lodge and be frightened that if she comes without an invitation from you, you would call in the Law. Let me visit Betty and if I'm not happy with things, I'll say so. Mikey is me dear own son, so I wouldn't leave him with just anyone."

"Well, I give my permission with reservations. You can call on her tomorrow morning. Go by the coastal path on your way to work. But, let me say, if you decide to employ Annie, it will be on a month's trial. Now, come, let us plan our trip to Chester. Our removal date will soon be here and we haven't even thought on our furnishings."

Chapter 21

It was pleasant walking along the path that would take her to Thistledown Cottage. It was the third week of June and nature had done the area proud, with its profusion of red campion, sea rocket, strawberry clover and pink thrift. Bushes of bilberry flowers lined her way and rowan trees swayed in the playful breeze. Over in the farmer's field the cows munched on a breakfast of tender grass, followed by a dessert of vetch and daisies to complete their meal.

Passing the gate of the colliery and only giving the place a quick glance, because there were men in a group staring at her, she came to the thicket. That meant in a few minutes Ruthie's cottage would come into view.

She began to feel a little nervous, wondering now if she was on a fool's errand. Did she really want any of the Tibbs family in her life again? But the picture in her mind of the poor under privileged Annie came to the fore. Where would she herself have been, if Betty hadn't taken her under her wing?

Ruthie was standing in her garden, staring up at an ancient tree. She was shielding her eyes from the glare of the sun and shouting.

"If yer up there, get down now, 'cos I told yer to go to the shops fer me, an hour ago."

Whoever was on the receiving end of her attention seemed to be ignoring her, because no one scrambled down obediently, or answered her. Ruthie scowled and hit the tree with the spade she was holding.

"Tis no use pertendin' yer not there, 'cos I know yer is. I saw yer pissin' from the branches only a couple of minutes ago. I'm waitin', our Ernie, and if yer don't come down, there'll be no dinner, 'cos me legs are givin' me jip again. Oh, it's yoo," she said, when she saw Maggie standing at her fence patiently. "Look Ernie, here's Lady Muck come down ter see us. Where've yoo bin then all this time? Heard yer livin' in a fancy house on that posh road and bin took on by that Miss Rosemary."

"Hello, Ruthie, nice to see yer too. It's Annie, I've come ter see."

"Well, yer can't, she's not 'ere. Works fer one of them private schools on the front. Taken on as a skivvy. Why, wot do yer want with 'er?"

She walked up to the top of the path, then glared at Maggie, balefully. Maggie had to move back quickly, as the smell wafting from her old neighbour was enough to bring water to the eyes. She was no longer dressed in the workman's trousers and jacket that she had always worn before. Now she had on a long brown serge dress, gathered round her waist, and a big dirty white frilled blouse above it. On her feet were a pair of cracked, worn hobnail boots, with no laces in. Her hands were ingrained with dirt, her finger nails chewed right down. She had tied her long, brown, matted hair back with a piece of string.

Her eyes narrowed, as she heard Maggie's reason for the visit, then slapped her hand on her thigh.

"So yer want to make a lady out of our Annie, do yer? That's like wot they say, making a silk purse out of a sow's ear! Did yer 'ear that, our Ernie? She wants ter take our Annie and mek 'er into a flamin' nursemaid. S'pose she'd get a fancy uniform, a little frilly cap and a striped blue dress? I've seen 'em on the front, pushin' them prambulaters. Well, let me say this, since our Solly got 'auled up on account of that money goin' missin', no bugger wants ter know us. Yes, 'e kept 'is job, Farmer woz very good to us, but everyone else turned their nose up and that's why Annie is out scrubbin' fer a livin'."

She went back to bang the tree with the spade again and Maggie had chance to consider what she should further say.

"How's Lenny and yer other children, Ruthie? Wouldn't they benefit, if their sister had a pleasant job and was bringin' better money in?"

"How much is the old woman paying then? 'Cos if it's better than that swanky private school, then Solly'll say she must tek it. Would she be livin' 'ere or livin' in?"

"Well, in the beginnin', she will be comin' in daily, because Miss Rosemary has to refurbish one of the bedrooms, to make it into a nursery."

"Refurbish? What's that then, when it's at home?"

"It's when you make somethin' new, out of somethin' old, I think."

"Well, by crikey, yer can learn somethin' refurbish every day!"

Maggie walked away, after getting Ruthie to promise that she would send Annie up to the dressmaker's shop for an interview, as soon as she could. It was strange that Ruthie had not commented on her widow's dress, but Maggie was glad that she hadn't. The woman was more interested in getting her rascal son out of the tree. She learnt that Katie was fine, Lenny still the same, and Danny had started as a screen worker at the colliery, whatever that was supposed to be.

She peeped over the hedge of her old cottage on the way. It was just the same, but the lilac bush was in full bloom and someone had planted a bed of pretty flowers against the cottage wall. The place was quiet and she supposed that the new occupants would be out working. At least someone else had been given the chance of a job, with Jack moving out of the vicinity.

Did a small regret appear at leaving there, she wondered, as she waited for a twinge? No, she felt happy. Happy with the new life, that she felt she had made for herself. Lilac Cottage had been only part of it all, a stepping stone to all that was to come.

The dressmaker's shop was full, when she arrived. Betty seemed grateful for her timely appearance.

"Can you see to this young lady, Maggie?" she asked in a relieved voice. "She wants to look at that bolt of organdie, the one in the corner, next to the green tarlatan. Come in here with me, Mrs Williams, I use the kitchen as my office now. I won't be a minute Mrs Brookes. Your dress is ready, but I have to adjust the tapes."

She came back a few minutes later, saying goodbye to her customer and turning her attention to the next client, who was waiting patiently. Ten minutes later they were sitting alone in the kitchen, with Betty giving her an up to date account of who had been in.

"That was Mrs Williams, one of your loan customers, Maggie. I've been wondering what to do about your little enterprise when we move to Selwyn Lodge. I am a bit worried at having so much money on the premises at any one time and, once we move in, I don't really want to be carrying cash up and down Burton Road. Perhaps we should consider a bank account for the Sheldon Loan Company? Put it on a proper footing. Though, then you will to have to sign any papers and I am a bit worried that the bank will think you rather young to have a business in your name."

"How much are we talkin' about, Betty?" Maggie asked eagerly, as it had been a while since she mentioned the money lending business and Maggie had felt it rude to ask. "The last time yer told me it was around thirty odd pounds, are we talking so much more since then?"

"A lot more, Maggie. It was seventy-one pounds and one shilling at the weekend, when I checked the contents of the tin. Word has got round so quickly. Of course, it was Ezra who started it, you know how he likes to gossip, and now the wives have accepted it, as part of their weekly life."

Maggie took in a deep breath and whistled. Such riches, but she dared not spend a penny of it. She would have had Constable Higgins on her trail, making out she'd stolen it from somewhere. An immigrant girl from Ireland, in his mind, could only be a thief.

"I wonder whether we should convert the upstairs room into a sort of office?" Betty continued briskly. "Put a sign up saying, 'Sheldon Loan Company' and employ a man to run it. I was thinking of offering vouchers. For example, we could give out something that can be cashed in at a big department store. The customer can get goods for, say, ten pounds. I don't know what, maybe a piece of furniture, table and chairs, a sofa, a bed, anything. Or maybe, if they wanted an outfit to go to a wedding or a funeral, they could take the voucher to a tailor and come here to us with the loan repayment and pay some of the interest. They could be called 'Bounty Vouchers' and you could charge a little more than you are charging now. For instance," Betty continued eagerly, "say I want a chiffonier for my front room. It will cost me seventeen pounds. I take this voucher to Frogerty's Furnishings in Chester, and they send a bill to you for seventeen pounds. The customer comes here and starts the repayment, plus the interest at ten per cent. You will make them sign a legal undertaking just as before, but this time, if we are talking about a larger amount of money, there would be something in the contract that mentions prosecution if the payment falls into arrears. Prosecution is a nicer word than big burly men, knocking at their door."

"Can we do all that, Betty?" Maggie asked, amazed, at the way Betty, only a woman in the scheme of things, could let her mind work. "It sounds as if it's a bigger thing than we could cope with, these vouchers. Shall we not just carry on with the company? All this talk of legal things frightens me, and can we really afford to pay a man to run an office?"

"Let me think about it for a few days, Maggie. Maybe I should discuss it with my solicitor, especially regarding a legal agreement. Perhaps a retired man, who has been used to working with figures, would give us a few hours a week. Just to cover the times when we're busy, because I still have to go each week to collect my rents. Of course a man would be ideal to do that for me as well!"

"I went to Ruthie's place earlier, Annie wasn't in," Maggie said, dazed by all Betty's plans, so deciding to talk about something she knew. "She's workin' at a school on the promenade, scrubbin', poor girl. I suppose that's all she can get, with Solly being put in the lock up like he was."

"And what did Ruthie say, because I'm not very happy with your suggestion regarding Annie coming to live with us. I cannot see that family staying away from our door, no matter what is promised by them."

"I know, I forgot how Ruthie is a law unto herself. She'd say she was checkin' up on the girl, but probably she'd have only come to make mischief."

"Well, we really could do with someone to do the straight sewing. Do you think Annie would be capable, if we showed her what to do? Is she a bright sort of child, do you think?"

"Oh she's sharp as a tack, but I really do want a nursemaid fer Mikey, and Annie is used to lookin' after her younger brothers and sister."

"But we could do with a young girl here to help us now," Betty said stubbornly, "and I am sure that Alice would be happy to continue to look after her grandson until we move into Selwyn Lodge. It would be no hardship for you to deliver him to her daily then, if we didn't employ a nursemaid. Have you mentioned that you are moving yet, my dear?"

"No, I'm frightened it will cause a row and I'll be landin' here on yer doorstep with me bags packed. I'm waitin' fer you to give me a date and then I'll tackle her. I was just thinkin' then of havin' a word with Mr Arlington. He's one of the lodgers and might know of someone from the estate office, who could give a hand runnin' the loan company. Maybe someone who's older and thinkin' of retirin'. I'm a bit worried though of how to go about it, 'cos Alice would be suspicious if I tried to take him aside."

"You can say that you are speaking to him on my behalf. We really do need a man to be our representative, especially as I've had another thought about combining my interests with yours. We could call it the Sheldon Loan and Property Company."

"Oh and how would that work, Betty?"

"Well, I think we may have problems opening a business bank account for the Sheldon Loan Company, because of your youth. If we merged both of the businesses together, we could have it in both our names. We pay all the money earned into one account, but we can both draw on it. We will need it for household expenses and you could pay Alice for looking after Mikey. We'd need to pay our representative, and any incidentals that we think of could come from there. Meantime the larger bills, for example, our employee wages, both our salaries and any major refurbishment of the house, can come from the dressmaker account. And I do really think we should have a man to set up our voucher system. It would seem so much more professional, and eventually could become a bigger concern than here!"

"Whew! It all sounds very complicated, Betty. I can't really get me head round it all, as yer takin' me breath away. But I trust yer with everything, yer know that. Because if it wasn't fer you, I wouldn't be sittin' here listenin'. I'd probably be like poor Annie, scrubbin' fer me money, or somethin' equally as unpleasant."

"Oh, Maggie, you don't have to keep saying that. My life took on a new meaning when you walked through my door. Yes, I could have started these projects on my own, but I needed someone to share it all with. As soon as I saw you, there was something about you, call it an affinity, that made me think we would get on well with one another. And we do, don't we?"

Maggie just nodded. She was too overwhelmed to speak.

She walked down the hill to Seagull Cottage later, her head buzzing with all that Betty had to say. An affinity? She wished Betty wouldn't use such big words. It was true, they got on very well with one another, but Betty, like Alice, was always in the driving seat. Ah well, decision making probably came with being older. She wasn't always going to be nearly eighteen and she really was going to have the world at her feet.

She looked along to the Middle Slip, where three women were coming up from the shore, sitting on their basket laden donkeys. At least she didn't have to break her back, gathering cockles when the tide was out.

Alice greeted her at the door, with a wobbly Mikey clinging to her hand.

"Look, Mama, I can walk," said Alice in a squeaky baby voice. "I've been practising with Grand-mama every day!"

Mikey smiled proudly at her and lifted his arms for a 'carry up'. Just seeing him looking at her so confidently brought a tear to her eye and a lump to her throat.

"So, how's me little man then, have yer bin good fer yer granny?" she said, using the term 'granny' because she knew it irritated Alice.

"Grand-mama, if yer don't mind, and yes, he's bin very good. He's a little treasure, aren't yer, son?"

She should have seen the signs then, Alice was binding her child to her tightly, but what options did Maggie have? The dressmaker's shop was no place for an inquisitive toddler, with needles and scissors and other sharp things. Besides, she needed to go to work to earn the money to keep her and Mikey. Betty had, when asked, given her a weekly allowance of ten shillings.

"Is Mr Arlington home yet, Alice?"

"Yes, he's sittin' in the parlour with a cup of tea, before I call him in with the others for their meal. Why, what do yer want him for? Oh, and I've somethin' to tell yer later, so after you've put Mikey to bed, come back down ter me."

Maggie carried Mikey into the parlour and sat with him, making them both comfortable in one of the high back chairs opposite to where Mr Arlington sat. He was reading the local broadsheet. He had taken off the jacket from his business suit and was sitting with his waistcoat unbuttoned, over his wing-collared shirt.

"Good evening, Maggie. Have you had a pleasant day?" he inquired, over the top of the newspaper.

"Yes, thank you, very pleasant. Mr Arlington, may I ask yer somethin' regarding a business aspect?"

"Business? Business?" he answered pompously. "What has business got to do with a young girl like you?"

"Miss Rosemary asked me…"

"Ah, Miss Rosemary, the dressmaker. Doing what women are good at. Dressmaking and cooking." He nodded wisely. "Business is best left to gentlemen."

Maggie could feel the anger coming before her eyes in a red mist after he had said that which was something she had not experienced in a very long time. But she managed to blurt out, "Well she wants ter see ye," before walking out with Mikey and her nose up in the air.

She had simmered down somewhat by the time she came downstairs later to the kitchen. She had avoided Mr Arlington's eyes when she had helped Alice serve up the lodger's meals. What a stuffed shirt he had turned out to be. Usually so polite and courteous, it must have been the mention of business, that had turned him into a prejudiced pig.

She knew that word 'prejudiced'. Betty had used it quite often, when she said that men were against women in business. It seemed that men liked their women at home, cooking meals, keeping their house clean and making a baby every year. It was the man's place to bring the money home and dole out the housekeeping to their wives. The housekeeping and the baby bit, Maggie remembered very well.

—

It was Seamus's turn to be in the dog house. He had announced that he and Danny had been over to Liverpool and had signed on with the White Star Line. They were leaving home the following weekend, to stay in the company's hostel, while they were shown the ropes, as it were. The pair would be given indentures, which would guarantee them work for the next three years.

Of course, Alice had been warned. Maggie remembered that fateful day, the 21st February, when Jack had sailed on the clipper ship. Seamus had said then he had wanted to be a cabin boy, but Alice had wrangled, shed a few tears, made the lad feel guilty for leaving, and he'd said that he would stay home after all.

"I've no one left, now," she sobbed dramatically, as Michael put a comforting arm around her shoulders and Maggie stared unsympathetically at the ticking clock on the wall. Perhaps Alice was beginning to understand the way that Maggie had felt, when she had been taken away from Molly. At least Alice still had the gentle support of her husband. Her own husband was a thousand miles away!

Suddenly Alice changed her tack, dried her tears and told Seamus brightly, "We'll come with ye, won't we, Michael? We'll take a packed lunch and make a day of it. I'd like to look around this hostel you and Danny will be stayin' in. I'll have to make sure it's what you're used to and that your bedroom is warm and clean."

"Leave it, Mother," warned Michael, seeing the horrified look on his son's face. Maggie had to look away to stop them from seeing her smiling, Alice had only been bluffing, to see what the lad would say.

–

"Well, my dear, you sent me a diamond of a man," said Betty, as Maggie arrived at the shop the next day.

"How do yer mean? Has Mr Arlington already bin in ter see ye? Did he know of someone who was about to retire?"

"No, Maggie," she exclaimed excitedly. "It is Mr Arlington who is going to work for us! He told me that his job with the estate management is far from secure, especially now the owner is selling off his leases and property. I told him that the job would only be from nine in the morning until one o'clock, but he said that would suit him fine, until he has built up the voucher business. He was very impressed with the whole idea and has even suggested that my tenants come here with their rents, although I have to admit I do like to go and have my little chats with them. Then, he said he knew of a sign writer in Birkenhead who will make a placard for the upstairs window and who will also be able to print the vouchers for us. Even the small amount of remuneration and expenses I offered him was acceptable, although I did say he would be paid more, if the bounty vouchers begin to succeed."

"Oh," Maggie said, dispiritedly. "When does all this begin?"

"The first Monday in August, because he has to give a month's notice to the estate office. Maggie!" she said in an exasperated voice. "Aren't you pleased?"

Maggie explained how Mr Arlington had treated her the evening before and that she was worried that any of their business concerns would get back to Alice. Especially if Mr Arlington found out who owned the company.

"I think it could be difficult fer me to work and live with him."

"Of course it won't be. He will be here in the mornings and you will be here in the afternoons and when eventually we receive a company cheque book, only I will be able to sign it anyway. But in any case, the cheque book will only have the company name on it, not our names."

"Oh," Maggie said again, and for the first time felt piqued, illogically, as if she was being pushed out of something. She could not put her finger on it, but it felt uncomfortable somehow in her mind. She had the biggest investment in the Sheldon Loan Company, but she wouldn't even be signing her name!

She boldly said as much to Betty, and in those next few minutes, Maggie found out what a hardheaded businesswoman, the dressmaker could be. Miss Rosemary stood back and regarded her coldly.

"You think that in some way I am trying to dupe you? Well let me tell you this, Maggie, you can take your seventy-one pounds, one shilling investment and see how far it gets you. Buy yourself a little house in the village and work somewhere else if you wish. Money makes money and, remember it was my idea in the first place to start the loan company. Left to you, your money would have sat in that feather mattress you told me about, probably found by your husband and spent inconsequently. My way was to use your money and make more and it has. My voucher idea will bring in untold wealth to you eventually and I mean to you. When we go to Chester next week I was intending to arrange for the business papers to be drawn up in both our names, so at the time of my demise, everything will come to you. The reason there was only going to be one name on the cheque book, is because I presumed, rightly or wrongly, that as you are under the age of twenty-one, you will not be allowed to sign as well. No, let me finish..." She held a trembling hand up, as Maggie had gone red with embarrassment at Betty's tirade and was trying to apologize. "Maggie, you are either very stupid or I have not explained myself properly, but please never think that I am dishonest. Remember that all this was done in the first place, just to help you out!"

"I'm so sorry, Betty, I don't know what ter say ter yer." Maggie stood there very flushed and unable to meet the dress-maker's eyes. "In me defence, all I can say is that, yes, I am very stupid, but I also don't understand yer very well at times. You use words that I've never even heard before and yer seem ter expect me to know exactly what yer talkin' about. Mr Arlington frightens me with his manner and I'm not sure that I'll be able to deal with him. Betty, can I throw meself on yer mercy and ask fer forgiveness for doubting yer? You've done right by me from the start and I'm very grateful. Yer don't know how much I owe to you."

"Maggie, you don't have to humble yourself to me," she said, back to being Betty, her gentle friend again. "Just understand that everything has been done in your best interests. Yes, I found Mr Arlington patronizing, to say the least, but he is a gentleman and I know we need someone like him to make our company the success it is going to be. If he is pompous, or tries to belittle you once he starts working upstairs, tell yourself it doesn't matter. Because you know something that he doesn't know. That his employer is really you!"

That evening, Mr Arlington was his usual polite self, but made no mention at the table of his visit to Miss Rosemary. Though that was probably because Alice had banned all talk regarding business at meal times. Alice's motto to her lodgers was, 'never take your personal problems with you to your place of business and never bring your business problems home.'

Around eight o'clock Alice asked Maggie to take a tray of tea into the parlour. Mr Arlington and Mr Peel were at home that evening, both being avid tea-totallers, whereas Mr Dickinson liked to have a drink at the Ship.

As she pushed open the door of the front room with her foot, she could hear Mr Arlington telling his companion about the new job he was about to begin. He had quite a loud boom of a voice, which matched his heavy build and serious looking face, though at that moment he was looking delighted at the recent turn of events.

"She needs someone like me there, Mr Peel," he was boasting, to the smallish, sandy haired young man, who was hanging on his every word. "Put the tray down there, Maggie, if you would. I was just saying to Mr Peel here, of the good fortune you put my way."

She looked at him in astonishment. Was he about to discuss the affairs of the Sheldon Loan Company with her? Suddenly she pricked up her ears!

"You can leave us now, Maggie, this is men's talk. Something you women know nothing at all about, but I would like to say thank you to you anyway."

He made a dismissive gesture with his left hand, never taking his eyes off the other lodger. Being the polite young woman he expected her to be, she nodded and backed away.

Maggie felt a rush of jealousy and miff towards him, as she closed the door behind her quietly. How dare he treat her in this uppity manner? He had only just been offered the job, now she wished she had the power to take it away. How was she going to put up with this self-important boar of a man, who was going to be in her daily working life, as well as the place that she still called home!

She had left the parlour door ajar slightly and hovered around in the hallway, pretending to be smoothing down the covers in the pram.

"Of course, with my contacts at the estate office, I will be able to develop the property side of the business." She pushed the pram a little forward. This was interesting to hear. "We will be able to pick up the leases cheap and buy some of the smaller houses outright. Miss Rosemary tells me that she has three properties already, which she rents out, and she owns a large dwelling on the Burton Road as well. You may have seen it. Selwyn Lodge, rather an impressive building, I thought. She intends to move in there in a couple of months, leaving the accommodation free for my office above the dressmaker's shop. She'll be sitting on a little gold mine, once she has the right person to guide her. And of course that person will be me. You know, Mr Peel, with my expertise and my development of these bounty vouchers, the concern will grow so quickly there might even be a position for you."

"My dear Mr Arlington, if only that could be true. And these bounty vouchers, what are they? How are they going to work?"

Maggie had to move away quickly then, as she could hear Alice walking to the kitchen door. So, Mr Arlington had big plans for her little company? She didn't know whether to jump for joy, or to sit herself down and cry.

Chapter 22

Maggie tried to voice her concerns, as she and Betty waited for the stagecoach to take them on their trip to Chester the following Monday. Alice had agreed to have Mikey for the whole day, though she couldn't understand why a woman of Miss Rosemary's importance should want to take Maggie. Surely the dressmaker would have business affairs to attend to and she would be in the way?

"Well, my dear, you should be pleased that we have found such a gem to help us with our business," Betty said, when she had been told what Maggie had overheard. "You say he has plans to develop the property side? That is wonderful! What is the matter with you today?"

Betty peered at the girl, as she stood beside her, because Maggie was frowning and looking close to tears.

"Oh, for heavens sake. I'm not going to put up with you in this mood all day. Cheer up or I am going to leave you behind."

Her waspish words, said in aggravation, caught the attention of the little queue that had formed behind them. Curious faces looked at the dressmaker and her assistant and the two women nearest pricked up their ears.

"I'm sorry, Miss Rosemary, I'm not feelin' very well."

She made sure her voice was loud enough for all of them to hear her words, then she began to talk in a whisper, so no one else could hear.

"It's that Mr Arlington. It's his manner. He's goin' to take over everything. You'd think he owned the business, the way he was talkin' te Mr Peel. Even said he could have a job himself, if the company got big enough. It just, well, annoys me!"

"Maggie," replied Betty, her voice pitched high enough for only Maggie to hear. "You are suffering from what they call frustration. I have had it often over the years. You know that, should we put our minds to it, we could equally do the job as well as Mr Arlington, but as I have told you, we live in a man's world and he is the man who can open all the doors. Imagine if you went to a large department store in Liverpool and put the plan of accepting bounty vouchers from their poorer customers. They would not even discuss it with you. You would be shown the door. I have had big problems in the past being taken seriously, especially when I wanted to buy a row of cottages. I had to rely on the bank's agent to complete the sale. Now, let's see a smile on your face and let us look forward to our day out together, and when we sit in the coach, just talk about day to day things, or everyone around will know of our business."

The black and yellow painted stagecoach arrived outside the Brown Horse and a scarlet coated guard got off his perch.

"Coach fer Chester, coach fer Chester. Four travelling inside, twelve on the top!"

He walked over to where Betty and Maggie stood, looked them both up and down and said, "Inside fer you, Madam, and on top fer yer servant? This way."

There seemed to be a collective intake of breath behind them, as everyone waited to hear what Miss Rosemary would say. But she smiled sweetly at him and said, "My companion is travelling inside the coach with me. Would you be so kind as to assist us both, young man?"

So, now everyone knew that Maggie Haines, the Irish immigrant widow girl, was the dressmaker's companion. That would be an interesting piece of gossip for everyone to tell!

They were helped into the shiny black and yellow painted road coach, along with two middle aged women, then a wooden folding ladder was erected, so that the roof top passengers could climb aboard. Whistling cheerfully, the guard began to collect the money for their passage. Two shillings for the comfort of travelling inside and one and sixpence, for an outside return.

He offered to take Miss Rosemary's valise and strap it into one of the luggage nets, provided between the roof seats. Of course, she declined. In it was a large amount of money, as she hadn't visited the bank in Chester for a while.

Maggie sat back and surveyed her travelling companions, as they settled down and waited for the coach to start. She was startled when a horn was blown by the guard, to say that the journey had begun. It then hit her that she had never travelled in a passenger coach before. Here she was, riding in style, instead of walking, and sitting by the side of an elegant, gracious lady too. Betty had dressed very carefully in a smart outfit of cream and lavender, and a matching poke bonnet, with lavender ribbons under her chin.

The women who sat opposite were not known to either Maggie or Betty. The fact that they were not patrons of Miss Rosemary's establishment was plain for them both to see. They looked like little brown sparrows, dowdily dressed in nondescript outfits, black laced boots, and with plain straw bonnets upon their heads. They only spoke to say good morning and to remark on the weather, which had turned out fine.

The coach circled Neston Cross, then began to climb the incline up Liverpool Road. Maggie looked out upon the passing view, tracts of farmland, arable and grazing, a little thatched cottage or a farmhouse, at occasional intervals along the rutted road.

The two grey horses strained and pulled, snorted and puffed, as the driver used his whip in an effort to get them to pull the carriage and its full load of passengers up the steep hill. With the track being dry and dusty, it was a daunting task and the horses must have been deeply thankful to arrive on the flat of the Chester High Road, a track well worn by the passage of time, as it was the main highway that bounded the small villages of Thurstaston, Heswall and Gayton nearby. Betty said it would be about an hour to their destination, as it was only fifteen miles away.

Maggie sat back in her seat and took the time to daydream, mostly about all of the things that Betty had said they were going to do that day. She had told Maggie that the city of Chester had been built by the Romans and, when the girl had looked at her blankly, she explained that there had been a Roman empire far away, over a thousand years ago. They were conquerors, who liked to leave their own land and set up cities far and wide. There were many such cities in England, but Chester still had the walls round it that the Romans had built to keep the marauding Welsh and Saxons out.

The main street names all had 'gate' on the end. Northgate, Eastgate, Westgate, Southgate because that was where the soldiers stood, to let people come in or out. Maggie had been fascinated at the story and couldn't wait to see the place, especially as the River Dee, the estuary that she could see from her window at Seagull Cottage, also flowed around the city of Chester. Such a lot to do, such a lot to see, Maggie wondered if there would be time, because the return coach was to leave at four. There was the bank to visit, the solicitor, the fabric house and furniture shop, and that was beside the sight seeing that they had planned to do. Betty had said that if they ran out of time, they could always come again, perhaps on a Wednesday or a Saturday next time, as that was when the market was held and country people came in to sell their wares.

Before too long, the coach had arrived in Chester, where Maggie looked at the black and white half timbered structures on the very old buildings with interest. Betty told her that the city's streets were soon to be lit by something called gas light.

The coach stopped outside the imposing cathedral, built on the site of a medieval abbey called St. Werburgh's, Betty said. The guard climbed down from the roof top and helped the women get down, telling them that they must be back by four o'clock, as the coach wouldn't hang about past then.

They walked for a few minutes, until they came to the Chester Bank, situated on Watergate Row. Betty told Maggie to let her do the talking when they met Mr. Hughes, the manager. He was very important and he only dealt with Miss Rosemary because she had a thriving bank account. Maggie wished then that she wasn't still wearing her dowdy widow's weeds. She should have gone to the shop before they started and put on the grand pearly grey dress that she had been working on.

Her heart began to beat fast and furiously as they entered the portals of that grandiose place, with its marble floors and wooden beams and clerks sitting behind a brown wooden counter in official black suits.

"Miss Rosemary." The grand personage himself came over to greet them, bearing down upon them like a strong dray horse that Maggie had seen in the street. "Good morning to you, dear lady, and what a pleasant morning it is for seeing the sight of you. Richards, come and take Miss Rosemary's valise from her. It looks too heavy for a lady to be carrying. You look as if you could be carried off in a puff of wind! Ah, this will be the friend that you were telling me about on your last visit? Mrs Haines, I seem to remember? Welcome, Madam. Now do come along with me to my office, ladies. Richards, bring the bag in here, then bring in three cups of tea."

They were taken to a side room, where the manager sat them down on comfortable straight back chairs. When Richards, his clerk, arrived with the tea, he was told to count the contents of the valise in an outer office and bring the receipt back in.

"So, ladies, how can I help you this fine and lovely morning?" Mr. Hughes boomed. "Was your journey an agreeable one? Did the coach arrive on time?"

He sat back at his desk, pleasantries over with, listening attentively while Betty told him of her plans for the enlargement of the Sheldon Loan Company. Soon to be known as the Sheldon Loan and Property Company. During this time,

Maggie just sat back and watched the proceedings, studying the manager's florid face, his bushy ginger side burns, his fair wavy hair and his long tapered fingers, with no dirt under the nails. She also noted the silver ink wells and leather bound blotting paper pad that were sitting in magnificent opulence on his grand mahogany desk.

"Does Mrs Haines understand that though she will be partner in the new company, she will not be a signatory, until she is twenty-one?"

Ooops, they were talking about Maggie, but had she been listening to anything they'd said? Betty tutted in annoyance and scolded, "Maggie, this is no time for you to be daydreaming, did you not hear what Mr Hughes said about being a signatory?"

"I'm sorry, yes, I know you told me that this may happen, but I will still get ter be asked about things, won't I? Yer wouldn't go ahead and do things without asking me?"

Maggie certainly didn't have a head for business at that time.

"Of course I wouldn't, Maggie", Betty replied sharply, sending her eyebrows skyward, as if to say to Mr Hughes that this is what their partnership was all about!

"Then, if Mrs Haines and yourself, good lady, are in agreement, I will have an account opened in the name of the Sheldon Loan and Property Company. Proprietors Miss Anne Rosemary and Mrs Margaret Haines."

"I think in this case I should be signing my real name, Mr Hughes. As you know it is Miss Elizabeth Brown. There will be new documents to be signed at the solicitor's and Anne Rosemary is only my trading name."

Maggie looked in surprise at Betty and paid attention. She had known her all that time and thought her name to be Elizabeth Rosemary, Betty for short. Perhaps this was going to be a day of learning many things!

"Then next time you visit our premises, a cheque book will be waiting for you," Mr Hughes was saying. "Ah, here is Richards with your deposit receipt and valise. May I wish you two ladies all the success in your new venture, and thank you for using the Chester Bank."

He saw them off the premises and Betty stood uncertainly for a moment, clutching the empty valise to her chest.

"I think we will visit the solicitor next, Maggie. If there are papers to be drawn up, we can get them done this morning and they might have them ready by the afternoon. Charming man, the bank manager, wasn't he? I have known him now for thirty odd years, when he came to the bank as a clerk at the start of his career."

Maggie didn't reply to that. He had scared her greatly with his pomposity.

They walked a little further on, until they came to a red stone building. On the ground floor there was a tailor, and within it was a set of stairs. They climbed to the first floor, where, barring their way, was a green painted half glass door. On the outside, etched in small gold letters were the words 'Hawkins and Harrison, Solicitors'.

A young clerk sat at a desk, writing in a large brown ledger. As the two women entered the room, he looked up from the ledger and asked how he could help them?

"Yes, my name is Miss Elizabeth Brown and this is Mrs Haines. Is it possible to see Mr Hawkins? He is my solicitor."

"I'll see if he's free." The young man disappeared through another doorway.

"Mr Hawkins will be free for the next fifteen minutes, Madam, if you would like to step this way."

Maggie was taken aback by this behaviour. At the bank they had been greeted at the door by someone of importance, not a boy of lowly rank!

They entered a room that hit Maggie straight away, as not being splendid or grandiose. The man who was standing to attention at his desk, was far from ebullient or smart!

"Good morning, Miss Brown, and who will this young lady be?" Mr Hawkins inquired. "Your niece or your god daughter, come to visit perhaps? I'm sorry, do sit down. I will get my clerk to bring you tea."

"Oh, please, don't bother on our behalf," Betty replied, Maggie thought a trifle nervously. "We know you are a busy man and can only spare us a little of your time. We'll get straight to the point. This lady is a friend of mine and recently she entrusted a great deal of money into my care. Rather than put it into my bank, I decided to invest it into setting up a small company. We have just been to the bank and opened a business account in the name of the Sheldon Loan and Property Company. We are the joint proprietors. Unfortunately for Mrs Haines, she is under the age of twenty-one and does not have a guardian. Her husband died recently. I understand that you would not be able to draw up a partnership agreement between us, because of my partner's age, but is there some other way we could draw up a legal document? One that states that if anything should happen to me in the next three years, Mrs Haines would be given her rightful share?"

Mr Hawkins frowned and seemed to be giving the problem all his concentration. He was a tall, thin man, with quite a long face, and he had black rimmed glasses perched on the end of his nose.

After a few moments of deliberation, he seemed to have an answer.

"I think we could draw up a sworn affidavit, Miss Brown, where you would swear on oath that if on your demise, Mrs Haines has not attained the age of twenty-one, she would be given her share."

"Excuse me," Maggie found her voice and this time she decided to put her two pennies worth in, as she didn't feel at all intimidated with this man and his surroundings at all. "How do yer mean, get me share?" She didn't like the sound of being 'given her rightful share', as Betty had put it. She continued, "The Sheldon Loan Company was set up with the money that I gave you, Betty. If the company was to do as well as you and

Mr Arlington say it will, what do yer mean, I'll get me share? Do yer mean I'll get me seventeen pounds back that I give yer, or whatever is in the bank at the time of your departin'? And who would get the rest, I'd like to know?"

Two pairs of eyes looked at her. Mr Hawkins looked astonished at her outburst, Betty looked rather annoyed.

"Maggie, I don't think we have spoken enough on this subject," she said. "Mr Hawkins, if you will forgive us, we will call back later, after we have decided what will be written in the affidavit. We will have an early lunch, do some shopping and be back about half past one, if that is acceptable to you, of course."

With that she put a hand under Maggie's arm and hustled her down the stairs, into the street outside.

"What's going on, Maggie?" she queried, in rather an irate voice, and when Maggie thought back to it later, she was entitled to be irate. "I thought all this was settled. Why didn't you say something in front of the bank manager if you were not happy from the start? Come, we'll go to the Blue Bell restaurant and discuss this over luncheon. I am very angry with you at this moment, that is all I am going to say."

They sat in very comfortable surroundings, with old oaken tables and spindle backed chairs, having ordered roast duck, new potatoes and vegetables, with a gooseberry syllabub for dessert.

When the small glasses of beer arrived that Betty had ordered, the discussion between them began. It all had to come out into the open, everything Maggie hoped for, or feared.

"Betty, yer know I'm grateful fer all yer do fer me, but what would happen if you did die before I'm twenty-one? What would happen to my part of the company? Yes, yer said, I'd get me share. I want ter know exactly of yer intention, before we go ahead with legal things." Maggie sounded apologetic, but after all her worries and misgivings, it needed to be said.

"Well, Maggie, I had intended to make you my heir, before all this mistrust from you started. I have no family, as you know, but I thought I would wait until you were twenty-one, before I made a will out in your favour. I am disappointed in you, to say the least, regarding your outspoken words in the solicitor's office. When will you learn, that I only have your best interests in my heart?"

"But, Betty, this is all words, not actions," Maggie persisted. "Don't yer see the position I am in? As yer say, I have no legal guardian. I am a widow at the age of seventeen. I own no property, have nothing of value. The only thing I have is a share in a company, that could be snatched off me at any time, 'cos I've nothing to prove that part of it is mine!"

Betty sat back in her chair. She seemed to be doing a lot of thinking after Maggie's outburst. Then she seemed to have an idea and, sitting forward again, she took her hand in her own.

"This is all about trust isn't it? And because you've had a few disappointments in your life, you are finding it hard to trust me? In your shoes, I would feel the same. Look, you are like the daughter I never had. I recognize in you the same spirit, the willingness to get on in life. Not to just sit back and let things happen. How would it be if we go back to Mr Hawkins and tell him that I want a will drawn up that says, on my demise, you will inherit everything? My dressmaker's shop, Selwyn Lodge, my share of the Sheldon Company and anything else I possess. There's no one else I would like to leave it to, no relatives lurking on a far off shore. Will that make you happy, Maggie? Will that put paid to your illogical fears?"

Of course, after that pronouncement, Maggie was flabbergasted! She couldn't believe her ears! But it seemed that Betty still hadn't understood her reasoning and again she tried to point it out.

"Betty, I think yer a wonderful lady, but yer don't have to go leavin' me everything in yer will. All I am after is a paper that says the Sheldon Loan Company belongs to me. Not the Sheldon Loan and Property Company and Selwyn Lodge, the share of the Sheldon Company and the dressmaker's shop. I want a piece of official paper with me name on it, that's all I'm askin' from you!"

"Oh, Maggie, what am I going to do with you? You're as stubborn as a mule, but I have to smile at your tenacity. Come, we'll eat this delicious dinner, then walk along to the fabric house."

Later, after choosing heavy velvet material and cream coloured linings for the curtains at Selwyn Lodge, and a few rolls of satin, muslin and serge for the dressmaker's shop, they wandered down to Frogerty's Furnishing with Betty's list.

It was a big list, because when Mr Freeman's assistant had cleared the attic at Selwyn Lodge of the furniture that had been put into store, some of the items were found to have wood worm. So, most of those lovely pieces had to go onto a bonfire, at Betty's instigation, though she couldn't stand and watch it as it burned.

"We'll start with the bedrooms, Mr Frogerty," Betty said, as the proprietor himself welcomed them and proceeded to note down their requirements. "We already have rugs down, Oriental and Turkish. My father went to many faraway places as a sea captain and brought them back with him. I have decided that I would like most of the furniture to be made from mahogany. So, three carved mahogany head boards, three bolsters and three feather mattresses, if you please. Oh, Maggie, perhaps Mikey would like a bed of his own now? He'll be growing too big, I'm sure, for his cradle. A smaller version too, if you have one, Mr Frogerty."

She went on to order occasional tables, a hall table, two sideboards, a writing desk, a curio cabinet, two blanket chests, a daybed, all plush in deep pink velvet, two bookcases, three chests of drawers, a dining room set of a table and eight chairs and several pink upholstered sitting chairs, to be distributed around where necessary. That just left a sofa and two fire side chairs to be ordered and a cheval mirror for each bedroom. Mr Frogerty was obsequious to the last. The order must have been worth hundreds of pounds to him.

"Of course we will deliver them free of charge, Miss Rosemary. In fact it will probably take three trips to Selwyn Lodge, but we will always be at your service, as you know. Now, just a small deposit on account if you don't mind and my driver will be there at nine o'clock sharp on the 29th."

That was the 29th July, as Betty wanted to make a start on furnishing the house, before Mr Arlington was to start his job, in the first week of August.

The choosing of the furniture had taken quite a lot of their time and they were late for the appointment with the solicitor at half past one. Maggie had still been turning over what had been said in the restaurant and she was determined she would get her way.

"Our apologies, Mr Hawkins," Betty said, breathlessly. "As you can see, we have come straight to you from another appointment. With the stagecoach coming to Neston only twice in the week, it is very difficult to do all one wants in the time allotted. We have had a discussion and the simple way is for me to make a will, isn't that so, Maggie?"

"Well, I would like ter tell yer it's a lovely idea and so I shall," she said stubbornly, "but I'm thinkin' a will could be torn up at any time. A little disagreement between us and off yer'll go and rip it up. Isn't that so, Mr Hawkins?"

"I have to say, Miss Brown, that Mrs Haines is right, and there's also nothing to stop you changing your will at a later date. The only way to safeguard her interest is a sworn affidavit which I took the liberty of drawing up while you were away."

"So you don't want my money, possessions and businesses when I die, Maggie?" Betty said, her voice sounding defeated.

"I've told yer, Betty, all I want is what belongs ter me. Now, let's please sign this affidavit thing and then we can be on our way."

-

They sat together companionably as the coach took them away from the city walls. They chewed on the fudge that Maggie had bought from a little sweet shop before their return journey and discussed the beauty of the cathedral, wishing there had been another hour to spare.

All animosity seemed to have gone, as Betty called herself a fool to have forgotten to order the oil lamps, to light up all the rooms. As they finished laughing at her forgetfulness, Betty nudged Maggie playfully and whispered in her ear.

"You're a plucky little devil, but I have to say I admire you. We should have a Latin motto put over our doorway at Selwyn Lodge, 'Never trust anyone, not even your best friend!'"

Chapter 23

The coach put them down at five o'clock at the Cross, where Betty and Maggie prepared to go their separate ways. Maggie was looking down the hill along the High Street, watching as Betty walked along, shouting back her farewell.

Maggie's eyes were drawn to the front of Anne Rosemary's, where she could see a little person all hunched up and sitting on the doorstep.

"Hold up, Betty, I'll come with yer," she shouted, as she recognized the figure, whom Betty was preparing to give a good talking to. "I think that is just the person I want to see."

By the time they had reached the doorstep, the little person had stood up to greet them. It was Annie. She looked as if she had been crying, because her dirty face was smudged, where she had wiped her tears away. She was still dressed in second hand clothing, a shapeless shift in a dark blue cotton and a ragged shawl that she was carrying over her arm. Her long brown hair was a mass of tangles and her feet were bare.

"I'm sorry, Maggie, that I couldn't come before," she explained timidly. "I only get Sunday morning off, when they give us time off to go to church. I sometimes slip away and visit me mam and little Lenny, if I get me work done early. Just fer an hour or so, but me hour is nearly up, 'cos I've bin waitin' here fer yer."

She turned an earnest face to Maggie, and in that moment, Maggie could see herself from two years before. It made her more determined that this tattered girl was to be given a chance. Be it nursemaid or apprentice sempstress. She looked at Betty, who exchanged a pitying glance. Of course, Betty's heart had softened too and gave in easily!

"Come in, the pair of you, and we'll have a cup of tea," she said, kindly. "Maggie put the kettle on, there might still be some biscuits in the tin. Now, Annie, have you ever done any sewing before? Do you know how to thread a needle? Because that is the job that I am offering, not the nursemaid position that Maggie spoke to your mother about."

"I thought we would give her the job of looking after Mikey, Miss Rosemary," Maggie interrupted, coming in from the kitchen, whilst waiting for the kettle to start boiling on the hob. She wondered whether to insist and get her own way, then thought better of it. Betty had put up with enough shenanigans from her today.

"Maggie, we are desperate for someone to help us with the flat seams and Annie has slim and nimble looking fingers. What's more, I'm sure her granny will have shown her the rudiments, before the poor lady died a couple of years ago. I remember your grand-mama, Annie. Wasn't your grandfather a blacksmith? He had his business on Bull Hill."

"Yes, they were me grandparents, only they died of the typhoid. But me granny used to say I would always have a skill in me fingers, though if you look at me fingers now, they're a terrible mess."

"I have some ointment that we can put on your hands, Annie," Betty said, as she glanced at the girl's raw looking hands. "We'll soon have them looking pretty again. Now, how much notice do you have to give the headmaster, because I don't want him up here, saying I'm stealing his staff?"

"I don't think the headmaster will care about a lowly skivvy, Miss Rosemary. It will be the housekeeper, Miss Pugh that will probably shout."

"Well, you see what you can do and just turn up when it suits you. The hours will be nine until five thirty and you will be paid one shilling per day. That is until you have become indispensable and then I will increase your wages. You will have Sunday off and every other Saturday, because Maggie, I think once we are settled in our new house, you must do your share here too. Luncheon will be provided, two smart dresses and a pretty mobcap. Maggie, you can measure Annie before she goes. Some of that black material in the corner would suit, and perhaps a white apron from that roll of cambric over there."

"Thank you, Betty," said Maggie, as Annie left the shop and began to hurtle up the road. "I knew yer weren't too happy about taking her on, so I'm really grateful."

"It's nothing, Maggie, I assure you. In fact, I've just realised something about Annie's grandma. She was a kitchen maid at Lorne Hall, when I worked for the gentry all those years ago!"

"Yer never talk about yer days workin' fer the gentry and I've never seen any of them ladyships comin' in here."

Betty laughed, then explained the hierarchy of the village. "There are no Ladyships any more, but we do have old families like the one that lives at Lorne Hall. I should imagine they still employ a sempstress, I can't see them being without one, can you? Then there is the minor gentry, people like the Millingtons and the Holt's, they have all made money in owning land or in industry. Then there's stuffed up folk like Alderman Cranwell. You remember, his daughter was in here a little while ago? Anyway, don't you think you should be running along home now, dear? Mikey will be missing you and Alice will be wondering where you are."

Maggie felt intrigued, as she set off for Seagull Cottage, thinking to herself that maybe there was something in Betty's past life she didn't want to share. She usually wasn't so quick to dismiss her and had coloured slightly when she mentioned the Cranwells, but she obviously didn't want to talk about happenings from thirty years ago.

"So, what time do yer call this?" was Alice's greeting, as she met Maggie in the hallway. "I've had absolute hell all day with that child of yours. I had to send Michael up to the chemist for more stuff to put on his gums and, left to you, I wouldn't have bin able to get a meal on. Thankfully, Michael took the poor little lamb fer a walk."

"I'm not much later than I usually am," Maggie protested, cut to the quick with the accusation. "Where is Mikey anyway?"

"His grandfather's sittin' with him upstairs in the bedroom, he seems to like someone nursin' him when he's in this state. I can't believe he's still suffering when he's nearly one. Both mine had more than four teeth through at his age. Must be takin' after your side of the family, I'll be bound. Well, now yer back from yer gallivantin', you can take over. Heaven knows what yer've bin up to in Chester all day."

"We went ter the fabric shop and then had a look around the city."

"Oh, so it was a sightseeing trip, when I've had to nurse your child all day."

"Well we…"

"Go and see to Mikey and take this chew stick with yer. I got our Seamus to go up to the field and cut a piece off the marsh mallow plant. It always helped mine when they were little. Oh, and Seamus is leavin' on Saturday mornin', so we'll have a special meal on Friday night, so make sure yer here."

"Make sure I'm here," Maggie muttered to herself as she walked up the stairs. "Where else would I be, you stupid woman? It's not as if I have a book full of appointments and I have to look ter see if I can fit it in."

She sat on the window seat later looking out over the estuary. Although it was gradually becoming dusk, she was still able to see quite far away. Mikey was asleep in his cradle, the two red spots that he had on his cheeks beginning to calm down. It was peaceful sitting there, gazing at the shore, where the seagulls were scavenging over pieces of rotting fish that the fishermen had left behind. She had fed Mikey with milk from one of the newfangled bottles, she had been forced to buy, against Alice's wishes naturally, as 'mother's milk was best'. But how could she work and be there to feed him as well? He was getting his teeth through, now though, so she was glad to have gone against the advice of her mother-in-law!

Maggie picked up the drawers that she was sewing for herself. When they were finished, she was going to hem a couple of blankets for her bed and for Mikey's. There was so much to think of in readiness for their move to Selwyn Lodge. Just for the two of them alone, there were cotton sheets to make, pillow shams, a quilt each, another nightdress and a smaller gown for Mikey to wear.

The curtains were to be made on the dressmaker's premises, but delivery of the material was not until the following week, so maybe Annie would make a start, as it was straight sewing. Poor Annie. She had looked so lost and uncared for. Her hands had looked red raw and her nails were all broken and chewed. Perhaps she would be able take the young girl under her wing, as Betty had done for her. She smiled as she thought of Annie as 'the young girl'. She was only three years older herself!

The next day, she called into Ezra's for a packet of tea. There wasn't much left in the dressmaker's tea caddy and it was an excuse to go and see him, as they hadn't spoken for quite some time.

His shop was empty for once and Ezra greeted her with a wide, happy smile. Maggie hadn't noticed before that he had such a fat belly. He usually had his apron on, but on seeing her, had taken it off and hung it on a handy nail. He wore his dark hair, slicked down, with a centre parting and he had let his sideburns grow thick and bushy. He was wearing a white collar-less shirt, with a waistcoat of very dark green.

"What can I get you, Maggie?" he asked, seeming very pleased to see her. "It's a few days now since I've seen you passing by."

"You've probably bin too busy, Ezra, though we were in Chester all yesterday. Miss Rosemary had a few things to do there."

"A beautiful city, Chester. The wife and I used to go there often. Our favourite place was sitting by the river and then going to a little cafe nearby for afternoon tea."

"We only saw the cathedral, regrettably. Miss Rosemary took me to the fabric house and then we went to Frogerty's to look at the furnishings."

"Ah yes, she said she was moving into Selwyn Lodge, all being well, at the beginning of September. In fact, she said that I was welcome to call on her at anytime and we must arrange a meal together, once she's moved in."

Maggie wondered then, if anything had been said about her own removal to Betty's house. What would Ezra think if he came calling and saw her and Mikey sitting there?

"You look a bit put out, Maggie. Didn't yer know that Miss Rosemary, my wife and I were friends for many years? Look, I know that you have been invited to live there as her companion, but she told me not to say anything, because your mother-in-law doesn't know. You'll have to tell her soon, Maggie. These things have a way of getting back to people, especially as Miss Rosemary is looking for staff for the place and she'll have to let them know who will be household members!"

"I didn't think of that. I just worry that Alice will throw me and Mikey out once she gets ter hear. Mr Dickinson, the lodger, is always waiting for me to do somethin' wrong, so me and Alice will fall out and he can have me bedroom. Though Seamus is leavin' on Saturday, so maybe she'll make us have his room. It's a lot smaller, but it still looks over the sea."

"You should tell her. Oh, and tell Miss Rosemary that I have a Miss Leason and a Mrs Kellett interested in working for her. Miss Leason has had experience working at a place over Gayton way and Mrs Kellett is applying for the cook's job." She nodded, as he turned to get the packet of tea she'd asked for.

"Maggie, before you go, can I just say. If you ever want to talk to someone about your bereavement... but of course you'll have Miss Rosemary to speak to."

Ezra had grown serious for a moment, where before he had looked full of the joys of spring.

He handed her the packet of tea with a smile and put his apron back on. A housewife had come into his shop and of course he wanted to look the part.

—

A few days later, Betty had got the staff she wanted. Joan Kellett was a widow with two grown up sons and Mary Leason had come home to her family for a rest, before she looked for another job. Both families were known to Betty, so she didn't ask for references.

It was decided that Maggie would meet Mary Leason on the doorstep of Selwyn Lodge at nine o'clock on the 29th. It would be their job to put the furniture into place when it arrived, light fires and do a little cleaning while they were there.

"I'd come along myself if I could," Betty said, "but Annie is to start next Thursday. Her little brother came to tell me before. I also want to start moving things from my living room upstairs. Mr Arlington won't be happy, if I've not made room for him up there."

There was still no mention of a nursemaid being looked for, to take care of Mikey, so Maggie assumed that Alice would be looking after him. Perhaps with Seamus leaving, she'd be happy to fuss over her little grandson.

—

Alice, of course, was in a miserable mood at the special dinner cooked for Seamus's departure. There were just the four of them, as Mr Arlington had said he would be late in, owing to business reasons. Mr Dickinson and Mr Peel had eaten earlier, the latter having gone to his room.

Alice had gone to a lot of trouble. With it being Friday, it was a day for eating fish at the household. Alice had been on the promenade early to see the man and his barrow, who went over to the Welsh side to catch salmon from the River Dee. There the fish sat in all its splendour, on a long china platter, after being slowly steamed in a large pan over the fire. For dessert she had made a rhubarb crumble, with a jug of fresh cream to pour over. There was silence as Alice picked at her food, although Seamus ate his with relish, before sitting back and saying with a grin, "I'll miss your dinners, Mam, I certainly will."

The wrong thing to say, Alice started to cry.

"Seamus," wailed his mother. "I'm goin' ter miss yer too. Whose goin' to look after yer like I do, when yer go away?"

"Oh, Mam, give over, will yer? I had to leave home one day. This is what me and Danny want ter do. Just think, I'll be home at least once every four weeks and I might get to see Jack when we get over to the Americas."

"I don't think so. The Americas are very big, or so I've heard, but if yer do see him, tell him his home is always waitin' here fer him. But, I don't know if 'is wife will be, 'cos I've heard she's movin' out pretty soon!"

Maggie's heart came up into her mouth! She gulped and took a breath to make herself steady. "How did yer find that out, Alice?" she asked, after taking a swig of water from her glass to settle her nerves. "It was meant ter be a secret, because I wasn't sure meself if it was goin' to happen."

"Mr Arlington told me. He said Miss Rosemary was removing from her premises, so that he could have her living room as his office upstairs. She said it had bin on the cards fer a while, this movin', 'cos she's had the builders in to renovate her house. When he said te her, surely she would be lonely in such a big place as Selwyn Lodge on her own, she said her companion was movin' in with her. I took a chance, Maggie, that it was you she was talkin' about. See, Michael, I said ter you it was probably Maggie, the way yer've wormed yer way in with 'er."

"That's not fair. I've never wormed me way in, as yer put it. She asked me one day if I would like to keep her company there and I thought with yer wantin' the space fer yer boarders, yer would be pleased to have the extra room. And yer will have now. My room and Seamus's room."

"Oh, no," Alice fired back. "Seamus's room will be kept exactly as it is for when he comes home on leave. It will be your room that will be given away and Mikey will come in with his grandfather and me."

"Oh, no, Alice, yer not keepin' Mikey. He's my child and we are goin' to get a nursemaid."

"Have yer got a nursemaid all lined up then, Maggie? There's bin no mention of it from Mr Arlington. He says there will be a daily maid and a cook there at Selwyn Lodge, no mention of a nursemaid to me."

"You can't do this to me, Alice. I can't just walk out and leave him with you. I'm his mother and Miss Rosemary made a promise of a nursemaid ter me."

"Maggie," said Michael, who had been listening to his wife and daughter-in-law wrangling. Seamus had got up and walked from the room, when he saw how the land lay. "Maggie, can I be the peacemaker here? Can't yer see that Alice is bereft, now that her youngest son is leavin' too. If Mikey moves out with you, she'll have no one. Perhaps you could keep him here, until proper arrangements have been made at Selwyn Lodge."

"I see what yer sayin', Michael, but I don't think there is anything anyone can do to stop me takin' him anyway. And she was moanin' only the other day, cos Mikey was teethin'."

"I can tell Jack," warned Alice bitterly. "He's his father, so he can stop yer legally."

"Get me a pen then. Do yer know his address? When yer do, let me know."

There was an uneasy stand off between the pair of them, until they went to St. Winefred's the following Sunday, when the priest preached a sermon about 'forgiving the minor irritations of family and friends'.

Their irritation with each other was resolved over the roast dinner, when Maggie decided that Mikey could stay with Alice, until a nursemaid could be found. Someone she was determined to find the very next day.

All much easier said than done. She said as much to Mary Leason, as they stood on the doorstep of Selwyn Lodge, waiting for the wagon to come with the first load of furniture.

The new maid was a slim, light haired woman in her late twenties. She had been persuaded to stay by Betty's inducement of higher wages than those of her previous employer's. That and the fact she could go home each night to be with her mother.

"I think Miss Rosemary will probably get round to finding me someone fer Mikey," Maggie confided, "but, I really wanted Annie to be the nursemaid. She's the girl who started as an apprentice sempstress yesterday, by the way."

"Things have a habit of turning out for the best, Maggie," Mary answered. "Look at me. I hated working away from home, especially now my dad is far from being well. I only got this job because my mother overheard Mr Williams say that Miss Rosemary was looking for a daily maid. I've not seen my mother run so fast down our lane, since our Albert was in danger of being bitten by a dog."

The wagonette duly arrived, driven by Bob, and his assistant, Harry. They left the two brown cart horses with their nose bags on, and brought in the first item of furniture, a mahogany writing desk, which they carried into the drawing room. Betty had given Maggie a diagram of every room and what she wanted in it, so within the first half hour the vehicle was unloaded and the men had set off to Chester again.

"While they're gone, I think we'll set to and light the fires in all the rooms," Maggie said. "I've brought a tinder box and

Miss Rosemary said there was plenty of kindling and logs in the storeroom. I think she must have got the gardener to chop some the last time he was here. By the time we've finished, the men should be back again. So, let's start in the kitchen, we could do with a cup of tea."

They worked together very well and by the final delivery of the furniture, they were quite satisfied. They even found time to sit on the paved area and chat, though Maggie made sure she wasn't too over familiar. Once she and Betty had moved in, Mary would be the servant and would have to take orders from her as well, or so she presumed. They watered the plants in the conservatory too, Mary being highly delighted with the indoor garden, as she had never seen a conservatory before.

They damped down all the fires before they left, including the one in the living room, though Betty was coming to over-look their handy work later, when the shop had been closed.

Back at the dressmaker's, Maggie spent a little time with Annie. The girl had been given a corner of the cutting out table to work on.

"Are yer enjoyin' yerself, Annie?" she asked. "I remember when I started here, I felt all fingers and thumbs."

"It's better than scrubbin' fer a livin', Maggie, and Miss Rosemary doesn't clat yer round the ear if yer make a mistake, like that one did up at the school. She's a good un'. She bought me a cream bun today to eat with me tea."

–

It was the 1st August, Maggie and Mikey's birthdays. The day started misty over the Welsh hills, but had cleared by the time Maggie had finished breakfast. No present had been sent by Jack from America, nor a message for Mikey, but had she really been expecting anything from him?

Alice fluttered about with little parcels. Mikey was given a stuffed toy, in the form of a little dog with a waggly tail. She had bought Maggie a light fringed shawl, pearl grey in colour, with red tassels. She couldn't help herself remarking that she was sure, once Maggie had left for Selwyn Lodge, that they probably wouldn't be seeing her wearing black again! How well Alice knew her, though she must have noticed her new pale blue outfit, waiting to be worn, on the wardrobe door.

In fact, Maggie had decided that she was going to wear the outfit that day. She had been invited to take afternoon tea with Betty, who was closing the shop at four o'clock, in her honour. Time to throw off drab colours and start thinking of blues and greens, or even a deep maroon material that she had seen. And she had decided to thumb her nose at everyone that day, just because it was her birthday. She would even wear her hair down and go hatless. Let's see what the gossips of Neston, would make of that!

Thinking it and doing it was an entirely different matter, so she compromised and pinned her hair up, though she didn't wear her bonnet and covered her new dress with her birthday shawl. For the sake of her young son, she had to nod to some convention. Getting a reputation as a hoyden wouldn't do for her future business, or do her son any good in the long run. And wasn't she glad, when she got to the Lodge, that she had changed her thinking? Because Ezra had been invited too and he wouldn't have approved of her appearance!

Mikey and Maggie stood in the doorway of Selwyn Lodge, while Betty fussed around, patting Mikey on the head and saying how clever he was to be walking at one year old.

"Come in, don't stand on ceremony. Remember, you'll be moving in here soon. Happy Birthday to the both of you. Wasn't that clever, timing Mikey's birthday, so you could share it forever. Come through, we have a visitor, Maggie. Our first one!"

They followed Betty through the dining room, then into the conservatory and there standing beside a tall potted palm was Ezra. Dressed in his best suit, his face full of smiles and two little presents on the table at his side.

Chapter 24

"What have you two been plotting?" Maggie asked, feeling that, since it was her birthday, she could be a little cheeky to these two good friends.

"Nothing, we just thought it would be pleasant if the three of us were together on your special day." This came from Betty, who had also brought two parcels and placed them at the side of Ezra's.

"May I say, Maggie, you are looking exceedingly well today, not that you don't always look your best. But a great improvement from when I first met you, nearly two years ago." Ezra took her hand and bowed over it.

Whew, they must have both been at the sherry, she thought.

"Can we go out into the garden, Betty?" she asked. "It looks lovely out there today and I'm sure Mikey would love to run around. He'll tire himself out and then I can put him in his pram and he can have a little sleep."

"Yes, but let him open his presents first," smiled Betty.

Both Betty and Ezra knelt down, to be on the same level as the wide eyed little boy. He ripped open the paper from the present excitedly, to find a solid silver rattle in one box and a wind up clown in the other. Ezra took the clown from him, wound the key and they watched it walk up and down.

Mikey was delighted, but then saw the open door of the conservatory. He tottered unsteadily through it, then proceeded to toddle round and round.

"Come Maggie, open your presents," Betty said. "I'll watch Mikey while you're opening them. I don't want him falling in the stream."

Betty had bought her a dressing table set in heavy cut glass. It had a jewellery tray and a matching kidney shaped bowel. They must have been in collusion, because Ezra had bought her a small vase to match and produced a little bunch of pretty flowers to go in it. She couldn't thank them both enough. She would keep them forever, she said. The sherry was produced and a toast made to 'Maggie's eighteenth birthday'. It was a day for her to remember. A very memorable one.

"I was thinking, Maggie," said Betty, as they sat out later on basket weave chairs, enjoying the sun. Ezra was playing hide and seek with Mikey, so he wasn't there to hear. "There seems to be no point in delaying our removal, now that we have the staff to help us, and Mr Arlington won't want all my possessions around him when he starts his job on Monday. What do you think? Would it inconvenience Alice if you were to move your belongings in here?"

"No, it shouldn't put Alice out, she'll welcome me gettin' out of the room. Mr Dickinson will have his bags ready and waitin' as soon as she lets him know. It's just that I'm goin' to have to leave Mikey behind, because we didn't get a nursemaid, like yer said yer would."

"Maggie, I didn't want to get just anybody to look after Mikey. It's important that we find the right type of young lady. Remember, these are his formative years. At the moment he is happy in the care of Alice. If you want, you can visit him every morning, before you come to the shop. That way you will have only left him overnight and probably by now he's sleeping the night through, so he wouldn't even notice that you have gone."

"I'll notice," she remarked sadly. "I won't be able to listen to his breathing and know him to be safely asleep."

"I'll be going into Chester next Wednesday, Maggie. I have some business to do with Mr Arlington and I'll call into a domestic agency and put our name down with them."

"Oh yes?" Maggie said, suspiciously. "Why are yer goin' to Chester with Mr Arlington then? I thought anything to do with business was between you and me?"

"It is. Now don't you start getting all excitable and jumpy. Someone has to go to Chester and do the banking and that will be one of his jobs."

"How do we know we can trust him? You've never complained of doing the banking and travellin' to Chester before."

"Has anything ever gone missing from Seagull Cottage? Have his previous employers caught him with his hand in the cash box? No, because he is an honest man and it will leave us free to concentrate on the dress making side of the business. I will introduce him first to Mr Hughes at the bank and then we'll see Mr Hawkins, as well."

"I suppose that will be to do with the bounty vouchers. I remember yer saying we had to get the wordin' of the agreement right."

"Yes, that is true. If we don't get the wording right, regarding where and how the voucher can be spent, you can guarantee someone will find a way of defaulting. Now, here comes Ezra and little Mikey. I think that's enough talking about business, especially today!"

"You know, Maggie, I think that colour of gown really suits you," said Ezra looking at the birthday girl, appreciatively. "Don't you think so, Betty?"

"I do indeed. I think, Maggie, that convention would allow you to relax your colours, now that it has been nearly six months since Jack departed. Of course it goes without saying, that you couldn't wear bright shades, and I like the way you have toned down the size of your crinoline by not wearing the under cage. Now, I had a special cake made at the bakery, a treat for you and Mikey. Come, I'll put the kettle on to boil and we'll have a slice with our afternoon tea."

Ezra lent a hand to remove Betty and her possessions on Monday, just as the morning sun was beginning to light up the sky. He and a local man pushed the grocer's handcart with the bed frame, mattress and headboard on board. Another trip carried a small wardrobe, chest of drawers and personal luggage belonging to Betty. They had finished in time for 'Miss Rosemary', to welcome Mr Arlington to his new job at the Sheldon Loan and Property Company, its existence now advertised on a placard placed in the window of the shop's first floor.

Maggie arrived at her usual time, to see Betty and Arlington disappearing together out of the front door, looking very friendly.

"Annie will let you know where we are up to, Maggie," Betty said, as she brushed past her. "We have to go out on business, we'll be back later, around half past four!"

"Do yer know he's 'ad me up and down them stairs all mornin'," Annie complained, once the new manager had gone up the High Street. "Annie, could you fetch my client and me a tray of tea? Would you be so kind to fetch me a pie from the bakery for my lunch?" She put on a deep man's voice and walked around the shop acting like Mr Arlington. "I'm goin' to suggest to Miss Rosemary that we give him a little bell. Even she seemed annoyed with him, 'cos he was takin' me away from what I was doing."

"And where've they gone now? Any ideas?"

The trip to Chester was supposed to be on Wednesday, so she wondered what the pair of them were up to now.

"No, they seemed to be doing a lot of talkin' upstairs in his office. She told me to tell yer, ter finish off the hem on that red dress over there and I've to carry on with the seams on this one here."

"Have yer had many people passin' through this morning and goin' upstairs to see 'His Nibs'?"

"I saw the man who has the tailor shop and one or two women that I've seen around the village. Why, was there someone yer wanted ter see in particular? 'Cos, except fer him and his shouting, I've had me head down, yer see?"

So, it seemed that Mr Arlington was already beginning to earn his money, with clients and customers coming in all morning, and now he had taken Betty off somewhere. It was probably regarding some property if she hadn't taken Maggie.

And so it was. When Betty came back later, minus her new employee, she had the details of several properties and shops up for sale. She looked flushed and excited and Annie was again requested to bring up a tray of tea to the office, but this time for Betty and her business partner, while they pored over all the unfamiliar words in the available property lists.

"There's something here about which shops and houses they want a quick sale on," Betty exclaimed. "What do you think, Maggie, shall we go for shops or some of these houses? See, there are some here on the High Street and one or two down Parkgate Road."

"I don't know, Betty. I don't know how much yer've got to spend, do I?" she replied, getting caught up in the moment and feeling very important. "It can't be from what we're gettin' in from the loan company and the bounty vouchers haven't started yet. You spent such a lot on the furniture fer Selwyn Lodge, how can yer afford to buy more property?"

"Money makes money, Maggie, and I've plenty sitting in the bank where it won't make very much interest. I think we'll go for six of these shops along here. The one next door will come in handy if we want to expand the dressmaker and, until the lease is up, we'll still have the rent coming in."

So it was decided that Betty would go ahead and bid for the properties she wanted. There was an auction at the Assembly Rooms the following week and Mr Arlington was to be her representative. When the paperwork was finished, six new acquisitions sat on the books of the Sheldon Loan and Property Company.

When Maggie got home later from her very exciting day, she found that her possessions had been put into the small back bedroom. There was no sign of Mikey's cradle, until she looked into Alice and Michael's room.

"What's this yer doin', Alice?" she shouted, as she ran down the stairs into the kitchen, where Alice was preparing the food for the evening meal.

"What do yer mean, what am I doin'? Miss Rosemary moved this mornin', so I thought you'd be on yer way."

"And do I not get a say in when I'm leavin', or is this just another excuse fer givin' Dickinson back his old room?"

"You said it. I've not had a penny piece off you for accommodation since our Jack went away in February. Yes, I agree yer've paid fer yer food and I don't begrudge our Mikey anything, but Mr Dickinson is a paying boarder and, as far as I'm concerned, yer can stay in the back bedroom, or yer can collect yer things and go."

"This wasn't what Jack said ter me before he sailed fer the America's. He said the house might be in your name, but I could stay here fer as long as I wanted to."

"But he didn't say yer could have the front bedroom, did he? Like yer said to me the other week, 'Find a pen and yer can write ter him.'"

There wasn't much to be carried out of Seagull Cottage the following day. Not many possessions to show for the eighteen months she had laboured, since she'd arrived from Killala. A large wicker basket, borrowed from Alice, held her dresses, nighties, cloak, underwear and birthday gifts. The irony was not lost on her, as she walked off to her new home. She had been allowed to take the clothes she had made, but not her little son.

–

The weeks passed by pleasantly enough, it was hard not to feel happy in the beautiful house she now called home. It felt good to be waited on by Mary and the food that Joan Kellett prepared was simple, but varied. Betty and Maggie would walk home together after they had closed the premises, have a glass of sherry in the drawing room, then talk over the day's events before sitting down to their meal. Sometimes Ezra would call and they would play a game of cards; sometimes they would sit in the conservatory and watch the sunset over the hills.

Her favourite time was sitting quietly, reading a book from Betty's extensive library. *Uncle Tom's Cabin* and *Pilgrim's Progress*, being two titles that fascinated her. Then there were the breeches and little shirt that she was making in her spare time, for Mikey. There was always something to do and she never felt bored.

The best thing of all was the bathroom. There was a bath, toilet and washbasin in white cast iron, the boiler chuntering menacingly on the outside wall. She could while an hour away in that bathroom, wallowing in her newfound luxury, massaging her body with scented soap and using proper shampoo on her hair. Her bedroom, which looked out over the garden and the estuary, held a single bed, a chest of drawers, a small wardrobe, a cheval mirror and a camphor blanket box. The room was large and airy, with plenty of space for Mikey's bed, but at the moment it was stored away.

There was an air of resignation on Maggie's part when she visited her child each morning. She remembered what Betty had said, when it was first spoken of, that she wanted her and Mikey to move in.

"If the child's welfare is tantamount in the arrangements for him, then legally you could be allowed take him away."

It seemed that his welfare had not been tantamount, Betty had never even interviewed a prospective nursemaid. It was as if Betty didn't want a child in her house.

One morning in September, Maggie was walking along the promenade after her usual daily visit to Mikey. Ahead of her was a young woman pushing a pram. She was easily recognizable as Miss Madeline.

"Wait fer me, Madeline," she cried and hurried to catch her. It would be pleasant to walk up the hill together and see the new baby girl or boy. "You've had your babby then, I see. Let me look, oh, he's a lovely little baby."

Indeed he was, all pink cheeked and handsome, not much hair, but what he had was going to be a chestnut brown, not a titian red like his mother, which made her think that Madeline might put a little something on her hair.

"So, what did yer call him? How old is he? A couple of weeks by the look of him."

"This is Edward Cornelius, so he'll either get Eddie or Con. He's two weeks old today," Madeline replied proudly, fussing with a frilly blanket that had been laid across the child.

"And how are yer? You must have bin up out of bed fairly quickly. Have yer had yer churchin' yet? Though I have to admit it's a long time since I've bin to St. Winefred's. So, yer've named the babby after yer uncle? It's good to keep to the family names. Mikey is named after his grandfather, Michael, and we also named him Patrick, after me dad."

She wondered why Madeline was looking at her in a puzzled way, after she had finished her sentence.

"Have I offended yer in some way, Madeline? Have I said somethin' I shouldn't have done?"

"No. Just then you asked if I had named my baby after my uncle. I've named my baby after his dad."

"His dad? But surely yer married ter Johnny, aren't yer? I saw yer both on yer weddin' day. Miss Rosemary and I were watchin', as you walked together into the church."

"How do you know Johnny? Are you the Maggie he was asking me about, because he said he knew a Maggie who had settled here?"

"I'm all confused now," Maggie said, and she was, totally. "So, yer not married ter Johnny? That is, Johnny Dockerty from Killala. A sea captain who used to run the cattle boats from Sligo to here."

Was it her imagination, or had her spirits begun to soar at her discovery?

"Maggie, shall we sit down for a few minutes?" Madeline asked, pausing by a low wall that they were passing. "Have you time to sit with me for a few minutes while we talk? I know you probably have to get to the dressmaker's, but I can't remember when I last sat and talked to someone. It's ridiculous really, because I live above a tavern where there's plenty going on, but Ted doesn't like me to mix with the customers and it can get very lonely, you know."

Madeline began to tell Maggie her story. How she was the eldest child of an estate manager on a large country manor, near Formby in Lancashire. She was walking the dogs along the windswept beach one morning when Ted Dockerty came along, out for his daily run. He liked to keep himself fit, because of the smoky atmosphere in the public house at Southport, where he was the landlord. He had confessed to her later that it was her glorious hair that had attracted him and, taken by her good looks, he started going to the beach every day. At first Madeline had ignored him, but then he made a point of shouting 'good morning' as he went running by. Of course, it was only manners to return his greeting, and suddenly one morning she found herself in conversation with him. She was bored at home. She had gone to a private school in nearby Churchtown, run by two gentlewomen who loved literature, needle-craft and the arts. Madeline had excelled herself under the careful guidance of her teachers and they recommended that she went to a finishing school in Paris, where she could concentrate on fashion design. Her father had been adamantly against it, saying that enough was enough and she could learn from her mother how to run a household. That was until a suitable marriage could be found.

Ted was a lot older than Madeline. She hadn't known by how much until he had arrived on her father's doorstep one day, asking for his daughter's hand. There was a massive row. How

317

dare a lowly publican come sniffing round? And eleven years older than their daughter at that? He'd set the dogs on him, have him horsewhipped, sent to jail, but Ted was to leave Madeline alone. By that time, Cupid's arrow had pierced Madeline's heart and one morning, before the family had stirred from their bedrooms, she had run away. Ted applied for the tenancy of the Brown Horse in Neston, far enough for her father to never find her. Ted was aged thirty-one and Madeline was twenty. They had to make up the story that Ted was her uncle, so that they could be together until Madeline was twenty-one. That was why she had to be careful who she spoke to. If her father had found out where she was, the chances were he would have dragged her back home again.

"So, then yer met Johnny, Ted's brother? How did that come about?"

"Well, Ted left home many years ago. His father and mother had a tavern in Galway, so Ted had been brought up in a public house and knew what the brewery trade was all about. Ted isn't a letter writer, so he never wrote to his mother, and it has to be said he was rather jealous of Johnny, because he was the blue eyed boy. As you said, Johnny used to come with the cattle to Parkgate and came to the Brown Horse with his crew. He was talking to the previous landlord on one of his trips and the man had told him he was leaving. He said that the brewery was appointing a man from Southport, he couldn't remember the name, but thought it might be Dockerty. Johnny thought it strange that the next landlord should share his name and vowed that next time he was over, he would make a point of calling in. Then the cattle orders dried up, so in the meantime Johnny had to sign on with another shipping company. It was another six months before he came back again, and he was delighted that he had found his brother, Ted. That was why you saw him at the wedding. Ted had asked him to walk me in, because we hadn't asked my father."

"And what of his mother, have yer ever met her? Have yer ever bin across to Ireland to see her?" Maggie asked eagerly.

"Well, no. Ted would have to get a stand in if he wanted a holiday and me expectin' hasn't helped. I suppose Johnny will have told her where Ted is now, so she could get in touch if she wants."

"I should write to her. It was Mrs Dockerty who taught me my letters and I've bin ever so grateful ever since, but I suppose I never thought to let her know where I am. It still hurts to think of Killala and those of me loved ones I left behind."

Madeline's baby began to stir from his sleep and started making little sucking noises.

"He's hungry now. If I don't go he'll set up a wail. Shall we walk up the hill together? I'll tell Johnny I saw you, next time he's here on leave."

"Before yer go, can I just ask yer somethin'. Has Johnny ever bin married or got a girl?"

"I've never heard of him ever being married, nor even having had a lady friend. I think it's because he prefers the company of men. Being with his crew all the time on his voyages, that is."

"Strange that. I prefer the company of women meself. Men are dirty and smelly and are usually only out fer themselves. Not that I don't love Mikey, and my father was good to me, but I've never met one that I thought I could trust."

"Oh Ted is alright, he'll do anything for me and he loves little Eddie. But I hear you are a widow. Surely you loved your husband too?"

"That's another story fer another day, Madeline. I'll ask Miss Rosemary if yer can come and visit at me new address. Now, I must get off or she'll be dockin' me wages. Look after yerself and the little one."

Later that week there were celebrations. The first bounty voucher customer came into Mr Arlington's office. A new suit had been ordered at the tailor's in the High Street, and had cost the man five pounds and ten shillings. The sherry came out, the toasts were made, even Annie was allowed to join in. In his usual boastful manner, 'His Nibs' promised that this was the first customer of many and assured them of the continuous success of the venture, under his very capable wing.

He went on to say that he had signed up Frogerty's Furnishings and Oakham's Department Store in Chester, Smallwoods, a household goods store in Liverpool, and he was yet to visit Birkenhead.

"He's a very determined man, Maggie," Betty said later as they relaxed at Selwyn Lodge. "He's happy to visit these places in his own free time, although I do pay him his expenses. And he is such a mine of information. Yesterday he was telling me that a man named Mr Singer has taken out a patent on something called a sewing machine. Instead of you and Annie hand sewing all the seams, this machine whips up and down them in minutes! He saw the article in his broadsheet. We'll have one of them as soon as I can find out where to order."

Chapter 25

One morning in early October, when the harvests had been gathered in and an autumnal nip was in the air, Alice stood in her doorway waiting for Maggie to visit. In her hand was a letter from Jack and she couldn't wait to find out what was in it!

Maggie opened the envelope slowly on purpose. Whatever was in it, it was bound to be trouble. He had been tardy in sending his letters in the past, not even caring for the welfare of his son.

"Has it got an address this time, Maggie?" Alice was getting impatient. "Wouldn't it be good, if we could let him know how we're all doin' so well?"

This was said, because Alice liked to boast now that her daughter-in-law was doing very well for herself, living in a grand place such as Selwyn Lodge.

"There's no address and you're not goin' ter like what's in it." Alice sat down with a worried look on her face.

"Oh no, Maggie, what are yer goin' ter tell me? Is he dead?"

"No, but Kitty May is. She died givin' birth to her baby. Well, not straight away, she died of milk fever nine days later."

"Oh Holy Jesus and all His saints," Alice crossed herself. "I wouldn't have wished that on anyone. So, what is Jack doin' about the baby? Was it a boy or a girl?"

"It says here that she had a baby girl and they named her Hannah Victoria."

"Well, he will have had ter give her up to the authorities. There's no way our Jack could bring up a little girl."

"It looks as if you'll be doin' that. He sent her over with a woman who's returnin' on the boat to Liverpool. Looks like they'll be here in a few days' time."

"So, I'm to have the care of his by-blow? Maggie, how am I going to do that? How am I goin' to explain her presence to everyone at the church?"

Alice had gone white. Even Maggie felt her knees weakening at the thought of the problems the presence of this child would create.

"Yer could say she's bin sent over from Ireland. The grand-daughter of yer sister and she's too old to have the care of it."

"I'm too old to have the care of it. You're his wife, you'll have to think of somethin'."

"Oh yes, that would sound very well. Me dead husband has sent me his illegitimate child from beyond the grave. I don't think so. Have yer ever heard of chickens comin' home to roost?"

Suddenly Alice's manner came over all wheedling.

"Maggie, yer know I'm even havin' problems lookin' after our Mikey. He runs me ragged at times. I was only sayin' to Michael the other day, perhaps we should think about helpin' you to find a nursemaid. If yer had a nursemaid at Selwyn Lodge, yer could have Mikey there all the time and this child of Kitty May's. I'd come and visit of course."

So that was the lay of the land. Mikey had become a handful, but because Maggie was there every morning, she was taking some of the responsibility away, leaving Alice to get on with her chores. Another child would really place a burden on her.

"Yer know, Maggie, I still have me lodgers to see to, and I'm not as young as I was."

"Well, let's see what happens when this woman brings the child here," Maggie said, unable to think clearly, as she had been given a shock as well as Jack's mother. "Meantime, I'll ask Miss Rosemary what can be done about a nursemaid."

The problem was though, what could she tell Betty? The truth? That Jack wasn't really dead. Would Betty be prepared to keep the knowledge a secret? Would she think any less of Maggie? She and Alice had deceived the church and all the community and been given sympathy, when there hadn't been the need.

She quickly made up her mind, then gave her decision to Alice. If she wanted Hannah to stay in the family, then Miss Rosemary would have to be told the dishonourable tale.

"I don't know if I want her to know our shameful secret. I have to admit that our Jack did abandon yer, but I still think you must take some of the blame."

An admission from Alice, but only wrung out of her, because she wanted Maggie to have the care of Jack's little baby. Still, perhaps it was best if the truth was told, then she could get rid of her double life!

"We've no choice, but to tell her, if we want her agreement to let me bring up Hannah, instead of you. I don't really know why I should though, because she's Jack's responsibility. Still, if it means I can have Mikey back, it will be just as easy, I suppose, to bring up two, as one. She'll be company fer Mikey, once they start ter grow, and it's better than the mite being put in a children's home."

"Jack would never forgive us if we did. I wish he would get the scribe to put his new address on. I'd love you to write and give him a piece of my mind."

"Perhaps he moves around a lot, but if we really wanted to, we could write ter Lord Belsham. Has Michael got any idea where His Lordship can be found?"

"I don't know. I can ask him, but let's keep that fer an emergency. I don't want to trouble Lord Belsham, in case Jack isn't workin' fer him now. Still, this woman will be able ter tell us when she arrives with the baby. I'd best prepare a room for her, in case it's late when she gets here. She can have your old room fer one night and we'll put Hannah in one of the drawers."

Betty wasn't pleased with the confession. They were sitting comfortably in front of the drawing room fire, drinking their after dinner coffee, when Maggie decided to tell all.

"The one thing we need in our relationship is trust," she had said sternly, after she had got over the shock of Alice and Maggie's skullduggery. "And when I think of how you were pointing your finger at me in the solicitors! My, you had a nerve, girl. Still, it's done now, but that doesn't excuse your behaviour. All this dressing in black and being the solemn young widow. You know it wouldn't have gone any further if you had told me in the beginning."

"I hated deceivin' yer, Betty. It was Alice who made me tell those lies, and what could I do, but go along with it? I was livin' in her house at the time."

"Then shame on Alice. But you are living in my house now and I think you could have told me when you moved in. A new life should not be built on lies. Do you know, even poor Ezra was taken in? Losing his wife the way he did, made him have a lot of compassion for you."

"Oh, please don't tell him, Betty. I couldn't look him in the face ever again."

"Well, I won't for your sake, but it's time you gave up this charade, at least between you and me. That black gown has to be vanquished to the back of your cupboard and I want to see you wearing lighter shades. Are you not worried that Jack will come back again? He doesn't know that his mother invented the sorry tale. It will rake up the coals if he was to surface again."

"What did yer used to say te me? 'Never trouble, trouble?' It will be Alice's problem if that happens, 'cos I can say it was what I was told."

"So can Alice really. The landlady at his lodgings said that it was Jack that she had buried. It could have been anyone! But let us put our minds to rearing this little baby. We really must employ a nursemaid now. I can't do without you at the dressmakers. I know that it's quiet now that the harvest suppers are over, but Christmas will soon be upon us and you know what that is like, with you being here last year. And I've plans afoot in my mind again. I'm thinking of leaving the premises we have in the care of Mr Arlington. He could do with our downstairs space now, so I think it is time for us to expand!"

"Expand?"

"Well, as you know, the bounty vouchers have really taken off. Oakham's has sent us five customers in the past three weeks. A customer of Frogerty's ordered all that furniture the other month and his repayments are the best we've had, up to now. We've just Smallwood's to send us a customer, but I suppose not many people around here travel much to Liverpool. Mr Arlington has high hopes of getting Robinson's in Birkenhead to commit to us soon."

"So yer sayin' yer want the dressmaking business to move?"

"Yes, the ship chandlers across the road would be ideal. It is double fronted and the man who runs it, says he may as well give up now the river is becoming silted. There's no call for his goods like there used to be. That is one of the shops we own, as you know, and Mr Jeffrey's is getting close to retirement age. Mr Arlington says he is so busy on the first floor that he could do with a young lady downstairs, to keep a filing system, greet our customers, and make his tea. I think the term used is 'office girl'. But, my plan for expansion rests on obtaining one of these sewing machines. In our quiet periods we could make gowns in popular sizes, seasonal colours and a range of styles. We could even ask our friend Madeline to help us with a few designs. If we are going to have a nursemaid, her child could be looked after with ours. She could be a great asset, with her penchant for fashionable clothing. Of course, she would need permission from her husband, because I would like her to work in the shop as well. You and Annie would continue to be the sempstresses and I could come in now and again to advise."

"Whew, Betty. I only asked yer about a nursemaid and yer three ideas ahead of me!"

—

Luckily Maggie was at Seagull Cottage a few mornings later when the woman who had been given the charge of baby Hannah, knocked on the door.

Sarah Osborne was a plain looking woman in her early thirties; her dark hair pinned neatly into a bun and wearing a blue striped dress and long blue cape, that befitted her nursemaid's role. She looked very weary and thanked Sam, the cab driver, gratefully for carrying the two large valises up the path behind her. In her arms was her precious bundle, all wrapped up in shawls against the chill of the morning air.

"You must be young Mrs Haines," she said, as Maggie opened the door. "I'm Sarah Osborne, temporary nursemaid to Hannah Victoria, engaged by Mr Jack Haines. I hope you received his letter, it was sent a week before we boarded the clipper out of New York. I do hope you are expecting us."

"Yes, my mother-in-law received the letter a few days ago. I must say we were taken aback that the child should be sent to us. Do come in though, it's not very warm standing there on the doorstep. Come into the kitchen and I'll make yer a cup of tea."

"I hadn't expected Parkgate to be so far away from Liverpool," Sarah commented, as she followed Maggie through the hall. "We docked at Huskisson in the early hours and I was told I would have to wait for the six o'clock ferryboat to Woodside and then catch a train to a place called Hooton. We were lucky to have seen the station trap setting down some passengers and you know the rest, because we are here. Poor little thing needs her bottle. She's been wailing on and off since Liverpool, though I think she's given up now and gone back to sleep."

"I'll shout Alice, that's Jack's mother. Alice! The lady's here with Hannah. I'm just makin' her a cup of tea."

"In a minute, I'm seein' to Mikey. Stand still yer little rascal, yer'll get a pin stuck in ye, so yer will."

"Can I see the baby, Sarah?" Maggie asked, as she showed her guest where to sit while they waited for the kettle to boil. Sarah smiled and handed the bundle over. A little girl with velvety looking brown eyes stared back seriously.

"Oh, you're beautiful," Maggie gasped, and Hannah began to smile slowly, as if she could understand her words. She began to unwrap all the shawls that surrounded the child and saw little dainty features that reminded her of a miniature doll and, strangely enough, of her sister, Molly.

She was dressed in an exquisite little gown, in pale yellow which suited her robust cheeks and curling blue-black hair. The dress was covered in layers of lace, with a row of pink buds along every one.

"She's got similar dresses in the valise. Mr Haines made very sure that she had a dress for every day of our voyage. Then there are the soil cloths, little pantaloons, bonnets and bootees, vests and little knitted coats. And he has also sent a money voucher to be cashed at the Chester Bank."

"All he needed was a nursemaid," remarked Alice, who had been standing with Mikey at the kitchen door. "Well, Maggie. Has the baby got a bottle? She'll want feeding by now, I'll be bound."

"I'm just going to heat her some milk, Alice. Hello, Mikey, would yer like some too?"

She reluctantly passed the little baby back to Sarah, then set about making up two bottles and three cups of tea. Alice sat at the table holding Mikey and there was quite a bit of tension in the air. "So, he sent you over with the baby. Has he told yer about its circumstance? Why yer've brought it here?"

"Yes, Jack told me what happened, that the poor mother died. I was working for a family out there, but I have to own up to homesickness. I thought I could manage a new life in a new world and that is why I emigrated with the Henderson family, but I couldn't do it. I missed my family, I missed the green fields, the rain, everything about England really. It's so different over there. Jack was talking to another man in the street as I was passing by, and just to hear another English voice, well Irish really, but you know what I mean… when I heard him I thought I must leave here. I must go back to England. So, I went up to him, brazenly now I come to think of it, but manners are so different over there, and I asked him where he was from and so it went on. I told him I was thinking about coming back and then he told me about the death of Kitty and how he wanted to send the baby home. It seemed fated somehow. Jack was prepared to pay my passage home and I have had a lot of experience with children. The Hendersons' had a little boy, a bit older than your boy, and a little girl of five years."

"But did Jack tell yer that Maggie here is his wife, and that Kitty was the woman he ran away with?"

"Well, he didn't quite put it like that, Mrs Haines, but I think I understand the circumstances. It's not my place to comment. I was just paid by your son to bring Hannah to you and that is what I've done."

"And where was this place that yer were livin', and where yer met our Jack? Did he give yer an address that we can write to?"

"The place we met was called Evanston. A long way from New York, I have to say. He took me to his lodgings, where the landlady was keeping her eye on the baby, but I didn't note down his address, because I wasn't going to be in touch again."

"Oh well, yer here now," sighed Alice. "When she's finished her bottle, I'll have a look at her. Then you can take her upstairs to change her cloths, she's stinkin' to high heaven!"

Alice came down a bit later with Mikey, who had been fascinated with this little person and the nice lady who had suddenly arrived in his world. Alice was looking rather flushed and agitated, but as usual was thinking about how she could take advantage of the situation. Here was a trained nursemaid and Alice had been given responsibility of another child.

"I've told Miss Osborne she can stay in the back bedroom fer a couple of days, while the baby settles in with us. I've lined one of the drawers with some bedding and she's put the baby in. Now she's havin' a wash and changing her clothes. I haven't said anything to her, Maggie, but she'd be the answer to all our problems. She'd have to swear though, that she wouldn't tell anyone about Jack or Kitty. We'll have to use the story of Hannah being sent over from Ireland by her grandma."

"She might not want to stay, she might want to go back to her parents, and I'd have to ask Miss Rosemary's permission if yer want them to stay at Selwyn Lodge."

"Well, it's what yer've wanted, havin' a nursemaid and Mikey there, so what's the problem? Yer'll just have an extra couple of mouths ter feed."

"Sarah was telling me that Jack has sent over a money voucher for the child's expenses, but I'll have to sort out with Miss Rosemary who will be paying the nursemaid's wage. As yer know, she only gives me enough money to pay you, fer havin' Mikey."

"Pooh, well that'll have to be your problem. Yer do enough fer that woman. She should be payin' yer as a companion help."

"Let's wait then until Miss Osborne comes down and we'll ask her what her plans are. No good surmisin', until we know what she wants ter do."

Maggie had to leave then, because it was time to walk to the dressmaker's. She left Alice to make the guest some dinner and, while doing so, sound Sarah out. It was no use making plans for the nursemaid's future, if Betty wasn't agreeable and it would be a squash in Seagull Cottage for Sarah and a nursery.

She took Betty aside, away from the ears of Annie. Maggie didn't want her business to become the property of Ruthie.

"So, can this woman be trusted to stick to the story of Hannah being a member of Alice's family from Ireland? Servants do like to gossip. They can't always keep confidences, my dear."

"She seems to be from a good family, Betty. She told me she was from a small village called Malpas, outside Chester. Her father is the local doctor there. She thought she would like to see something of the world and that is why she went with her employers to America, but she couldn't put up with the hot summers and cold winters. She prefers the four seasons that we have over here."

"And what about followers? Is there a man friend spoken of, because I don't want young men hanging around Selwyn Lodge?"

"I was only in her company a short time, but there was no mention of one. I couldn't imagine any man on the scene, because she's bin in America fer two years."

"And how do you feel? Taking on the responsibility of another woman's child?"

"I must say I felt aggrieved that Jack didn't keep his baby-making tackle where it should be, but I wouldn't like the little mite to have gone anywhere else, but here."

"Oh Maggie, you show such a hard shell to the world, but inside I know there is a soft centre. That's why I admire you so much. I don't think that I could be so forgiving, if I was in your shoes." Betty decided to become practical again. "I have to take it on your authority that this woman is what we are looking for. But, if it doesn't work out, I will have to ask her to leave and the children will go back to Alice. Then, there is the question of payment for the young woman. As you know, I haven't got a bottomless purse and we did say you would pay for a nursemaid, out of the Sheldon Loan Company."

"Jack has sent a money voucher for Hannah's expenses. I don't know how much it is, because Sarah hasn't given it to me yet. It is to be cashed at the Chester Bank, so if I gave it to you, you could pay it into the Sheldon account."

"It will be a big problem though, now that Mr Arlington is doing the banking," said Betty thoughtfully. "He will wonder, when he sees it, what it is all about. Now, I can ask for a bigger allowance to be taken by me before the banking's done, and say that I have increased expenses. That will cover the nursemaid, but I'd have to make an excuse next week and go alone to Chester, to pay the money voucher in. Alice will have to sign it on the back. I presume it was sent to Alice, as he won't know that you have moved out to live with me. It's a good job I've always had my business statements sent to my home, and I haven't made bookkeeping part of Mr Arlington's job."

"Oh, I'm sorry, Betty, to be puttin' yer to all this trouble. What can I say? You've always bin so good te me."

"I'm only doing it because I want you to be happy, Maggie, but I won't be so accommodating if I don't get any peace. We'll ask Mary to prepare the front bedroom. It is the largest one, so we can put in a single bed and Mikey's bed, and Hannah can have Mikey's cradle. It can be the nursery, and I'll have a chest of drawers and a blanket box put in there. You'll have to get someone to bring the cradle up from Alice's house and any bedding that Alice can spare. Now, I think you can run along back to Seagull Cottage. It's quiet today and I'm sure you have much more pressing matters on your mind."

After Maggie had gone, Betty examined her conscience. If truth was told, the Sheldon Loan and Property Company was doing better than Maggie was aware. The account had just tipped over the two hundred pound mark. Even taking Mr Arlington's wage and expenses out, the company was coming on in leaps and bounds. Her dressmaker's as usual, just paid for its existence by supporting Selwyn Lodge, its staff and their allowances. It was imperative in Betty's mind that her business had to do some expanding. And the shop across the road would be just the place to attract a more wealthier clientele.

Sarah Osborne was quite taken aback when Alice spoke to her about a nursemaid's position. She had been looking forward, at the end of her long voyage, to spending some time with her family. She had three younger brothers and a married sister and was thinking that a rest and her mother's home-made cooking would put her in a better frame of mind.

Sarah wasn't sure if she wanted to keep on looking after other people's babies. It would be pleasant to have a home of her own, as she was coming up to thirty-three. But, Hannah was a sweet, compliant baby and perhaps she would enjoy working in this peaceful corner of Cheshire. She had to admit she would like the healthy sea air and the magnificent view over to the Welsh Hills. If Mrs Haines Senior was to be believed, the house that Sarah would reside in was nothing short of sumptuous, and there were other servants employed as well. Not that Sarah thought of herself as a servant. A 'paid help' were the words that came to mind. When the younger Mrs Haines arrived back and offered a wage that was quite handsome, she accepted. She asked for paper and pen and wrote home to her parents instead.

Chapter 26

It was lovely having Mikey with her again, Maggie thought, as she lay in bed one morning. She listened to him laughing in the bathroom next door, as Sarah got him ready. The nursemaid had settled in well and got on famously with Joan and Mary. She was deferential with Betty, who was head of the household, and kept Maggie involved in the welfare of both the children.

Baby Hannah was coming on in leaps and bounds, she had a smile for everyone and Mikey was her slave. The pram was in daily use, weather permitting, Hannah cosily wrapped up inside and Mikey perched on the apron surveying all around him. He would come back from his walks with Sarah, his cheeks red from the wintery air, talking incomprehensibly to anyone who would listen. Hannah had blossomed into a little doll. She had huge dark brown eyes, black hair falling into curls and a calm, sweet nature.

Maggie couldn't resist making her tiny lace trimmed dresses in her spare time, with matching bonnets, little knitted jackets, and bootees and mitts. In fact, secretly she was beginning to treat Hannah as the daughter she'd never had with Jack. But for an act of fate, the child could have been her daughter. It was just that Jack had made her with somebody else! When Sarah had her day off, sometimes on a Sunday or one day in the week, then Maggie took over her duties and had the children all to herself.

There had only been one slight problem, early on in Hannah's residence at Selwyn Lodge. Had the child been christened? No one knew, but the priest asked Alice when the family turned up one Sunday to worship. It was coming up to Christmas and Maggie decided that, although she wouldn't go to Confessional, in case she confessed something she shouldn't, it wouldn't harm her to go to Mass and introduce Hannah to the congregation. No one had thought of a story, and the three of them looked in dismay at each other.

"Was anything said, Alice?" Michael stuttered, wishing a hole would open and swallow him up. They were on Holy ground after all.

Alice shook her head and said, "We didn't think to ask about it, Father. Surely as she's from a Catholic family, she probably will have bin."

"I think if you're not very sure and we haven't got a certificate, then maybe I should christen her. Have you any idea of her birthday, when she was born?"

Again, all three of them shook their heads and hoped that the priest wouldn't start asking for details of the child's background.

So, the following week Hannah was christened. Hannah Victoria Haines. Though it was Alice's side of the family she was supposed to come from, nobody queried the name.

Maggie had enjoyed that particular Christmas. It had been a really special time. Part of the household went to worship at St. Mary's (that was Betty, Sarah, Mary and Joan) and Maggie had taken Mikey and Hannah to join Michael, Alice and Seamus at St. Winefred's. Then they all trooped back to Selwyn Lodge for an early Christmas dinner, so that Mary and Joan could go home to their families, and the rest of them could go to Seagull Cottage for Christmas tea.

It had felt good to be part of it all. Maggie felt settled and contented, listening to Mikey's excited chattering, as he opened his parcels, and seeing his delight when he saw all his toys. She noticed also how Seamus had grown in confidence, as he told them tales of the antics he saw in some of the upper class cabins. Then Ezra had called in with a small wooden rocking horse, trimmed with a leather saddle and little leather reins and a pot doll that looked like Hannah, which was whipped away from Mikey's probing fingers, of course. Ezra stayed and kept Betty company, as Betty said she was feeling too tired to walk down to the shore.

Sarah went with them for Christmas tea, so that she could help with the children. Her time to herself was New Year, when she would visit her parents for a few days. To top it all, Maggie wore her brand new outfit, guaranteed, said Ezra when he saw her in it, to cause all heads to turn. The skirt was of a heavy velvet, maroon in colour and gathered at the waist to fall in pleated folds. She wore a cream blouse, trimmed with the same maroon material and topped it off with a long sleeved bolero, also piped in maroon. Let Alice argue at my choice of colour, she had thought, as she dressed herself that day.

–

It was February 21st. The anniversary of Jack's supposed funeral. Maggie wondered briefly where he was, as she lay in her bed listening to the sounds of the household wakening. Was Jack well, was he happy? Would she and the children ever see him again?

Later that morning Betty and Maggie had an appointment. Mr Jeffries, the ship chandler from across the High Street, had closed his business down and Mr Arlington had been given the key. It was full speed ahead to get the new shop ready to open at Easter.

They were meeting with Mr Freeman, the man that had refurbished Selwyn Lodge, to tell him how they wanted the place modernizing and to discuss fixtures and fittings with Madeline. She had received the necessary permission from her husband, 'to amuse herself' for a few hours each day and, as the pub didn't open until the evening, Ted was happy to keep an eye on their baby. For the moment, anyway. There was always the nursemaid at Selwyn Lodge to look after little Eddie, if Ted couldn't cope.

That day would be a bittersweet one for Betty, as she didn't own 'Anne Rosemary' (Dressmaker) outright any more. Maggie had found her a few weeks before, hunched over her bank statements at her writing desk in the drawing room. Feeling concerned, she asked her what was the matter, as Betty looked quite pale and worried, as she studied her accounting book.

"I have to be honest with you, Maggie. The money in the dressmaker account is going down at a very alarming rate. It is the upkeep of this place, the staff, the food, the maintenance, and everything, and I spent more than I should have done on furnishing? Now I am committed to Mr Arlington to put his plan of expansion into operation. Sheldon Loan and Property Company cannot go forward unless the dressmaker's shop moves across the road."

Maggie stared at her friend in amazement. Betty looked as if she had aged another ten years. The serenity in her face had gone, to be replaced by a careworn look, with frown lines etched deeply between her brows.

"Maggie, what am I going to do?" she whispered. "Everyone here relies on me for their living. If we took on a smaller place, there would be only enough room for you and me."

Maggie had to consider her words carefully, because it was possible Betty wouldn't follow what Maggie was talking about. "How is the Sheldon Loan and Property Company doing?"

"Marvellously."

"And is it having to pay out for doing up the new shop that bothers yer, or generally that the dressmaker's isn't makin' enough money to pay the bills?"

"A bit of both really."

"Then how would it be if Sheldon bought Anne Rosemary? Can it afford to do that? Then you could pay rent back to Sheldon, then we'd have both our names on everything!"

"Why, Maggie, that sounds the perfect solution to everything. It just goes to show that hidden in that head of yours, lurks a mind with business acumen. I don't know why I didn't think of it. We could keep the shop name, pay a nominal rent and perhaps find a tenant to live in the premises above."

Of course, Mr Arlington had to be told of the new situation, and there was a trip to the solicitor for Betty and Maggie again. Betty continued to do her own accounts and paperwork but now, when people looked at her, she was her poised and elegant self again.

Unbeknown to Betty, though, Mr Arlington also had plans for using some of the Sheldon company's resources. He had inside information that a railway line might be laid from Hooton to Neston. He could see the sense in buying parcels of land and was keeping his ears open for the announcement of an auction.

The two women stood outside the old chandler's shop waiting for Mr Freeman, the builder, to arrive. It was a chilly, blustery day and both were grateful when he turned up a few moments later, saying he had got tied up estimating someone else's job.

The shop inside was even colder, run down and very dirty. It was hard to imagine the place being turned into a warm and welcoming fashion house.

"So, what I want today," said Betty, no doubt feeling pleased that they were about to embark on a new challenge, "is for everybody to put forward ideas of how they would like the shop interior to look. We'll discuss it over a cup of tea later, and I would like Mr Arlington to take notes. Madeline, as our designer, you can begin."

"I have been giving it some thought and I see canopies of Regency stripe positioned above each gown rail and down both sides of the shop. Cream and gilt upholstered chairs at various points throughout, a polished wooden floor with a large Eastern rug. Colours to be pink, cream and green and the walls to be painted white, with just a hint of a something in it. At the back of the shop, I see three changing rooms, big enough to accommodate the crinoline, with long mirrors attached to the walls within. In each window, I would suggest draped organdie and a little material from the canopies, with only one model on a dais, elegantly dressed in whatever fashion we decide."

There was a little applause from her listeners, who had tried with their imaginations to visualize.

"Annie, your turn next," said Betty. "What would you like to see?"

"If possible, I don't want ter be seen. I would like a room that kept me out of sight and then the jumble I get meself into wouldn't be on show." Everyone laughed at this, as Annie was a messy worker, leaving pieces of unfinished work all over the place.

"Maggie?"

"Well, what Madeline and Annie have said I could agree with, but maybe from Annie's point of view, it would be best if we made a workroom for her upstairs. You see, if we had a tenant upstairs, we are probably talking of a rent of three or four shillings. I feel a better idea would be to create an independent sewing room, that would be able to do alterations on clothes that have been bought elsewhere."

There was a stunned silence from everybody. Annie giggled nervously, Madeline and Betty smiled, but Mr Arlington had a face like thunder. Why, no one seemed to know.

Madeline decided to come to her rescue and fill the pause with another proposal.

"Advertising, I think, is what is needed. It is no use having a splendid establishment and having only passing trade. I think that now the train comes into Hooton from Chester, we could advertise in the Chester Courant and mention there's also an excellent station trap service to our front door. I know it would be expensive to begin with, but worth it in the long run if it also attracted the carriage trade."

"Yes, well, thank you everyone," said Betty happily. "Shall we adjourn to your office, Mr Arlington? Mr. Freeman could get his men to start with some cleaning and washing down of the walls. You know where I am, if you need me, Mr. Freeman? Just across the way. Maggie and Annie, do you want to take your lunch now and we'll talk later, and Madeline, thank you for coming and I'll see you very soon."

"I think I would like to see Mrs Haines in my office, if you don't mind, Miss Rosemary. There are one or two things I would like to discuss."

Mr Arlington glowered at Maggie for some reason known to himself, but she stood her ground and didn't turn away meekly.

"As yer wish. Now, or after I have had my lunch break, Mr Arlington? Only I'm rather hungry, as I came from Selwyn Lodge in a bit of a hurry today."

"Now, Maggie."

He turned on his heel and stalked away. Annie and Madeline looked at each other, filled with dread. Betty laid her hand on Maggie's arm as if she was about to caution her, but she simply smiled back. It was going to be very satisfying to do what she had in mind.

"Before you go, Maggie," said Madeline, "can I have a quiet word?"

"That's fine, Maggie," Betty said. "You stay and talk to Madeline, Annie and I will go to the bakery and bring you back a pie."

"I've been so excited about today," Madeline told her, "that I forgot to say that Johnny is staying at the Brown Horse with us. He said he would like to renew his acquaintanceship with you."

Maggie's heart began to thud, and it wasn't because of her appointment with Mr Arlington. Foolish, she knew, because what was Johnny to her now? The son of a friend that once helped her down the hill to Killala. It seemed like eons ago. But gone was the ragged girl with no hope in her life, who had been dependent on a husband with doubtful aspirations. Now she was a genteel young woman, who had all the comforts she could wish for, with a vibrant up and coming business and the love of her little son and the adorable Hannah. Johnny wouldn't even recognize the girl he had cruelly snubbed that day on the quayside. So, what did he want with her? Curiosity? A friendly visit so he could report back to his mother? She told Madeline that she would receive him after supper, around eight o'clock that evening at Selwyn Lodge.

"Yes, come in," snapped Mr Arlington, when Maggie knocked on the office door, after she had taken her time eating her pie and sharing lunch time with Betty and Annie.

He was sitting at his desk with his back to the window and he motioned that she stand before him. He didn't even bother providing her with a chair. His tone was menacing, as he asked her, how dare she interfere with the running of the Sheldon Loan and Property Company? How dare she suggest a new venture to be carried on from above the new dressmaker's shop? Who was she to say what rent should be paid up there?

"I think you get carried away with yourself, just because you are Miss Rosemary's companion and reside at Selwyn Lodge," he thundered. "If I had my way you would be dismissed, but I have to bow to the owner's judgement. It isn't up to me who I can sack."

Maggie took in a deep breath and exhaled slowly. She could see the familiar red mist drifting in front of her eyes, but she had been waiting for this moment ever since she had been belittled by him that evening at Seagull Cottage, and now she was going to watch him eat those words he had just tried to berate her with. Her voice was fairly steady, though she was burning up with anger, but she managed to give the impression of a woman in control.

"I'll let yer into a little secret, shall I, Mr Arlington? Miss Rosemary is not the owner of the Sheldon Loan Company. I am. If there is any sacking to be done, I will do it. Yer seem to have got above yerself, though I have to admit yer have done a very good job for me."

Maggie watched, as he looked at her in disbelief. Then he laughed as if he had just heard a good joke.

"You?" he said, pointing a finger at her. "You? An Irish immigrant without a penny in your pocket, taken pity on by the Haines family and brought across to here. Oh yes, Alice told me. You would have rotted in that hovel of yours, if Jack hadn't found it in his heart to have married you and given you a new life. Then you latched on to Miss Rosemary and everybody knows the tale from there. Well, I think we'll have the owner up. I can hear her coming through the front door now. If she doesn't verify your story, I'll make sure you are dismissed. I've never heard such cock and bull rubbish in all my life."

Betty came up the stairs as fast as she could make it, when she heard Mr Arlington shouting. From the look on both Maggie and the office manager's faces, she could see there had been a massive row. Maggie was looking mutinous, Mr Arlington snorting and pawing like a bull, though what she had expected, knowing that the man had called her friend into his office, without her being present, Maggie would never know!

Maggie could see from her face, that she knew she was going to be called on as the peacemaker, as both of them had things to offer her in the end.

"Is this about the ownership of the Sheldon Loan Company, Mr Arlington?" she asked gently, as he helped her into a chair. The man nodded, irritably.

"Yes, I can confirm that Maggie Haines is the owner, she invested the money when it started out. She also owns half of the property side, which means she has a share in the dress-maker's shop."

Both of them thought the man was going to have a seizure, as he slumped back in his chair, loosened his cravat and pulled at the collar of his shirt.

"Oh, dear lady," he breathed, his words coming out with difficulty, as he gazed in Maggie's direction. "How can I apologize? Oh, what a gaffe I've made. It's just... from what my landlady told me, it couldn't possibly be the truth!"

"When Maggie's husband made a lot of money from his pugilistic activities, he asked her to keep some of it for him,"

Betty explained, sticking partially to the truth, as it was really none of Mr Arlington's business, as to where the money had come from. "Then, as you know, he went away and Maggie was scared to be holding on to such a sum. She came to me for advice as to what she should do with the money. I said I would invest it for her in my name, because she is under twenty-one. Then a while ago we put the whole thing on a legal footing. So, if you want to, you can ask for the truth at the Chester Bank."

"Oh no, Madam. I believe you," he said, mopping his brow with a pristine handkerchief. "I am truly sorry, Mrs Haines. I will clear my desk straight away and you can appoint another in my place. I'll be sorry to go, because I have enjoyed my job and found it very challenging."

"No, don't do that," Maggie said, thinking that if he left, they would never find a man of his calibre to replace him. "Apology accepted. Stay and carry on." She waved a hand airily in his direction, then turned to Betty. "He's made us a lot of money and we do appreciate that, don't we? In fact we were thinkin' of a little bonus for you, Mr Arlington. I'm sure once you've got used to the idea of me being a proprietor, we shall all work together very well."

Later she confessed to Betty that if she hadn't come up when she did, there might have been a murder to mop up.

"I would have hit him if yer hadn't come up and put a stop to his shenanigans. The ignorant eejit was coming out with that rubbish that Alice had fed him. But, he's bin put in his place and, let's face it, we do need him. He'll probably work even harder, just to show us poor lowly women that we need a man to front this place."

To be honest, Maggie had enjoyed her moment of glory. The man truly had a high opinion of himself.

That evening, as the two women sat sipping their sherry before being called into dinner, Maggie remarked casually to Betty that she was expecting a visitor. She had dressed carefully in her purple gown and matching bodice and had draped a shawl with the same colour fringes around her shoulders for warmth. She was planning that she and Johnny would sit out in the conservatory and, at that time of the year, it was rather cold.

"I'll need yer to, what's the word, to chaperone us, Betty. It's a man I met in Killala, the son of a lady I used to call on. He's Madeline's brother-in-law. Do yer remember when we went to the wedding and he got her out of the carriage with that huge dress and train? Well, while he was staying at the Brown Horse, he asked Madeline did she know of a young girl who had come over and settled in Neston? She said she didn't, but one day we were talking and it turned out that the person was me. He's home on leave again, Madeline let me know this morning. He's a sea captain by the way, and he's comin' ter see me, ter renew our acquaintanceship, he said."

"A sea captain, you say? Oh that's very interesting. My father was a sea captain, as you know. We'll make him quite welcome, dear and you can catch up on each other's lives since you last saw him. But remember you have a secret and, if I were you, I'd keep it to myself."

Johnny walked up Burton Road just after half past seven. He had been persuaded by Madeline to wear the clothes he wore at her wedding. He had left them at the Brown Horse, because he had no occasion to wear such fancy clothes on his sailing ship. He was rather nervous, silly really, because he had no reason to be. But what if he got to this Selwyn Lodge place and found that the girl he had spoken of wasn't the same one? He looked over the hedges at the houses that he was passing by. They were splendid dwellings, grand and imposing. The Maggie he knew from Killala couldn't possibly live in one of these!

He thought back to that day when she had pleaded with him to be taken back to Ireland. A ragged, tattered girl with enormous tears in her eyes. He had been so unsympathetic, only wanting to be off to the tavern with his crew. But, she had been married to a fellow by then. It was her husband who should have had the responsibility of her. Then Madeline had told him that the husband had been found dead in his lodgings across in Liverpool. His conscience still troubled him of his promise to meet her the following spring, just to check that she had settled in, and to report to his mother that all was well with her. His mother still asked if he had sighted Maggie, when he chose to visit Killala on one of his leaves. The company he had worked for had abandoned the delivery of cattle over to the River Dee, so, he had switched to the transatlantic run from Liverpool and captained a cargo ship instead. It was easier than what he had been used to, and he had a good bosun on his crew. For every trip he made, he was given two days leave, while the ship was checked, loaded and made ready for the away.

Johnny stood at the top of the driveway. The plaque on the gate post said 'Selwyn Lodge'. For a moment he felt like turning back. Then he saw a small child peering out of an upstairs window. It couldn't be where Maggie lived, she didn't have any kids. He straightened his cravat nervously, ran his long tapered fingers through his curly brown hair, then cleared his throat. Time to get it over with. If it wasn't the Maggie, he used to know, he had the rest of the evening to down a few pints.

Chapter 27

"Answer the door please, Mary, if you would, then take yourself off home," cried Betty. "We'll see to our visitor. We can pour him a sherry or make him a cup of tea."

Mary did as she was told and opened the front door to the handsome stranger. His appearance told of an expensive tailor. This was no labourer standing there.

"Good evening. I have an appointment with the lady of the household. Would you be so kind as to tell her that a Mr Johnny Dockerty, has come to call?"

"Certainly, right away, Sir. Would you like to step in and I will take your coat? Ah, here she is, Miss Rosemary. This gentleman says he has an appointment, Madam. Do you want him to be shown into the drawing room?"

"I can do that, Mary."

Betty walked forward, extending her hand in welcome.

"Good evening Mr. Dockerty, I am very pleased to meet you. My name is Miss Rosemary and you are Johnny, I believe?"

Johnny stood formally and shook her hand. Inside he was in turmoil. Would you look at this hallway! You could put a whole cottage in it, for a start. No, Maggie couldn't possibly live here. Madeline had sent him on a wild goose chase.

"Er, I was told, Madam, that you have a young girl residing with you. Her name is Maggie. We knew each other way back, she being a friend of me mother's."

"Yes, I know, she's expecting you. Mary, I said you could go!"

Betty had noticed her servant standing close by, open-mouthed.

Johnny was ushered into the drawing room, where Maggie stood waiting to greet him. He looked as if he didn't believe it was her! The vision she was hoping he saw was arrayed in purple, looking confident and proud.

"I can't believe the change in you," he exclaimed. "When I think of the last time I saw you…"

He walked up to her and bent low, as he took her outstretched hand to shake it formally.

Betty coughed behind him and asked if she could get him something to drink? He seemed as if he was in a daze, perhaps a little alcohol would do the trick.

"Oh, yes please, anything will do." He couldn't take his eyes off Maggie as he said it and stumbled as he went to sit in a chair.

From her point of view, Johnny was just as he was when she had seen him at Madeline's wedding, though he didn't seem as confident and his hand had been trembling when he had held hers.

Betty took herself from the room after she had served Johnny his brandy and left them together to talk. He looked around the room, as he sipped his drink politely, noticing the quality furniture, the curtains, the Oriental rug and the opulence of the beautiful room.

"How's yer mother, Johnny?" she ventured. "I think of her often. Well, when I think back to me days in Killala anyway. Is she well, still livin' in the cottage there?"

"Yes, she's still livin' in the cottage, manages to cook fer herself and tend her little garden. She's as well as can be expected, Maggie, considerin' her age. I try ter get over to see her when I can, but it's difficult now my home port is Liverpool. There are new people at the Filbey's now and the wife looks in on Mother, checks that she's all right."

"And what of Killala? Does anyone still live down there?"

"That I can't say, Maggie. My visits take me through Ballina, so I've never taken a trip down to the River Moy."

"It's probably gone to rack and ruin," she said speculatively. "I don't think Aunt Tess was plannin' to stay there very long."

Just then, there was a little scuffling outside the door, then it swung open. Mikey was standing in his night clothes, looking at them with his thumb in his mouth. He was closely followed by a very apologetic Sarah, who scooped him up into her arms and began to tell him off.

"He heard voices in the hallway, Madam, as I was settling him in his bed. I turned away to see to Hannah and he shot off down the stairs. I'm sorry, he's just learnt to come down on his bottom and it's his favourite game. I'll take him back straight away. I'm sorry to have disturbed you."

Maggie got up from her chair, laughing and calling her son a little imp. Johnny would have seen the closeness, the love they had between them that typified a mother and son relationship. And Sarah had mentioned another child, Hannah. No doubt Johnny was thinking that her husband had been busy before he'd gone off and died in the way that Madeline had described. Maggie caught a glimpse of Johnny's face, as he watched her with Mikey. He seemed to be dismayed by the distraction that the child had brought along.

Johnny felt trapped, Maggie found out later. He was wondering what he was doing there, sitting cosily with people he didn't really know. He was glad he had left her that day, when she had pleaded with him to take her back home again, as she had probably been expecting Jack's child as well.

There was nothing for it, but to finish the brandy and get on his way. He'd go back to the port next morning, as suddenly he'd begun to miss his crew. Maggie may well have turned out to be a bit of a looker, but he wondered if maybe it had been a set up, one of those womanly wiles. Madeline was always on at him to find a wife, give up the sea and settle down. But while his mother was still alive, he had no intention of doing so.

Betty came in then, presumably thinking they'd had time to break the ice between them, and began to tell him of her seagoing father. Before Johnny knew it, he was being offered little biscuits, slices of ham and thin cut bits of bread. There was more brandy to follow, and so he decided it hadn't been such a bad evening after all, as he wove his way back to the Brown Horse later. Of course, inevitably Madeline had been waiting up when he got back there, all agog and excited that Maggie was the person he used to know.

"Yer want ter get in there, brother," Ted advised, very seriously. "The auld one is worth a fortune and there's no one around ter leave it to, except that young widow you've just bin visiting."

–

"So, Maggie, that turned out to be a very pleasant evening, don't you agree?" said Betty, after Johnny had gone and they had enjoyed another glass of sherry each. "A charming man, polite and well mannered. Just the type of man you would expect to have the respect and loyalty from his men. And he was so interested, wasn't he, in my father's trips to the Orient? Now, get the dreamy look off your face, my girl. There's no sense in wanting something that will never be."

"Betty," she protested. "I was just going over the evening, mulling it over in me mind. It was different having male company for a change, but I'd admit he's very handsome all the same."

"If you feel we lack male company, I'll invite Ezra over more often. He's quite good-looking for a man of nearly fifty. You can feast your eyes on him!"

–

The following weeks were just a blur, and hard for Maggie to remember in fine detail. Except that the Singer sewing machine that had been on order, arrived. Annie and Maggie took it in turns to use it and completed yards and yards of

348

seams. Madeline's designs were soon turned into reality. Not as outrageous as her milkmaid outfit, but plenty of layers, flounces and frills. Betty had told her not to be too creative, as they still wanted to attract the local custom as well. So a range of white frilled blouses were made that could be worn with a colourful sash and a choice of a plain cotton or wool skirt.

The preparation of the new premises came on in leaps and bounds, as each day the workmen, dressed in short jackets, grey worsted trousers, aprons and billy-cock hats appeared.

On the day of the 'grand opening' there were enough ready-mades to satisfy the most discerning customer, though it had to be said the advertising in the Chester broadsheet had been a disappointment. Only one new carriage-owning customer was attracted by the advert. The rest of the customers were existing clientele, wanting to look over this new fashion house they now had in their village. Ever optimistic, they began to take orders for Ladies' Day. It was what Betty called their 'bread and butter' custom and would keep them all busy for those next few weeks.

–

One Sunday, Ezra came to visit and was invited to stay for afternoon tea. He and Maggie sat comfortably in the conservatory, overlooking the garden that was full of swaying daffodils. Betty was in the kitchen making a cup of tea for the visitor and the children were in the nursery having a sleep.

"It's been over twelve months now since your husband passed away, Maggie," Ezra remarked, playing with the leaf of an exotic plant that was inches from his side. "It gets easier, doesn't it? But I still miss having someone in my life. Have you thought of ever marrying again?"

Her heart missed a beat and she wondered if he was gathering the courage to propose to her. She thought he must be thirty years older than her at least!

349

"Er, I've not thought on it, Ezra, because I'm happy as I am. I have me work and me children. I'm quite contented without a husband. Why do yer ask?"

"I would like to get married again, I think. I have my shop and the church, I like singing in the choir, but sometimes I get lonely and I do miss my wife's home cooking. Yes, I would like someone again in my life. I have got a young lady in mind, who I think would be suitable, but I have to admit I'm a lot older than her."

Oh no, she thought. He's definitely working up to asking me to be his bride!

"Do I know the young lady?" Maggie held her breath, waiting for his reply.

"Yes, it's Sarah. Sarah Osborne, the nursemaid who works for you. I've seen her worshipping at our church and I've heard her singing too. She's good with children and she's kind and pretty. I think she would make an excellent wife for me."

Maggie exhaled slowly when she heard his words. Thank heavens, Sarah Osborne, phew!

"I wouldn't like to lose me nursemaid, Ezra. She's very valuable to me and yer don't even know her properly, do yer? She might not be ready to marry and settle down yet."

"I've had a little conversation with her, when she's been attending church alongside Betty. Do you think she'll want a bit of courting? I suppose she will. I'll ask her out next time I see her. I'll ask if she would like to take a walk with me. We could go for a stroll along the promenade, then I'll take it from there. And if I get as far as proposing and she agrees to marry me, I promise I won't steal her away. At least not until she starts our family anyway!"

-

The days were getting longer, so one evening Maggie decided she would take the children down to Seagull Cottage to visit their grandma. Since Mr Arlington's outburst she had kept away from the boarding house, only seeing Alice and Michael if she decided to go to church.

That day had been a fraught one, as the money outlaid in the creation of the new fashion house, seemed an unnecessary expense to her. Their customer base had hardly increased and she had said so at the weekly meeting with Betty and Mr Arlington.

"It's because yer had to have an empire, Mr Arlington, that we moved across the way. But Miss Rosemary's was at its best when it was a simple business. Just a dressmaker and her clientele. Now no one hardly sees her and they have to make do buying from the rail."

"Maggie, let's be fair about it," Betty intervened. "Sheldon Loan and Property Company could not have grown without the aid of Mr Arlington and he had to have room for a reception downstairs and space for ledgers. We took a chance, I know, moving in to a double fronted shop, but give it time. Village people are renowned for being parochial and they're very loathe to change."

"It's a question of choice, Mrs Haines. Do we expand the Sheldon Company or the scope of the dressmaker's? Which one makes us the most money in the end?"

"Well, naturally it's the bounty vouchers that are bringing the money in, but I feel yer could have managed, without all the fashion house expense."

"Give it a few more months, Maggie," Betty said. "As you know, Rome wasn't built in a day. I'll try to come in more often, but I thought Madeline was doing very well?"

"She is with the younger customers, the ones that are wanting the wider skirts and the crinolines, but the older women want to see you, not buy one of the readymade skirts that have to be taken in or shortened. They want what they call 'bespoke' and they don't want the ministrations of an upstart Irish girl like me."

"Oh, I'm sure, you are mistaken, Maggie. Isn't she, Mr Arlington? Except for your diction, which has improved dramatically since you arrived here, your needlework is just as good as mine."

Maggie heard Mr Arlington snorting at this, which he turned into a sneeze when she looked inquiringly at him. They suffered each other for the sake of the business, though she still thought him pompous and she knew he considered her an upstart, taking Miss Rosemary for a ride.

Maggie turned all that over in her mind, as she walked with Mikey toddling at her side and Hannah asleep in the pram. She had seen the latest bank statements and he had not. Mr Freeman and his men had not come cheaply, paid by the hour and not by the job. It meant a lot of idling could be done by his labourers and they were often seen coming back from the pub. Meanwhile, the Sheldon company had gone from strength to strength, with a balance of four hundred and ninety three pounds, and that was after all the wages and bills had been met. The conclusion she had come to was that taking over the dressmaker's had not been a good move. She should have quelled her emotions and let 'Anne Rosemary' stand alone. But, it had been done, a lesson learnt and Betty had been good to her, letting her and the children stay at Selwyn Lodge, and not even paying rent.

"So, here yer are on this fine summer's evening," Alice exclaimed, as she saw who was at the door. "I'd forgotten what yer all look like. My yer've grown, our Mikey. Have yer come ter see yer Grand-mama?"

"Alice, yer only saw him two weeks ago. I know he's growin' quickly, but not that much since then."

Alice ignored her and, taking Mikey by the hand, went into the kitchen to get him a drink of milk. That was what she always seemed to do, make a fuss of her first born grandchild, whilst she ignored the second one.

"I'm glad yer called, Maggie," she said when she followed her into the kitchen, after she had taken Hannah from her pram. "You've saved me puffin' up the hill to the dressmaker's. I got another money voucher from Jack, and this time he's written a few words. Will yer read them to me, while I make a cup of tea?"

"It says he doesn't work fer Lord Belsham any more," Maggie said, sitting down at the table and perusing the missive. "He's become a promoter himself and he's moved into the city of New York, where there's plenty of raw new talent moving in. He's teamed up with a trainer and they run a gymnasium, fer sparring partners and practising. He says he's makin' so much money that he'll soon be able to visit home! He sends his love to Mikey and Hannah and hopes that she has settled in."

"Has he sent an address this time?"

"No, he says he will do, when he gets himself a permanent address. At the moment he has a room, but it's only for a short while because the area isn't very nice. That'll put the cat amongst the pigeons, if Jack turns up fer a visit. Remind me to take a holiday when he writes ter say when he'll arrive!"

"But don't yer see, Maggie, if we can get an address, Seamus could find him when the ship puts its passengers down at that Ellis Island place, yer know the one he said you have to go to before they let yer in? Well, when his ship goes into the harbour, he's allowed to go ashore. He could tell our Jack how we're doin' and Seamus will see how our Jack is doin' as well."

"If yer say so, Alice. Don't get yer hopes up. He's bin gone well over a year now and we don't often get a word."

"Oh, I know I'll see my boy one day. It'll be in my lifetime, I know it will!"

Maggie dawdled a little before they set off back to Selwyn Lodge. She and her child stood hand in hand on the promenade, looking out across the estuary, while Hannah settled back to sleep again. The tide was in, but not quite lapping the promenade wall. Maggie liked that time of day in the early summer, the sunset streaking across the sky, all pink and yellow, promising fine weather for the next day.

How she loved that place. Jack could keep his foreign land and talk of good money to be made. He wouldn't have her view of craggy mountain tops and the quilted panorama of green fields, dark forests and brown arable land. There was a stillness about the place, only broken by the squawk of seagulls, as they came to rest on the roof tops, the occasional call of a curlew and the plopping of little boats as they were lifted by the waves. Contentment filled her soul and she felt the thoughts of her trying day disappear into thin air.

–

A few days later, Madeline came into the shop, breathless in her eagerness to impart to Maggie, what was being planned for Ladies' Day.

"Johnny will be home and Ted and I were talking. How about if we all go together to the fairground after the parade? We can watch the parade with the children, visit the fair, then in the evening put the children with your nursemaid and go dancing behind the Bowling Green?"

"It sounds wonderful, but Sarah might have plans to meet Ezra. They're walkin' out together now."

"She's your nursemaid! Surely you can tell her that our plans come first? Or what about Miss Rosemary keeping an ear out for them, or better still taking them all to your mother-in-law's home?"

"I don't think that will go down very well with Miss Rosemary or Alice. Miss Rosemary is beginning to feel her age. She likes to be in bed by nine o'clock, she likes to turn up the oil lamp and read."

"Alice then."

"Alice couldn't manage Mikey and two babies. Even with Michael helpin' they couldn't cope. No, if I promise Sarah she can invite Ezra to sit with her in the conservatory, she'll be happy to listen out fer the children. I'll tell her you'll be bringin' Eddie and she can line a cupboard drawer fer him."

"I'll bring the pram, he can sleep in there. He'll be used to his own smells in there. A strange cupboard drawer will unsettle him."

"As yer wish, you're his mother. Now what time do yer want us ter meet? Are yer sure Johnny will be happy with yer plan?"

Maggie wasn't sure that she was. It was playing with fire to be seen in the company of a handsome man. Tongues would wag and lurid stories would be made up about the fighter's widow walking out with a seagoing man. What the local gossips didn't know, they would invent. She was also worried how Betty and Alice would react when they got to hear about it.

Betty was quite understanding, when she explained that it was going to be a family outing, though not so supportive when she heard of their intention to dance at the Bowling Green, later.

"All I can say is, be careful that you don't encourage him, Maggie. He only knows that you're a widow, not that Jack is lurking somewhere in the wings. Make sure you are never alone with him. Stay with the others, then tongues can't wag."

Sound advice, and she recalled it as she put on the lightest coloured dress that she had made yet. It had many layers of creamy tulle, over a crinoline cage, topped with a ruched over-skirt in deepest pink. The bodice was fairly roomy, gathered into the waist with a band. The neck was trimmed with a little lace collar and the sleeves ballooned into a large open bell. She carried a pretty cream shawl over her arm, edged with the same deep pink fringes. On her feet were off white, kid leather, laced ankle boots, which she knew would be scuffed and dirty by the time she got home. But, that was the price of fashion. She would never have dreamt of purchasing such a pair of frivolities two years before. She knew, though, that Madeline would be dressed up to the nines and she didn't want to feel dowdy.

Nor did her children escape her ministrations. Mikey was dressed in corduroy breeches, black patent leather shoes, and a white frilled shirt with a little bow. She carried his little blue velveteen jacket in a small valise, in case he got cold. Hannah, as always, was made to look her prettiest, in a lacy layered lemon dress, matching bonnet and yellow cardigan.

It had rained earlier that morning, but the sun had come out by eleven o'clock and there were the makings of a fine day. By the time they had reached the Brown Horse, the crowd had swelled to large proportions and she was very grateful when Madeline suggested that they sit in the upper window of the tavern, with its vantage point of all below.

Johnny greeted her stiffly. There was a coolness about him as he took her hand and he didn't meet her eye when she said 'hello'. The children distracted them, though, and there wasn't time for her to wonder at the chill of his greeting.

Mikey nearly fell out onto the pavement, he was so excited at hearing the band. They ooompah pahed along the High Street and down to the Anglican church, the ladies with their colourful staffs and Sunday best dresses following on behind. The procession was as good as the year before, though the crinoline was still in the minority.

When the street was quiet, the crowd having either gone to the church or the fairground, Ted suggested that they all walk along to the fairground too. He didn't open his premises until six o'clock and he had engaged some evening cover. Madeline and Maggie pushed their prams ahead of the men, with Mikey tugging excitedly at Maggie's hand.

"Come on, man, get yer face straight," Ted advised quietly to his brother. "She won't want ter be courted by someone who has a face that looks like sour cream!"

"Who's to say that Maggie wants to be courted, brother? She may be content as a widow. We're assuming that Maggie would like to be married again."

"Oh, Johnny, women are placed on this earth to be bearers of our children. That's all they want out of life, to be happily married and to have babies every year."

"Well, it seems to me that Maggie is happy having her job and leaving her children with a nursemaid. Anyway, I told you. I don't want to settle until our mother has gone."

Chapter 28

Mikey was attracted by the hurdy gurdy man and toddled across to listen to the melodies. The two young mothers followed at a leisurely pace, as pram pushing was difficult with the muddy ruts in the field. They settled down at a refreshment table, while the men wandered around, looking at the stalls. For a moment, Maggie felt nostalgia grip her, as she remembered Jack and Michael at the rifle range. Was that really only two years ago, when she had sat with her great big belly, as Jack planned out their removal to Liverpool and they waited for Mikey to be born? So much had happened since then.

She looked around the field that they were sitting in. The gypsy wagons were over by the trees, gaily painted wooden vehicles on four large spindle wheels. The merry-go-round, the swing boats, the hoopla stall, the big fat lady, nothing seemed to have changed. But her life had, dramatically, since her chance meeting with Miss Rosemary.

Thinking of Betty brought her to a sudden jolt. This was the field Mr Arlington had spoken of? This and another across Raby Road. He was trying to persuade them to attend a land auction, to be held at the Assembly Rooms, the coming July. The rumours were strong. A track could be laid to bring the train to Neston, and the people to benefit would be the ones who had bought up pieces of land. It would be a pity to take the gypsy field away, though. She had heard that the gypsies had been coming to the village for many a year. It was an event that everyone looked forward to, that and Ladies' Day of course.

She was deep in thought, when Madeline shook her arm impatiently.

"I said, shall we go and have our future told? There's a gypsy woman telling fortunes over there."

Maggie shook her head decisively.

"No, Madeline, I think it's against our religion, I've read something somewhere about that."

"Pooh, it's just some mouldy old priest, who's trying to stop our fun."

"Well, you go if yer want to and I'll stay and look after Eddie. Mikey, come back here now, that little animal is getting cross with you!"

Mikey came running back to her, his eyes twinkling happily, as Madeline, full of excitement, dashed away across the field.

"Mama, the mun-kee danced for me. Did you see it, come with me and see it now!"

"No, Mikey, sit and be good fer Mama. If you are, I'll get you one of those ice creams, when yer Uncle Ted and Johnny come back to join us."

She looked over to where the two brother's were standing, talking. It looked as if Johnny had the weight of the world on his broad shoulders and she wondered what was bothering him. Whatever it was, it wasn't her business. She didn't know him well enough to offer him her help.

Her mind wandered again. This time to thoughts of what it would be like to be wed to Johnny Dockerty. Seeing his handsome face above her, as they made a baby in their marriage bed. Feeling his hard, lean muscles as he held her closely. Feeling warm, comfortable and loved, as she lay there in his arms. She could still hold onto her business, he would be away a lot at sea. Goodness! What was she thinking about? She was still married to Jack, even if he was thousands of miles across the sea. She took an ivory fan from her reticule and wafted her blushing face away.

"Maggie!" Madeline came rushing back, breathlessly.

"The gypsy said you're to go over. She says she wants to tell you something you should know! Have you got a sixpence? That is what you have to cross her palm with. A silver sixpence. Do you know, she told me I was going to have seven children? Not much else, seven children and a happy life."

"I don't want ter have me future told me, Madeline. God won't be happy if I go and get told."

"Tosh, it'll only take a few minutes. Go on, scaredy cat. I'll look after the children, like you looked after Eddie for me."

She felt drawn then. Maybe fate took a hand in people's lives, just as religion did. She walked slowly, watching the gypsy as she beckoned. Then the gypsy disappeared into the wagon, so it seemed the deed was to be done!

Maggie climbed up the wooden steps precariously, because her crinoline hoop was swaying and she was in danger of falling to her knees. She could hear the woman laughing softly, then she pushed open the bottom half of the door for her. Maggie had just managed to squeeze herself into the wagon and was amazed when she looked around!

The interior was fitted with mahogany cupboards and doors. A locker seat with a chest of drawers and another seat ran along one wall. At the end of the wagon was a window and underneath sat a double bed. On the other side was a wardrobe and a cupboard, next to it a stove for cooking and another seat, where the gypsy was sitting, staring at her boldly.

Everything was bright and sparkled with cleanliness, as if Gypsy Petunioni was proud of her home. The woman was dressed in a gaudy red skirt, white short sleeved blouse and a red bandanna over her long black hair. Her skin was swarthy and weather beaten, and she looked to be in her forties and very, very slim.

She beckoned to Maggie again, this time to sit on a stool on the other side of the table. Then she took hold of the girl's left hand and traced some lines with a forefinger. Seeming satisfied, the gypsy then looked into a big glass ball that she had placed in the middle of the table. It looked milky, until she caressed it slowly with her hands, then it went crystal clear.

"I see two men in yer life, Maggie."

Her eyes widened in surprise. How did the gypsy know her name?

"One man is fair haired, the other is dark. Danger is lurkin' there. You will travel over a great expanse of water. Another child will be born ter yer. Riches are fer the takin', but beware of a parasite in yer life. Someone close ter yer will die in horrible circumstances. Yer will have a long life."

Then the woman stood up abruptly, as the ball turned back to being milky again. She held out her hand for her money, which Maggie thrust into her palm, shakily.

She stumbled down the steps, with the gypsy's words ringing in her ears, as she blinked in the bright sunlight, for it had been a little dark in there. She walked back to Madeline and the children slowly, contemplating all that had been said and trying to make some sense of it. Would she really be travelling across the water to Jack, to live in America and, have another child? Would she share in the riches of Jack's promoter business? A dangerous business, if truth was told. But she didn't want to do any of it. She wanted to stay there in Neston, reap the rewards of her loan company and be settled in her life.

"Someone close ter yer will die in horrible circumstances." Well that could be Jack as well. His job was dangerous, mixing with all those fighters. He could be landed a fatal blow. Then she could marry Johnny and have his child. The expanse of water to be travelled could be over the Irish Sea!

What fantasy. She glowered at Madeline when she drew level, for insisting that she should go.

"That's why it warns yer in the Bible, not ter get mixed up with mediums and fortune tellers. I'm all confused now, Madeline, after what the gypsy told me. It's best ter take life as it comes."

"Oh, what did she tell you?" Madeline's curls bobbed merrily, as she waited excitedly to be told. "Are you going to

361

have lots of babies like I am? We'll have to get busy, me and Ted. You know she never mentioned anything about my dress designs."

"Well, she wouldn't, would she? How would a gypsy know about how good yer are at designing dresses? She'll only tell yer about women things, because that's all she's goin' to know. And I'm not goin' to say what she said, but I won't be making baby clothes. Except fer you, that is."

Ted and Johnny came ambling over. Madeline regaled them with the gypsy's forecast, but told them Maggie wouldn't let her know what had been said to her.

"Come on, Maggie," Ted said, teasing.

"Are yer goin' ter meet the man of yer dreams? Share that big place at Selwyn Lodge with him?"

It was said in a joking manner, but both Johnny and Maggie looked uncomfortable. He was poking fun at them, they could see, because he made a point of looking their way.

"Would you and Mikey like one of those ice creams?" Johnny asked her gently, trying to bridge the awkward silence that had sprung up between them. "Then afterwards we could take him on the swing boats. I used to love them when I was a boy and the gypsies used to come to Galway."

They spent the rest of the afternoon companionably, sampling the delights that the fair had to offer. Later, Maggie took the worn out Mikey back to the arms of his nursemaid. He and Hannah had nursery tea, then were tucked up in bed tenderly.

She sat with Betty in the drawing room. They were to have their meal together, then Johnny was to call for her around half past seven. The gypsy's words had upset her and she confided in the older woman, relating what the gypsy had said. Of course she was told off soundly by Betty, who didn't believe in dabbling with the hand of fate.

"I don't want me life to change in any way, Betty. I'm happy here with what I have. I'm not looking fer riches, though I'd be happy with a handsome man! This expanse of water she was talkin' about, makes me think I'll be joining Jack in America, and that is certainly what I really don't want te do."

"I've told you, Maggie, that fortune telling is all a load of twaddle. How can someone see into the future? If they could, they would become a millionaire. Now, you might think the dark haired man is referring to your sea captain friend, but believe me when I say, that nothing can become of your friendship. You must talk to him this evening, in case he has other ideas. To change the subject though, Maggie, isn't that field where the gypsies camp the field that Mr Arlington was talking of? That and the one across from it? It would be as well to consider buying both the fields, and there are also a few for sale along Liverpool Road."

"Has he shown yer a list yet, Betty, because I don't really want us buying that field fer business use when there might be others we could buy instead. Those gypsies have bin comin' to Neston for a very longtime and we'd make a lot of people very disappointed if they stopped coming. All because of a new railway line."

"Tut, tut, Maggie. To succeed in business you must put a different hat on. Business and emotion do not mix."

"Betty," she smiled, tickled with her choice of platitude, "that's a corker, that is, coming from you!"

She changed her bodice to a creamy blouse, got rid of the crinoline cage and wore starched underskirts instead, then pinned up her hair and sat a small pink bonnet upon it. She put her black lace up boots on, then surveyed herself in the cheval mirror, pinching her cheeks to heighten their colour, proudly telling herself, that she would do.

But, why was she going to such lengths over her appearance, she thought, remembering her earlier conversation with Betty? There was no future for herself and Johnny, even though she knew she hadn't imagined that look he had given her that afternoon, when he had walked at her side to purchase ice cream for her. It was one of appraisal, a measured look, as if he was considering her to be a possession. Something he wished to acquire.

Nothing like the look he had given her when they had parted on the sea front, when she was a ragged immigrant and he was running the cattle boat. That look had been bordering on horror, in case she was going to become a limpet in his life. A clingy person who would take up his time. Of course, she had now become desirable to him. Gone was the dirty, tangled hair that she had worn any old how, gone was the shabby, threadbare clothing and the smelly bare feet. Instead, she had become a clean, wholesome young matron with money in the bank. Ted and Madeline would have told him that, she knew, because they wouldn't be able to keep that information to themselves.

"Mrs Haines," called Mary, tapping on the door of the bedroom and disturbing her preoccupation. "Mrs Haines, your visitor's here."

"Thank you, Mary, I'm coming now. I'll be down in just a minute. Tell Mr Dockerty that I'll be with him soon."

The maid set off at a fast pace, to give the message to this fine upstanding man, who she had shown into the drawing room. Then she flew into the kitchen to tell the cook that Mrs Haines's fellow was there again!

"Good evening, Maggie," he said, as she presented herself before him and handed him her velveteen cloak to settle around her shoulders. "May I say you are looking particularly beautiful tonight." (That advice had come from Madeline, women liked to be complimented on their clothes.) "I am looking forward to spending the evening in your company." (That was advice from Ted) "Shall we walk down to the entertainment? I have to admit I'm not an experienced dancer. I hope you don't mind." That was from Johnny's heart. He had two left feet as far as dancing was concerned.

"No, it doesn't bother me. The last time I was dancing, it was at a ceilidh with me mammy and dada. We can sit and watch and I can catch up with whatever you've bin up to."

Johnny was looking his handsome best. He had changed his shirt for a white one with pin-tucks and around his neck he wore a black cravat. He put out his arm for her to link him, as they walked together to the hallway.

"Don't be late," shouted Betty, from the conservatory, as she hadn't bothered on that occasion to stir herself from her after dinner coffee. "And don't forget what I told you!"

"Do I sense a mystery, Maggie?" Johnny inquired, as they strolled down Burton Road.

"No, it's just Miss Rosemary doin' her chaperone act. She'd come with us if it wasn't fer her aches and pains. I'll have te get the doctor in, she's bin like this now fer days."

Madeline and Ted were waiting. They had grabbed a table and some seats, so the four of them could sit comfortably together on the paved area at the back of the Bowling Green tavern. The married couple had agreed a plan, that after an hour or so they were going to disappear. They all watched as people danced happily to the music provided by a local three piece band. Sometimes a waltz, then a square dance. Everyone was having a really good time.

As if by prearranged signal, Madeline said that it was time to check that the pub towels in the Brown Horse were up on the beer pumps, which meant that the customers knew that it was closing time.

It had become a little chilly once they had gone and Johnny drew his chair up closer to Maggie.

"I keep wanting to apologize about that day you met me on the cattle run, Maggie. It was unforgivable, the way I neglected my duty towards my mother's friend. She took me to task when I got back home and I told her what I'd done. She said you should have gone to her for help, instead of being whisked away by the Haines's. I'm sorry, my dear, that is all I can say. I could have saved you such a lot of hardship if I'd listened to my heart instead of joining my crew at the inn."

"Johnny, yer don't have ter apologize. I'd made me bed by then and on it I had to lie. I was expectin' Mikey. I didn't know it then, but if I had to live me life all over, I wouldn't want to be without him."

"Yes, he seems a great little chap. You are very fortunate. So, how did you manage to fall on your feet? Living in that great big house like you do?"

"It's all down to Miss Rosemary. She took pity on me and helped me make a cloak, when it was winter and I didn't have any decent cover to me name. Then I found some money. Do yer remember that feather mattress yer helped me down the hill with? Well, I found it in there. I hope yer not going ter tell Ted or Madeline any of this. It's a private conversation." Johnny shook his head and assured her it would go no further. "So I took the money to Miss Rosemary fer safe keepin'. It wasn't a lot, but she invested it for me and it will all be mine when I'm twenty-one."

"Which is when?"

"Oh, I haven't had me nineteenth birthday yet. It's in August. Mikey and I share the same day. But 'til then, the money buys property, keeps the household going, goes out in loans and keeps comin' back again."

"So you'll be a wealthy woman when you're twenty-one? That is astonishing, when you think you had nothing two years ago."

"Well, it's shared with Miss Rosemary, that's why I live at Selwyn Lodge with Mikey and Hannah. I'm like a companion to her, now she's old and got no one."

Johnny stood up, pulling up the collar on his jacket purposefully, as the wind from the sea had started gusting, causing many of the revellers around them to pause in their enjoyment.

"It's getting late, we must be heading back. I'm leaving in the morning. Another trip, with a cargo of coal this time. It's a dirty, sooty job for the crew, but it pays good money. May I presume on your kindness and call on you next time I'm here? I must away to see my mother on my next leave."

"Of course yer may, and do give yer mother me good wishes."

Johnny escorted her back to Selwyn Lodge, then hurried, no doubt, back to the Brown Horse and Ted, presumably to tell his brother of all he'd been told.

–

Next day, at the weekly meeting, Mr Arlington was very insistent regarding a decision on which parcels of land he was to bid for in July.

"Well, I don't think it should be that land on Raby Road," Maggie began.

"This is because Maggie went to the gypsy fair yesterday," explained Betty, inconsequently.

"Why can't we buy land on Liverpool Road?" Maggie, persisted. "It's only pasture there and there's plenty of that around. Anyway, Miss Rosemary, can we afford it? How much land can Mr Arlington bid for? Remember we still have all our bills ter pay."

"I think we can stretch to three parcels. We'll leave the gypsy field, if it is going to cause you consternation, but we'll have the one on the other side of Raby Road. Plus Mr Arlington can bid for two fields in Liverpool Road. Now, Maggie, are you satisfied with that arrangement?"

Of course she was! It was good to see 'His Nibs' trying to look deferential. He must have thought that Maggie was a bit mental to put the gypsies before financial gain.

Later, as she and Betty sipped their tea in the fashion showroom, Annie busy treadling away upstairs, Maggie was asked if she had enjoyed the dancing.

"Yes, but Johnny said he had two left feet, so we just sat and watched the others."

"Did you tell him about Jack and why he disappeared?"

"Afraid not, but I did tell him that I found the money in the mattress and how I would get my investment when I'm twenty-one."

"Oh, Maggie," Betty groaned. "You know nothing about this man. You've taken him into your confidence, just because his mother was your friend? Let me tell you a little story that might help you to make up your mind about him. I have never told anyone about the humiliation I felt, long ago when I was a young girl in my early twenties.

"During my time as a sempstress at Lorne Hall, I fell in love with a footman. He was very similar in appearance to Johnny and that's why this memory springs to mind. Nothing seemed to upset him, he was always cheerful and easy to get along with. He was the only man I thought I could spend the rest of my life with. But he had a roving eye and I have to admit I wouldn't give in to his pressure, for a bit of a tickle in his room above the stables. So he pursued one of the under maids instead. I won't tell you her name, because you'll know then who I'm talking about. Eventually, she found she was expecting, and that left me heartbroken. As you know, my father made a lot of money selling the goods he brought back from the Orient and we eventually moved into Selwyn Lodge. Well, that young man plagued me then. He brought me flowers and little gifts, hung around Burton Road waiting for me to come out, followed me, even though I had told him that I wanted nothing more to do with him, and generally made a nuisance of himself. Eventually my father had a few strong words with him, which seemed to do the trick and he took himself off to marry the unfortunate young girl who had given birth to his baby. The reason I am telling you this, Maggie, is because I think that Johnny is a bit of a cad. You told me of his unsympathetic attitude towards you, when you asked him for his help, but now you have become an attractive proposition to him, two years on. He did not look like a man who was at ease in your company, but I noted he was impressed with your surroundings when he came to call.

"So, what do we know about him? He isn't married. Why not? Most men are at thirty-one. Why hasn't he grown through the ranks of a successful shipping company, like my father did?

He's still only the captain of a small cargo ship, after running a cattle boat for so many years. It doesn't seem as if he has much ambition, but through you, he could give up going to sea and still have it all.

"In my opinion, you should nip it in the bud. Even if you are in love with him, you have to tell him of the whereabouts of Jack. It will cause a bit of consternation amongst the church people and the villagers, as I'm sure Madeline's husband would be the first one that he would tell, but eventually gossip dies down and people look for other things to talk about. You are not in love with Johnny, are you my dear? I can tell. If you were, you'd be constantly dreamy eyed."

"It's true, Betty. I'm not in love with him, not that I know what love is, properly between a woman and a man. But I am attracted to him, he's a handsome man and courteous with it, and I'll spare your blushes and not go into detail of what he does to my insides. But truth ter tell, I don't really want a man in my life any more. Why do I need one? If I were free ter marry and he came ter live here, he would become a drain on our income. He would soon take over and start giving his orders and we've already got Mr Arlington, who tries to do that. All we have worked for would feed his fancy lifestyle. He'd want expensive clothes, the best in brandy and even a carriage and pair! If I was destined to have a man in me life again, I'd choose Jack. He's the father of Mikey and Hannah and the nearest I will ever get to feeling a certain love. But, I never want ter give up what we have between you and me, Betty. Our friendship, our loyalty and the care we have fer one another."

Both women sat quietly with their thoughts, then tears began to well up in their eyes. What had been said was the truth of the matter, when a chance meeting had drawn together their precious souls.

Author's Note

If you have enjoyed reading *A Woman Undefeated*, look out for its sequel *Dreams Can Come True*. It's the continuing saga of an Irish immigrant's story, when she returns to her homeland to lay a few ghosts to rest.